I0766157

Storm Princess

— 1 —

USA TODAY BESTSELLING AUTHORS

JAYMIN EVE & EVERLY FROST

Frost, Everly
Eve, Jaymin
Storm Princess: Book One

Cover design by Covers by Aura.

Page edges by Painted Wings Publishing Services.

Chapter art and scene break illustrations from Samaiya Art.

For information on reproducing sections of this book or sales of this book, go to
www.jaymineve.com
www.everlyfrost.com

jaymineve@gmail.com
everlyfrost@gmail.com

For those who tame the storms.

May you live as gently as a summer rain shower,
as powerfully as thunder,
as brightly as lightning in a clear sky,
and as eternally as the air we breathe.

PROLOGUE

BAELEN RATH - 7 YEARS AGO

I can't feel my legs.

Light shifts beyond my eyelids. It's a soft glow, not sharp or blinding like the final flash of lightning that blasted my senses, turning my world into fire and pain.

I inhale, trying to focus on my breathing as my bedroom comes into focus, blurry at first, awash with sunlight, calm and quiet. My training kicks in and I take inventory of my body: vision impaired, hearing damaged, head throbbing like liquid magma, arms and hands still functional, status of my legs… unknown…

I'm alive. I know that much for sure.

I fist the sheets, blinking at my surroundings, trying to put together the pieces… *Marbella's blue ribbon twisting in a sudden gust of wind... a crack of lightning that split the sky above us... her scream piercing my heart...*

Marbella!

I struggle to sit up, pushing with my hands and elbows, confused about the dead weight from my waist down. *What's wrong with my legs?*

My father leans over me, his green eyes full of worry, his firm hands on both my shoulders, pressing me back to my pillow. He's the only one strong enough to restrain me, but still I struggle, fighting him.

His grip tightens. A stern order leaves his lips. "Baelen, be calm."

Panic spreads like wildfire through me. "Where's Marbella? Is she okay?"

His jaw clenches. He doesn't let up on the pressure on my torso. "She's gone, son."

"Gone… where?"

"The Storm chose her."

The Storm…

"No…" I shake my head. "No… the lightning hit but—"

My father squeezes my right shoulder, but this time it's sharp like a warning. Shapes move at the edge of my room. I force myself to focus, testing my vision, waiting for the figures to become clear. Finally, their features become sharp again.

Several men wait quietly around my room. The one who steps forward wears his golden-blond hair dead straight and tucked behind his ears. His arms shimmer with faint golden tattoos. I recognize him as Gideon Glory, one of the five Elven Commanders. I've met all of them. As the last of my line, I have a right to a seat on the Elven Command when I reach age twenty-five —that's if they don't force me to lead the army like they forced my father, keeping him at arm's length and at their beck and call.

Gideon's voice is deceptively gentle as he asks, "What do you remember, boy?"

The time for calling me a 'boy' has long passed, but he does it anyway. It's just another way for him to reduce my status in the eyes of the onlookers—his entourage, each of them opulently dressed in robes decorated with gold embroidery. Except one who is dressed plainly…

I consider the man who stands apart from the others. His white-blond hair is shaved short around the back and sides but is long on top, and his eyes are pale olive. He is striking in an overly perfect way and far broader in the chest and shoulders than the other elves. In fact, he could rival me in size and build, which is a rare thing among elves.

He ignores the conversation around him, fixating on the open window, head tilted, listening intently to the birds outside my window as if they are more important than Gideon's questions. One hand shifts at his side, fingertips reaching into the beam of sunlight streaming through the window.

I don't know him. I've seen the other elves in Gideon's entourage before, but not him. Every now and then, the others glance at him, shuffling as if they don't want to stand too close to him.

I squint at Gideon, pretending to think, eventually shaking my head. "What did Marbella say?"

"Not much—" my father begins.

Gideon interrupts him with a snap. "Marbella Mercy is riddled with nightmares." He leans down, his expression pinched as he narrows his eyes at me. "All she does is scream for you, Baelen Rath. It's a mockery that the Storm chose such a weak princess this time."

Rage builds inside me that he would talk about Marbella like that, especially when she's hurting. She is the strongest woman I know, the most determined, kind, intelligent…

Damn. Not the Storm. Please not the Storm…

My father squeezes my shoulder again. It's amazing how a single touch can carry so many warnings. "Marbella said she dared you to climb the cliff. She said you fell and hit your head. Then the Storm came for her."

I lower my eyes, staring at the ivory sheets that cover me all the way to my armpits. A lie is more effective when it's corroborated by an admission of guilt.

Without looking up, I say, as if I'm ashamed, "She didn't dare me. I dared her."

Gideon huffs, waving his hand at my face. "So she is not to blame for this, then?"

"For what?" I'm genuinely confused now. If he'd gestured at my legs, it would have made more sense. At the back of my mind, a fierce storm of my own emotions is growing. If I can't feel my legs… if I can't use my legs…

Shock is threatening to destroy me. A roar of pain and loss grows inside my chest. If the Storm chose Marbella, then I've lost her. I've… lost her….

I refuse to let my feelings show. I am a Rath. I'm trained to step back from every situation, view my options, consider the most strategic response, and deliver it with deadly precision—

Gideon gives me a cold smile. "Take a look in the mirror, boy. That's if you can walk to one."

Fuck precision. All I want to do is smash Gideon Glory's smug face right now.

Without another word, he saunters from the room, taking his entourage with him. The man with the short hair follows but pauses in the doorway, dropping the emotionless mask he was wearing to study me with an expression I have difficulty reading. It's not pity because pity would be insulting and there's nothing offensive about the look he's giving me. It's not arrogance or mockery, either; it's not even coldly clinical.

He checks for Gideon, waiting a beat for the hallway to clear ahead of him before he says, "You will walk again." He nods as if he's certain. "If you want to."

Giving my father a respectful nod, he turns to follow the others.

My father lets him go.

Keeping my voice low, I ask, "Who was that?"

My father presses his lips together. I don't think he's going to answer me, but then he says, "Someone who knows what it's like to live in a cage."

For a long time after that, Dad sits in silence on the edge of the bed as we both listen for the sound of horses and the clatter of carriages down the wide cobbled path that tells us our unwelcome visitors have gone.

"Baelen?" Dad finally asks, worry flooding his expression. "Can you feel your legs?"

For the first time, I notice how gray his hair looks, how drawn his face, as if he aged overnight. Yesterday was Marbella's eighteenth birthday. I was supposed to leave for military school today. Now… everything is uncertain.

I shake my head, whispering, "No, sir. I can't."

He drops his head to my shoulder. The enormity of my situation threatens to burst out of me, but I control my responses. I control myself the same way I control my actions in a fight, the same way I control my choices in every step of my life, because rage—ruthless rage, the kind that's part of my bloodline—can only lead to destruction.

"What really happened, Baelen?"

"I can't…"

I can't tell him. If Marbella is gone, then I can't trust anyone with the truth, except maybe the most important part. "She's everything to me."

My father draws back, gripping my shoulders again. "You have to forget about her now—"

"No."

"Baelen—"

"No!" I drag myself up to a sitting position, using only my arms, pulling my legs with me as I try to get out of the bed.

He releases me. I'm even taller than my ancestors—warriors all of them, male and female alike. I'm strong, every muscle in my body honed from years of brutal training, but I have never used my position or my strength to hurt anyone.

Now I shove him away from me. "You can tell me what to do in every other aspect of my life. I will do my duty to my House, be the warrior I'm supposed to be, burn my drawings, defend the border until I die. I'll even walk again—just watch me. *But you will not tell me who to love.*"

Tears glisten in his eyes, shocking me. The only time he cried was the day my mother and baby sister died. A tear drips down his cheek as he swallows, his shoulders sunk low.

"Marbella Mercy is the Storm Princess now," he says. "She's out of your reach, Baelen. At least… until she turns twenty-five. Then, if you still love her, be prepared to fight to the death if you want to be with her."

I level my gaze with his. "If that's what it takes, that's what I'll do."

1

MARBELLA

NOW

The first crackles of lightning scatter across my skin as the perfect storm swirls above me. It's been building since yesterday—from the moment I last subdued it.

The Storm Vault is so high that normally I can't see the eye of the storm, but this one's growing so fast that the dark center is an expanding mass before my eyes.

It's coming for me.

The Vault is constructed of thick stone hundreds of feet high and wide and lined with about a million protective spells. There's only one way in and one way out—through a small waiting room that leads to another airtight room. There are three sealed doors between me and the rest of Erawind.

I don't kid myself. It's not the doors or spells that keep the storm under control.

It's me.

I call the powerful force to me, coaxing it down, ignoring the intense fear that rises inside me.

Curse my survival instincts. If I listened to them, I'd run as far and fast as I could away from this place. But there's no escape from my daily task.

Centuries ago, the gargoyles conjured dark magic to create the perfect storm to wipe out the elven race. Hundreds of elves lost their lives while the Elven Command tried to subdue the storm—

but they couldn't destroy it. Realizing they had no choice but to contain its fury, the elves created the Storm Vault and tried to trap the storm inside.

But even their most powerful spells couldn't keep it here. Right when the storm's fury would have destroyed the last spellcaster, her young daughter burst through the Vault's defenses and ran to her. That's when a miracle happened. The girl absorbed the power of the storm into her body. And the storm calmed for the first time.

That girl was the first Storm Princess. I'm the fourth.

I'll stay in my role until another princess is revealed and replaces me. There's no retirement. No choice. If I try to leave, the storm will follow me.

Until it latches onto another Storm Princess, I'm a living, breathing lightning rod. And if I die before another princess is revealed, the storm will be unleashed. We're connected, the storm and I. As long as I'm alive, the perfect storm remains under control.

I control it. Even if it doesn't feel that way.

I murmur, "C'mon, Beast, what have you got for me today?"

I've been calling it "Beast" for as long as I've been coming to the Vault—every day since the storm chose me. That was seven years ago. I was eighteen at the time.

I stand firm as a streak of lightning blazes from the distance, striking me as fast as I can blink. It zaps the soft spot between my shoulder and collarbone, and despite my preparedness, a soft "oh" escapes my lips. Somehow, it always knows where it can hurt me most. I roll my shoulders and focus on my breathing, knowing that if I stay calm, the strikes won't hurt as much.

My job is simple: absorb the elements. Take the worst of the storm into my body to keep it from exploding from the Vault. I do this every day. Every day the storm calms, and then it builds again. Again and again, I come here to calm it. I should be used to my daily ritual, but somehow the storm always finds ways to surprise me.

Right now, it's the lightning I need to worry about.

Another strike licks fire across the back of my neck and I know it's time to move. I lift my hands above my head, slowly drawing them down and across my body, controlling my breathing as I step into a warrior's routine.

The princess before me was a dancer named Mai Reverie. I don't have the grace for dancing. Combat moves are the closest I get.

The next strike falls directly through the circle of my arms, but it curves at the last moment. It follows the angle of my arms, curling to match my form, traveling an inch above my skin, moving with me instead of against me.

Another strike follows, joining the first and spreading across my body, curling around me in a white and blue light show. Strike by strike, the lightning follows my movements. As fast as I absorb one strike, another one hits, but the contact is soft now. Sometimes I feel like the storm is an angry child who only wants to be noticed and cared for.

The first time the lightning moved with me, nobody believed me. Only my personal advisor, Elise, is allowed into the waiting room to watch me through the large glass panels on that side of the Vault. One day, my bonded partner will be allowed in here too, but for now Elise is my only witness and even she struggles to believe what she sees.

The lightning plays across my skin and taps my shoulder.

I grin. "Oh, you want my attention, do you?"

But my smile quickly fades, because the light show disperses, and I realize that the tap to my shoulder was a warning. The atmospheric force bearing down on me is stronger than ever. It presses against me with suffocating density, like a blanket through which I can't breathe. I gasp against the sudden pressure. Then, just as fast, it lifts.

I look up and wish I hadn't. Storm clouds gather at unnerving speed. The lightning gives way to something worse.

Rain.

I never feared rain before I became the Princess. Sure, it's wet and cold, but the rain produced by the perfect storm is something else—sharp as needles, intense, *drowning*.

I take a deep breath. It's the last one I'll get for a while.

A blast of thunder tears my hearing to shreds, then the rain buckets down. I can't absorb it the same way that I absorb the lightning. All I can do is hold onto it like I'm some sort of rain magnet.

Water fills the space around me as if I'm standing in an invisible orb. There are drains beneath me, but they're never fast enough. In moments, I'll be swimming…

The rain sweeps down, flattening my hair against my back, drowning my clothing in ice. Sometimes the rain is hot like lava. The first time it burned me, it shocked me to my core.

Today, it's cold. Very cold. I shudder so hard I lose my warrior pose.

That's when the rain's tone changes.

My brow furrows as I continue holding my breath.

A whisper reaches me through the pounding flood of water. I strain to identify the words, but can't make them out.

My feet are covered in the deluge, and it rises to my calves, then my waist. As new raindrops hit the surface around me, I sense a melody in it, sounds I've never heard before, but I'm not sure how that's possible.

I stretch out my arms, palms upward to the strange new beat. Raindrops smack my skin. I struggle to focus on the swooshing whispers, trying to hear…

Curse, curse, curse…

Your husband…

If the rain wasn't pushing down on me so hard, my eyebrows would have risen into my hair. As it is, all I manage is a wonky, single eyebrow lift.

I don't have a husband. Not yet.

But my twenty-fifth birthday is a month away and I'm required to bond. All Princesses must because there comes a time when we can't control the storm on our own anymore. We need to share the physical burden and only the strongest male elf can share it with us. He can't control the storm like we can—he can't use its power—but he acts as an extra buffer, an extension of our own bodies so to speak.

I dare to take a breath, inhaling needles of cold water, and shout into the growing wind. "What do you mean?"

Death.

Not by choice. By curse.

Death? What the…?

If I die and another princess isn't waiting to replace me, the elements will break out of the Storm Vault and tear Erawind to shreds. It's the reason everyone treats me like I'm made of porcelain. My death would unleash the fury that killed so many elves long ago and nearly destroyed our home.

A dozen curse words rest on the end of my tongue, but I don't let them loose. Elves believe that language holds power and a word spoken aloud in anger returns that anger to the speaker. I can swear inside my head as much as I like, but a spoken curse word is just that—a curse. And right now, I'm already hearing "curse" way more than I want to.

"How?" I scream.

Your husband will kill you.

Not by choice.

I freeze. Still it repeats, over and over, and the message is loud and clear: My husband is going to kill me. It won't be because he wants to. He's going to be cursed.

Against my will, I'm shaken to my core. Still the rain pours down, and I can't listen to it anymore. I slap my hands over my ears. For the first time, my resolve slips. I've been calming the storm for so long that it's a part of my life. A strange part, that's for sure, but something I do to keep my people safe. Now I want nothing more than to escape.

The rain is talking to me, for heaven's sake!

Fear gives way to frustration and something else I haven't felt for a long time—panic. I struggle against it. The last time I felt panic this intense, I hurt someone I cared about.

I struggle to push the emotion away, but it clouds my logic and rises like the rainwater, rushing against me.

The orb of water has almost reached my neck. My hair floats behind me. My arms are immersed. I can't feel my feet. It's so cold that my toes have turned numb. At the same time, the lightning returns.

It crackles around and through me. It glows like electric eels in the water, lighting me up. And still, the rain whispers to me… *Kill, curse, husband, kill, curse…*

"Enough!"

With as much strength as I can muster, I push my arms upward, willing the lightning to follow my movement like it did before. The glowing strings of electricity speed upward, leaping from the water like spears. The lightning doesn't stop there. Airborne once more, it strikes upward, lashing into the heart of the storm above me. Striking itself with my will.

An enormous *crack* slams into my hearing so loudly that I scream.

Instantly, the rain stops. The water drains away through the floor. The thunderclouds disperse. All that remains is a wisp of white fog.

The storm is gone.

If I weren't so exhausted, I'd be astounded. I stopped the storm, but not in the way I usually do. Normally, I wait patiently for it to do its thing. Today, I fought back.

Somehow, I turned the storm on itself.

I drop to the floor, exhausted and drenched, hands loose at my sides, hair streaming down my back. There was a time I thought it would be fun to conquer the Vault wearing boots and leather, like some kind of warrior princess. It turned out that was a good way to ruin expensive leather and chafe myself in all sorts of uncomfortable ways. The Princess before me wore a flowing, white dress and floated on the water, meditating, even through the lightning strikes.

These days I opt for a black, full-body swimsuit made of thick material. Unfortunately, all attempts to waterproof it turned out to be useless. But it saves my dignity when I emerge from the Vault looking like a wet cat.

I drag myself to the first door, my whole body filled with worry, barely glancing up to see Elise pressed against the glass. Her hand moves, but I'm too tired to interpret what she's trying to signal. She steps back as I push the door open. It's spelled to open only for me, so nobody else can get through it.

There's enough light for me to see the worry written across her face. "Princess, you need to—"

My panic resurfaces and I babble over the top of her. "The storm's gone wild, Elise. I can't predict what's going to happen in there anymore. I don't know how much longer I can contain it on my own." As much as I hate to admit it, I need to bond. Although, if

I believe the whispering rain's prediction that my husband will kill me, getting married is the worst thing I could do.

I shake my head and then freeze, realizing what Elise was trying to warn me about.

We aren't alone.

Two male elves wait in the shadows near the far door, one taller than the other.

Before Elise can speak again, the taller man steps into the light, but his head is down so I can't see his face. In a single fluid movement, he drops to one knee, both palms raised toward me.

I stare in shock at the red stone he holds out to me in his open hands.

Every elven House has a heartstone. All of them are priceless, irreplaceable, but this one is legendary.

The size of my fist, the rock casts ruby light around us from a thousand carefully cut facets. There's no mistaking it. It was the first heartstone ever created—the first true heart.

This stone belongs to the House of Rath.

My heart jumps. My heartbeat suddenly rages in my ears, not because of panic or fear, but with the sudden, unbearable need to reach out and close the distance between me and the man kneeling opposite me. His head is still down. All I can see is his hair: light brown, with a telltale kick on one side. I fight the impulse to reach out and run my hands through the strands.

It's been so long…

I haven't seen Baelen Rath since we were teenagers. Or, more accurately, since the day I almost killed him.

The memory should drive me away from him and make me want to put as much space between us as I can. After all, it would take only a touch now that the storm's power has filled my body to cause him severe physical harm or death. I'm deadly to everyone near me right now.

My upraised hand freezes in the air as I force myself to ignore the need to touch him, but his name passes my lips before I can stop myself. The nickname I called him when we were much younger. "Bae."

If he heard me, he hides it. His arms don't waver. But his hands close more tightly around the stone he's holding up to me.

The heartstone glints at me. An unnervingly beautiful light, all crimson and bright, nothing like the pain suddenly filling my heart while Baelen remains silent.

I'm about to say his name again when the man beside him steps into the light, unsmiling, staring at me. "Princess, the stone is offered to you."

I blink at him. "What?"

The man's forbidding expression turns to confusion. He sputters as he spins to Elise. "Is she not aware of the protocols?"

Elise is ashen, her face paler than I've ever seen it. She doesn't touch me—that would be dangerous right now—but her hand lifts in my direction. "Princess?"

The protocols...

Oh no...

I nearly take a step back, but Baelen looks up for the first time and I catch my breath, my heart stopping altogether. His green eyes pierce mine. The cut of his jaw is unyielding. I follow the shape of his high cheekbones to his chin and the pulse at his neck. Following all the strong lines of his face that I once ran my fingertips across. A mouth that once spoke my name and, in that single word, said so much. A body that once gave me everything I could ask for.

Then he tilts his head to reveal the scar that cuts from his right temple down the side of his face and curves behind his ear. The scar splits at his jawline and slashes beneath his chin like a curling vine. As if a single wound wasn't enough.

I did that. He wears that scar because of me.

His voice is emotionless as he turns the scar fully into the light. "This is what you wanted to see?"

"I... No..." My own voice fails me. Shocked that he thinks I'd care about something as superficial as a scar, while my chest hurts to see the extent of the wound. He's wrong. I don't want to see the scar. I want to see that he's okay despite it.

But the fact that he's holding his family's heartstone out to me—offering it to me—means that he intends to be a champion in the fight for my hand. He intends to fight for me. By taking the stone, I will show him that I accept his nomination.

The thing is, the protocols force me to take it. The whole process is designed to make it look like I have a choice, but I don't.

If I refuse to accept him as a champion, I'll dishonor his entire House.

The problem is… he's the only one left. He's the only remaining Rath. The fight for my hand isn't all about battle. It's a game of wits first and strength last. But the final fight between the two remaining champions is to the death. It's designed that way so the loser doesn't live to challenge the marriage bond. If Baelen fights and dies, his House will die with him.

The scar is a painful reminder that I almost ended his life once. I won't do it again.

Hardening my heart and burying my memories, I take a step back. "I can't take the heartstone you offer me."

His advisor freezes beside him. I recognize the male elf as the same one who served the late Commander Rath. Baelen's father passed away last year. I attended the wake, and it was my first chance in seven years to speak with Baelen. But a funeral is one of the times that a Princess's wishes don't hold sway and despite trying to reach Baelen, I'd barely seen him from a distance before my personal guard whisked me away.

His advisor's voice rises. "Does the Princess intend to offend the House of Rath?"

"My lord—" Elise hurries to defend me, but I stop her with my upraised hand.

I don't touch her. That would be lethal with the storm's rage still filling my veins.

As much as I feel like a mere vessel for the storm sometimes, the reality is that I control its power afterward.

My outstretched hand glimmers with lightning. The forces I've absorbed want to be released. It's my responsibility to subdue the storm each day, but doing so gives me the power to wield its fury.

Technically right now, I *am* the storm.

With a trickle of fear, it occurs to me then to wonder how long Baelen and his advisor were waiting inside the room; how much they saw. It's common knowledge that I can tame the lightning, but what I just did—stopping the storm in its tracks—was entirely unexpected. I know I can trust Baelen, even with our history, but I'm not so certain that his advisor will keep this secret.

Despite the power raging inside me, I'm tired. All I want is to slump in a warm bath and wash off the cold rain and its ominous message about my husband killing me. I want to reach back into the past and change what happened, and I want to reach into the future and ensure the rain's message doesn't come to pass.

More than anything, I want Baelen to lower his hands.

I can't take the heartstone from him without talking with him first. I can't let him risk his life like this. Not for me. Not for anything.

I address his advisor. "My lord, you mistake my intentions. I *can't* receive the heartstone right now. I've just come from the Vault. If I touch the stone, I'll destroy it."

Drawing myself upright with my remaining strength, I focus on a point past the advisor's face. "The power inside me will destroy the stone *and anyone holding it.*"

I lower my eyes to Baelen's, hoping he hears the message in my next words because I may not get another chance to say them. Try as I might, I can't stop my voice from breaking a little as I speak. "I won't be responsible for the death of the last Rath."

My focus switches to the exit. I step up beside Baelen, fighting the resurging need to reach out to him like I was once able to do. I force my expression blank and keep my distance from him but close the gap between me and his advisor.

The advisor seems to have taken my warning seriously and takes a hasty step back.

I sense Baelen shift, his face turned to mine, but I don't have time to assess his reaction—whether he's as offended as his advisor or whether he heard the fear in my voice and understood it.

I need to move away from him before these impulses overcome me.

I snap at his advisor. "I will kill any elf I touch right now. Get out of my way and come back at a more appropriate time."

He makes way for me as I push through the door and stride into the next room. Elise stays close on my heels. As my personal advisor, only Elise is supposed to be allowed inside the Vault's waiting room. She's the only one who sees what I go through to keep my people safe. How Baelen and his advisor got inside is something I mean to find out.

The members of my all-female personal guard, also known as

the Storm Command, wait outside the final door. I prefer to think of them as the *nunnery*. They'll surround me once I reach them, making sure nothing and nobody comes near me. That includes any male elf or even female who isn't part of the Storm Command.

I can't imagine what Jordan—the head of the nunnery—will say about me being approached by a man in the Vault's waiting room. It's her job to keep all elves away from me. Until one of them wins the right to marry me, all contact is forbidden. Even the heartstone protocol is supposed to take place in a very public arena under intense scrutiny.

I risk a glance back at Baelen through the open doors between us. He's on his feet, turned in my direction. The stone rests in his fist at his side. I'm amazed at how it disappears inside his big hand.

His head is tilted a little to the side, that slight wave falling across his piercing eyes. The scar he wears across his jaw seems to blend and disappear into his features. A scar belonging to a warrior.

Now that he's standing, I'm struck by the breadth of his shoulders, the width of his biceps, his lean waist, and powerful legs. His muscles are even more developed than they were seven years ago. He may be fully clothed, but it does nothing to hide his physical strength.

He was always the tallest, the strongest, the biggest. All Raths are built for war. Fighting. Protecting. Stepping into danger.

It's the reason they're all dead.

I clench my jaw. *I won't let you die, too.*

Turning away from him, I push on the final door and Jordan immediately assaults me. The nunnery snaps to attention, ten strong female elves forming a wide circle around me in the broad corridor. They don't dare come within five feet of me on any side, and they won't let anyone else come close either.

To my surprise, Jordan's expression is as worried as Elise's—not a look I'm used to seeing on her face. Jordan is always confident, composed, and in control.

Now, her face is flushed. She holds out her arm horizontally to her chest and rests her forehead on it in a gesture of remorse. "Princess, I ask your forgiveness. I had no power to stop him."

My eyes narrow in wary contemplation of her meaning. As the

head of my personal guard, Jordan is ranked higher than any other military officer. She doesn't control the army—only the nunnery—but no other elf can give her orders except for me. It's a necessary precaution to ensure that nobody can get to me.

The only military position of higher authority than Jordan's is the Commander of the Elven Army—again for my personal safety: it's important for the leader of the army to communicate directly with me without obstruction from my guard. Baelen's father used to fill that position, but he stayed away from me. After what I did to his son, I didn't blame him.

Luckily, the gargoyles have been quiet for the last seven years, so it was possible for him to keep his distance. After his death, a temporary replacement filled the position, but to my knowledge, the Elven Command hasn't announced a permanent replacement yet.

"Jordan?"

"I received word while you were in the Vault. Baelen Rath is now the commander of the armed forces."

And the only man allowed near me.

My legs almost fail me with shock, but at the same time, a thread of relief flows through me. Maybe now I'll have a chance to have a proper conversation with him and convince him not to be a champion.

At least it explains how he got past Jordan and made his way inside the waiting room.

She steps back, her focus shifting to a point behind me, and I suddenly realize that the door didn't close when I passed through it. I'd thought Elise was right behind me, but she's hovering against the wall near the door.

I sense Baelen's presence in the doorway like a force stronger than the lightning. I twist to assess the distance between us. The logical part of my brain tells me I can't endanger him, but from the moment I first saw him, I've been fighting to keep my distance to keep him safe.

The illogical part of my mind wants me to close the gap between us. Now that he's standing so close to me, facing me fully, memories I've been pushing away for seven years threaten to bring down the shields I've built around myself.

He steps forward, allowing the door to close behind him, moving far closer to me than anyone else would dare. I check for the heartstone, but it's nowhere in sight now.

His expression is no longer emotionless. Whatever mask he was wearing when he offered me his heartstone, it's gone. He was always honest, never playing games or wanting any part in politics. Now, his gaze flows freely across my face, lingering on the dripping strands of my auburn hair, following a droplet of water down my cheek to my lips before returning to my blue eyes.

His voice is low, and his eyes don't waver from mine. "Marbella Mercy."

It's strange to hear my name spoken aloud. Everyone else calls me "Princess" or worse: "*the* Princess", even if they're speaking to me, as if I'm a thing. It's been a long time since I've heard my name associated with my House: The House of Mercy. When I became the Princess, I had to leave my home and family behind. My mother is allowed to visit me once a year, but I'm not allowed to see my father and brother.

"I meant what I said," I tell him. "I could hurt you right now."

If he's worried, he doesn't show it. "Danger never bothered me."

Spoken by anyone else, those words would sound conceited, but from a Rath they only ring with truth. I try to quell the smile forcing its way onto my lips. "I learned that about you a long time ago."

Jordan clears her throat, her face flaming. Her eyes dart left. We're blocking the corridor and, although it's not a frequently traveled path, elves are gathering on either side, unable to get through. Jordan's expression makes it clear that we're creating a spectacle.

On the eve of the marriage protocols, a spectacle is a bad thing.

I remind myself that I'm not a girl anymore. I can't catch Baelen's hand in mine like I once did, can't tell him my secrets, can't even smile at him.

Again, I force myself to take a step away from him. He might outrank Jordan, but he doesn't outrank me. Damn that logical side of my brain. I want to stomp on it and kick it into a corner.

Swallowing hard, I speak loudly. "Commander Rath, you will

attend the War Room to discuss your appointment. My Storm Command will be in attendance. I expect you there in two hours."

I spin without another word, asserting my authority. He may be the commander of the army, but as a potential champion, there are rules he has to follow. I catch his acknowledging nod, the barest hint of a smile that could stop my heart, and I feel his unwavering gaze on me as I turn away.

Everything within me screams at me to go back, to tell him everything I need to tell him, to rage against the chains that cage my existence, and give myself choices that have been taken away from me. But they're imaginary choices that no longer exist. It took me years to accept that what I want, and what I can have, are two entirely different things.

I keep walking.

The nunnery closes around me, filling all the gaps that someone could step through, protecting me even from myself.

I'm supposed to be alone, untouched, pure, and pristine.

Only Baelen Rath knows that I'm not.

2

BAELEN

I force my feet to remain planted where I stand, fury pounding inside me as torrential rain rises to Marbella's neck inside the Vault, threatening to drown her.

I'm not allowed to help.

After seven years away from her, I don't know much about the rules, but her advisor, Elise, stands in front of the door into the Vault, sending a clear message that I am not to approach or interfere.

Damn it all. Give me an enemy I can fight. Give me a bloody battle against raging beasts. I'd rather face any of those than stand by and watch Marbella hurting.

My grip on my family's heartstone tightens. I'm in danger of crushing it, but I don't let up. Can't let up. I have to channel my fury somewhere.

Inside the Vault, rainwater has nearly reached her neck, her brilliant auburn hair floating on its surface, her body immersed. She shivers so hard, I can see it from this distance. The water must be freezing. I can't hear anything, but her head is tilted as if she's listening carefully—and becoming angrier by the second...

I will her anger to increase. It's how she'll get through this. Her anger... she was always furiously determined, never revealing vulnerability even when she had a right to. I only saw her downtrodden once and I felt privileged that she trusted me enough to ask for my help. Well, not exactly *ask*. I offered and she accepted, allowing me into her life.

Lightning streaks from the ceiling to wrap around her, lighting up her body, her narrow waist, the curve of her legs and arms. She pushes her arms upward and the lightning follows her movements, taking the water with it.

The burst of light inside the Vault is breathtaking. Most elves don't believe that she can control the lightning, but I never doubted it for a second. If anyone can conquer the Storm, it's Marbella.

Lightning explodes from her hands, striking the heart of the thunderclouds above her. The walls shudder as if reacting to a giant explosion while Marbella drops to the wet floor, curling over. I can't hear her, but I can see that she's screaming.

Her scream... My worst fear...

I step forward, prepared to break down the wall if I have to.

My advisor's arm knocks against my chest, attempting to stop me. He's a tall elf, his skin tinged golden like the members of his House—the House of Glory. His robes swish against the floor as he moves, the intricate golden tattoo across the back of his hand catching the fading light from the Vault. His name is Gannon and his expression remains blank, pinched, always stern.

I glare at his arm, restraining myself. He doesn't have the strength to push me anywhere I don't want to go. I could snap his bones with a single twist. If he were my friend, a trusted advisor, I would never consider retaliating, but this man was appointed by the Elven Command to be my father's advisor. I didn't choose him, which means I can't trust him. I can't trust his motives for keeping me from helping Marbella right now.

When I turn back to the Vault, Marbella is dragging herself to her feet, her hair streaming down her back and clinging to her curves. Her black storm suit is torn across one knee, a bloody gash visible between the flaps, but she doesn't seem to notice as she stumbles across the Vault and bursts through the door.

Her advisor rushes to speak first, but Marbella talks over her, an edge of fear in her voice. "The storm's gone wild, Elise. I don't know how much longer I can contain it on my own."

Her fear is like a punch to my stomach. Nothing prepared me for her presence. Now that the spelled wall is no longer a barrier between us, all I want is to hold her, make sure she's okay, make her smile, breathe in the scent of her hair…

Gannon lowers his arm and I nearly move toward her. I nearly forget why I'm here, that her choices are not her own anymore, that I have to fight for her harder than I ever did before. If I want to stand beside her inside the Vault, fight the storm with her, I have to earn it.

I have to become a champion and fight, ultimately to the death, to be with her.

The first step is now.

I'm moving before I know it, taking a knee, raising my family's heartstone up to her, an offering held in both palms.

If she takes it, I'll know that the last seven years haven't destroyed us, that she still wants me in her life. I'm not afraid of the lightning still crackling around her, the tiny pulses caressing her fingertips and neck.

She freezes while the crimson stone glistens between us. With my head down, I can't see her face, don't know her reaction, other than that she doesn't move a muscle. A thin trickle of blood slides down her knee, the only movement.

She doesn't take the stone, doesn't speak, and my heart… slowly sinks, cracks a little.

I try to search for reasons… any reason other than the one staring me in the face—that she doesn't want me to fight for her. Maybe she doesn't recognize me. I've changed a lot. Maybe she senses the wild that has crept into me, the wild that became my life while I was away from her. Maybe it scares her. Maybe *I* scare her. I try to stop the shudder running through my body. I never want her to be afraid, let alone of me.

She whispers, "Bae."

I inhale the sound of my name, beat back the memories of the hundred times she said it before, a tiny spark of hope rising inside me, but as the silence stretches, my heartbeat slows and my hope fades again.

If she were going to take my heartstone and accept me, she would have done it by now.

Gannon steps into the light, his voice cold. "Princess, the stone is offered to you."

A brief glance at her face tells me her brow is furrowed as if she's waking from a dream. "What?"

Gannon spins to Elise, chastising her about something to do with protocols, but their conversation washes over me. Now that I'm looking up, I can't drag my gaze away. Her hair has come loose from its tie, wet strands framing her face. Her lips are slightly pursed and the turquoise flecks in her eyes catch the light.

I'm shocked to discover that I can't read her expression to know her thoughts. There was a time when I could tell what she was thinking, every little change in the way she pressed her lips together, every small shift in her gaze, the presence or absence of the slight crease in her forehead telling me if she was worried or happy.

Now… she's blank, her feelings hidden.

She studies me intently, following the contours of my cheekbones to my chin, pausing at my neck as if she's searching for something.

Ice fills my heart as I realize she's looking for my scar.

I swallow, my jaw clenching, turning that side of my face into the light. The wound stretches from my temple all the way down to my ear, cutting in both directions along my jawline—behind my ear and also toward my chin. It's like a thick, twisted rope, the kind of scar that is too brutal to be passed off as a mark of honor or symbol of power. It makes other elves uncomfortable, especially female elves.

I search her eyes for the girl I used to know, the one who didn't care what I looked like, didn't care how many fights I won, or how much power my family had, who saw more than the Rath name. I fight my fear that that girl is gone, destroyed by seven years of raging against a never-ending storm and surviving the Elven Command's political intrigues as they retain their poisonous clutch on power.

I should have come back sooner.

I shouldn't have left her here. I should have broken down this Vault and taken her—and the Storm—away from here. A crazy thought. A desperate thought.

Fear that I've lost her turns my voice to ice. "This is what you wanted to see?"

Her eyes widen. "I… No…" She stares at the heartstone, a fierce, trapped stare as her focus returns to my scar.

She steps back. "I can't…"

Gannon's face turns purple with rage. "Does the Princess intend to offend the House of Rath?"

My forehead creases while Elise hurries to speak. I'm still learning the rules, but I'm starting to think I haven't been properly informed. The way Gannon spoke makes it sounds like Marbella doesn't have any choice except to take my heartstone. But I thought it was voluntary, an acceptance of my wish to become a champion, not a mandatory protocol, as if she didn't have any say in it at all…

A dozen curse words pass through my mind. *What if I've gone about this all wrong?* What if I'm not supposed to be in this room at all? Now that I think about it, Marbella's Storm Command was extremely flustered when I asked to see her in the Vault. They let me through, so I thought it was okay…

For the first time, desperation enters Marbella's expression. She addresses my advisor, her voice brittle. "I *can't* receive the heartstone right now. I've just come from the Vault. If I touch the stone, I'll destroy it *and anyone holding it.*"

She lowers her gaze to mine. I see her again—finally—the woman I knew, the one who climbed mountains, stood on the edge of a cliff with me, and valued me more than my power.

Her eyes glisten with conviction. "I won't be responsible for the death of the last Rath."

My lips part. I want to tell her that she won't be. That she doesn't have to be afraid.

I was built for war. I was built to fight. I've spent the last seven years making myself stronger than ever because I knew this day would come.

Lightning crackles around her fingertips as she steps up beside me. The power radiating from her up close is intoxicating. I lean toward her, into the danger instead of away from it, drawn closer, but she pulls away from me.

Without looking at me, she says to Gannon, "Come back at a more appropriate time."

Gannon hurries out of her path, stumbling to avoid the light swirling around her as she strides through the first door into the second room.

I stand to watch her go, squaring my shoulders, lowering the heartstone to grip it in my fist again. She turns back at the final door, her gaze flashing across the distance, no less worried. Then Jordan Splendor demands her attention.

Jordan's flushed face and gesture of failure aren't lost on me.

I definitely wasn't supposed to be in here.

I growl at Gannon as I pass. "Get me whatever rulebook governs the Storm Princess's movements as well as the Heartstone Ceremony protocols."

His lips pinch, likely because he knows I've seen through him. If the rulebook confirms what I think it will—that nobody is supposed to enter the Vault—then it will confirm my suspicion that he's an Elven Command spy. He used me for the opportunity to get a look inside the Vault. No doubt, he'll hurry back to Gideon Glory to report what he saw. Either way, I won't be taking his advice again.

"Yes, Commander," he says.

I don't give him the heartstone, not trusting him with it. Instead, I slip it into the pouch at my waist. With a polite nod to Elise—a nod I hope conveys my regret—I take a deep breath and follow after Marbella.

I catch Jordan's final words as I stop inside the open doorway. "Baelen Rath is now the commander of the armed forces."

Marbella wobbles but doesn't reach for anything to steady herself, doesn't ask anyone for help. I guess she was serious when she said she could hurt anyone she touches right now…

Jordan notices me, her eyes widening, and Marbella swings back to me. She immediately assesses the distance between us, adjusting it so she isn't anywhere close enough to touch me.

I want to apologize, but her fierce gaze obliterates every rational thought in my head. Everyone around us disappears. If I thought for a second that I had her permission, I would close the gap between us, brush the hair from her cheek, and ask her how she really is.

The corner of my mouth hitches up the tiniest bit. I hope she'll respond with a smile, even a hint of one. "Marbella Mercy."

It doesn't look like she does a lot of smiling these days.

She remains gravely serious. "I meant what I said. I could hurt you right now."

I shrug my shoulders. I ask myself why I'm not afraid of the power crackling around her, but I have no answer for that. "Danger never bothered me."

There it is. The hint of a smile, the smallest gesture that tells me she still remembers us. "I learned that about you a long time ago."

Jordan clears her throat, pointedly indicating the blocked corridor.

I hope that Marbella will look left and sees who is waiting farther along the hallway. I want to give her a moment of happiness. My gift to her…

I bury my disappointment when she swings back to her ladies, throwing a clipped command in my direction. "Commander Rath, you will attend the War Room to discuss your appointment. My Storm Command will be in attendance. I expect you there in two hours."

I don't miss the fact that she emphasized she won't be alone.

Watching her walk away is harder than watching her fight the storm. I battle the sigh that rises to my lips as I clear the doorway, allowing Elise to hurry after Marbella to join the Storm Command surrounding her.

Gannon also slips past me. "I will bring the books to your quarters, Commander."

I give him a nod, pausing to make sure he's gone before I head in the opposite direction.

Marbella's brother steps out of the shadows farther along the walkway. She hasn't seen him since the Elven Command ripped her away from her family after the Storm chose her. She and her brother used to be close; in fact, her whole family was. If I could give her anything right now, it would be time with him. I guess it wasn't meant to be today, but I'm determined to reunite them one way or another.

"I'm sorry, Macsen."

Macsen shrugs his shoulders, but he can't hide the sadness lurking behind his eyes. It's the same sadness that crept into his parents' eyes after Marbella was gone.

"How is she?" he asks.

I shake my head, not afraid to let my guard down. There are only a handful of elves I trust. Macsen Mercy is one of them.

"I honestly don't know. If what I saw is any indication, she goes through hell inside that Vault but doesn't say a word to complain about it. She ordered me to meet her in the War Room in two hours."

"Ordered you?" Macsen grins at me, his easygoing nature resurfacing. "I wish I'd seen that."

I huff, quietly appreciating that he's trying to make light of a dark situation. "She's different… changed."

"It's this place," Macsen says, his smile disappearing as fast as it appeared. "She has to play by their rules."

"And so do I," I growl. I run my hand through my hair as we walk down the corridor. "I miss living in a place where truth is respected."

Macsen arches an eyebrow at me. "Is that where you were for the last three years? In a place of truth?"

I give him a scowl that tells him nothing. "Maybe."

After teaching myself how to walk again, I went to military school like I was supposed to. But after that, I had to leave, get as far away from everything as I could. I want to tell Macsen where I was, but I have to be careful.

He shakes his head at me. "You disappeared after military training. For three whole years. Where did you go?"

My fist clenches. "Away from Marbella. As far as I could get."

Macsen considers me for a moment. Then his hand flies out and catches my shoulder, forcing me to stop walking. There aren't many elves who would dare confront me, let alone have the strength to stop me in my tracks. Marbella's brother used to be tall and lanky. Now he's an axe who hides his true strength behind a casual façade. He's unexpectedly dangerous, which is just one of the reasons why I trust him to watch my back.

His eyes narrow, his tone accusing. "She didn't accept your heartstone, did she?"

I grind my teeth. "She said she wouldn't be responsible for the death of the last Rath."

He releases me, exhaling. "She thinks you'll make it to the final fight. She's scared you'll die—"

"I won't."

"You could. Have you thought about that? Is that what your father would have wanted? To see the House of Rath die out once and for all? After what happened to your mother—"

"I won't walk away from Marbella."

"You did once."

Rage spirals up inside me. My scar suddenly burns like the night it happened, a hot wound, but not the worst. "You call that walking?"

He pales. I sense the curse words he wants to speak aloud but doesn't. "I'm sorry, friend. That was unforgiveable."

I exhale my anger, releasing it into the quiet corridor. My knowledge of the protocols may be almost nonexistent, but I do know one thing. "I don't have a choice, Macsen. I'm the last. My House has to offer up a champion. Even if I wasn't…" I give him a furious grin. "I'd fight any living Rath to the death for the chance to be with her."

Macsen levels his gaze with mine. "The other Houses won't make the trials easy for you. Remember how it was in military school? They heard you were injured and moved in for the kill. Multiply that by a thousand."

I attempt a smile. "That's why I have you, brother."

He nods, grinning. "I'll watch your back."

As we exit the corridor, I ask, "What news about the border?"

Macsen's expression turns grim. "The gargoyles have reached Baldor Peak."

"That's closer than I expected," I say. "I have to warn Marbella."

3

———

MARBELLA

As we sweep along the wide corridor, Jordan keeps pace on one side of me and Elise walks on the other. They're my constant companions, and I count myself lucky that I can also call them my friends. To be chosen for their positions, they went through a set of protocols seven years ago, similar to the ones my future husband will go through over the next few weeks: tests of emotional and physical strength, intelligence and, most important of all, compatibility. But even if I wanted to tell them everything, there are some things nobody can know.

Such as what really happened on the night I became the Storm Princess.

I can't be alone with Baelen Rath.

If I'm alone with him, my shields won't hold.

"Jordan, it's important that you remain with me at all times." I try to soften my order with an attempted smile.

"I understand, Princess."

I glance at her and the grim look she gives me tells me she really does understand. The rulebook setting out the champion protocols is inches thick. It starts with dictating how each House chooses their nominated champion and ends with orders about my wedding night. I struggle not to roll my eyes about that.

There are so many rules it makes my head spin. I remember the

30

first time I laid eyes on the giant book and I'd asked, "What happened to falling in love?"

Back then, Elise gave me the only stern response she ever spoke to me: "A Princess does not love. She does what is right for her people."

That was when I banished all thoughts of Baelen from my mind. Or, at least, I tried to.

I turn to Elise next, but I don't have to say anything. Her expression tells me she's way ahead of me. The way her eyes fill with worry, the slight furrow of her forehead. She's thinking hard about my situation right now. Baelen Rath is an added complication to what happened in the Vault—what I did with the storm.

"We need to talk about the weather," she says and I know it's code for: We need to talk about the storm, Baelen, and basically everything that seems to be going wrong today.

The biggest question for me is: Did anyone else hear the rain? I don't think they could have because the Vault is soundproof—it has to be to contain the thunder. The vibrations produced by the perfect storm can cause whole buildings to collapse.

Because of that, I don't think Elise would have heard the rain's warning. For a moment, I debate whether I should tell her. I need to talk to someone about it. As much as I love Jordan, she can't know about any of it. The rules again—only Elise can know what goes on in the Vault.

As we emerge from the corridor into the light, I flip my head back and growl my frustration at the sky. There's enough thunder inside me to rumble past my lips and scare the nearby civilian elves. They scatter away from me as the Storm Command—and me inside their circle—takes the paved path through the gardens.

Above us, the artificial sun shines high in the afternoon sky. A thousand years ago, when the elves were forced from the surface of Earth, they used deep magic to create an entire ecosystem between the layers of Earth, complete with a sun and moon, forests and rivers. We were at peace with the gargoyles then, and we divided our new home into two parts: Erawind for the elves and Erador for the gargoyles.

The humans don't know we're here. Since we descended into

this world, elves with visionary powers have seen images of Earth's surface. There's a city of metal and bricks far above us. According to the Visionaries, the humans call it Chicago.

The Storm Vault itself is contained inside a citadel, in the middle of our highest place of learning—the heart of Erawind and home to priceless spell books. The elves would never have chosen to build the Vault here, but the storm was deliberately sent to this place to destroy all our most precious knowledge. The elves had no choice but to contain its fury in the closest building possible— which turned out to be the stone tower where young spellcasters used to take lessons.

It means I'm surrounded by both warriors and scholars at all times. It's an uneasy cohabitation. The passing professors bow deeply to me, but I know they still mourn the loss of the sanctity of their school and resentment lies beneath the respect they show me. The perfect storm is a constant threat to their most precious belongings, as well as their lives.

I leave puddles in my wake. I'm dripping and my body temperature is dropping. As a spellcaster, Elise has the power to warm me, but magic doesn't mix well with the storm's fury. It won't be safe for anyone to touch me for at least another hour.

My plight is my own.

I sigh. I'm desperate for that hot bath.

"Princess!" The shriek from the side of the gardens breaks through my thoughts.

Jordan and Elise immediately close ranks around me. The Storm Command maintains an impenetrable circle. I sigh with frustration, because they're all taller than me. At a little more than five-feet-three-inches, I have no hope of seeing over the protective barrier they've formed to identify the source of the commotion.

"Princess! Princess!" As the crying woman draws nearer, I recognize her voice.

"Let her through, but don't let her touch me for her own sake."

The Storm Command's circle opens so suddenly that the running elf skids through it. Jordan catches her at the last moment before she slides into me.

The newcomer's red hair flows around her. Elves come in all shapes, sizes, and skin colors, but only female elves in the House of

Reverie have hair the color of blood. My own hair is auburn and a pale comparison.

I keep my distance as I address her. "Rebecca, what is it?"

"Princess, you must come at once. Mai is ill."

Mai Reverie is the dancer who used to meditate in the rain. She never told me, but I sensed that she had a similar connection with the rain that I have with the lightning.

"She's asking for you. She won't speak to anyone else. Only you."

My eyes widen. "She's refusing help?"

"She is. She won't let anyone help her until she speaks with you."

Beside me, Elise's worried eyes meet mine and I wish I could read her thoughts. In ancient times, spellcasters had the ability to sneak into another elf's mind and catch their thoughts, but that practice was exposed and outlawed when the last elven king died. It was his scheming that turned the gargoyles into our enemies. He was the first to die in the storm and because he had no children, the heads of the elven Houses agreed to form a new Elven Command in which all the Houses had representation and a vote.

I race after Rebecca, trying not to connect with anyone as I move. The Storm Command quickly clears a path for me, and I marvel at their efficiency. Three women dart forward, clearing the way ahead, while the others close ranks and keep perfect pace with me.

Mai's quarters are on the other side of the square. She's the only other former princess who's still alive. The other two lived for hundreds of years each, hanging on until the Storm chose its next princess.

My own quarters are on the opposite side of the square—Mai vacated them when the storm chose me. There's never any resentment on the part of the vacating princess. We have no real political power—that rests with the Elven Command. And besides, who'd want to spend their days fighting with a storm?

I still remember the look of relief Mai gave me when I met her for the first time. Her relief was so huge that it terrified me to consider what I was taking on.

I race through the outer wall of her quarters, through her personal garden and its neatly sculpted stone and sand arrangements. I slow my pace as we run toward the inner rooms. I call the Storm Command to slow down, too. "Go carefully."

The female elves become like wraiths, their footsteps light, barely perceptible. My own are heavier because of the weight of the storm I absorbed and my boots squelch on the pristine marble floor.

Jordan gives my feet a glance and I shrug my shoulders. I'm noisy, but there's nothing I can do about it.

Besides… the energy radiating from Mai's greeting room tells me she'll sense me coming no matter what. Her inner quarters are surrounded by indoor plants—vines full of red roses curling across the top of the door and internal windows. The House of Reverie is known for its ability to cultivate plants in any environment.

Jordan signals for the elves to halt and turns to me. "Her door is open."

She describes it to me because they're still blocking my view. An open door, at least, is a good sign, because in elven society it's a sign of good faith. Mai isn't hiding anything.

"Open." The Storm Command obeys me instantly, shuffling back into a crescent keeping my back safe, so I have a direct view of Mai's quarters through the door. It fills me with faith to see how much they trust my commands.

Mai and her husband Darian sit on the rug in the middle of the room. Mai's legs are in an awkward position, making me think she collapsed in that position, while Darian supported her. Beads of sweat rest on her brow and her dress is shiny as if she went swimming in it.

I step forward, but Elise is quicker. "No, Princess."

I spin to her.

Her forehead is creased with worry. "Princess, if there's illness inside that room, you can't be exposed to it."

I shake my head. "I'm full of storm, Elise. I'm as strong as I'll ever be. Mai needs my help. I can feel it. I'm not backing away from this."

"I don't expect you to, but please let me come with you."

I'm surprised she thought I'd go in without her. She's not only my advisor but my best friend. "Of course."

Rebecca hovers beside me. "She said she'd speak only with you, Princess."

"I understand, Rebecca, thank you for telling me, but the rules are the rules: a member of the Storm Command must be with me at all times."

Rebecca bows her head and clears the way as Elise and I step into the room. The Storm Command forms an impenetrable barrier behind me and spreads out to guard the windows on either side.

I turn to Elise. "But that doesn't mean everyone has to listen."

"I understand." Elise turns her hand to the side and passes it across the doorway as we step inside the room. I trust her to create a sound barrier between us and the watching elves.

Darian lifts his head while Mai reaches out a hand to me. Her skin is much paler than normal.

"Marbella," she says. "I'm sorry to greet you in this state."

I drop to my knees. "What happened, Mai?"

The concern on Darian's face makes me envy the love between them. He allows her to lean against him, supporting her in an upright position.

"She collapsed while she was gardening," he says. "I carried her in here, but then…"

He glances at her as if seeking her permission.

In response, Mai places her hand on his. "It's all right. I can tell her."

She turns to me. "I started to rain."

Elise's forehead creases. "It started to rain?"

"No," Mai says, "*I* started to rain."

I'm sure I misheard. "You started to… What?"

In response, Mai leans back onto Darian, turning her head into his shoulder, whispering, "Will you help me show them?"

"I will always help you," he says, but he turns to us first, his expression stern. "She's weak and I'll only assist her to do this once. Then you have to get help."

He wraps his arms around her waist and lifts her to her feet, pulling her upright. Her legs wobble, but he keeps her straight long enough for me to see what I need to see.

Her dress changes color halfway down, dark and saturated from her ribcage, but dry at her shoulders. Her hair, too, is completely dry. Wispy strands float around her. But her hands and feet…

Water drips from her fingertips and puddles around her feet. I can tell from how dry her head and shoulders are that the water isn't falling from anywhere above her. It's dripping from her fingers and toes. It's coming from her.

I meet her eyes and I know there's more. It was the rain that spoke to me in the Vault, and Mai always had an affinity for the rain.

Her fingers move. The change is so slight that I barely perceive it, but then…

Everything slows around me. Elise is half-turning, her eyes wide, one arm rising to point at the water falling from Mai's hands. Darian is about to speak, his mouth half-open. Then everything… stops.

Even the water droplets suspend in mid-air. Except for Mai and me.

"What did you do?" I ask, barely breathing.

"I used the power of the thunder to suspend time."

"You what? But you're not the Princess anymore. How can you channel the storm? That's…"

"You have so much to learn about the power of the storm, but they won't let me teach you. You'll have to learn on your own like I had to."

"Who won't let you teach me?"

"Marbella, you need to listen to me. We only have a few moments. The rain spoke to me. Someone's cursed the protocols."

"It spoke to me, too!"

I edge toward her. Glimmers of lightning wrap around my fingers, but I push them down. Mai isn't a threat to me.

She looks relieved that I already know. "Then you know your husband will be cursed to kill you."

I suck in a deep breath. "The rain told me. But I don't know what to do."

She doesn't hesitate. "You have to fight for yourself."

"What?"

"Be your own champion. Win the challenges. Accept no man as your husband. It's the only way."

"But I need to bond. The storm's getting stronger. It's too strong for me."

"No, Marbella, no. You already have everything you need to control it. The Elven Command wants you to believe that you aren't enough—that you need to share the burden. But you'll discover once you marry that it's all a lie. The other Princesses weren't alive to tell me, but I'm telling you. *You* are all you need."

She glances at Darian. "I love him, and I wouldn't change my marriage for all the world. And, yes, he has supported me and been my best friend, but the moment he stepped into the Vault it almost killed him! I'm forbidden to speak of it, Marbella. But the truth is that *we* are the storm. Only us. Only our bodies. And now... the storm is choosing to connect with me again, trying to send you a message through me."

"We have to get you help."

She gently shakes her head. "Soon. I promise I'll be okay. But you need to understand your power."

"But... why? Why does the Elven Command make us marry if it doesn't help us?"

"So we are never seen holding all of the power ourselves. So we are not *all*-powerful." She grimaces. "I can't hold time much longer. Promise me you'll fight for yourself. Promise me!"

I have so many more questions. So much to ask her.

But at the heart of what she said is the answer to saving Baelen: I will fight for myself. Even though confusion whirls through me about everything Mai revealed to me, I'm filled with intense relief.

As everything speeds up around us, I say, "Thank you, dear friend."

She nods and collapses against Darian.

I spin to Elise. My advisor shivers beside me, running her hand through her hair as if she's pulling off cobwebs. She's a gifted spellcaster and will be able to sense that something happened, but she won't know how. She doesn't understand the power of the storm. As it turns out, I don't either.

I know I should tell her what just happened, but Mai spoke only to me for a reason. I meet Rebecca's eyes across the room. She's Mai's advisor—she would have seen what happened when Darian accompanied Mai into the Vault.

She must know the truth about the marriage protocol. Her lips are pressed together. I know she won't speak a word of it.

I spin to Elise before she can say anything. "Mai needs help now. Call the healers, please."

Elise waves her hand, lifting the cloak of silence around the room, and the message is relayed back through my Storm Command. Two of my elves separate from the others and sprint away, their lithe bodies a blur of movement. Of the ten, they are my message bearers, chosen for their speed. Every one of my Command is highly trained and hand-picked to excel.

I'm afraid to touch Mai in case the power inside me could hurt her, but I kneel and lean as close as I can. "I'll do as you say."

I will fight for myself.

4

MARBELLA

We leave Mai in the hands of the healers. I want to stay, but my Storm Command takes up so much space that I'll hinder their efforts. There's nothing else I can do to help. Mai gives me a nod and I'm grateful that she'll accept help now.

I head for my quarters across the square with only ten minutes to spare before I'm supposed to meet Baelen in the War Room. There's no way I can face him without a hot bath to calm my nerves and wash away the storm.

Elise takes one look at my face and sends one of the Storm Command ahead to prepare the bath, and another to the War Room to let Baelen know I'll be late. I give her a grateful smile for doing both. It's better that I don't cause the House of Rath more offense than I already have today.

She leans in as we reach my quarters, her voice gentle. "Princess, once you deal with the Commander, we need to talk about what happened today."

"Yes, thank you." I appreciate the way she always remains calm. Sometimes it makes me wonder if there's more to her simmering beneath the surface, because she never panics or becomes angry. As much as I hate all of the protocols, they definitely worked in my favor to give me an advisor who balances out my emotions.

Inside my room, I strip off the storm suit and hang it over its special rack in the bathing room that adjoins my bedroom. I sink into the bathtub of water, immersing myself completely, even my head. The last of the cold rainwater washes out of my hair as I try to shake the images of Mai's raining body and the way she suspended time.

The bath is the only place I'm allowed to be alone. Elise and Jordan wait for me in my bedroom and my Storm Command lines the hall outside. My home is more of a soldier's barracks than a home. My room is the largest and sits in the center of the square structure. There's only one door to my room but hallways on every side. My Storm Command sleeps in rooms all around me—twenty elves rotating on and off shift in such a way that there are always ten of them with me and I get to see all of them throughout each week.

Light reaches me through two skylights—one in the bathroom and one in the bedroom.

I drop the mask of control I always wear and allow myself to accept the fear rising inside me.

Becoming my own champion means defeating the smartest, fastest, most skilled male elves in Erawind—elves who've been training for years for the chance to take my hand.

Every elven child is taught sword skills, archery, and hand-to-hand combat from an early age. I was too, and I remember a lot of it, but my training stopped when I became Storm Princess. Metal and lightning don't mix so I'm forbidden from touching weapons containing iron or steel. On top of that, nobody is allowed to touch me, so even fighting with practice weapons, like wooden swords, is out of my reach.

I tried to maintain my abilities by running through combat drills in the Storm Vault, but the skills I learned as a child are bound to be rusty. After seven years without practice, I know how to wield lightning much better than I remember how to wield a sword or shoot an arrow.

I tell myself it will all come back to me, but I want to scream in frustration. My promise to Mai suddenly seems empty. I can try to fight for myself, but how can I win against the strongest men?

I acknowledge my fear, dispelling it from my lungs, breathing it out as I lift my head out of the water again. Every elf in my Storm

Command has a skill they can teach me. Ways to reignite what I used to know. I just have to find a way for them to do it.

Nobody can know my intentions until the Heartstone Ceremony in a week's time. The most difficult part will be learning all I need to know in such a short time. Impossible. But I have to try.

I dress as quickly as I can, choosing a flowing silk dress, and pull my hair into a loose braid that drapes between my shoulder blades and reaches my waist. I don't have time to dry it, and it drips down my back, but it serves as a reminder of Mai and her message to me. For the same reason I don't touch weaponry, I also don't wear a crown or other jewelry.

Elise and Jordan stand together outside my bathing room, their heads together in quiet conversation. They look up at the same time with identical expressions of concern.

"I know," I say. "You can't leave my side."

In response, Jordan spins. "Storm Command! To the War Room."

I stride within their circle, heading east until we reach a set of buildings not too far from my quarters. The War Room is located at one end. When we reach the big oak doors that open into the room, I curse my height once again. I have no idea what awaits me.

Finally, the protective circle stops and opens, spanning out like a wave on either side of me. Elise stands directly to my right and Jordan to my left.

I draw to a halt. I'm ten feet away from Baelen Rath who stands alone in front of the War Table. His advisor isn't here this time. I keep my distance, my skirt swishing around my legs when I pause.

He catches me in his gaze, takes a step forward, but stops. For some reason he looks thrown, surprised, but then a blank mask drops over his expression. That damn, blank mask he never used to wear in my presence, but I've seen it twice now. It betrays nothing of what he's really feeling. Now, the only indication that anything's wrong is a single clench of his jaw and a slight crease between his eyes as he appraises me.

He's dressed in light armor and looks right at home in this room dedicated to war and strategy. I, on the other hand, had been so deep in thought about how to overcome my rusty battle skills that I hadn't paid much attention to how I look.

I'm badly underdressed.

I lift my head high, overly conscious of my damp braid. "Commander Rath, please report."

His voice is a low growl. "The gargoyles are on the move."

It's the last news I expected him to deliver. Shocked murmurs ripple through my Storm Command. The gargoyles haven't made a move in hundreds of years.

All my other worries disappear in an instant. Nothing is more important than defending Erawind against another attack.

I stride toward the War Table and circle behind it. Its top is carved into an elaborate map of our country, Erawind, and the gargoyle's country, Erador. "Show me."

Baelen moves to stand beside me. Again, he stands much closer than anyone else would dare. If I extended my arm, I could brush his side. I'm close enough to feel his body warmth. Close enough to turn into his arms. He seems completely unaware of how many rules he's breaking, and it's distracting in ways that send shivers through me.

He's focused on the map. "The mountains on the border behind Rath land have always been our weakest point."

I nod. It's one of the reasons that all descendants of the House of Rath are trained mercilessly for battle—even if they don't want to be. While other houses indulge their children's interests, the sons and daughters of the House of Rath were never given a choice.

For a moment, I remember Baelen sitting at the edge of the cliff behind his home, his legs dangling over the edge like it wasn't thousands of feet in the air, pencil and paper in his hands. He'd turned and given me that half smile that lifted only one corner of his mouth but somehow lit my world with sunshine. He'd handed me his drawing book and said, "You may as well see it before my father burns it."

Now, Baelen's forehead is creased in concentration as his hand sweeps across the map, pointing at various spots in the mountain ranges. "We've known for a while that the gargoyles are nesting on the western side of the peaks—inside their own border and as far from our side as possible. We've tolerated their presence there because they've kept away from the east. But in the last week there have been sightings as close as Baldor Peak."

My forehead creases with concern. "But that's on our side of the border."

He nods and points at another mountain that rests within the boundaries of Rath land. "Last week, a full nest was found here."

I can't stop the shiver of surprise that shoots through me. "That's only fifty miles away from us here in the city. What are the chances they'll form an attack?"

"Unlikely in the next six moons. Reconnaissance across the border tells us the encroachment into our territory is sporadic right now. They aren't swarming behind their border and the nests that have been identified so far are fledglings and spread too far apart to indicate that a coordinated attack is imminent."

"But it's possible… when? Within the next year?"

He nods. "Which is why the Elven Command decided it was time to appoint a permanent Commander of the armed forces. I know this is the last thing you want to hear right now, but we need to prepare for war."

My heart sinks. The marriage protocols and my own fate pale in comparison to the threat of battle.

Baelen pauses. "*You* need to be ready for war."

His gaze returns to me. His mask is gone and his brow is furrowed again. Fiercely, this time.

Is it because I kept him waiting? With news this important, I can understand that the delay must have been frustrating. I try to find my voice as his gaze burns the sound right out of my throat.

"I apologize that I was late," I say. "I understand this is very important."

The crease in his forehead remains. "Mai Reverie was ill. You did the right thing by attending to her."

I chew my lip. "Then… I've done something else wrong."

"It's…"

I wait for him to finish his sentence. "Commander Rath?"

"I wasn't expecting you to be so unguarded," he says, the furrow in his brow deepening. "When you came out of the Storm Vault you were prepared for battle. You were as I expected you to be—the Storm Princess—but now…"

My own brow furrows as I glance left and right at the swarm of warrior elves around me. The War Room is big enough to accommodate a hundred guards. Five of the Storm Command have already moved to stand behind me while the other five remain watching us from the other side of the table.

"I'm always guarded," I say.

"No. This." He gestures. I try to ignore the fact that he stretches his hand out far enough that it almost brushes my arm. He's still standing much too close. So close that the movement of air tingles across my skin.

"The storm's power is gone but you aren't wearing armor," he says. "No body shield. You don't carry any weapons."

It's true that I look like I could be out for a stroll. It's a far cry from the storm suit he saw me wearing earlier, and I already know I'm underdressed. Still, I scowl. "You expected me to come here prepared for battle? You're not my enemy, Baelen."

His expression becomes even more concerned. "Of course not. But you're too trusting. What if I meant to harm you?"

I blink at him in surprise. Then in challenge. "Do you?"

"No."

"Then I'm glad we got that out of the way. In the future you will refrain from commenting on my choice of clothing."

"No, I will not."

I pause, my blood boiling now. Elise and Jordan both stiffen on the opposite side of the table. Elise's hand twitches at her side, and I guess she's two seconds away from teaching him a lesson for his insolence.

Of course, it wouldn't be good for her to strike the commander of the army, even in the defense of my pride. I gesture for her to stand down as I draw away from Baelen, putting a good two feet between us. "No?"

"My job is to protect Erawind and that means protecting you," he says, his voice intense. "You can't trust anybody. Not even me. You may have an excellent guard—"

"I do have an excellent guard."

His jaw clenches. "That doesn't mean they can't be breached or defeated. The gargoyles killed our most powerful spellcasters and decimated an army of our most skilled warriors. My entire family was wiped out. The Raths were fierce, unbreakable, but the gargoyles got through. They can defeat your guards too."

Every word he speaks threatens to break me. Where he wore a mask before, now his emotions are raw and plain to see. Worry, rage, and pain. So clear and honest that every member of my Storm Command has suddenly slumped as if they feel the weight of what the House of Rath has sacrificed to protect us all.

I don't want to accept that he's right. I want to believe that he's being disrespectful by commenting on my clothing because that would give me the right to be angry. To disregard his feelings.

But the gargoyles nearly wiped out our race.

They killed his family.

Now that his father has passed away, he has nobody left.

I never expected him to talk about that. He never did when we were young.

And now his meaning is clear. He doesn't care that I'm wearing a dress, the same way he never cared when we were younger that I came from one of the poorest, lowest elven Houses. Even though he was a Rath, one of the oldest, most powerful Houses.

What he cares about is exactly what he's saying: I'm not wearing body armor, I don't carry a weapon, and without the storm's power, I'm unprepared for an attack.

He is a Rath through and through. Fighting, stepping into danger, and above all: protecting.

My Storm Command looks to me for a response. I'm proud that none of them have risen to anger because of what he said. I'm glad they'll wait for my command before acting. But in a moment of clarity, I realize that Baelen Rath has given me exactly what I need.

I take a deep breath and choose my response carefully. "You're right," I say. "My training stopped when I became the princess. I don't think about war, only the storm. I spend my days either in the Storm Vault or recovering from it. I value my Storm Command as a precious gift. I trust them with my life. There was a time when I had the skills they have. But I can no longer do what they do."

Jordan crosses the distance to the table, standing directly opposite me on the other side. "Princess, you have only to ask, and I'll share what I know."

"Thank you, Jordan. I would appreciate that."

I spin to Baelen. "Commander Rath, I trust you will support me when I seek permission from the Elven Command for my Storm Command to train me?"

His forehead creases. "Why do you need their permission?"

I stare at him in disbelief. "Training me involves touching me. That's forbidden. I need their permission—"

His eyebrows shoot up. "I'm sorry, what?"

"I need their permission to…" I shake my head, exasperation suddenly billowing in my chest. "Everyone knows the rules. Nobody's allowed to touch me. Where have you been all this time?"

His response is so quiet I almost don't hear it.

"Trying to stay away from you."

As his words register, my voice chokes in my throat. There's no anger in his voice. Nothing cruel in his expression. He's answering me as he always did—with the truth. But his honesty hurts more sharply than the burn of lightning or the needles of rain I endure each day. Tears burn at the back of my eyes.

I guess this is why he'd turned away from me at his father's funeral. I don't blame him for putting as much distance between us as possible. He might have offered me his family's heartstone, but he doesn't have a choice. If I refuse it, I will dishonor his House, but if his House fails to offer a champion, then it is a higher dishonor. It would be better for him to fail at the trials than not offer himself as a champion.

I look away—to the floor, to the map, staring at it, clenching my fists and willing the burn behind my eyes to stop. I need to get the conversation back on track, to make sure I can get the training I need, but first I have to regain control of my emotions.

For the first time, I wish I'd come directly from the Storm Vault, because in those moments I'm untouchable and indestructible. Not like right now, when eight words from Baelen Rath can cut through my heart like a blade.

I hate that I feel this way. But worse, I hate that I don't know if he stayed away from me because he blames me, is scared of me, or hates me. Fear doesn't normally enter the equation for a Rath, so I'm assuming blame or hate. Both would fit, especially given that, as the only member of the House of Rath, he has no choice but to fight for my hand.

Confusion builds inside me, but it's better than the sadness I'd felt a moment ago.

He steps up to me. Close. Closer than before. If he lifted his arms, he could wrap them around me. He's suddenly too close and I don't understand why. Not when he told me he deliberately stayed away from me.

I don't need to look up to know that the Storm Command has bristled like thorns. The soft clang of metal tells me they've reached for their weapons. Baelen Rath may be the Commander of the Elven Army, but their duty to protect me comes first.

I stand perfectly still, the breath freezing in my lungs, afraid I might lean just a little too far to the left and make contact with his chest. I want to. *May the ancients forgive me, I need to make contact.*

"Marbella." His head tilts down to mine, his voice soft, a bare whisper, his breath a caress against my neck. "I never needed anyone's permission to touch you but your own."

The breath stops in my throat.

His long-ago voice echoes back to me. *You may as well see it before my father burns it.*

I'm burning right now. A need I've suppressed for years heating my body and tugging at my heart. So irrepressible that I turn my face toward him, my lips only an inch from his.

The Storm Command presses inward and, at that moment, Jordan draws her sword, the steel ringing in the quiet room. But they can't have heard what he said. If they had, all hell would have broken loose already.

Baelen steps away in the nick of time, and I let out my breath, feeling both relief that I didn't break the rules and deep frustration that these rules bind my existence.

He speaks to the room as much as to me as he says, "You shouldn't need anyone's permission to defend yourself."

I don't know how to answer. *I have no choice. The rules are there so I don't accidentally hurt anyone. The rules are there so I don't bond with the wrong elf and give him access to the power of the storm before the Elven Command allows it.* Although, after what Mai told me today, that isn't true after all.

The weight of Baelen's gaze lifts as he turns to Jordan. "The only reason you let me into the Storm Vault today is because I have the power to command you, isn't it?"

She gives him a stiff nod, her lips compressed in an unhappy line. She seems to remember her sword and slides it back into its scabbard.

He continues to her. "Even the Elven Command can't give you orders. Is that also correct?"

"Yes, Commander Rath. Only you and the princess can command me."

"And what's the punishment for disobeying me?"

"That would be treason, Commander. Punishable by death."

He pauses. "Then I command you to train the princess. Each day. In this room."

He turns in a circle, speaking to the entire Storm Command. "Each one of you will train the princess in the skills she needs. But not one of you will speak a word about it."

Elise's jaw hit the floor so hard I'm sure I heard it crack. "But—"

"You too, spellcaster. Not one word."

Jordan's sword is suddenly nowhere to be seen. A grin breaks across her face. She appraises Baelen with a rare expression of admiration. "It will be my pleasure, Commander Rath."

I'm suddenly not sure what I've got myself into.

5

MARBELLA

When we return to my quarters, Elise is more agitated than I've ever seen her. She draws me to the meeting room at the end of the living rooms on the second floor and seals the room tight against listening ears.

"Princess, forgive me, but I need to know what I don't know."

Every bone in my body wants to pace the floor, but I draw a chair across the floor to face the glass paneling looking out over the forest and the river beyond it.

I sit. "I knew Baelen Rath when we were teenagers."

She nods. "I know the story. You used to climb the cliffs together behind Rath land. Your mother was a servant in their House. Apparently, there was a dare about who could climb highest."

That was the story I told everyone. A child's account that they would accept. Close enough to the truth to be believed.

I push away the images in my memory as I say, "The Storm found me there. It knocked Baelen down and he hit his head on the rocks. It was my fault because I dared him to climb in the first place."

The beautiful green forest slips from view as I drop my head into my hands, scrubbing at my eyes. "I don't want him to be a champion."

"Because you don't like him?"

49

"Because I don't want him to be hurt again because of me."

There's silence beside me. When I look up, a ghost of a smile plays around Elise's mouth. "That sounds a bit like the opposite of not liking him."

I swallow my embarrassment and try to cover what I just said. "Actually, it's more like not wanting him to be killed. He's the last Rath. I can't have that on my head."

"I see." She peers at me and, for a moment, I'm afraid she'll see through me to what lies beneath: feelings that I've never forgotten, snatched moments that I've kept wrapped up inside my heart.

"I'm afraid there's nothing you can do to stop him," she says.

"I know. But he doesn't seem to understand the rules. I can't predict what he'll do next."

Given the fact that he wasn't aware of the rule about touching me, I wonder if he knows *any* of the rules. Even if he deliberately avoided me all these years, he had to have heard other elves gossiping about the marriage protocols. Even the order of events on my wedding night is public knowledge.

Elise leans forward. This is the moment when, in another life, she would have taken my hands in hers—an act of comfort I can't experience.

"I've been doing some research on the potential champions. The identity of the final men is kept under strict secrecy so it's guesswork. Some I believe are obvious: Simon from the House of Splendor and Eli from the House of Elder. The others are harder to guess, but it was easy with Commander Rath because he's the only possible champion from his House."

"What did you find out?"

"After the storm, it took him a year to recover. He didn't just suffer a head wound. His spine was damaged too."

I gasp. I knew about the wound to his head because it was visible, but nobody ever told me about his spine. I clench my hands in my lap as sadness washes over me.

She continues, "The spellcasters did what they could but they were worried he might not walk again. He proved them all wrong."

I blink away the tears in my eyes, but they keep coming.

Elise reaches for me but drops her hand. She keeps speaking as if she knows that what I really need right now is for her to distract me from my thoughts.

"He spent three years at military training. For the first year, the men in the other Houses saw him as a target: an injured Rath, vulnerable for the first time. It was their chance to assert dominance. But Baelen Rath had a surprising ally."

She's smiling at me, and I don't know why. "Who?"

"Your brother."

"My brother made it into military training?" For as long as I could remember, my brother, Macsen, had wanted to join military training but men from minor Houses had to work twice as hard to make it in. My mother never mentioned this to me on her yearly visit, but maybe that's because it would also mean talking about Baelen and my mother knew that would be too painful for me.

"Apparently, they became quite a formidable team and over time, they gathered other men from minor Houses to join them. Baelen Rath is said to have created his own loyal army there, many of whom now serve under him in the Elven Army."

"I know that my marriage protocols aren't exactly taught at military training, but still… there would have been talk wouldn't there?"

She shook her head. "Well, apparently not. It's said that there was an incident when another man mentioned that he thought you would…" She coughs. "Make a good wife. Well, that's a nice way to put it. Commander Rath apparently took him to task. After that, nobody dared mention you or anything to do with you, including the protocols."

"But after that, after military training…?"

"After he completed his training, Commander Rath disappeared. For three years."

"What? Where did he go?"

"Nobody can tell me. But what I know from the brief discussion I had with his advisor is that he is doing his best to inform Commander Rath about the protocols."

"Then he doesn't know any of the rules."

"That sums it up, yes."

I sigh. "This is dangerous."

"That is also true. I agree that you should refresh your defensive skills, but you need to be very careful. Which brings me to the next thing."

She stares at me pointedly. "What happened in the Storm Vault this afternoon? I've never seen you repel the storm like that. In fact…" She takes a deep breath. "I've never heard of any Princess doing that."

I shudder. She's right. As far as I know, Princesses don't fight back; they simply absorb and control. I don't know how it happened so I focus on the thing I can control—telling Elise about the storm speaking to me. Mai doesn't want anyone else to know about it, but I can't shoulder this secret on my own.

"The rain spoke to me," I say.

Elise's eyebrows shoot up. We've both had a lot of surprises today and I'm hoping this isn't the one that finally destroys her calm demeanor. "What?"

"It spoke to me, Elise. But what's worse is what it told me. It said that my husband is going to be cursed. He's going to kill me."

Her eyes are huge saucers and all color has left her face. "But… that's… no… If you die, the storm will be released!"

"I got so angry at what it told me that I fought back—and the fact that I could fight the storm shook me up too—but I need you to look into this for me. Is a curse even possible? Aren't there protective spells cast over the protocols? If a curse is possible, could it be the gargoyles? Could it be someone in the elven Houses? Who would gain from my death?"

"Not an elf! Surely not. No, this can't be true."

I stare at her. "Okay, if there's anything I need from you right now, it's that you have to believe me."

She lifts her hands. "I do. I believe you. But the only ones who could gain from unleashing the storm would be the gargoyles."

"Then maybe that's why they're nesting close to the border. They're preparing for an attack without raising too much suspicion."

"That's the most likely scenario. We have to tell Commander Rath. Oh wait…"

I shake my head. "We can't. You've taught me enough about spellcasting that I know the curse could be lying dormant in all the champions and will only ignite once my husband's chosen."

She nods. "As a champion, he could already carry the curse and if there's a failsafe built in, it could kill him if he finds out about it."

"I need your help."

"I'll do as much research as I can, as much digging as I can. We will stop this. We have to."

She leaves me then, racing away to her spell books. I sink further into the chair. The distant forest blurs in my field of view. I didn't tell her my own plan of attack—to fight for myself.

Nobody can know until the Heartstone Ceremony.

That way nobody can stop me.

6

BAELEN

Everyone knows the rules. Nobody's allowed to touch me...

Marbella's rebuke echoes around in my head as I toss and turn in my bed. The room is larger than I'm used to, twice the size of an ordinary bedroom, with a massive desk resting under the wide windows on one side. Maps cover the walls, strategic routes through the mountains. Many of the drawings contain messages hidden in plain sight, some left by my father, some drawn by me.

Only Macsen and a handful of trusted soldiers know how to read the secret messages contained in them—locations of gargoyle nests and hidden stores of supplies.

After meeting Marbella in the War Room, I spent the afternoon preparing the troops for the arrival of the other Houses. As commander of the armed forces, it's my job to meet each House at the gates and escort them safely inside to their allocated quarters.

No matter how much I throw myself into my work, I can't get Marbella's face out of my mind, the way her damp hair rested across her back, the material sticking to her skin, the little droplets gliding down her neck when she leaned forward... I wanted to reach out, ease the furrow in her brow, but the accusation in her eyes was fierce.

Where have you been all this time?

I didn't abandon her. She doesn't know how hard I fought

54

against everyone around me, everyone telling me to forget about her, telling me that she was out of my reach, that she's untouchable now… I never dreamed they meant literally.

I thump the bed and throw back the blanket with a growl of frustration. Being this close to her is like having a rope stretched between us and it tugs at my chest, pulling me beyond endurance.

Sleep is not possible. I have to train.

I pull on a pair of long pants and a shirt made of supple material, easy to move in. As a last thought, I also attach my weapons harness and check the blades that sit neatly inside it. I'm wide awake by the time I head down the corridor of the imposing sandstone building. I've trained my body to go without sleep; all it takes is a little fire of anger inside me and I can function for days. I was trained for war from the moment I could walk—whether I wanted to be or not—but since that night on the cliffs, it's been like something shifted inside me. I can fight longer, stay awake longer, think more clearly during battle, as if everything is crystal clear and sharply focused.

The military compound never rests. Guards are posted at every entrance of the sleeping quarters. The armored soldiers tap their fists to their hearts as I pass, greeting me the same way they used to greet my father. "Good evening, Commander Rath."

It's a sharp reminder of the faith they have in me—a reminder that I'm not only here for Marbella. Darkness is creeping into Erawind and I need to get to the heart of it.

I return the soldiers' greeting and continue on my way, heading straight to the training room on the eastern side of the compound, relieved to find that I'm alone here.

I stretch first before I run through a set of warrior's moves, the kind I can usually lose myself in, but not tonight.

Her voice keeps repeating inside my mind.

Where have you been?

I take my frustration out on a training post that has multiple thick pieces of wood jutting at horizontal angles. Every time my fist hits it, I'm in danger of splitting my knuckles, but over the years I've given myself calluses to avoid the worst pain. Beating up a wooden post isn't nearly as hard as standing close to Marbella and knowing there's a massive rift between us.

Thinking about her isn't helping. Fire billows through my chest, energy that I struggle to keep contained. It's a pit inside me full of rage like molten lava that wants to destroy everything in my path.

My fist crashes into the post with a crack, fissures splitting the wood, but I don't stop. Can't. With an uppercut, I hit one of the horizontal wooden posts and it cracks right off, flying through the air. My vision turns crimson, as if the fire in my heart has taken over my mind. My left fist follows, slamming into the middle of the training post, traveling straight through it. Wood shatters like glass, exploding outward. Pieces crash up against the wall behind it, while others clatter to the ground.

I stare at the broken post, my chest heaving, my fists tingling but not in pain. An energy I don't understand courses through my chest and arms. I bend, pick up one of the broken pieces at my feet, and study the burned edges. It's almost as if a fiery dagger cut through it, not my fist—

"Baelen."

Swinging, my instincts take over as I draw a dagger in one swift movement, ready to pitch it.

Macsen's hands fly up in a gesture of surrender. "Whoa, brother. It's only me."

I don't guard my thoughts from Macsen. "Never creep up on me," I warn.

I drop the wooden shard and return the dagger to its holster, my movements deliberately slow to give myself time to calm my breathing.

"A Rath through and through," he says with a wry smile. "Attack first, ask questions later."

"It didn't help my father." The bitter statement is a truth that hurts. Dammit, where did that thought come from?

Where have you been?

I have to face my own regrets. Marbella's question struck right into my heart, but not only because it relates to her. I left my father, my only remaining family. I wasn't there to watch his back. He was always a mighty warrior to me, invincible. Stronger than me, more skilled at every weapon, every battle strategy, even more adept at hiding in the mountains.

But that's because I saw him through a boy's eyes, literally looked up to him.

Macsen considers me quietly. Today was the first time he demanded answers from me. Until now, he left me alone with my thoughts, even at my father's funeral.

"You asked me where I was, but the more important question is where I wasn't." I meet his gaze. "I wasn't there when my father was killed."

His expression falls. His response is quiet. "Neither was I." After military training, he was posted in the mountains, guarding the border between Rath land and Erador. I waited to find out his posting and then I left, believing that Macsen would take my place, defend the border as fiercely as I would.

He did. But it wasn't enough.

Macsen speaks quietly into the silence, shadows playing across his face in the lamplight. "Nobody was there. We didn't see it happen. He went into the mountains on routine reconnaissance. He left all his reinforcements behind, said he didn't need backup. Luckily, he told me what path he was taking or we never would have found him…"

Macsen stops to peer at me. "We didn't know where to find you, but you came back the very next day. It was like you somehow knew…"

He wants to know how I knew that my father was dead. I can't even begin to explain it to him. It's not much of an answer, but I say, "I was busy saving other lives. Just not my father's."

Macsen considers me for another moment before he digs into the satchel at his waist. "I came to bring you this. I think you need it."

He hands me a thick book with elaborate golden script across its leather cover: *Storm Princess.*

Macsen explains, "Gannon brought it to me. He said he couldn't find you. I took a guess as to where you'd be." He coughs a sudden laugh. "Judging by the size of that book, you'd better start reading right away or you won't get through half of it before the ceremony."

I run my hand across the cover. There's no book in the world that will explain Marbella's thoughts to me. I also don't need a book to tell me the strongest oath I can make to her. My father made it to my mother and he never broke his vow.

I grip the spine. "I don't need this book to know what I have to do."

Macsen tilts his head. "What are you talking about?"

"I need her to know that I didn't abandon her. That I never will."

Macsen's eyes narrow. His gaze flicks to the book and back to me. "Baelen… if you're thinking of doing what I suspect, please rethink. That's a death sentence for a champion, brother. She's not the only one who needs you. Erawind needs you too. You have to remember that."

The furious pit inside me opens up, but I push it away. "A life without her is a death sentence. I've spent the last seven years dying."

Macsen's response is a rapid tensing of his jaw. He's holding in all the curse words he wants to shout at me right now. He won't speak them, but his furious gaze says it all.

Before I can say anything else, a bell chimes. I tense before I recognize it. "One of the other Houses is here."

He gives a confirming nod. "I heard a rumor that Splendor was on its way."

Despite my position, I'm not told who will arrive and when. I just have to be prepared at all times. Glancing back at the mess I'm leaving behind, I feel bad about not cleaning it up. Being a leader isn't about having others clean up the mess you make. My father used to tell me, *"Actions have consequences. You can't hide from them. You clean the blood off your own sword, son."*

In this case, I'll have to send someone in to sweep up the broken training post.

I stride from the room, the book tucked under my arm. "I'm glad it's Splendor. I need to speak with Sebastian."

Macsen dares to place a hand on my arm, a brief warning as we exit the room. "Be careful, Baelen. The Elven Command is concealing the situation with the gargoyles at the border. They don't want the news to spread."

"You don't trust Sebastian?"

"I don't trust his grandfather. Teilo Splendor is a member of the Elven Command."

I shake my head. "Sebastian won't betray me."

"No, but you have to be careful around his House. Remember that his cousin Simon is likely to be chosen as a champion. If it comes to a fight to the death between you and Simon, Sebastian's loyalty will be tested."

Damn these protocols.

As we leave the building, I'm pleased to see a battalion already gathered in the courtyard at the center of the military compound, ready to ride out to greet the arriving House.

Tonight, it's Splendor. Soon, it'll be others. Not all of them will be a welcome sight.

7

———

MARBELLA

My training begins at the break of dawn. I don't have to go to the Storm Vault until early afternoon, so I have all morning to train. I hadn't expected to be awoken before the sparrows, though.

"Good morning, Princess. Rise and shine." Jordan pushes the lever that covers the skylight above my bed, her tall form a silhouette against the dim light beyond.

I crack open one eye. "The sun isn't up."

"No, but the city's awake. The first of the major Houses arrived last night and we're expecting three more today."

During the week leading up to the Heartstone Ceremony, the major Houses have the right to arrive first, while the minor Houses have to wait—until the last day or even the last moment if the majors take their time. It's all a game of strategy—get here first or wait to make an impression.

I scrub at the grin threatening my face. Baelen Rath beat all of them. I'm not sure why that makes me happy, but it does. Although... there's one rule that he did follow, which is that the House of Rath has the right of first nomination as the highest House. But approaching me in the Storm Vault was definitely a first.

"Which House arrived last night?" I ask.

"The House of Splendor."

I sit up. "Splendor!" A larger grin breaks across my face. "Is Sebastian with them?"

Jordan's serious facade disappears for a moment as a smile replaces it. The glow in her eyes lights up her face. She tugs at the end of her long ponytail, her dark brown hair a smooth cascade over her shoulder. "He's with them."

I bounce out of bed. "That's the first good news we've had all week. It's been too long since you saw him." My forehead creases at what she's wearing. "You can't see him dressed like that."

She stands tall in her gray body suit. It's lightweight and flexible —standard issue. But boring as anybody's business. Not that Jordan doesn't look good in even the most unflattering clothing. Constant training has honed her body to a lithe grace. She glides everywhere she goes without even realizing it.

"Sebastian Splendor knows that I'm the Storm Commander," she says. "He respects my position."

"True. But you're a woman first and he needs to see you as one."

Her shoulders sink a little. "Until the Heartstone Ceremony, I'm not allowed to speak to any male elf. Just like you can't."

I grin. "That doesn't mean he can't *see* you. My training starts now, right?"

"Yes, and don't think I haven't guessed you're stalling."

I throw my hands up as I stride to the bathroom. "Does Sebastian still like to start his day with a run?"

She tilts her head. "As far as I know, yes."

"Then I think we should too."

"Princess?"

"Trust me. Call the Storm Command. I'll be out in two minutes."

I splash water over my face as soon as she leaves and pull my hair into a ponytail similar to the ones my Storm Command wears. Then I choose a simple suit of light material that matches Jordan's: gray in color, strong but supple. I grab an apple from the fruit bowl beside the door and devour it in a few big bites.

Jordan gave up everything when her House, Splendor, nominated her to be a member of my Storm Command, including her budding relationship with Sebastian. I've set myself on a course to avoid marriage, but I'll do what I can for her to have a normal relationship. Well, as normal as it can be.

I emerge and call the elves to me, marveling at how fresh they look despite awakening before dawn. My own eyes are still half closed. We navigate the corridors until we reach the clearing leading out to the river.

There's a scenic path along the river that Sebastian ran the last time the House of Splendor visited the city. For the most part, the major Houses occupy their own lands throughout Erawind and only visit the city on formal occasions. Members of the minor Houses don't own their own land, but work on the land of major Houses. I hate the social division, although I'm painfully aware that I never would have been friends with Baelen if my mother hadn't worked in the House of Rath.

Now, I pause with the river on my left until I sense movement a short distance behind us. Perfect timing.

"Run." My command is quiet in the stillness and my ladies move, fluid and graceful around me. "Three file, please. Jordan to my outer right."

My guards split into three lines, with me in the middle of the central one. It's easy for them to reform the protective circle if they need to. Each pace-keeper at the front will move to the back of the line after five minutes, sharing the responsibility of keeping us in unison.

I don't look at her, but I sense Jordan's eyes on me for a moment as she obeys me and moves to the line on my right, closest to the grass at the edge of the path. If the male elves want to pass us, they will have to move right by her.

For a minute, I sink into the rhythm of movement while the river sparkles to our left and the grassy slopes glitter with dew.

A moment later, the heavier footfalls of male elves reach us. While we run in quiet stealth, they sing as they jog, making their presence known. I close my eyes for a moment because there's nothing quite so gorgeous as the unguarded harmony of male elves singing. While the House of Reverie is known for its ability to cultivate plants, the House of Splendor is known for its voices.

"Spin gold, shelter silver," they sing. It's a warrior's song that can be adapted to any context. Right now, spinning gold is about welcoming the rising sun, and sheltering silver is a tribute to the waning moon. In battle, the meaning is far more gruesome: spill blood and bury the enemy.

They veer out from behind us onto the grass. Our identities are concealed in the dim light, but our silhouettes make it clear we're women.

As they draw level with us, their harmony becomes respectful of our gender. "Welcome the light and honor the life-giver."

The House of Splendor is also known for being more progressive than the other Houses, encouraging its women to take up positions traditionally reserved for men. It's particularly prosperous as a result. I can't help but smile as the men speed up to draw level with us and then slow to match our pace. The expanse beside the river is wide enough to accommodate multiple jogging groups.

One of the men breaks off from his group, jogging closer to Jordan. It's hard for me to see, but elves in the House of Splendor have very pale eyes, reflective like a cat's, and I'm sure I recognize the unusual silver-green of Sebastian Splendor's.

I know it's him when Jordan tilts her head and gives him a formal nod. He does the same and settles into stride with her. The male elves sing about gold and silver again, but Sebastian's voice is louder than the others when he sings the next verse. "She is worth more than both."

They may not be able to speak to each other, but he found a way to tell her he still loves her. For the first time in days, my heart swells. There's not a lot I can do to control my own destiny, but I'm determined that my friend will find happiness.

We run together for the next thirty minutes until the sun breaks across the horizon. In this formation—and because my Storm Command rotates on and off duty—it's easy for the men to assume that I'm not with them. Now that the sun is rising, that illusion will be hard to maintain.

I don't need to signal Jordan for her to know this. As soon as the sky brightens, she calls for the Storm Command to break away from the men, turning as a group and cutting across the slope to take the shortcut back to my quarters.

As I turn away from the sun, a shadow passes across it. I squint back to identify it. I shake my head. I'm sure it was just a bird.

Once we're back on the main path, the elves form a protective circle around me again.

"I'm not as fit as I thought I was," I say, raising some eyebrows. "I think we should start the day with a run tomorrow too."

Jordan smiles. "Thank you, Princess."

I shake my head at her. "I wish you'd call me by my name."

She grins. "One day, Princess."

When we reach the War Room to begin my training, Elise is waiting for us. She's the only thing I recognize in the room. The members of my Storm Command who stayed behind from the morning run have been busy transforming the space into a training center. My jaw drops at what they've achieved. Shelves full of wooden weapons rest against the walls. There are mats everywhere, along with climbing equipment and archery targets.

Elise steps forward.

"Anything?" I ask her, hoping she'll understand that I'm asking if she's discovered anything about the curse.

"Not yet. But I found an answer to the problem of touching you while you train. I've cast a shielding spell over each member of your Storm Command. It cloaks their skin and places an invisible barrier between you. They will be able to touch you without making any real contact."

"I didn't know you could do that."

"It's not easy to conjure and it wears off," she warns. "You have three hours at most, but I suggest you keep it to two hours just to be safe."

I turn to Jordan. "Is that long enough?"

"It's probably for the best. You can't be too tired to face the storm this afternoon."

I'm not sure. I've got a lot of training to catch up on. The last time I fired an arrow was, well, far too long ago.

When I begin to argue, Elise steps in. "You can't take any chances today."

Her words are pointed. I haven't forgotten the storm's power yesterday. It feels like a lifetime ago that the storm spoke to me. So much has happened since then. But I can't forget that the storm is getting stronger.

Jordan's posture changes. She transforms into relentless trainer mode right before my eyes. "Are you ready, Princess?"

"More than ready," I say.

8

MARBELLA

The barrier between our bodies works a little too well.

Fighting my Storm Command feels the same as fighting pieces of wood. It's not like touching living, breathing creatures. On the positive side, I stopped seeing my ladies as elves. I stopped worrying about hurting them the way I've been trained to fear hurting others ever since I became the princess.

By the end of the week, one day before the Heartstone Ceremony, Jordan has beaten any remaining fear or uncertainty out of me. I've also discovered my weapon of choice.

As ten female elves surround me, I see only targets.

The blows come lightning fast, but I feint left, then right, duck and slide, retrieving my wooden staff from the ground several feet away. I return to my feet, swinging my weapon at foot level while I'm down.

As the wooden staff sweeps the ground, two of my Storm Command are swept from their feet with it. I quickly follow up with whip-like blows to both their torsos, forcing them down as I leap upward. Three more are upon me but I shove the weapon at one, hearing the air leave her lungs, as I quickly withdraw and swing it left at the other, connecting with a crack against her ribs. I kick out at the one approaching from my right, losing myself to the rhythm of the fight.

I leap and spin to avoid the next dagger, the next sword, using the staff to disarm and attack at the same time. I love how much distance it gives me, keeping my attackers at bay and if they get too close, I use my legs to force them backward.

One of them decides to fight fire with fire, coming at me with her own wooden staff. The two weapons thud and crack against each other, back and forth as we continue to avoid each other's attacks. An arrow whistles in from the side and I deflect it, vaguely aware that there are only two more women still standing. I jab the staff left, but don't give it everything. The woman avoids my attack by feinting right but I'm too quick for her, casting my weapon in that direction before she can adjust. It connects with her shoulder with a savage thud, and she stumbles backward.

The final two women race toward me at once, swords in hand, one ducking under the staff, the other flying upward. I rotate left, my weapon passing between them, but I'm already spinning it. It catches the leaping elf across her legs, knocking her off course and the second across her cheek, cracking against her head so loudly it jars me back to the present.

I drop my weapon and race to her. "Are you okay?"

Every one of my ten Storm Commanders lies on the ground. They alternate between wincing and grinning at me. Laughter and clapping follow from the ones who have managed to begin rising.

The one I clobbered in the head rubs her scalp, but she's smiling. "Nothing a bit of ice won't fix, Princess. It's an honor to have fought you."

I spin to Elise, still concerned, but she nods. "The cloaking spell protects them from wounds as well as touch. Don't worry, she'll be fine."

I exhale and help the woman to her feet. "I think I've gotten a bit *too* strong."

Jordan jumps to her feet from where she stood on the sideline. She wears a giant grin. "There's no such thing as too strong. Well done, Princess. We'll train again after the Heartstone Ceremony, but only when you're not needed for the protocols."

I bite my tongue before I tell her that I won't be able to train again at all. "Thank you for helping me regain my skills."

I help pack up the weapons. Then I have time to visit Mai at the healing center one last time before I have to head to the Storm Vault. The good news is that she's doing much better. A golden sphere rests on her stomach: the spellcasters devised it as a way to capture the Storm's remnant energy and draw it safely out of her. They promised me she will be better in a week, but she won't be able to attend the ceremony tomorrow.

On the way out of the healing center, Elise creates a sound barrier around her and me. She's grown more and more subdued as the week progressed, and I expect her to tell me that she has no new information—more than anything I want her to tell me that a curse isn't even possible. All of me hopes that's true.

She gestures at the sky. "The magic that holds our home together is deep magic; the kind that existed at the beginning of time. The ecosystem around us isn't created by spells made up of words and spellcasting but by the ancient magic of creation. It's only through the deepest magic that our world can exist between the layers of Earth."

She studies the sky for so long that I prompt her. "What is it, Elise? I doubt you intend to give me a history lesson right now."

She wraps her hair behind her ear. "I made a mistake, Princess. When I was searching for a curse, I looked in the spell books—even in the Heartstone Protocols—and I found nothing. I convinced myself it wasn't possible. I didn't want to believe that the curse could be something far worse."

"Now you're scaring me."

"A curse shouldn't be possible because the Heartstone Protocols can't be breached. As soon as a champion hands you his family's heartstone, the protective spells wipe clean any previous spells cast over him and prevent any new ones from being placed. It's created that way so a champion can't win by casting spells over himself. But… the protocols don't protect against deep magic. They can't."

My heart sinks. "You're telling me the curse is made from deep magic? But deep magic can't be countered."

She nods. "It would be like trying to stop the sun from shining. The curse may as well be sunlight—"

"More like *death*-light…"

"—shining around the champions. When the final protocol is

complete and your husband is chosen, the curse will activate in the same way that our sun rises."

"Then nothing can stop it."

"Only you can," she says.

I miss a step. "How?"

"You have to kill him before he kills you."

If there was any lingering doubt in my mind about fighting for myself, it disappeared with those words.

Now more than ever, I'm determined that no man will claim me.

9

———

BAELEN

The night before the Heartstone Ceremony, the city is alive with celebrations. The revelries have become more boisterous as the week drew on, but I have no interest in joining in. All of the serious contenders are waiting in their allotted quarters, conserving their energy and mentally preparing themselves for what might lie ahead. The arrogant ones, on the other hand…

I head up patrols through the city, particularly in the entertainment precinct, where I break up drunken scuffles between puffed-up men who throw taunts and the occasional fist at each other. I can't help but be quietly surprised by the fact that most of them are so overconfident, they don't take note of my ability to physically subdue them.

On my final patrol of the night before the Ceremony, I pass through a busy tavern at the edge of the city. My brow furrows when I see one of the Major House contenders at a table inside. Rhydian of the House of Valor leans back in a chair while a woman stands behind him, rubbing his shoulders. Another sits on his lap, feeding him berries.

I turn to leave but stop when I see Sebastian drinking alone at a table in the far corner. A tavern like this is the last place I expected to see him.

I ask the soldiers in the patrol to remain outside while I step

70

inside. The buzz of voices inside the tavern quiets when I enter, but the patrons quickly return to their drinks and conversation.

I slide into the seat opposite Sebastian.

"Friend," he slurs, his normally glistening silver-green eyes focused on a spot on my shoulder. "It's the last night of free will."

I consider the five full glasses set out in a neat row in front of him, the empty one he clutches, and the slouch of his shoulders. I try to make sense of his statement. What I know is that he shouldn't be drinking, let alone in a place like this. Most of elven society is governed by rules and propriety, but not all. This is not the shadiest tavern, but it's not the best.

"You've had enough, brother," I say. "Let me help you home."

When I attempt to take the glass away from him, he grabs it with a terse, "No!"

I lean in, forcing him to meet my eyes. It's not like him to get drunk. In fact, I've never seen him drink at all. "Why are you here?"

He scrubs at his eyes with his free hand. "I trained with Simon for years. I was his sparring partner. Beat him a fair share of times too. I never dreamed…"

He slumps over his cup, resting his chin on it, staring off into the distance.

Getting information out of Sebastian is like pulling a healthy tooth. I guess I know how Macsen feels each time he asks for answers about my disappearance. "You never thought what, Sebastian?"

He shakes his head. "You'll find out soon enough."

I exhale slowly. "Come on. I'm taking you back to your family."

I reach for his shoulders, but his hands fly out in a surprisingly alert gesture, gripping both my forearms. "You're my friend, Baelen. We went to the military academy together, stood side by side against all the others. I will never betray you. You know that, right?"

Of course he won't. I trust him like I trust Macsen. "I believe you."

"Then leave me be, friend. I promise I'll be sober in the morning."

It's not him I'm worried about. I wouldn't put it past Rhydian to try to settle some old scores while Sebastian isn't at his best.

I take a glance back at Rhydian, discouraged to find him standing several paces away, his cheeks flushed with drink. I haven't spoken to him since military school. His family sent a lowly representative to my father's funeral.

Rhydian scratches his nose, not hiding his sneer. "Baelen Rath. Crawled back from whatever pit you fell into."

Patrons at the nearby tables clear out as soon as Rhydian starts speaking, a move that makes me sigh. I guess they're expecting violence.

For the first time since I returned to civilization, I miss the string of trophies that used to rest around my neck, each one a reminder of a kill that saved a life—a reminder of my purpose. I left it behind because civilized elves wouldn't understand it. Hell, it would scare them more than my scar already does.

To show him that I don't want trouble, I hold my hands deliberately wide of the array of daggers that I carry, as well as the sword strapped to my back. I'm dressed in light armor, nothing like the armor from my House, but it'll protect against most attacks.

Rhydian carries a single dagger and his hand is already twitching over it. A quick sweep of the crowd tells me that two men have inched their way toward us. I recognize them as members of his House.

"It's good to see you too, Rhydian." Slowly folding my arms, I take up a casual stance. Behind me, Sebastian rises from his seat, surprisingly steady. Unlike me, he isn't carrying any weapons. Just like me, he doesn't need them.

Rhydian takes a step before he spits at my feet. "You should crawl back into that pit."

I ignore the taunt. My father trained me well: *Only the weak respond to insults, son. Watch for the knife, not the words.*

I peer around Rhydian to the women who hover, uncertain, in the background.

I say, "You should get back to your friends, Rhydian."

His hand drops to his dagger. He jeers. "Those whores? They're nothing. Just wait until I get a piece of that sweet Princess ass—"

His dagger flies toward me. I guess he thought mentioning Marbella would distract me. I feint right and Sebastian darts left, both of us avoiding the weapon, which thuds into the wall behind us. Not a smart move on Rhydian's part to lose control of his only weapon.

Sebastian leaps toward the man approaching from the left, ducking the elf's sluggish right hook and landing a quick succession of blows that puts the guy on his backside within the blink of an eye.

Now that Rhydian is disarmed, I tackle him right in his flabby middle. He's a brute, but he's let himself go since I left. I hoist him bodily into the air and drop him onto the surface of the nearest table, cracking it right down the middle. He thuds to the floor, caught between the two pieces of wood.

I spin to the remaining man, glad to see that most of the patrons have cleared out now. The last thing I want is a bystander getting hurt. I swipe a dagger from my harness and the man is so busy watching it that he doesn't notice my other hand.

My free hand whips out, grabs his shirt, pulls, twists. Moving swiftly while he's off-balance, I yank the shirt over his head, drag him backward to the next table, kick the back of his knees to force him down, and slam my dagger through the shirt into the table's surface, pinning him there without leaving a single mark on him. He scrabbles to free himself, but he'll have to rip his shirt to do so.

I return my attention to Rhydian, who stumbles to his feet, shoving at the broken table with an angry roar. He rages toward me, taking a swipe at me, but I dodge it.

"Go home, Rhydian!" I shout.

He knocks into another table before he pulls himself upright, licking his lips. "I don't take orders from you, Rath."

Despite his declaration, he spins and walks past the women as he heads toward the door. At the last moment, his hand whips out, grabbing the blonde woman by her hair. "You're coming with me."

She cries out, her eyes squeezing closed in pain as he drags her forward.

I move in a flash, crossing the distance. Any blow to his body will make him jolt, which will hurt the woman. My focus narrows. As she struggles to be released, my hand wraps around Rhydian's wrist.

Energy flows through me from my chest down my arm to my

hand, an unexpected heat that scorches my fingertips. He shouts as I twist his wrist and force his hand to fly open.

He retaliates with a punch to my face, but I deflect the blow, land a kick on his thigh, and force him to his knees.

I blink away the crimson haze that descended over my vision and it's gone in an instant, some sort of trick of the light.

The woman lurches back, clutching her scalp, tears streaming down her face.

"Go," I say. "Take your friend."

The woman grabs her friend and they rush from the tavern. Seconds later, the patrol swarms inside. Several of my soldiers are missing—they will make sure the women make it safely home.

"Rhydian Valor, unless you want to see the inside of a cell tonight, I suggest you take yourself home," I say.

Now that there are multiple swords pointed at him, Rhydian surrenders, spreading his fingers wide to show he won't fight me again.

I release him, but the hatred in his eyes is unmistakable. "Don't expect to survive the trials, Baelen."

I don't respond, making my way back to Sebastian instead.

He gestures to the five glasses on the table behind him, three of which now lie on their side, knocked over in the scuffle. "I'm done here."

Walking with Sebastian back to his quarters, I don't press him to speak. I take several of the patrol soldiers with me, including the captain, trusting the others to take care of the scene at the tavern.

When we arrive, Sebastian's mother greets us at the door. She's a quietly-spoken woman who is well-respected in her House and others.

"Thank you, Baelen," she says, placing a grateful hand on my arm that tells me she was concerned about her son's welfare. It doesn't seem to matter how old he gets, she still worries. I wonder if my own mother would worry about me if she were still alive.

Sebastian disappears inside the building, his shoulders no less slumped than when I first saw him.

The captain leans in to speak with me as we head back along the paved street. He's an older man who always thinks before he speaks and is skillful with a sword.

"Commander Rath," he says, giving me a respectful bow. "We can continue the patrol. You should get some rest."

I've been avoiding sleep. Every time I fall into bed, I dream of the past. I'm wearing thin and I don't know what the first trial will be. I acknowledge his offer with a nod. "You're right. Thank you."

I force myself to return to my quarters, barely undressing before I fall onto the bed, afraid of what I'll see in my dreams, all the moments I left behind, some I cling to like torturous dreams and others I don't want to remember.

10

MARBELLA

"Wake up, Princess." Jordan whispers to me from the far side of the bed. She's already opened the skylight.

I untangle myself from the sheets as I squint at her.

I bolt upright. Today is the Heartstone Ceremony.

Before I give in to the panic rising inside me, Jordan leans forward, grinning like an elven cat. "We have a surprise for you."

I slide out of bed, my dressing gown trailing behind me, but she gestures for me to stop in the middle of the room.

"Close your eyes."

I lift an eyebrow, but I trust her. I place both hands over my eyes. There's a click as the door opens. I sense footsteps, light, female, at least five... no, more than ten. There's a dragging sound too, like something being pushed across the floor.

All sounds stop. "Can I open my eyes now?"

There's a pause. Then, "Yes."

I open my eyes to find that all of my Storm Command has squeezed into the space around me. Some of them sit on the bed and others stand in the doorway to the bathing room to make room for all twenty to fit into my room.

I catch my breath at the object they've pushed in front of me. It's a dummy like the ones from the War Room but it's covered in armor.

I take a step forward, running my hand over it. Fine, gold-

76

colored plates are connected together in an intricate pattern to form a chest plate that wraps around the dummy from neck to groin. Plates have also been fashioned to cover the outer thighs and shoulders. Beneath it, a full body suit of silvery-blue material shimmers from beneath the dummy's chin down to its toes.

I spin to Jordan. "Are those Shimmer Beetle husks? And the suit under the armor—is it made from Elyria Spider web?"

She hasn't stopped grinning. "Yes and yes. It's for you. We've been constructing it for the last seven years. It took that long to source enough of the web and husks."

The suit under the outer layer is spun from the web of the Elyria Spider, whose web is unbreakable even by the sharpest sword, and the plates are fashioned from the golden husks that the Shimmer Beetle sheds only once each year. The husks are as tough as iron but light as feathers.

I don't even bother trying to hide my tears. They drip down my cheeks in fat rivers. "It's not metal so it won't interact with the storm. I can wear it even when I've come from the Vault."

I'm surprised it only took them seven years to make the armor because both animals are extremely rare and only live in the highest peaks behind the…

I freeze.

"But they only live on Rath land. You can't take anything from another House's land unless you pay or trade for it."

Jordan shifts uncomfortably beside me. "We didn't have to pay. We had permission. In fact… it was an order."

"From whom?"

"From the late Commander Rath. Baelen Rath's father."

So much shock hits me that it's like a physical force. I teeter backward to sit on the bed while the Storm Command rushes to make room for me.

"Rordan Rath ordered you to make this? Why?"

I shake my head in disbelief. Baelen Rath's father avoided me, never spoke to me, hated me as far as I knew.

"He came here a month after you were officially announced as Princess. He stood outside your door, sort of just staring at it. I wasn't sure what to do but he finally asked how you were. I told him the truth: that you were still recovering, that you hadn't said much, and…"

Jordan glances at me and there's sympathy in her eyes before she goes on. "I told him you were still having nightmares."

I shudder, taking a deep breath. "And?"

"He said he knew he could give me orders, but that he was only going to give me one. He said that I was to send the Storm Command every fall and spring to collect the abandoned Shimmer husks and Elyria webs from the highest peaks on Rath land and that I was to fashion them into a suit of armor for you to wear."

I swipe at the tears still swimming in my eyes. "I don't understand why."

She drops to her knees on the floor in front of me while the Storm Command watches on. "He said one last thing that might shed light on his actions. He said his son's sacrifice had to be for something and he was damned if he wasn't going to do everything he could to protect you."

I drop my head into my hands. Tears stream between the cracks in my fingers. Baelen Rath's father had forgiven me. I'd never expected such mercy.

I make a decision. I'm pretty sure it's a rash one, but it feels like the right thing to do.

I speak into the quiet room. "Baelen Rath is going to offer me his family's heartstone today. If his life is threatened at any time during the trials, I order you to protect him in the same way you would protect me."

My announcement is met with shocked silence. Nobody moves.

Jordan remains kneeling in front of me. She jolts back on her hands like I struck her. "But Princess…"

"I know what I'm saying, Jordan."

I hold up my hand to stifle any argument. Then I stand, smoothing down my dress. "You all need to be on full alert. These won't be ordinary trials."

I close the gap to the armor. "You've made me proud, each and every one of you. Thank you all for this gift."

I smile at the glimmering suit. I'm about to put it to good use.

11

MARBELLA

The indoor arena is packed. All the Houses have arrived. The five members of the Elven Command stand in a line on the dais. They're members of the five highest Houses: Elder, Splendor, Glory, Valor, and Bounty.

Baelen's House, the House of Rath, is technically highest of all, and as such, a member of his House should also be standing on the dais. But no elf is permitted to occupy a position in the Elven Command at the same time as they act as Commander of the Elven Army. Since Baelen is the only living Rath, his House's position on the Elven Command remains vacant.

The men standing on the dais are a dazzling display of beauty and wealth. It's mid-morning but the spellcasters have adorned the arched ceiling with spun silver and gold, lanterns hanging high above us under a false night sky.

There are fifteen major Houses and fifteen minor ones. While most of the crowd remains behind a golden barrier further back, there are thirty squares set out at the front, one for each House.

The Houses won't reveal their chosen champions until the last moment when the man carries his heartstone to me, so there are at least two extra men with an advisor in each square acting as decoys.

The whole place is churning with elves.

I wait with Jordan in the entrance room reserved for me. My Storm

79

Command is already in position on either side of the dais. A golden chest sits on its own raised platform on the far side of the dais. Each time I receive a heartstone, I will place it in the chest and the magic will bind the champion to complete the trials until he's eliminated.

A purple cape sweeps around me, tied at the front. I hold my family's heartstone—a lavender-colored rock that is pale and washed-out. My family is the only House that can't submit a champion in case we're related. But my mother, father, and brother will be in the crowd. Jordan stands with me, but Elise is yet to return from her sweep through the champions.

Music starts playing to quiet the crowd, a fanfare of trumpets and chorus of elven voices from a choir positioned on the far side.

The noise in the room finally dies down as Elise joins me, a little out of breath. "Your mother and father are here. When you're on the dais, look to the right. They're in the elevated seats at the back of the stadium."

I grit my teeth. My parents should be on the dais with me. They should be treated like royalty instead of shoved in with the crowd like every other onlooker. "My brother?"

She swallows. "Your brother stands with the House of Rath. I believe he's agreed to be a proxy for Baelen during the trials."

Shock ripples through me, but also happiness. The House of Rath is located right at the front, which means my brother will stand mere feet away from me. I haven't seen Macsen for seven years and to be this close to him means the world to me.

Elise chuckles. "He's changed a lot. You won't recognize him."

I don't have a chance to reply before the five members of the Elven Command cry in unison: "We call the Storm Princess."

I take a deep breath and step onto the dais. The entire room becomes quiet. I take my place in the center and lift my left hand with my family's heartstone in it. My right hand rests at my side, palm out, visibly empty. I place a pleasant smile on my face.

I finally have a chance to glance around the room.

Elise was right. I barely recognize the warrior standing at the foot of the dais, but I do recognize the smile my brother gives me. He's filled out from the lanky boy he used to be, broad in the shoulders, as tall as Baelen.

Baelen's expression is a far cry from my brother's. His face is blank, guarded. Like all the potential champions, he's dressed in black robes with his family's crest across his shoulders and chest.

I lift my voice. "Let the Heartstone Ceremony begin."

On cue, one of the Elven Command steps up to my left. Each of the five will take turns calling the other Houses forward one at a time. This time, the first Elven Commander to speak is Gideon Glory. His hair is golden blond, straight, and tucked behind his ears. In the right light, the skin of elves in the House of Glory shimmers as if they're made of the jewels that are found on their land. If my brother's presence next to Baelen concerns him, Gideon doesn't show it.

"I call the House of Rath," he cries.

The first time Baelen offered me his family's heartstone, he'd approached me with his head down, offering it up to me like a sacrifice. Now, he doesn't take his eyes off me. I shiver, unable to look away. My heart speeds up as he steps onto the dais and stops in front of me, tall enough that I have to tip my head back.

His chest rises and falls. He keeps the heartstone at his side as he glides onto one knee, never breaking eye contact with me.

"I am Baelen of the House of Rath. I offer you my heartstone."

I wait for him to lift the stone up to me, but he doesn't, clutching it in his fist at his side instead. The red rock glints between his fingers, catching the light around us.

He holds it beside him for so long that the crowd begins to murmur. The other Houses lean forward. I sense the Elven Command pressing in behind me.

With a shock that almost drives me to my knees, I wonder if, for the first time, Baelen Rath is about to follow the protocols.

Except that this is one protocol I never wanted him to follow.

I can't tear my eyes away from his, but everything around us suddenly becomes crystal clear. My heart pounds double time in my chest, roaring in my ears.

Slowly he lifts his fist to his heart. Instead of offering me the stone, he presses it to his chest. All I can do is watch as if I'm in a dream over which I have no control.

Every elf gasps. Only my brother stands perfectly still. He must have known Baelen was going to do this. Had they talked about it? Does Baelen know the danger?

No, Baelen! Don't! Don't say the words!

His heartstone begins to glow. Blood-red light shimmers at its edges, tendrils reaching through his robe, seeking to make contact with his skin.

No champion has ever done this before because it binds them to me and dooms them if they fail the trials. If I had any hope of saving him before…

My hope crumbles with every flicker of light from the heartstone. He holds my eyes, and his voice becomes fierce. With every word, firelight from the heartstone pulses into his chest, binding him to his promise.

"Marbella Mercy, Storm Princess, I give you my heart," he says. "I will love you, protect you, and honor you until the end of time. Until death."

Soft, green eyes from another time and his voice asking me: "May I have your permission?"

My legs fail me.

I drop to my knees in front of him, my purple cloak billowing around me, my own heartstone sinking to my lap. I don't care that my reaction causes a stir. Let them think that I'm weak, that I'm in shock, that I want to scream out my fear for him.

Baelen, what have you done?

He draws the heartstone away from his chest and I'm horrified at the way the light grips him, stretching from his heart until the last moment when it sinks back into the stone.

He's just bound himself to me for life.

Until death.

All I want in the world right now is to reach out my hand and close the gap between us.

He waits for me to respond. There are words I'm supposed to say, but I never memorized them. I never expected to need them. Once spoken, they will complete the binding.

My own voice sounds like a death knell.

"Baelen of the House of Rath, you are bound to me, live or die, succeed or fail. You will never love another."

In the time since he first offered me the heartstone in the Storm

Vault, he hasn't smiled once. Now he does. It's a half smile, a lifting of one corner of his mouth like he's uncertain about my reaction but knows what he wants.

He holds the heartstone out to me. I turn my palm up to receive it. He lowers it into my hand, pausing before letting it go. I close my fingers around it, force myself to rebalance, and draw to my feet. He follows me up.

My voice wobbles as I say, "I accept the House of Rath."

Baelen nods and spins on his heel to return to his square. The space he leaves behind is so enormous that I almost topple as if my world is suddenly unbalanced, as if something has been taken from me without me knowing it.

I stare at his retreating back, wanting him to come back to me. He pauses mid-stride and half-turns with a puzzled expression on his face, as if he sensed my need, but he keeps walking.

I make myself rise up to all of my five feet and three inches, forcing my mind blank. I have to deposit the stone in the chest and then return to the center of the dais. I turn to my left, ignoring the stares from the Elven Command. The heartstone case is open before me. Inside, it's divided into thirty compartments marked for each House and protected by spells. As contenders are eliminated, they will come to retrieve their stones.

I place the Rath Heartstone into the top left compartment, unwilling to let it go. I force my fingers to unfurl, leaving it there.

Then I return to my place in the center of the dais.

The next House is the House of Elder. The two cousins Eli and Ethan wait in their square. Elise's investigations revealed that they're both clever fighters, lean, not exactly built for war but excellent with strategy. It doesn't look like Baelen's pledge to me worried them—or if it does, they aren't showing it.

Eli steps forward, revealing the heartstone in his hand. He takes the step up to the dais lightly. He drops to one knee, holding it up to me.

"I am Eli of the House of Elder. I offer you my heartstone," he says.

I take it from him, saying, "I accept the House of Elder."

After placing the blue heartstone into the chest, I wait for the House of Splendor. Elise had told me about Simon who is predicted to be the champion from this House. Sebastian and another man wait with him as decoys. I sense Jordan's gaze on Sebastian. She hasn't been able to speak to him, but thankfully after the ceremony that ban will be lifted.

As expected, Simon steps out of the square, but so does the other man. My forehead creases as they both step forward... and then they step aside.

Sebastian holds the heartstone in his hand.

I jolt, seeking Jordan where she stands with the Storm Command on my right. She's frozen, pale, one hand half-raised. She clamps her mouth shut and steps back, staring at the floor, her chest visibly heaving as she drags air into her lungs.

Sebastian reaches me and I check his expression. I need to know if he wants this or not. His free hand is clenched. A muscle ticks at his jaw. His eyebrows are drawn down. He drops to his knee and holds the emerald up to me without meeting my eyes.

He pauses and whispers, "Please tell her this is not my choice."

Then he raises his voice. "I am Sebastian of the House of Splendor. I offer you my heartstone."

I don't accept!

Anger rises in me for the first time, hitting me square in the heart. I seek Baelen across the room. He looks from Jordan to Sebastian and back again. *He knows.* He knows this is killing them both.

Then his eyes meet mine and it's as if his presence calms me. I'll find a way. Just like I'll find a way to save Baelen.

"I accept the House of Splendor," I say.

The remaining twenty-six Houses present their champions. I memorize their names and faces, knowing that any one of them might meet Baelen in the final battle. But as the last champion leaves the dais, I turn my focus to myself. The hardest part of the ceremony is about to begin—nominating myself.

My heartbeat picks up. The armor I'm wearing under my robe suddenly feels weighted. It's my last chance to back out. Once I nominate, there's no going back.

Gideon Glory returns to my side, staying at a respectful distance. "Princess, do you agree that all Houses are properly represented?"

I'm supposed to say "yes." That one little word means the ceremony is over and the Elven Command can announce the first trial. It's such standard protocol that Gideon almost doesn't wait for me to speak.

"No."

"Thank you, Princess, then we will…" He stops and turns to me. His brow furrows. "What did you say?"

"I said, 'no.' The House of Mercy is not yet represented."

He gapes at me. "Princess, you know that your own House can't be represented in the protocols."

"Actually, the rule states: 'No *man* from the House of the Princess may be a champion.'"

"Well, yes, but…"

"And there is no rule that states that only a man may be a champion. That happens to be tradition only."

He splutters. "That is also true but…"

I spin to the onlookers. The crowd is murmuring, the Houses are shuffling, and the existing champions appear wary. My brother stares at me with a questioning look on his face. Only Baelen is quiet, half-turned, waiting for me to speak.

I take a deep breath, knowing I need to speak clear and true. I raise my hand with my washed-out, old stone in it. My brother breaks into a grin. Far away from me, my parents jump to their feet; my father clutches the railing in front of him and my mother holds her hand over her heart.

For the first time, Baelen looks at me with wonder.

The memory of thunder fills my voice as I say, "I am Marbella of the House of Mercy. I offer my heartstone."

I pause, my family's heartstone held high, as everyone in the room waits for me to say the words that will bind me to the protocols.

"And I accept it."

Suddenly everyone's shouting.

12

MARBELLA

The Elven Command is in an uproar, but they aren't allowed to touch me. And for the first time in the history of Marbella Mercy that works to my advantage.

While they shout at me, I walk right past them and carry my stone to the chest. I place it into the bottom right compartment, the only remaining space. As I step back, the magic takes hold and the lid slams shut.

The bang startles everyone into silence.

"What's done is done," I say.

I return to the dais, but instead of remaining in the center, I remove my cloak and hand it to Jordan. She takes it, her face streaked with tears and now with shock.

"Princess…"

"He loves you. He's being forced to do this."

Before I return to stand on the dais, I seek Elise across the room. She nods. She knows why I'm doing this. Revealed in my armor for the first time, I raise my voice to the clambering elves. "My people, if you expect me to be your Storm Princess, to fight for you and protect you, then understand this… I will fight for myself first."

A female voice in the crowd cries, "We honor you Princess, but the princess can't fight to the death!"

"In a battle between myself and another elf, either of us may

86

exercise the right to yield. I believe the Elven Command will support that change in the circumstances."

The Elven Command sucks in their breaths. I just rewrote the rules and they're all chewing lemons right now. More than one of them looks like they're about to spit. The final battle is always to the death. Yielding isn't an option. Or, at least, it never was before. But they can't let me die.

They huddle behind me, whispering. Gideon Glory and Pedr Bounty eye me with distrust. Osian Valor and Teilo Splendor are the calmest but they're both shrewd, clever men whose intentions are difficult to read. It's the frosty expression on Elwyn Elder's face that really worries me. Even though every elven House has an equal vote, Elwyn holds the highest seat, second only to the vacant Rath seat, so in a deadlock he currently has the deciding vote.

It's Elwyn who steps forward. "The Princess may yield at any time in any trial. However, if she reaches the final battle, and wishes to win, she must kill her opponent."

His features are unyielding as he speaks.

"And…" He glances at the others. "She must not forget her duty to the Storm Vault."

How could I ever forget? "I won't."

His posture doesn't change, tense and unyielding. "Then there's only one more question before we begin the trials: does the princess wish to exercise her right to veto a champion?"

Before each test begins, I have the right to veto a particular champion. It sounds simple, but it's dangerous.

To veto a House is to dishonor that House, so as a way to alleviate the shame, that House has the right to ask something of me in return. It can't be something I'm not capable of giving, but it can be something that I might not want to give. Gold and silver are the obvious penalties, but there are dangerous requests too like admitting a female elf from the vetoed House into my Storm Command even if she isn't compatible or skilled.

Also, the veto power can only be used once, and only up until the time when there are three men left. I can veto one of the three, but not once there are only two—because if used at that time, then I could effectively pick my husband.

On top of that, it has to be used strategically. Using it now, at the beginning of the trials before I've seen what any of the champions are capable of would be foolish—I could use up my veto power on a man who was going to be knocked out in the first round anyway.

The trials for Mai's marriage protocol are recorded publicly, so I know she didn't use her veto power at all. When she was asked the final time whether she wanted to use it, she said, "My heart was sealed the moment Darian Gild walked into this room. I don't need to use the veto power because I know he'll win."

I was always in awe of how clever she was. Darian won, of course, but it made me smile to think how she'd subverted the protocols, effectively undermining the other two champions without owing their Houses any compensation. If either of the other two champions had been kind-hearted, I would have felt sorry for them, but the records of the protocols showed otherwise.

I shake my head. "No, I don't."

"Then, we will now reveal the first test. This is a test of physical endurance. It is not a battle against the other champions, but a battle against yourself. Each of you will be transported to a spot that is an equal distance from Scepter Peak in the Revenant Mountains. Those who reach the peak within twenty-four hours will proceed to the next round. Those who don't will be eliminated. The trial begins at the third hour this afternoon."

His gaze flicks to me. That gives me less than half the time I need to subdue the storm and get ready.

"Any champion not present in the courtyard at that time will be eliminated. Go in peace." He swivels to me. "Princess, you must subdue the storm before you leave."

I narrow my eyes at him. They didn't know I was going to compete so I can't assume they set it up to make me fail, but it doesn't give me much time to prepare for the climb, let alone recover from the Storm Vault first. I'm definitely at a disadvantage. "As I said, I won't forget my duties."

I wait for them to file from the dais. The Elven Command leaves first, the spectators second, the champions third and, lastly, me. In the distance, my parents are the last to leave the stands. My father and mother both tap their chests and hold out their hands to me, a symbol of their love. I copy the gesture, tears burning at the back of my eyes. Down in the champion's area, Baelen nods to my brother as the other champions leave and he joins them. My brother remains at the edge of the dais until the others have gone. Jordan, Elise, and my Storm Command wait in the wings so I'm not as alone as I'd like to be right now.

I cross the distance and sink to my knees at the edge of the dais so I'm at eye level with my brother. "Hello, Macsen. Brother."

He bows his head more formally than I expected. "Princess." But then he grins at me. "Sister."

I smile. "There's the brother I know."

"You've put yourself in the path of danger by becoming a champion."

"I'm in greater danger if I don't compete."

He tilts his head, questioning. "Whatever you face, Baelen won't let anything happen to you."

"Unfortunately, Baelen's strength doesn't help me right now."

His smile vanishes. "Well, now you've really got me worried."

"I wish I could tell you more." I force a smile onto my face. "Actually… I really wish I could give you a hug. I have a feeling you'd tower over me now."

"That I would, big sister."

Elise clears her throat from the side. My time's up. "Are our parents well?"

"Much better for seeing you."

I draw to my feet, and he takes a step back. I can't leave until he does. It's my job to take the chest to my quarters where my Storm Command will guard over it.

Macsen pauses. "I don't know what happened between you and Baelen. But he won't let you go without a fight."

With that, he spins and strides from my sight. I blink away my surprise. I have to focus on the trial now. When I reach Jordan, my brain is already working a million miles an hour.

"Winning this test is as much about preparation as endurance," I say. "I need clothing to withstand the climb and protect me from the weather, as well as food and equipment. I'll need to survive a night in the mountains. And I don't have as much time as the other champions to prepare because I need to subdue the Storm."

She keeps pace beside me, calling the Storm Command to bring the chest. "We still have packs prepared from when we climbed the Rath peaks to collect webs and husks. I'll modify the contents of one of those. And you can wear the same climbing suits we used—they're light but thermal to guard against the cold."

"I'll gather food," Elise chimes in.

"No, please, I need you with me in the Vault. I have a feeling it's going to be hell today."

13

———

BAELEN

The three friends I trust most in the world wait for me in my room—the room I'm starting to call the Map Room because it feels less like a place for sleeping and more like a place for plotting the future.

I close the door. "Everything's changed."

Sebastian sits in one of the chairs, his head in his hands, his features drawn, and his eyes dull. "I'm sorry I couldn't tell you. I fought them, Baelen. I fought them hard, but my grandfather insisted I had the best chance of making it through the trials."

I level my gaze with his. "You're the strongest warrior in your House, Sebastian. Don't apologize for something you have no control over."

He doesn't let it go. "I know what Marbella means to you."

I place my hand on his shoulder. "I know what Jordan means to you. We will make it right, but right now, we have to focus on the first trial."

Macsen leans against the table. "The plan's changed, hasn't it?"

I nod. "The Elven Command won't allow me to tell anyone about the new gargoyle nests, but I've found a way around their rules. We need to bring Marbella into it."

The third man steps forward. He's calm and reserved, a clever fighter, and one of the most compassionate elves I've ever met.

91

Other men often misinterpret his compassion as weakness, thinking they can best him in a fight. They always regret it.

"Jasper." I greet him with a warrior's grip. He's the champion from the House of Grace, but as it's a minor House, he wasn't allowed to arrive until a few hours before the Ceremony.

He asks, "Are you sure that's the right approach, Baelen? You'll be asking her to risk her life."

"She's strong, Jasper. She can do it. Particularly because you'll be watching her back."

His lips part in surprise, then form a determined line. "It will be an honor. Thank you for trusting me with this, Baelen. I won't let you down."

Trusting him is easy. Surviving the trials will be harder, not least because Rhydian Valor was chosen as the champion for his House.

I push away my fears and doubts. Risking my own life is so much easier than risking my friends'.

"I'll see you at the start of the trial," I say.

Then I turn on my heel. It's time to return to the Storm Vault.

14

MARBELLA

The wind picks up first, wailing around the walls of the Storm Vault. It's so fast and thick that it looks like water streaming against the walls. The center where I stand is totally calm. My heart sinks. The storm's only done this once before—the day of Rordan Rath's funeral—the day I tried to see Baelen.

I'm not an unwitting victim this time and I don't wait for the Storm to build. I know what's coming and it's not pretty. I hold my hand up high, drawing the lightning down to me, waiting for it to encompass my arm and torso like an armor made of light. I feel stronger with it around me. Then I scream into the clouds. "Why are you doing this, Beast?"

A small but visible wind tunnel separates from the wailing wind spinning around the Vault. It's a mini tornado and it shoots right at me, screaming sound as it moves.

Your husband will kill you.

I duck. The tornado speeds past my ears and does a U-turn right back at me.

"No, he won't! I won't have a husband. I'm fighting for myself."

The tornado strikes at me like a snake. I throw my hands up to ward off the blow, expecting the pain of the lashing wind.

Everything stops.

He won't be himself.

The whisper comes from right in front of me. I release my crossed arms and open my eyes to find the mouth of the wind tunnel paused in front of me.

It repeats: *He won't be himself.*

I shudder so hard my arms shake. Of course, a curse takes over and the person doesn't know what they're doing.

The mouth of the wind tunnel widens, opening and rising above me. It crashes down on me, sucking me upward at the same time. I don't have time to defend myself as it pulls me across the Vault, knocking me into the wall.

The air leaves my lungs. Pain courses through every bone in my body. Now I'm caught in the larger hurricane beating around the room. The centrifugal force pins me against the walls. I could bear it if the walls were smooth, but they were originally made of rock and stone and the surface grates against me, shredding my storm suit in patches. My skin will be next.

I push against the force as hard as I can, pulling my knees under me, scraping them at the same time, ready to spring out of the wind. It takes every muscle in my legs, but I fling myself backward and toward the calm center.

I'm free for two seconds before the smaller wind tunnel picks me up again. It throws me upward, hurling me into the air. High up, there's calm. For a moment, I can see everything beneath me: the wind whooshing around the walls, the smaller tornado writhing like a serpent, the lightning trying to curl back around me.

It's time to fight back.

I harness the lightning as the ground races toward me, drawing more and more of it toward me. Thunder suddenly rages above me. I draw the sound in, and at the same time as I hold the lightning, I release the thunder beneath me.

It thuds between me and the ground, the force halting me several feet from where I was about to smash against the floor.

I lower myself to the ground, drawing more and more lightning to me with my arms and hands. The lightning in my hands changes color. It's no longer the usual blue. Instead, it streaks dark red like streams of blood run inside it. The force grows in my hands, raging and pulsing. Tendrils reach beyond the sphere, trickling along my arms and across my chest. It burns like acid. If I don't release it soon, it will consume me.

The wind tunnel looms over me again. With a scream, I release the burning mass into the wind tunnel and the raging storm above me.

The sphere explodes into the darkness, staining the air, and for a moment, a shape is revealed in the roiling darkness. The outline of a woman's figure burns in the sky above me before it fades.

I sink to my knees. The wind stops wailing. It must have started to rain at some point during the fight because water drips around me and from my hair. I've collapsed in a puddle of rainwater that's quickly turning icy—a last reminder of the storm's power.

I force myself to stand before my legs go numb. My storm suit is shredded in places and my knees are bleeding. I'm not sure how I'm going to regain my energy before the trial begins in another hour. I drag myself across the Vault. I don't even have the energy to squeeze the water from my hair as I push through the first door.

I stop short inside the waiting room.

Baelen stands in the center of the room while Elise waits to the side.

His head is down, his eyes closed, feet planted, and hands formed into fists at his side. There's something about his posture that alarms me—an incredible tension in his muscles, as if he's fighting a battle inside his mind that I can't see.

"Baelen?"

He raises his head, slowly opening his eyes and, for a second, his green eyes are flecked with red. It's the same color as his family's heartstone. Crimson light trickles across his irises, flowing across his cheeks and down his neck. The color fades as he refocuses on me.

"The Storm's growing stronger," he says. "You shouldn't have to fight it alone."

I'm cautious, not sure if what I just saw in his face was a trick of the light—some sort of visual disturbance caused by my own actions with the lightning just now. "I wish I didn't have to."

He nods, accepting my response. The light is gone from his eyes and his expression is piercing, focused now. "The Elven Command won't drop me anywhere near you for the first trial. They'll place me on the other side of the mountain."

I can't stop the smile playing around my mouth. "I don't need your protection, Baelen Rath."

"No, but you need my knowledge. The Elven Command will do everything they can to use the marriage protocols to keep us apart. This might be the last conversation we manage to have."

He's right, but not only about that. This might be the last moment we ever share in private. I have no idea what the future trials will involve. Elise has stepped to the other side of the room. She won't take her eyes off me, but it's the most privacy she can give us.

"What do I need to know?"

"There are gargoyle nests on Scepter Peak."

My eyes widen. "But… No… We have to warn the Elven Command."

"They already know."

My mouth drops open. "What? They know they're about to drop the champions on a mountain with gargoyle nests?"

"To kill the gargoyles. There are enough champions to do it."

"But the nests are where the gargoyles raise their babies. Killing them would be an act of war."

He shakes his head. "The gargoyles shouldn't be there. It's our territory and the Elven Command can claim ignorance—they'll say that the champions simply defended themselves. Male gargoyles protect their children with the savagery of a wild animal. It won't take much to provoke one."

Shock strikes through me. "But the Command *does* know and that's worse than war. That's… murder. How many nests are there?"

I'm not sure why I care. The gargoyles have always been our enemy. They almost wiped us out. And yet… I've always held the elves to a higher standard. I've always expected the elves to fight with honor. We would never attack children. For the Elven Command to deliberately send warriors into a place knowing it could turn into slaughter is cruel and wrong.

"Only two. One on each side of the mountain."

I catch up fast. "And there are two of us. You want me to make my path alongside one of the nests so none of the champions will come near it."

He nods. "I know I'm asking a lot of you, but if you wait for the other champions to pass you by, they won't discover the nest."

"But that could mean losing."

He smiles. "Will it? The other champions might underestimate you, but I don't."

"I guess it could work in my favor. Make them think I can't handle the mountain."

"When I know you can."

I swallow. I grew up climbing the Rath peaks. The image of Baelen sitting at the edge of the cliff returns to me.

He continues. "I haven't figured out why yet, but there are forces at work within the Elven Command that want to disrupt the peace between us and the gargoyles."

I can't help glancing back at the Storm Vault. It told me that my husband would kill me and release the storm. Now Baelen is saying that someone in the Elven Command is looking for war. There's no doubt in my mind that it's all connected.

My forehead creases as I realize something. "When you showed me the gargoyle nests in the War Room, you didn't point to Scepter Peak."

Frustration enters his voice. "Because the Elven Command refuses to make it public knowledge. They forbid me to tell anyone."

"Then how can you tell me now?"

"Because I bound myself to you. My oath to you comes before everything else. Even if you hadn't chosen to be a champion, your life is in danger."

So that's why he bound himself to me. I try to focus on the problem, but my reaction is too strong. I can't stop myself from saying, "You only bound yourself to me so you could tell me secrets."

I'm shocked by how bitter that makes me feel. Disappointment rises like the storm inside me. My fingers tingle with remembered lightning and my chest suddenly aches as if icy rain has gathered inside it.

He draws nearer to me. His gaze burns me. "Telling you secrets is just a happy consequence. I bound myself to you for many reasons."

I want a real answer, but I'm not sure how far to push him if he doesn't want to tell me. "But, Baelen… if you lose… you won't have the chance to love another elf. There must be… someone… in your life now?"

He shakes his head. He pauses, glancing at Elise, and I suspect he's choosing his response carefully, the same way I always think before I speak.

He asks, "Do you really not see it?"

"See what?"

He turns his head. He points to the scar running the length of the side of his face. "This."

"No. I don't." I scowl. "Are you telling me that not a single elven girl came near you because of that?"

He taps the scar with his finger. "I learned very quickly that *this* changes everything."

"Why?"

My response makes his brow furrow. He stares at me. "It really doesn't make a difference to you?"

"I don't see it and I don't care about it." I stop, because that sounded wrong. "Of course I care that you were hurt. I care that you almost died. I care…" My voice chokes, but I force myself to keep speaking. "I care that I was the one who did that to you."

His eyebrows draw down, but it's a thoughtful expression, not an angry one. "You blame yourself for this."

"Yes! Of course I do! It was my fault. I never should have been on that cliff with you. But I wanted to see you before you left for military training. Then the storm came for me, and I thought you died. I thought I lost you…"

I gasp. He's taken two steps forward and suddenly we're standing a mere inch apart. He's so tall that I have to tilt my head back to see his face. His head slants down to mine but his hands stay at his sides.

He doesn't close the gap between us. "I bound myself to you because I want you."

My heart thumps inside my chest. A shock of lightning travels through my spine in both directions: up across my shoulders and down to my toes. It comes from deep inside me, triggered by his voice and the nearness of his body. I forget that I could hurt him—kill him. The lightning reaches out. It wants to connect. I lean forward, but what he says next makes me freeze.

"My father told me you had nightmares."

I swallow, keeping my voice low. "Elise told me they thought you wouldn't walk again."

"I almost didn't," he says. "Then I thought of never standing beside you again."

"But you disappeared, Baelen. You stayed away from me."

"I had to. I forced myself to keep moving in the opposite direction of you because if I didn't, I'd find myself here, tearing down these walls to get to you."

The red light reappears in his eyes. Nobody has ever invoked the heartstone bond before, so I don't know anything about its effects, or what it looks like, but the light in his eyes, and the way he looks at me, draws me closer to him. Dangerously close.

I whisper, "I don't get to choose who I love."

"Is that why you nominated yourself? So you can control the outcome?"

"Yes." It's true, but I can't tell him the real reason why. "But what if it only makes things worse?"

"Nothing could be worse than being this close to you and not being able to touch you."

Heat builds between us. Physical, tangible heat. The gap between us is so narrow, so delicate, that any movement might close it. The glow from the corner of my eye tells me that I'm not in control of the lightning right now. Light twists along my arms and legs, reaching through my dripping and ripped clothing, wisps of it reaching out toward him.

For the first time, I wonder why Elise hasn't stepped in, raced forward, kept us apart, and that's when I realize…

Nothing else is moving. She's frozen beside the wall, one leg raised as if she was in the process of taking a step forward.

I've used the thunder and slowed time. I'm not sure when I did it, but relief floods me. I exhale and it's like breaking chains. For the first time, I can speak freely.

"I can't lose you again, Baelen. I thought you died once, and it killed me."

"You won't lose me." The corner of his mouth turns up in that rare half-smile that makes my heart thud. "I made sure of that when I took the oath."

"But when you bonded to me, you made yourself a target—"

His smile disappears. "I'm already a target. I'm the last Rath. I have a right to a seat on the Elven Command, but they won't let me near it. They've kept me away by electing me as the Commander of the Elven Army instead. Just like they did with my father. I command the army, but they command me. They *choose* to keep me at arm's length, away from the decision-making. And you…"

His gaze passes across my face like a caress. "You defied them today. You have no idea how afraid they are of you."

My control on time is slipping. Elise's foot begins to lower, and I know she'll separate us in a matter of seconds. I have so much to ask him, like where he went all those years that he disappeared, and what is his plan for finding out what's going on with the Elven Command. I want to tell him about the curse, but I can't. And that's my worst problem. Baelen doesn't know about it, but he knows I have the right to yield in battle. If, somehow, we make it to the final two, he trusts me to yield instead of killing him.

He trusts me.

He steps back: one step, then two, pulling away from me, and part of me goes with him. The light in his eyes fades and the lightning playing across my body turns dull and sinks back into me, left lifeless by the distance between us. The separation stabs every nerve ending in my body like a thousand needles.

"Spin gold, shelter silver," he says. "You are worth more than both."

Elise's foot lowers. Suddenly animated, she races forward only to stop and blink at us. Baelen has positioned himself several feet away—a very respectable distance—which is clearly not what she thought she saw. She clears her throat as he bows to her. He spins on his heel and exits through the door before she can say a word.

Her eyes narrow at me. "I'm missing time." Her accusation is sharp. "And it's happened before. You need to tell me what's going on."

I opt for honesty. "I can't call it at will, but the thunder lets me slow time."

Her eyebrows rise.

I add, "I think there's a lot more to the storm than anybody knows."

"I think you're right." She draws herself up. "Well, we'll have to deal with that later. Right now there's no time to waste. You need to get back to your quarters and get ready. Obviously, I didn't hear everything you said, but I did hear that there are gargoyles on Scepter Peak. If you order me to, I will alert the other advisors. We need to prevent a fight."

"No. As much as it's wrong, the Elven Command will know that Baelen told me. That will only put us in more danger. I'll follow Baelen's plan. But I need you to find out everything you can about gargoyle nests in the next half an hour."

I take a deep breath. "I want to be prepared."

15

———

MARBELLA

The Storm Command escorts me to the open field beside the assembly area. I carry my wooden weapon across my back and wear gray clothing that will camouflage me against the rocks on Scepter Peak. I debated wearing my armor, but I'm going to need to run for a long distance and I haven't tested it enough to know if it will weigh me down. I've timed my arrival to the field so that all the other champions are already present, accompanied by their advisors. Baelen stands on the far side, but I keep away from him. If I show allegiance, it will only make him more of a target.

The champions become quiet as I approach. There are men everywhere. The amount of testosterone in this field right now could fill an ocean.

"Storm Command, separate please."

My ladies draw apart so there are gaps in their formation that I can see through. I need to let the champions know that I mean business. The ones I pass cast me curious glances. They've never been this close to me outside the Heartstone Ceremony.

Having just come from the Storm Vault, lightning crackles in the air around me and I don't try to disguise it, letting it play around my fingertips and torso. It seems like an unfair advantage but so far none of the Houses have complained. I'm guessing they

102

have no idea how much I can control the storm since I'm the first Storm Princess who can.

"Now, now," Jordan laughs, speaking loudly enough to be heard. "You're scaring the competition."

I join her. "They should be afraid. No man will claim me."

The ones nearest to me jolt, immediately looking to their advisors who give me sharp glances. I don't know why they're surprised. My declaration to fight for myself should have told them I'm not aching for a husband.

One of the champions steps forward, forcing my Storm Command to stop. He's a big gorilla of an elf, shorter than Baelen but broader in the shoulders and chest. He takes up the entire gap between my ladies. I recognize him as Rhydian Valor. Not my favorite House.

He looks me up and down, focusing too long on the lightning curling around my chest.

I'm up here, you buffoon.

"I like a woman with fire in her," he says.

My ladies bristle, taking up defensive positions, weapons immediately in hand. He doesn't even acknowledge them.

I narrow my eyes at him. "You've had a few fiery women already, have you?"

I catch sight of his advisor, hovering in the background, his face slowly turning red.

Rhydian doesn't blink an eyelid. "Most women like a man with a bit of experience."

I press my lips together. "Well, I'm not interested in someone else's leftovers."

My dislike for him sinks into the silence around us. His advisor appears to be choking beside him, but Rhydian isn't deterred.

A sly smile creeps across his face. "I'm certain I can change your mind. After all, isn't that what you want? To be out here so we can all get a taste of you?"

Shock rockets through me. Is that what they think? That I became a champion for the chance to mix with the men? A quick glance around the field confirms my fear. Most of them give me the same knowing look as Rhydian.

Only a handful look shocked at the insult he just paid me—

Sebastian Splendor is one of them. He angles toward Rhydian, dark anger spreading across his face.

Jordan reacts faster. "How dare you insult the princess!" With a scream of rage, she launches herself at Rhydian. Her body is a blur as her fist connects with his jaw faster than he can defend himself. Her boot follows it, knocking him off his feet. In the time it takes him to hit the ground, she lands two more blows, lightning fast, the crunches heard above his shout.

Just as fast, she leaps back and away from him, putting a clear few feet between them. There's a reason she was chosen as the head of my Storm Command, and she just showed them all why.

He lands on his butt, thudding to the grass, shaking his head. His muscles bunch as he pushes himself back to his feet. He tests his jaw, snarling at Jordan.

She hasn't broken a sweat. She stands tall, her hands relaxed at her sides. "Do you want to go again?"

He hesitates, glances at me, and then shakes his head.

"Then stand away from the princess."

He steps back, but as Jordan signals for the Storm Command to move forward, he leaps for her, his big hands going straight for her throat. It's a coward's move. It takes Jordan the shortest moment to adjust, but it's long enough to put her in danger.

Silent as a predator, Sebastian Splendor appears beside Rhydian, grabbing his outstretched hands and sliding around him, using the other man's momentum to spin and shove him in the opposite direction. Where Jordan's attack style is all *crunch*, Sebastian's is fluid and seamless.

Another man steps in and forces Rhydian even further back. This new man has his back to me, and I can't identify him, but he grips Rhydian firmly and doesn't let go. Rhydian is suddenly much further back in the crowd, too far to pose a threat.

Sebastian spins to Jordan. She's frozen to the spot.

"Warrior of the House of Splendor," he addresses her with respect, not taking his eyes off her. "Please forgive my trespass into your space."

I can only see half of her face, but I know her well enough to see the battle she's hiding. It breaks my heart to see them finally able to speak to each other but not free to say what they want. She clears her throat, takes a deep breath, and whispers, "All is forgiven, Sebastian."

His gaze remains on her for a moment, brittle and breaking. She just forgave him for being a champion, but it looks like her forgiveness is breaking his heart. Then he nods and pushes backward, forcing the elves behind him to step back too. The man who helped him joins him to form a barrier of sorts, allowing us to pass.

I assess the man standing beside Sebastian as we move on. He's from one of the minor Houses: Jasper from the House of Grace. He has straight brown hair, shoulder-length but tied back, and brown eyes. He has a lot of courage to step forward against one of the major Houses.

The advisor from Rhydian's House rushes after me. "Princess, I apologize on behalf of the House of Valor."

I don't stop moving. "Your House should choose its champions more wisely. You can tell your House and any other House that will listen: any man who comes near me will forfeit his life, and I won't regret killing him."

My Storm Command glares at every man within glaring distance. By the time we reach the place where the Elven Command is supposed to give us further instructions, my ladies are having a full-on glare fest. Nobody comes near us now.

I seek Baelen on the other side of the clearing, not sure how much he saw or heard. All of it, by the looks of things. He nods at someone behind me before he turns away and I'm surprised to see that it's Jasper who remains within a few feet behind my ladies.

At that moment, Elise races toward me, pushing through the crowd.

Jordan leans into me. "I'll tell Elise what happened after you're gone. She'll deal with the other advisors."

I know she will. I just wish I could be there when Elise gives them all the what for. The Storm Command opens for Elise who hands me a piece of folded paper. "You'll need this."

I lift the corner of the paper. It's a map. The location of the nest will be inside it. "Thank you."

She hesitates. "Are you sure, Princess?"

Am I? I'm about to deliberately seek out a gargoyle nest and deter the other champions from going near it. Then I have to complete the challenge and make it to the top of Scepter Peak after giving everyone else a head start. Not exactly what I saw myself doing when I woke up this morning. "I'm sure."

The Elven Command files onto the field but there are no grand speeches this time. Teilo Splendor is the only one who speaks. "All advisors must now leave the field."

Jordan hesitates beside me, her fists clenching. "I've never left you before, Princess. I don't know if I should."

I swallow. "I'll be fine, Jordan."

She holds my eyes. "Whatever you do, don't underestimate the others." She spins on her heels. "Storm Command, file out."

Elise and my ladies leave me for the first time. And for the first time ever, there's space around me. It's a shame it's filled with arrogant men. At least none of them dares to approach me now.

Teilo continues. "Champions, remember that you must reach Scepter Peak by this time tomorrow or you will be eliminated. Now... choose your transport!"

He steps back and for a moment there's silence. Then the faint whoosh of flapping wings fills the air. High in the sky, animals soar toward us.

My jaw drops. Winged stallions sail through the air, circling overhead. Golden griffins join them, followed by giant eagles with white-tipped wings. Some are smaller than others, but their wingspans are all massive. As one mass, they swoop toward the field.

The champions brace. As the first flying beast reaches us, the nearest man begins to run, pacing himself with the gliding creature, leaping neatly onto the Pegasus' back when the horse draws close enough.

Choose our transport? More like *catch* our transport.

The animals don't land, and they don't slow down. Several more men leap to their chosen animals and take to the sky.

None of the creatures come near me. Just like any sensible animal, they're spooked by the storm, veering off before they get too close.

In the distance, a griffin flies down to Baelen but he hesitates.

"Go," I whisper. If he doesn't take his chance, there might not be another one. He's already let two animals pass him by, waiting for me. There are only a handful left.

Most of the other champions are airborne.

I close my eyes and reach out with the storm, becoming quiet enough to sense my own heartbeat, to calm the sharp lightning and try to subdue it. I need to quell the storm or nothing will come near me.

The edges of my senses prickle. The hot lightning rears up again. I try to push it down, but at the same time I sense the wind at my back and the sudden deep thud of outspread wings. I open my eyes but only enough to run, pacing beside whatever creature is brave enough to align itself with me.

The rush of wind close by tells me I have one chance to leap onto its back. I glance left, judging the distance and the shape of its body.

I almost stumble.

A vast, red-feathered bird flies beside me, larger than any of the eagles. It's so bright it looks like flames lick off the surface of its feathers. My lightning leaps out to greet it and I inhale air faster than ever before, my heart pounding. Somehow I've called a creature to me that by rights can never be called. But it's the only creature that would never be afraid of me.

The Elven Command are stony-faced, staring at what I've done. The champions who are already in the sky circle back on their flying creatures, leaning over their animals to see the blazing creature. Their disbelief is palpable from here.

I pick up my pace. I don't hesitate. I leap onto the back of the phoenix, landing safely, and together we soar into the sky.

I LEAN FORWARD OVER THE FIREBIRD'S NECK. ITS FEATHERS ARE LIKE both silk and sunlight. It covers the distance faster than the other flying creatures and soon we're ahead of everyone else.

I pull out the map Elise gave me, holding on tight as the wind buffets me. There are two spots marked on the western side of the mountain, many miles apart. One has an "M" marked next to it, so I know that's the one I'm supposed to go to.

I stroke the phoenix's neck. "The question is: Where are you going to drop me?"

The bird tilts its head, eyeing me with an amused expression. Its voice sounds like wind chimes inside my mind. *I can fly you to the top of Scepter Peak, if you like?*

I try not to fall off its back. I shouldn't be surprised that it can communicate with me, but still… "I'm supposed to start my journey at the same distance from the peak as everyone else."

Who says?

I laugh. "I should have guessed that the Elven Command can't spellcast you to follow their rules."

I answer only to the deep magic.

I scoff. "Then how did you come to me?"

The bird coasts for a moment. *You are the Storm.*

We're passing over Bounty land now. Scepter Peak is the highest peak in the Revenant Mountains, which rest on the border between Rath land and Bounty land. The landscape beneath us is green and lush with fruit trees and orchards, but it will soon change as the countryside turns into mountains.

"I saw you before, didn't I? You were flying over the city one morning last week. That's how you arrived so fast."

I've been waiting for you to summon me.

"So I have the power to summon a phoenix because I control the Storm."

The bird tilts its head toward me again. *There's only one of me. And you can summon me because you are the Storm.*

"Isn't that what I said?"

The phoenix chuckles. *Not quite.*

I consider it for a moment. "Did Mai ever summon you?"

She wasn't the Storm.

My forehead creases. "She was a Storm Princess. The same as me."

The phoenix glides. *No, there has never been one like you.*

"Somehow that doesn't sound like a good thing."

What do you know about deep magic?

I fold my arms over my chest, ignoring the fact that it

unbalances me. The phoenix adjusts to steady me and I'm guessing it won't let me fall. "Not enough, apparently."

The phoenix glides toward the mountains. *When humans forced the elves and gargoyles from the surface of the Earth, many gave their lives to create this new world. First, the gargoyle king became the force that separated the layers of the Earth. Then, the elven king became the sky. The elven queen became the sun and the gargoyle queen became the moon.*

"I've heard that story."

It's not a story. I flew both Queens into the sky myself. After that, many more lay down on the ground and from their bodies sprang mountains, trees, and grass. You see, deep magic is life itself.

The phoenix shakes its beak. *The Storm is deep magic too. It was created by a gargoyle who gave her life for revenge.*

I jolt. "I saw a woman in the storm today. Was that her?"

The phoenix lifts its wings, the closest to a shrug that it can manage while flying. *I can't tell you what you saw. But something happened on the night you were chosen. Something happened between you and the Storm. When I look at you, I don't see an elf like Mai or the others.*

It cranes its neck, slowing its flight to study me. *When I look at you, I see... something else.*

I shudder, clearing my throat. This conversation has gone places I'm not prepared for. I bury my head in the map, ruefully eyeing the top of Scepter Peak. It would be so easy to fly straight there. "You should drop me on the southwestern side of the mountain. I'll show you where."

We travel more slowly after that, and the phoenix doubles back a couple of times to allow the other champions to catch up. I need any nearby elves to see my path and avoid it. I also need to start at a similar distance from Scepter Peak so the other elves think this is where I was supposed to land.

Finally, we approach the ground three miles out from the nest, but the phoenix doesn't give any signs of landing. I glance left to check the other champions. I can see two of them, each a quarter of a mile apart. The first one stands, balances, and leaps from his eagle, rolling to the ground in a flurry of snow. The second one casts himself sideways, equally graceful, diving and also rolling.

It looks like jumping is the way to the ground. I check that my pack is secure. I can't afford to lose it or leave anything behind. I opt for efficiency over elegance, standing and balancing. Before I leap over the side, I pause for a moment, the wind rushing past me. It's a *normal* wind. Not a storm wind.

I breathe it in, filling my lungs. "Thank you for bringing me here."

I'll be hovering over you, Marbella Mercy. If you need me, call me.

Without another word, I cast myself off its back, grateful for the snow to soften my landing. I roll to my feet and don't look back. The wind swirls around me as the bird returns to the sky.

After that, I pace myself, jogging through the shallow snow, seeking a better pathway toward the nest. I keep my map hidden, having memorized the distance to the nest, constantly checking side-to-side that the other champions are keeping their distance. So far, so good.

I lose sight of the others as I enter the heart of the mountain, the craggy pathways obscuring my line of sight. Rock faces soar around me, the snow cover is heavier, and the sun will set within another hour or so. It should only take me another half an hour to skirt around the nest, make sure none of the other champions have followed my path, and then I can keep going. To make it to Scepter Peak in time, I'll have to travel through the night.

Exhaustion from fighting the storm sweeps through my bones now that the exhilaration of flying has worn off. I try to conserve my energy by slowing down, reducing my speed to a slow prowl as I approach the location of the nest—a cave within the maze of rocky crevices.

The signs Elise told me to look for are warmth and a lack of snow since gargoyles give off more body heat than elves. There would also be an increase in spider webs because the warmth attracts insects that in turn create a food source for spiders. Like moths to the flame. Apparently, the gargoyles don't mind.

My heart rate's already thumping by the time I press against the cliff face only fifty feet from the nest. A quick glance around the corner tells me that the cave opening is wide enough that I'll be seen if I try to sneak directly past. Not that I was planning on doing something that risky, but it will take me longer to skirt around it.

I grip the edge of the rock face, ready to take another glance, replaying the first image of the open cave mouth in my head.

Something isn't right. I'd looked straight at the cave. There weren't any spider webs obscuring my view.

I check again. Snow is built up around the area. The path is clear. There are no signs of life. My hands shake as I check the map again. I can't have got it wrong…

According to the map, I'm in the right place, but the nest isn't here. The gargoyles must have moved. I have to find the new location… and fast.

I sprint past the mouth of the empty cave and up the incline opposite, seeking higher ground to get the best view of my surroundings.

Twenty minutes later, I find myself at the edge of a cliff, facing outward. Further to my left is a fissure between cliff faces—a narrow pathway. If I don't want to go between it, I'll have to scale the cliff somehow. I study the valley below, then cast my gaze to the opposite peaks. Some of the other champions have already lit lamps. The golden lights bob between crevices and trees.

If I were a gargoyle, where would I nest? I'd want to be able to take flight easily but still have cover. I would need a deep enough cave but not one that stretched too far into the mountain in case there were other openings that compromised safety further along. I wouldn't go down, only up.

I take the pathway to the left. As I suspected, the cliff face is too steep to climb, and the narrow pathway is the only way through. I check my pack, pull out my lamp, and light it, but I can't see very far down the path before the shadows close in.

I'm only about halfway along when the gap suddenly widens into a clearing. I freeze, because I've just walked through a cobweb, and on top of that, I'm sure I heard… growling.

I'm suddenly aware of a wide opening on my left. The mouth of a cave yawns like dark jaws only five feet away. I spin toward it, lifting my lamp high.

A creature shifts in the darkness. It steps into the light, lips drawn back over sharp teeth, standing eight feet tall on its hind legs. Its wings stretch the entire distance across the cave's opening.

I guess I found the nest.

16

MARBELLA

I pull my weapon from across my back. I suddenly feel stupidly unprepared facing a gargoyle holding nothing but a wooden stick and a lamp. I reach for the lightning, but it's gone. The Storm can't save me now.

The gargoyle's lips curl as he hisses, "Elf!"

He thuds forward, his wings angled toward me. I backpedal as fast as I can. I need to avoid the daggers at the points of his wings as well as his fists. He swipes at me, faster than I anticipated, more agile, stepping lightly as I try to avoid his attack. I barely avoid the fist that hits the rock beside me, cracking the surface easily, as if the gargoyle's body is made of steel.

My eyes widen as his fist lands a hairsbreadth from my cheek. His hands are the size of my face. He has muscles on muscles. He's way more lean and nimble than I anticipated. And he's about to pin me against the rock where I won't be able to move.

I leap into action, dropping the lamp and whipping my weapon upward, whacking the beast hard beneath his chin, followed by another three, quick strikes that force him to take a step backward. That gives me just enough space to slide into the clearing where I can swing my weapon more freely.

I jab at his chest, legs, and thick neck, but the gargoyle avoids each blow, my weapon sliding harmlessly by. Even though I don't make contact, I'm one painful step at a time closer to the way out. I need to escape back the way I came and hope the gargoyle doesn't follow me.

I strike once more, but this time he snatches the weapon out of my hands, pulling it instead of avoiding it, bending at the same time and snapping it across his knee.

I stare in shock at the stump in my hands.

Stupid wooden weapon!

I turn to run, but the gargoyle snags me, a claw dragging against my back, ripping the top of my suit. I arch as pain rakes between my shoulders. I swallow the scream that will draw every nearby elf.

Maybe I *should* scream. Maybe I—

The gargoyle shoves me back against the rock wall and all thought stops. He presses me into it, jagged rock edges poking into my back. The daggers at the tips of his wings slide deep into the rock beside me, cracking the surface. The edges of his wings seal against the rock face on either side of me.

I'm trapped inside a cocoon made of his steel-colored wings, the gargoyle's face leaning down to mine. His nose is small and his chin angular, like it's carved out of stone, but his ears are pointed like mine. One of his fists pins my left shoulder. His other hand wraps around the right side of my waist. Both press me into the rock.

The creature inhales, his nostrils flaring. His breath washes over me as he inhales and exhales again.

I'm winded and pinned. I can't move. The only thing keeping me from panicking is that he didn't kill me on the spot when he could have. That has to be a good sign. Unless he likes to play with his prey…

I stay very still as he drops his head to mine, studying me. His nose wrinkles. "You smell like… the air before it rains. Most elves reek of flowers and perfume but you… are clouds and ice. Why is that?"

I try to breathe around the pressure of his hand on my waist pushing against the base of my ribcage. "I'm told I'm not like other elves."

He narrows his eyes at me and snarls. "State your intentions."

I seriously want to ask him the same thing. Is he going to kill me? "I didn't come here to fight you or harm you. I'm here because…"

There's a soft snuffling sound from within the cave across the clearing. The gargoyle shifts uneasily, his eyes lifting from mine, flicking left.

A baby cries. It sounds just like a newborn elf, but it isn't.

The gargoyle snaps back to me. He thrums like a plucked chord. He strains closer to me, a growl rumbling in his throat, his daggers pushing further into the rock. "No elf has ever been this close to my children and lived as long as you have. You are testing every reserve I have."

I'm pretty sure I've stopped breathing. My mouth is completely dry, and my voice is a bare whisper. "Why haven't you killed me?"

His brow is deeply furrowed as he shakes his head. One dagger retracts and smacks into the rock closer to me. One strike will shatter my chest. The daggers penetrate rock—my bones will be like butter. It's a reflex. He wants to kill me. I don't know what's stopping him and I don't think he does either.

A growl rips from his throat as he demands, "What are you?"

I find my voice, but barely. "I'm the Storm Princess."

"Storm…" The gargoyle's eyes widen. He sniffs my neck, and his breath is oddly soft, sending shivers down my spine. Some of the tension bleeds out of his shoulders. "You speak the truth."

He presses closer and I'm suddenly aware that there's a whole lot of man across from me right now. I've never seen a gargoyle in real life. The only images I have are pictures drawn by elves showing angry beasts with red eyes and dripping teeth—creatures that sit on their haunches and hunch over the bodies of dead elves. This gargoyle is nothing like that. He's lean, powerful, and graceful. His thighs press into mine as he continues to sniff my neck, tickling my ear with every exhale.

The reality of what he is shakes me.

That, and the fact that he's the first living creature to touch me in seven years.

"I…" I glance at his hands. His claws are retracted and nowhere to be seen. His palms have softened against the suit protecting my shoulder and waist, becoming gentle.

He withdraws them slowly, loosening his hold in degrees.

"I can't kill you." His wings peel away from the rock face, daggers drawing out as he steps away from me. I cling to the solid surface behind me to stay on my feet.

He sweeps his wings upward and they fold at his sides. "You will leave now."

I nod rapidly. "Yes. I'll go." I stoop to retrieve the lamp, angry at the way I miss the pressure of the gargoyle's hands on my shoulder. Angrier that I want Baelen's hands and can't have them. "No, wait."

The gargoyle swings back to me, wary edges showing again.

"There are other elves on this mountain tonight," I say. "They don't know you're here, but they'll attack you if they see you. You need to stay out of sight."

He draws himself upright, muscles rippling without effort. "They won't defeat me."

"I believe you, but I can't leave until I know you're safe."

His demand is swift and sharp. "Why?"

"Because I promised someone I'd make sure we didn't start a war tonight."

The gargoyle studies me. "Then you'll need to douse your lamp."

It's still burning at the base of the rock. I'm lucky it hasn't caused a fire, but there's not much to burn around it other than rock and moss. I kill the flame and wait for my eyes to adjust.

A smile plays around the gargoyle's mouth as he sees my reaction. My jaw drops as I realize how much I was missing because of the lamplight. Elyria spider webs glow like threads of silver across the rock inside the cave, drawing me toward it. I pause beside the gargoyle and point to the side of the opening.

"I'll wait here until they've passed by and then I'll—"

The air leaves my lungs as the gargoyle sweeps me up inside his wings. It's warm and surprisingly comforting inside his arms, even though the contact is brief. He deposits me just as quickly inside the mouth of the cave.

He growls in my ear before he thuds to the other side of the cave, "You may as well see what you're protecting."

It's impossible not to see the nest with the two small bodies inside. One of the babies is a miniature of its father—skin like smooth, grey rock and jagged wings folded at its side. But the baby sleeping beside it has skin as soft-looking as an elf's. In fact, it's identical to an elf except that its ears are rounded.

It looks… *human*.

I spin to the gargoyle. "That's a human baby."

To my surprise, he laughs, closing the distance to the nest, and leaning over the child. "Look closer."

I peer at the baby, its arms and one little foot peeking from its silk blankets. Tucked neatly behind its back are gauzy wings, delicate like finely-spun silver.

"But… it's beautiful."

The gargoyle runs his finger across the child's wispy hair as it stays soundly asleep. His hand is twice the size of its head. "You've never seen a female gargoyle."

I shake my head, gazing at the little girl.

"Our women give birth only once and always to twins: a boy and a girl. The boy is what you recognize: skin as hard as steel, face as sharp as flint, and deadly wings." He grins at me, shaking his wings and showing his teeth as he speaks to demonstrate his features. "But our women are more beautiful than the most beautiful of your kind. They are moonlight." He hesitates. "Just like you are storm."

I shake my head. "How did I not know this?"

His grin fades. "It's easier to hate something if you think it's ugly."

All those pictures of vicious gargoyles… I never once saw anything that looked like the baby girl sleeping in front of me. I rest my hands on the edge of the nest. It's built out of rock, but covered in silk blankets. "Why are you here inside elven borders? You must know it's dangerous."

The gargoyle inhales sharply, the growl returning to his voice. "It's less dangerous than my home. Crossing the border is the only way to keep my daughter safe. The threat of elves is nothing compared to…"

His head snaps up. He spins to the mouth of the cave, nostrils flaring. "An elf comes. I will kill him."

"No, don't. I'll make him go away. Stay here."

I race to the entrance, seeking the source of movement. I strain to hear anything, impressed by the gargoyle's senses. It must have heard me traipsing through the snow for ages before I arrived.

A figure appears at the far end of the clearing holding a lamp—the opposite side to the one I arrived through. I half turn back to the gargoyle, lifting my hand. I'm not exactly sure what I'm gesturing. Definitely to stay put. Possibly goodbye. I'm not ready to leave, but it might be the only way to draw the elf away.

I take a deep breath and stride forward, leaving the cave behind, and closing the distance to the newcomer as quickly as I can. "Identify yourself."

He pauses and holds the lamp up to reveal his face. "It's Jasper Grace, Princess. Forgive me, I didn't mean to startle you."

I retort. "You'll have to ask the Elven Command for forgiveness. We aren't meant to cross paths."

He drops his eyes, but lifts them again. "Possibly Princess, but I follow Commander Rath first and the Elven Command second."

I advance on him. "You do, huh? And what did Commander Rath tell you?"

"Not to let you out of my sight. I've failed that task for the last two hours. I won't fail again."

I glance backward, sensing the air shift. The gargoyle won't tolerate the male elf's presence any longer.

"Well, now you've found me. I've lost my lamp, so you'll have to lead the way. Let's go." I stride toward Jasper, deliberately lifting my arms, making myself wide, to force him to turn back the way he came. He backpedals to avoid touching me, spins, and strides along the path, glancing back to make sure I'm following him.

I shouldn't look back to the cave, but I can't help it. The Elyria webs are invisible again because of the lamp's light but I imagine I can see the gargoyle's silhouette against the far stone, quickly disappearing from view as I push forward. I rub my shoulder where he touched me. I have to shake it off. "Where are the other elves?"

"They're all further ahead than us. We have a lot of catching up to do."

Relief floods me that the gargoyles are safe. Now I can focus on beating this trial.

As we follow the pathway between rocks, Jasper continues. "The night will determine who makes it to the peak tomorrow. Anyone who sleeps will lose."

I hear all the questions in his voice: am I tired? Will I need to rest? How much will I slow him down?

Half the champions are only here to prove a point—to rank themselves against each other: to score points, especially those from minor Houses. The other half want the prestige that comes from sharing the power of the Storm. Only a handful are actually interested in me. Or perhaps... there's only one who is truly interested in me.

I grit my teeth against the annoyance and distrust that rises inside me as I follow Jasper along the rocky pathway. If it wasn't for his actions earlier and Baelen's signal to him, I wouldn't even believe him right now.

I snap, "Commander Rath may have asked you to look out for me, but that doesn't mean he thinks I'm fragile. Don't make that mistake, Jasper Grace."

We come to a crossroads between pathways. Jasper holds the lamp high, studying each path before he turns to me. His jaw is set, his eyebrows drawn down. He doesn't wear fine-spun clothing like I do—his jacket is knitted, and his pants and boots are standard issue. It strikes me that he must be cold, but he hasn't said anything about it.

Without warning, he kills the light in his lantern, leaving us in darkness. A bright spot remains in my vision. I can't see, but his voice suddenly consumes my senses.

"I know exactly who you are, Marbella Mercy. You come from the same place I do. Scrubbing floors for the major Houses. Mucking out stables, feeding their pigs, taking the brunt of their bad tempers and wayward whips. We're supposed to accept it because we're full of *mercy*, full of *grace*. There are many stories about the night you became the Princess, but there's only one that I believe."

I wait for him to tell me which story it is, but he doesn't. As my eyes adjust, his silhouette becomes clear against the moonlight. He stands taller in the dark, shoulders back, feet planted firmly despite the uneven ground. Somehow, he's transformed by the absence of light.

He points, his arm steady. "This is the way, but we need to run. We can't rely on the lamp, only our senses. There are predators in the rocks and trees, and ice will settle on us before the sun rises. We have to make it over this peak, through the valley, and then up again. Are you with me?"

I swallow my surprise. "I'm with you."

17

BAELEN

The cold bites through my thermal suit, the temperature plummeting as I run as fast as I can, arms pumping, up the craggy slope.

The griffin dropped me farther out than it should have. I watched other animals fly by with their champions, transporting them farther up the mountain, while mine landed and refused to rise again.

Curse the Elven Command. The animals were spellcast to bring us here. It wouldn't matter which one I chose, it would have dropped me in the same place. I have to travel twice as far, twice as fast, to make it to the gargoyle nest before anyone else chooses the pathway that veers past it.

It's foolhardy to use up my energy at the start of the trial. I should be pacing myself, but I don't have a choice. I don't have time to take care on the slippery slope.

Gritting my teeth, I push my body to move faster, flying through the powder of snow cover, leaping over rocks and debris, boots thudding on jagged stone as the sun sinks below the horizon. I grew up climbing the mountains behind Rath land, learning how to read the landscape, to know a sure footing from a perilous one. I draw on every instinct, every second of concentration, as I dart around the increasing boulders, my heart burning, my lungs expanding, the muscles in my thighs and calves screaming.

One by one, I pass the nearest elves, each one a figure in the distance. They pause, no doubt observing my speed. I know what they're thinking: I'll burn out. They won't be that stupid. They'll shake their heads and continue to pace themselves.

They're right. I will burn out, but not for another few hours. They didn't spend the last three years of their life hunting vicious creatures in desolate places.

I push on, finally approaching the last elf closest to the nest. He's headed right toward its location. I recognize him as Gwynn from the House of Bounty. He's Pedr Bounty's grandson. *Does he know about the nest? Did his grandfather set him on this path?*

We're equidistant from the fork in the path that will either take him right past the nest or away from it. Elves think gargoyles have low intelligence, but they don't. They're incredibly clever and nest in the hardest-to-reach places along the difficult paths. Having wings means they don't have to worry about ground access.

The easier path through the mountain heads away from the nest, but I can't assume Gwynn will take it.

I fight my fear and force myself to focus. Focus on my breathing. Focus on running, increasing my speed, even though the slope gets steeper. I'm close enough to Gwynn to be in danger of breaking the rules. Whatever I do, I can't cross his path.

Up ahead, a group of high boulders will force me to do just that.

Unless I run over them.

A pair of gargoyle wing daggers wouldn't go astray right now. I could pierce the rock and give myself leverage to fly over the rocks. *Hah, wings would be better.*

Running left, I head for the lowest boulder—even though it will take me farther off course—judge the distance, and leap. The wind lifts beneath me and I land exactly in the center of it, using it as a literal stepping stone to leap onto the next highest rock. From one boulder to the next, I judge each jump at lightning speed, traveling higher with each leap. I sail over the final boulder, somersault, and land on my feet on the other side.

Having cleared the boulders, I dart forward past the fork in the path, well ahead of Gwynn. I sense him freeze fifty paces behind me. He didn't even see me coming. I'm sure he thinks he's the one who nearly broke the rules.

A quick glance back tells me he's eyeing my choice of path with distrust. I've obviously chosen the harder way through the mountain. I can't tell for sure from this distance, but his confused, frozen stance feeds my hope that he didn't know about the gargoyle nest after all.

But of course. It would ruin the Elven Command's plan if the gargoyle nests weren't a genuine surprise. It makes my blood boil that they would endanger their own family like that. Male gargoyles are formidable opponents who aren't to be trifled with.

Which is why my path now is even more dangerous.

Relieved to see Gwynn trek away from the nest and disappear toward the other side of the peaks, I finally slow my pace. I take care around the next corner. Darkness has fallen but I don't light my lamp, watching for the Elyria web that will tell me the nest is close.

A scuffling up ahead makes me freeze. The sound greets me through a narrow opening. The air is still freezing, not warm like it would be if gargoyles were present, but the nest should be right through the opening…

A soft whooshing sound breaks the silence. *Wings?* I tilt my head, listening intently. It sounds like wingbeats, but it's not the deep swishing sound that a gargoyle's wings make…

My memory stirs a moment before a bird caws, a sharp shriek that cuts through my heart.

There's only one bird that makes that sound: a talon crow. A dangerous predator that can rip a fully grown man to shreds. Children don't have a chance. If it got inside the nest already…

No!

I sprint toward the opening, drop my pack, and pull a dagger from my harness as I run. Without slowing, I twist sideways and speed through the opening, ducking and rolling back to my feet.

My dagger flies straight and true toward the enormous black bird as it swoops across the clearing outside the cave entrance situated on my right-hand side. The gargoyle's nest must be inside the cave, but I don't have time to check.

The bird shrieks again, a shrill cry this time, as my blade hits its outer wing, right in the joint where its wing bends. Its body is as big as a panther's and its wings stretch nine feet across the clearing.

Every feather is fashioned like a blade to cut its victims. Tusks rise from each side of its beak, giving it the ability to gore anything it clutches in its talons.

Rage burns through me. Even the fiercest gargoyle struggles to fight a talon crow. The average elf doesn't stand a chance.

But me… I've had practice.

The crow changes direction from the cave entrance, sweeping toward me instead. I crouch, whip out a second dagger, and run, aiming my weapon for the joint in its other wing. I let my dagger fly as the bird soars forward. The blade hits true, a precision shot.

Just as the bird's talons would grab me, I drop and slide beneath it. One talon cuts through my thermal suit, making a large tear, but I don't have time to assess the damage. Right now, I don't care. The wild rises inside me again. I move by instinct, a pit of fire fueling my actions, the same rage that got me through the last seven years.

I grab the bird's talons as it sails over me, yank the animal down, and flip it onto its back. It flops, wings outspread, flailing and trying to retract them to counter my move. The daggers in its joints make its movement clumsy.

Before it can recover, I launch myself forward, one boot landing on its wing across its upper bone, my foot pressed next to the blade. My other boot does the same, pinning the other wing.

It shrieks again, its beak wide open. It won't stay down for long. I have only a moment before it recovers. Quickly reaching down with my bare hands, I grab a tusk in each and twist in a savage movement.

The bird's neck snaps.

I stare down at it, rage boiling at the back of my mind. It shouldn't be here. Not in elven country. Talon crows are gargoyle predators. The presence of gargoyles on this side of the border must be drawing the predators here.

The cold air chills my heart. The faint sapphire glow of Elyria web tells me that gargoyles were once here, but if they were still alive, the air would be warm. Preparing myself for the worst, I force my feet to move to the entrance.

Inside the cave, a nest has been built up out of rock, but it's empty, silken swaddling cloths torn and strewn across its surface.

Scattered belongings lie around the cave—a satchel lies open, its contents spilling out, a broken hairbrush, a yellow ribbon…

I spin to a figure that moves in the darkness on the left of the cave. There are no Elyria webs on that side—either the spiders didn't spin there or the webs were ripped down deliberately to drop it into darkness.

A man stands in the dark, gripping a silken blanket in his fist. It flutters into the light while the rest of him remains concealed in the darkness. The absence of wings in his silhouette tells me he's an elf.

"You're too late to save them," he says.

The bottomless pit of rage opens up again. I pull out my last dagger, the soft ring of steel breaking the heavy silence.

I take a dangerous step forward, my voice a snarl. "Did you kill them?"

"Me?" His head flies up as if he's genuinely surprised. "My kills are clean." He gestures to the chaos around us, his hand entering the light, revealing the edges of golden runes on his forearms. "This was messy."

He points to the various spots around the room—a woman's dress, a man's belt—and finally he lifts the swaddling cloth he clutches in one hand.

He echoes my thoughts as he says, "There was a male, a female, and two babies." He circles the side of the cave, keeping to the darkness, stopping before he enters the light. "But there's no blood. They weren't killed. They were taken."

I consider the chaos—plenty of broken objects but no sickening scent of blood. The question is: *Where were they taken?* I'm not sure which is worse: to be killed by elves or returned to the horror that awaits in gargoyle territory.

I lift my chin, peering into the dark. "Who are you?"

The male elf finally steps into the light. He's nearly as tall as I am, almost as broad in the chest and shoulders. His platinum-blond hair and the golden runes tattooed on his bare arms glow softly in the light.

"You taught yourself to walk again," he says.

I allow my dagger to lower to my side. "You visited my home with Gideon Glory, but I don't know your name."

He casually watches my blade's descent. I could use it in an instant, but he seems unperturbed. He doesn't carry a single weapon but considers me with an impossible confidence. "Didn't your father tell you?"

I consider his reaction carefully as I speak. "My father said you lived in a cage."

His eyebrows rise, and then he gives me a nod, as if he's surprised by the accuracy of the statement. "Your father was an astute and perceptive warrior. I was sorry about his death. I wanted to attend the funeral so I could pass on my condolences but... it wasn't to be."

He still hasn't told me his name and now I'm wishing I had pressed my father for more information. I put aside my questions about this man's identity. Right now, his motives are more important.

"If you didn't kill these gargoyles, why are you here?"

Questions plague me. *How did he get here?* He's not a champion, despite the fact that his physical appearance clearly says he could be one. In fact, the way he moves, stealthy, graceful, and the careful thought he puts into his speech, tells me he would be a formidable opponent. Yet he is not the champion for his House.

He studies the cloth in his fist, crushing it. "I'm not supposed to be here. I heard Gideon say that gargoyles were hiding on this mountain. I've wanted to see a gargoyle for a long time. I finally had the opportunity to... slip out... while Gideon was distracted with the trials, so here I am."

I take a step forward, my hand hovering over my blade again. "Do you expect me to believe that you're here out of sheer curiosity?"

He grins. "A warrior as intelligent as yourself would never believe such a thing, Baelen."

"Then why?"

His smile becomes bitter. He opens his fist and drops the cloth into the nest. "Because it felt like freedom. Because maybe I know what it's like for these gargoyles, trying to escape what lies behind them."

Does he know what they're escaping? That seems like a dangerous question, so instead, I ask, "Why do you live in a cage? If you're confident enough to stroll into a gargoyle's nest, then what's stopping you from leaving?"

His eyes narrow dangerously. "And leave the only family I've ever known?"

I take a guess. "Gideon isn't your father. He's not your grandfather, either."

"You're right, but he's the only reason I'm alive. The only father I've known. I owe him…" He takes a deep calming breath. "I owe him my loyalty."

Until that moment, I considered whether I had found another man I could trust. I believe that he didn't come here to harm the gargoyles. I also believe he could be an asset in a fight—I haven't seen him in action, but I can tell at a glance that he would fight like a demon if needed. But… his loyalty clearly lies with the Elven Command.

He sighs, leaning forward, his palms pressed against the top of the nest. "Loyalty is a tricky thing, isn't it? Would your men still trust you if they knew where you were for the last three years?"

I'm wary. His question implies that he knows, but that's impossible. "They would trust me no matter what."

He folds his arms. "You have more faith in elves than I do."

Laughing cautiously, I shake my head. "Only in some." I push away from the cave wall, crossing the distance to scoop up the swaddling cloth.

He freezes as I approach, then he carefully steps in the other direction, maintaining the gap between us. He reminds me of Marbella, the way she shifts away from people because she's afraid of hurting them.

He gestures to the cloth. "They wrap their children in cloths made of silk, yet they wear rough clothing themselves."

Sadness wells inside me. "Gargoyles value their children above all else."

He's silent. So silent that I consider him carefully. Just like the day I first met him, I can't read his expression. I suddenly realize that's because it's an expression I rarely see. Most elves are naturally confident, especially the elves in the House of Glory, pompous and self-important, believing themselves to be better than others.

This man is the opposite.

He is full of self-hatred.

"Then a child would have to be truly worthless for them to abandon it," he says.

My caution increasing, I murmur, "Only death separates a gargoyle from their child."

"Ah." His expression is blank now. He circles the cave, staying at the edges, well away from me before proceeding to the entrance. He pauses there, a silhouette against the growing dark outside. "My name is Grayson."

He disappears into the darkness and I let him go. If he got here on his own unscathed, then he'll find his way home. I try to shake off my disquiet about how much he seemed to know about my past.

Now that I'm alone, I slump against the nest and allow my emotions to show.

I was too late. The gargoyles are gone. If the nest were empty, it would mean they had relocated somewhere else, but the broken belongings indicate a fierce struggle.

Failure weighs heavily on me, pressing down on my heart.

I thump my fist against the rock. I have to refocus now. I've burned up a lot of energy and I have to make it through the valley tonight and up Scepter Peak before the trial ends. The talon crow is a sharp reminder that the mountains are deadly. If I had more time, I would take one of its talons with me as a reminder of the danger. As it is, I'll have to keep my eye out for other predators.

I race from the cave, scoop up my dropped pack, and leave the empty nest behind.

18

———

GRAYSON

I crouch silently at the edge of the rock overhanging the cave. Below me, Baelen Rath disappears into the darkness. He's a stealthy figure who blends into his surroundings, reminding me to pull my dark mottled coat over my head to ensure I'm camouflaged from spying eyes. The dead talon crow lying in the clearing was merely a vessel. One of the Elven Commanders would have been inhabiting the crow's body, using its eyes to spy on the mountains. Luckily, Baelen killed it before it saw me here.

Gideon thinks I stay in my cage. He *trusts* me to stay in my cage where I won't do any damage.

I exhale my feelings of guilt.

Below me on the ground, Baelen picks up a steady pace and doesn't look back.

I envy his freedom. I envy the way he sees the world with clear boundaries of trust and loyalty. I envy the way he seems to belong —even in this wilderness.

Me… I live in the gray, in the space between.

Drawing upright, I inhale the crisp air, the scent of the wild around me, but it's not mine to keep. Only to experience for a short time.

I wonder what my life would have been like if I'd taken up Rordan Rath's offer all those years ago. I was only ten years old when he first found out about me. He took one look at me and

128

immediately asked Gideon for permission to train me in combat, saying I could be an incredible asset to border defense. It's true, I'm physically stronger than other Glory elves, even stronger than Garrett—the one the House of Glory chose as their champion.

Rordan Rath turned to me and asked if I wanted to come and train in the House of Rath with the chosen few from the major Houses.

I wanted to say *yes*. So badly.

For the first time in my young life, someone was offering me something that could be mine, but then I saw the expression on Gideon's face. His smile. His nod. He wanted me to say yes.

I love Gideon, owe him everything, but he made no secret of the fact that he would do anything to bring down the House of Rath. I would have been an instrument of destruction. Rordan had no idea the danger he was putting his own son in by asking me to train beside him.

But if I had said yes... *what then?*

I catch myself before I consider the impossible.

Friendship is not an option for me.

I take a moment to consider my next move, drawing on the power inside me, my senses tingling as it rushes through me like a waterfall. I could visit the other side of the peaks, catch sight of the Storm Princess for the first time, but no doubt that would be a waste of my time. Gideon may have had reluctant respect for Rordan Rath, but he has nothing but scorn for Marbella Mercy. He says she's the weakest, most self-centered princess we've ever had. Still, it would be interesting to see her for myself. The fact that she chose to fight for herself in the trials is intriguing.

Just as I take a step off the ledge, preparing for the burst of my power that will carry me to her location, I catch sight of another creature slinking through the distant snow.

Its eyes shine deadly silver in the dark like a warning that I've stayed out too long already.

It's time to return to my cage.

Power rushes through me and then I'm gone.

19

MARBELLA

Jasper and I run for an eternity through the cold and dark. By the time we reach the first peak, it's close to midnight and the breath wheezes out of my lungs. Of all the challenges, running uphill is killing me.

"Rest." Jasper drops his pack to the ground and retrieves a water flask. I'm stupidly pleased to see that his chest is heaving as much as mine.

I reach for my own water and gulp some down, taking it slow, waiting for my breathing to get back under control. Sometime this century would be nice. I pace to the other side of the clearing, grateful for the bright moonlight. The snow cover is patchy and thin. The cold won't get really bad until we descend into the valley at the base of Scepter Peak.

"I think we should take this path down to the valley," I say, pointing between the trees. "It's more exposed, but I don't like what could be hiding in the trees if we go through the woods."

There's no answer behind me.

"Jasper?"

I turn to find him on one knee, one hand reaching for his pack, the other held out to me: *stop*.

My gaze shoots left where he's looking.

Two silvery eyes glow in the darkness at the edge of the clearing. For a moment, I'm terrified it's another gargoyle, but no...

this new beast can't be reasoned with.

The creature slinks on four legs toward us, the largest cat I've ever seen, its fur streaked with silver, its claws like steel, and its teeth long and curved… *shadow panther.*

I freeze, trying not to provoke it as Jasper's hand slides into his pack. I hope he has an arsenal of weapons in there because I have none now that the gargoyle broke my wooden weapon.

Too late. The cat is a blur of silver as it speeds straight at him, leaping for his throat. He pulls a dagger from his pack a moment before the animal knocks him to the ground. Luckily, he curled his knees under it and uses his legs to shove it backward.

The creature regains its footing, leaping back at him before he can get up. He slashes at it, but it swipes the weapon clear out of his hand, knocking him down again. As the animal snaps at his throat, he pushes against it, his own hands wrapped around its neck.

He isn't going to win. The creature's weight gives it an advantage and its sharp teeth only have to pierce his vulnerable neck in the right place to kill him.

And yet… he hasn't looked to me for help. Not once.

I'm running before I know it, snatching up the dagger. The handle is wooden, but the blade is metal, and it extends into the center of the handle. Electricity flows through me. Lightning that I couldn't call on my own is suddenly out of my control with the touch of steel. My hand lights up and so does the blade.

The shadow panther senses its peril and tries to twist away, but I plow into it with a scream, slicing cleanly through its neck with the electrified knife. At the same time, I shove the panther away from Jasper, knowing that the lightning could kill him if it flows through to him.

The panther spins backward, rolls, and comes to a stop, dead, ten feet away. I land neatly on one knee, the blade in my hand pointed at the ground. Electricity flows through my arm and shoulder, tingling through my neck and down my spine. It lights up the clearing, casting colors across Jasper's face.

He leaps to his feet as I jump to my own. He can't seem to stop staring at me, watching the light show curl around me.

I don't exactly want to let the blade go. I'm shocked to realize that I miss the lightning. Having it near me is like regaining a strength I lost. It takes all my willpower to pitch the blade into the earth so Jasper can pick it up. The light fades from my arm and so does the unwavering strength.

Jasper strides toward me, fists clenched, stopping at what I'd call a "Baelen distance" away from me. Which means he's far too close. I eye him warily.

"Where are you hurt?" he demands.

"What? It didn't touch me."

"Shadow panthers are only drawn by the scent of blood. They only attack wounded animals. I'm not hurt so that means you must be."

I'm almost certain my eyes are saucers now. He's right. The gargoyle drew blood when it grabbed me before. The site of the wound has been numb for a while, so I've been able to ignore it. Reluctantly, I turn my back to him and reach to open the top of my torn suit at the back of my neck and between my shoulder blades.

I can't see his reaction. There's silence behind me.

"I… fell against a rock and cut myself," I say.

His response drips with disbelief. "You fell? The elf who just now killed a shadow panther with one swipe and landed on her feet at the end of it? I can't see you ever falling."

I ignore his comment, knowing I can't give him any real answers. "I don't think it's a bad wound. Is it?"

He exhales with enough force that his breath washes across my skin and I realize that he's bent to inspect my back. He growls and it's evident that the state of my back is causing him frustration. "This needs patching to mask the scent of blood, but how am I supposed to help you when I can't touch you?"

My pride rises in indignation. "You don't have to help me. I'm fine without help."

"Okay, let's take all the helping-of-Marbella out of the equation. There are more shadow panthers out there and they can smell you a mile away. We need to do something about this." He sighs. "Is there some way I can attach a patch without touching you?"

"I doubt it. Sorry. Give me a minute and I'll try to do it myself. Then we need to get moving again."

I plod over to my pack, pull out the medical pouch Jordan packed for me, and choose the largest square of patching I can find.

It's made of soft, thick material and has adhesive gum around the edges so I won't need to bandage it in place.

My suit is ripped from the neckline to beneath my shoulder blades, but the wound goes further down since the gargoyle's claw dragged the lower half of my suit instead of cutting it. That's a good thing because it means my clothing isn't ripped to shreds, but it makes it very difficult to get the patch on. I try to keep the suit open, but the adhesive on the patch sticks to the material.

I peel it off and try again.

Argh, seriously?

I close my eyes. "Jasper?"

He strides to my side, eyeing the patch half stuck to my back, the other half stuck to my suit.

I take a deep breath. My face burns with every word. "It turns out that I'm going to need to take the top half of my suit off so I can get this patch on."

The moonlight is behind him so it's hard to see, but I'm pretty sure his expression doesn't change. I've never met a man who could hide his reactions so well. Even his voice remains monotone. "You want me to give you space."

"Sort of requires you to take your eyes off me. Can you do that?"

Without a word, he spins and presents me with his back. "Yes, Princess."

So we're back to "Princess." I guess I'll have to live with that.

As quickly as I can, I pull the top half of the suit down to my waist, shivering in the cold. My hair is tied up in braids to keep it out of my eyes and prevent it from snagging on anything. My only regret is that I can't swing it forward to give myself some warmth and cover. As I swivel my neck, I freeze at what I see on my shoulder.

There's a gargoyle-palm-shaped bruise across it, and another one across my waist on the other side. It's obvious that a living creature has touched me, even if it was through my suit and not skin-to-skin. I glance at Jasper, relieved that he's keeping his word. Nobody can see these marks—if they do, the uproar I caused at the Heartstone Ceremony will seem like a stroll through the forest in springtime.

I arch back, swiftly placing the patch over the wound, pressing it as best I can around the edges. I slide my suit back up, push my arms through it, and clear my throat. "All done, thank you."

He doesn't wait for me, retrieving his pack and heading toward the path I'd picked before. I join him, matching his stride down the rough terrain, happy that he doesn't feel the need to talk.

WE'RE HALFWAY THROUGH THE VALLEY BEFORE THE SUN BEGINS TO rise. By then, we're both covered in icy particles, our breath frosting the air, and our steps labored. The trees around us are white with ice. It would be pretty if it wasn't so deadly. The only way to survive is to keep moving, but the cold… All I want to do is lie down and sleep.

Most of the tension leaves me with the first rays of the new day. It's not enough to warm us yet, but it's a hint of the warmth to come. My teeth chatter, but I manage to form sounds. "N-n-no more shadow panthers."

He chatters back at me. "No more s-s-snakes."

"Wh-what snakes?"

"Two miles back. Big. Black. Behind you. Ah, never mind." He waves it away.

My jaw loosens as the sun finally hits me, unlocking me from the cold. I shake the ice from my shoulders and hips, thumping the thicker layers to crack them. "You didn't call for help when the panther attacked you last night."

He sucks in a breath, his chest filling out. The sunlight slants through the trees across his face and eyes. Snowflakes still sparkle on his eyelashes. He swipes at them. "I fight my battles alone. Always have."

"We have that in common." I study the path ahead, wondering if it's safe to run again. It would definitely be easier to run on the flatter land and conserve our energy for the climb. "The Storm Vault is my daily battle. Nobody else can fight it for me."

"What's it like?"

"It's violent, strong. It pushes me around until I push back. It's moody and unpredictable. Sometimes it feels like…" *A person.*

I used to call it a beast, but now after what the phoenix told me, I wonder if I should call it… a girl?

I continue. "It's powerful, but it's also part of me. A really strong part."

"I saw that last night when you killed that panther. I'm not exactly sure…" He stops, shakes his head, and keeps walking.

"Not sure what?"

He presses his lips together. Glances at me. "I'm not sure how any man has a place in that."

I can't speak. My footsteps suddenly crunch too loudly in the quiet. He isn't joking. In fact, I've never seen him smile. Not once. He strides away from me, but I don't let him go. I catch up and stride beside him, forcing my shorter legs to keep pace. "You never told me the story you believed—about the night I became the Storm Princess."

"No, I didn't."

I wait for him to say more. "You're not going to, are you?"

"Not today." He still doesn't smile, but maybe there's a hint around his mouth of something that possibly, maybe looks a little bit like the start of a smile?

"We should run while we can," he says.

We take off again. By mid-morning, we've started the trek up Scepter Peak. We can see other elves now, some ahead of us, some behind, and the fact that we can see them means that they can see us. I recognize Sebastian Splendor as one of the elves ahead of us. Rhydian Valor is nowhere to be seen. But neither is Baelen. Half the elves would have been dropped on the other side of the mountain so not seeing them doesn't mean they haven't made it this far.

Silently, Jasper and I separate so it doesn't look as if we're climbing together. There are two pathways up Scepter Peak. The safest, but longest, is the winding path that meanders around the mountain until finally you reach the top. The other, faster path, cuts straight up the middle, but it's steep. Really steep. Almost vertical in places.

From a distance, Jasper pulls climbing picks out of his pack and holds them up with a questioning look. I forage around in my pack and pull out two of my own. The steep path it is then.

I wish I could take a deep breath, and prepare myself somehow, but I'm already way past exhausted. I can't say how my legs are still functioning let alone my arms. I haven't had any sleep and a bare minimum of food.

As I face the first steep surface, jamming my climbing picks into it, I start counting. Every step makes a difference. Too soon, weariness takes over. My movements become mechanical. I stretch and pull, lift, consider my next move, ram my climbing picks, place my footrests, stretch up, and lift again. Every now and then, I glance at Jasper, registering the sheer concentration on his face. I'm close enough to see the strain in his hands and the way his muscles bunch in his arms and legs through his clothing. I try to ignore my own bleeding fingernails.

Every so often, he glances my way, indicating with his hand or the tilt of his head, a better place to anchor my pick, an easier surface to scale. I return the favor as often as I can, keeping pace with him.

The sun rises high in the sky, and I have no idea whether we've missed the deadline already. I don't even know what the sign will be. Some sort of fanfare, blaring trumpets, a storm of confetti, maybe a chorus of elves will suddenly appear to sing us home.

Around me, everything has slowed. We're all tired. The other men are fighting their own demons. A man to my far left suddenly slips, swinging from his climbing pick, and almost loses his grip. He scrabbles with his feet before finding his hold again. My heart stops. A fall from this height means death.

Further above me, Sebastian Splendor cranes his neck, watching the man who almost fell. Then he looks in my direction and locates me holding on for my life.

He rams his climbing pick into the surface of the rock, suddenly roaring. "One more!"

I glare at the rock face in front of me, mottled gray and brown. I'm not sure if I can do it. To my left, Jasper pauses. Then he reaches up and strikes into the rock, lifting himself upward. He shouts, "One more!"

Just one more.

The man who nearly fell rests against the rock face. I can see him shaking from here. I reach upward with my own climbing pick, adding my voice. "One more!"

The roar takes up around us until we're all shouting, a chorus of voices, each of us fighting our fatigue, hauling our bodies like dead weights up the mountain.

There's a ledge above me. Sebastian has already disappeared over it. Two more steps.

One more. Just one more.

I pull myself up and roll over the edge, lying on my back, heaving, the meager contents of my stomach returning to me. There's no way I'm throwing up here. I have to keep going. I can't give up.

I roll onto all fours, taking deep, shuddering breaths.

Sebastian kneels a few feet away, his head tipped back to the sky. Jasper pulls himself over the ledge ten feet away from me, rolling onto his back and staying there. The man who almost fell appears over the edge to my left, collapsing against the rock, nursing his injured arm, his eyes closed. I finally recognize him as Eli Elder: the heartstone I accepted after Baelen's.

I lift my head. Look up and around.

Sky stretches everywhere without end.

It's not a ledge. It's the top. I'm at the top of Scepter Peak.

Further in the distance, another man stumbles toward us. Baelen's steps are slow like he's wading through water, but he doesn't stop until he reaches me. Then he drops to the rocky surface, both arms hanging at his sides.

His clothing's torn. There's a gash across his chest. His eyes threaten to close with exhaustion but they don't leave mine. I hold on to the look in his eyes, to the half-smile he gives me, to the whisper of my name, "Marbella."

We made it.

20

MARBELLA

Giant eagles carry us home.

None of us are able to stay upright on their backs so they swoop down and carry us away in their talons. I try to count how many of us made it, but my vision blurs. Twelve? Maybe more?

The bird delivered a water flask into my hands before it lifted me up. I grip the flask with the last of my strength, sipping fluids as slowly as I can. The flight back takes long enough that I fall asleep against the bird's talons, waking to find myself in the courtyard outside the Storm Vault as the eagle sets me down in the circle of my Storm Command.

It takes flight, giant wings beating up a whirlwind, leaving me on the cobbled stone as Elise hovers over me. Her eyes brim with tears as she looks from my face, to my hands, to my patched back. "Princess, I'm so sorry…"

"I know." It's time. I have to subdue the storm. I try to stand but my legs buckle, and I crash to my knees. I have to make it into the Vault and I have to do it on my own two legs. Elise can't use a cloaking spell for me to lean on my ladies because other elves will see us. Even now there's a crowd gathering, curious elves pointing and whispering.

"Close," Jordan orders, concern brimming in every angle of her body as she casts glances back at me. The Storm Command responds by forming as close a barrier around me as they can, protecting me from prying eyes.

Jordan's anger washes over me. "She's hurt. She needs help. The others get to rest, but she doesn't. It's not right!"

I close my eyes and bite my lip as hard as I can. I force myself upright and take a step. Tears of pain drip down my cheeks. My legs are screaming and it's all I can do not to scream out loud. I take another step. Somehow I make it to the corridor, across the marbled floor, and to the first door. I lean against it, my knees bent. Elise opens it gently so I can slide inside.

"Please Elise, now that nobody's looking, can you…?"

"Cloak myself. Already done."

As she slips her arm around my shoulders, it's like being wrapped in wood but it's better than walking on my own. I didn't think I needed another elf's touch, but after the gargoyle, my body aches for normality. A hug. Someone's hand in mine. An arm around my shoulders that I can actually feel.

I stumble through the next two doors. She can't follow me into the Vault itself, so I fall into it, sliding to the floor. I curl into a ball at the edge and close my eyes, tears leaking onto the floor. I don't try to stop them. Very soon the rain will wash them away. Or the wind will cast them back at me like a slap in the face.

I speak to the storm. "Do your worst."

A breeze slides across me, caressing my skin, cooling the burning wound in my back. It lingers over my shoulder and waist where the bruises from the gargoyle remain. The wind swirls like ice, forming patterns above the surface of my skin, mirroring the shape of the gargoyle's palms. The storm was a gargoyle once. The way it mimics the shape of the gargoyle's palm is almost reverent. The shapes remain for a moment, great icy paws, before dispersing into the air.

The breeze becomes stronger, strong enough to push me upward, turning me onto my side, dragging at the material around my shoulders. Something rips from my back—then the patch floats over me. It's soaked in blood. Blood I didn't know I was losing.

Lightning crackles, striking the material while the wind holds it, burning it mid-air, destroying it.

I try to call the lightning to me, but I don't have the strength. I sink back to the floor, my hand dropping, as a bright bolt of lightning streaks from high above me, thick and white and sharp at the end that's pointed at me.

Before I can move, it strikes the wound in my back.

Pain explodes through my shoulders and down my legs, burning my back, and leaving me screaming. Just as suddenly, icy rain pours down around me, putting out the flames, and easing to a soft patter like a sun shower. The pain eases as the ice numbs my back.

Confused by the storm's behavior, I open my eyes, squinting upward, but the rain shushes me.

Your wound is cauterized, it says. *Sleep now.*

21

BAELEN

Marbella lies so still inside the Vault that I'm afraid she isn't alive. Her hair is matted, her eyes tightly closed, her sleep so deep that her chest barely moves. The suit she wore to Scepter Peak is pulled down across one shoulder, a yellowing bruise in the shape of a giant palm resting across it.

A gargoyle's palm.

I asked Jordan to double the guard around the corridor entrance to the Vault, but as soon as I saw the bruise, I asked her to triple it. I shouldn't have been concerned about their desire to protect Marbella though. Her Storm Command are beside themselves with worry. Many of them refuse to leave, not even to sleep.

I lean against the viewing glass, my breath frosting across it. When we arrived back from Scepter Peak, I followed Marbella in here to make sure she was okay, but she didn't see me before she stumbled inside. She's been asleep for nearly two days. In that time, the storm hasn't raged once.

I jolt as the door flies open behind me.

"Baelen!" Elise hurries toward me. "The Elven Command is about to announce the second trial. They're calling all the remaining champions to the indoor arena."

She casts a worried glance inside the Vault, where Marbella hasn't stirred.

Unlike when I first arrived, I've now caught up with all the rules and protocols. "Don't worry," I say. "Her presence at the announcement isn't required. But you should come with me as her proxy."

Elise hurries beside me as we exit the Vault.

Jordan gives me a nod as I leave. "Nobody will go inside," she says. "I promise you."

When we leave the corridor behind, I say to Elise, "I'm grateful that Marbella has such a loyal Storm Command. And such a wise advisor."

Elise swallows, her long legs keeping up with mine. "She is more than our Princess, Baelen. She's our friend. We will defend her with our lives."

She presses her lips together, as if she's thinking hard about something. As we pass beneath a copse of trees in the middle of the courtyard, shadows fall across her face.

"You can speak freely to me," I say.

She gives me a small smile. "Your visits to the Vault haven't gone unnoticed."

I stiffen, then force myself to relax.

"I'm not telling you to stay away," she says. "Just warning you. Marbella has made a difficult choice for good reasons. I know she cares… deeply… for you. She doesn't want to see you get hurt."

I stop in the middle of the pathway. "Elise…" I meet her eyes. "I have no expectations. I only offer Marbella my heart and soul. It's her choice what she does with that."

The worry doesn't leave her eyes. In fact, it increases, but she remains quiet until we reach the indoor arena.

The Elven Commanders stand on the dais inside the arena. I try to get a sense of their mood, an unsettled feeling creeping into my stomach when I see that they're all wearing self-satisfied smiles. They're far more relaxed than I expected them to be. Not only did Marbella defy them by entering the trials, but she saved the gargoyle on her side of the mountain. They didn't get their war. The fact that they're not more upset right now tells me they have something up their sleeves.

The remaining champions and their advisors mill around the

arena, which is completely bare of decorations. There are no spectators like there were for the Ceremony.

I catch Jasper's eye before I find a quiet spot at the side of the crowd with Elise. He and his advisor stand at the back and they both appear uneasy. I seek Sebastian in the crowd. He casts me a warning glance a moment before Rhydian Valor stalks directly toward me with a vicious smile on his lips.

I refuse to react, settling into a casually defensive stance. Rhydian turns away at the last moment, abandoning his attempted intimidation to take up a spot at the front of the group.

Osian Valor raises his hands for silence. "We will now reveal the second test." He beams at us. "This will be a test of combat."

I stiffen. A murmur starts among the champions.

"Combat…" Elise whispers at my side. "It's supposed to be a test of wits second. Combat shouldn't happen until the end…"

Osian continues, "The remaining champions will present to this arena at the eleventh hour of the morning for a mass battle."

"A mass battle!" Multiple advisors shout at once. "This is unacceptable!"

One of the advisors shouts above the others. "Surely, you don't expect the champions to kill each other?"

Osian gives him a benevolent smile. "Of course not. The champions may use any means necessary to force their opponents to yield. Any champion who yields will be eliminated from the trials."

Elise is pale beside me. "*Any* means?"

"What means are acceptable?" Rhydian shouts. He glances around at me, a dangerous grin settling onto his features.

Osian says, "Maiming, wounding, anything less than death."

Fear strikes through me. *Marbella…*

I push through the crowd. "What about the Storm Princess?"

Silence falls around me. Deathly silence.

Osian's smile is victorious. "The Princess is not immune. Any methods may be used to force her to yield."

Anger like lava boils inside me. My fists clench. I fight the crimson rage threatening to shade my vision. "You will not allow anyone to harm the Storm Princess."

Osian spits. "She chose to compete! She knows what will

happen if she's too injured to subdue the Storm. It's her duty to decide what's more important. We have already bent the rules to accommodate her. If she is afraid, she can bow out." He casts around. "Where is she? Perhaps she has given up already."

He waves his hand in a dismissive gesture and each Elven Commander turns their back on us and stalks off the dais, leaving the arena in an uproar. It's not just about Marbella. None of us expected to be fighting each other this early. None of the Houses are happy.

Elise places a trembling hand on my arm. "Baelen… you have to protect her."

I cover her hand with mine. "With my life."

22

MARBELLA

I awake on the floor of the Vault. The Storm's gone. It's quiet. Except for that annoying thumping vibration slamming through my head…

I open one eye. My head is pounding. I'm thirsty, but the storm told me the truth: the wound on my back is nothing more than a nasty scar now.

The thumping vibration hasn't stopped. If anything, it's getting worse and more erratic. I spin to the transparent panels at the side of the Vault.

I recognize Elise. She's pounding her fists against the paneling. Her mouth is moving as if she's shouting, but the Vault is soundproof so I can't hear her. Something's definitely wrong. Adrenaline shoots through me and I jump to my feet, racing to the door and pulling it open.

"Princess!" she cries, drawing breath. "The next trial! The next test is about to start."

My eyes widen. "How long was I asleep?"

"Two days. I've been trying to wake you…"

"Oh no." I'm already running, flinging open the second door. "Which way?"

Elise is on my heels, her silk robes flying out behind her. "It was supposed to be a game of wit, but they've mixed things up. It's a mass battle in the arena."

I skid to a halt in front of the final door. "They want us to kill each other?"

Her face is pale. "Maim, wound, defeat, and force to yield, but not kill. Those were their words."

My lips curl in disgust. "Then it's a test for a torturer." I slam my fist into the last door, frustration and anger burning through my nerve endings. "They're doing this because of me. Aren't they?"

"The whispers are that the idea originated from the House of Valor."

Worry shoots through me. "Did Rhydian Valor make it through the first test?"

"With only a moment to spare. But yes, he did."

"Then, it's about revenge. He'll go after Sebastian and Jasper first for humiliating him, and then he'll come after me."

Now that we've stopped running, Elise shakes beside me, trembling so hard I can see her arms and legs wobbling. I've never seen her so scared. "Elise, what is it?"

"The other champions won't be cloaked. They're allowed to touch you. They're allowed to do anything they want to force you to yield."

I stare back at her. Wait… anything?

She clutches the door. "You weren't there when the Elven Command announced the trial. Rhydian Valor asked for clarification of the rules and the Elven Command gave permission for any methods to be used. I wasn't allowed to speak. Commander Rath was silenced. He tried to speak for the other champions as well as you. This is bad for everyone.

"Please, Princess, I knew you'd never forgive me if I didn't wake you, but please… Don't go to this trial." She reaches for me, her fear is like a solid force. "Please stay here where it's safe."

"Safe for how long?" The storm's whisper echoes around my head: *Your husband will kill you.* "Either they cut me to shreds in this trial, or one of them tries to kill me in the end."

"Cutting you isn't the worst they could do."

"I know!" I scream against the wooden door. "The Elven Command is trying to force me out. They want me to be so afraid that I won't compete. Tell me one thing: while I was asleep, did the storm rage?"

She shakes her head. "I've never seen it so calm."

"Then I might not have its power." I need to curse. I need to shout and scream. But more than that... "I need my armor. How much time do I have?"

For the first time, there's a glimmer of hope on her face. She opens the door, revealing my Storm Command waiting in a protective semi-circle. Jordan holds my armor out to me. But her face is as pale and afraid as Elise's.

"You hoped I wouldn't open this door," I say.

"I did."

"Cover me, please." They close ranks as I strip right there, sliding out of my damaged climbing suit and into the light-as-air armor. It covers me from my neck to my toes. I feel braver inside it. Let any man try to cut his way through this.

Elise says, "You have three minutes before they close the doors."

I wish I could ask her to cloak my skin, but the spells that protect the trials won't allow any spells to be cast over me.

I don't have to say anything. I start running and so does my Storm Command. Two of them sprint ahead to clear my path, giving me a clear run through the courtyard and out to the arena. Crowds of elves press around the outside of the building. The upper levels must already be full. No doubt word has travelled fast, and nobody wants to miss the spectacle. Spectators obstruct the doors. If I don't make it inside in time, it will be because of these elves outside.

My Storm Command screams ahead of me, the tips of their spears sporting blunted covers so they can use them to push elves aside. "Out of the way! Clear the doors!"

Elves scramble backward, hurrying to obey, whispering and pointing. "The Princess."

From inside the arena, someone shouts an order. I recognize Elwyn Elder's voice amplified by the spellcasters to be heard above the noise. "One minute to go. Close the doors."

I'm not going to make it in time. There are too many elves in the way. But the doors are large enough that there's space above the elves' heads...

"Jordan, boost!"

She sprints ahead of me with one of my other ladies. The circle around me opens up to allow passage through the front. Jordan drops to her knee in the gap and so does the other elf, facing each other with their hands laced over their knees. I race to them and use their hands as a springboard. At the same time, they stand up beneath me, propelling me into the air.

I fly through the gap of the closing door, angling sideways to make it through. I roll on the other side and bounce up onto my feet.

Elwyn Elder pauses on the dais as my arrival causes a stir. His hand hangs mid-air as if he was about to give the signal to begin. He's *definitely* not happy to see me.

An hourglass rests on a table beside him. It's full of sand at the top already drizzling to the bottom. I'm guessing that means our time has started. It's too late for me to scream a veto at Rhydian Valor. Even if I could, eliminating him won't do me much good—he has too many friends.

The arena has been set up so there's a protective shield around the dais at one end—a grand viewing area for the Elven Command. The rest of the crowd sits high above me on the upper levels, also protected by a shield. I'm assuming it's in case of wayward arrows.

Down at floor level, the space has been spellcasted to resemble a forest. The other champions stand at intervals around the arena. I count twelve, including Baelen, Jasper, and Sebastian. I take note of Rhydian Valor, especially the fact that he seems to have been placed in an advantageous spot behind a boulder where he can take cover.

Well, I guess that makes me lucky thirteen.

"Princess," Elwyn says, his voice still amplified. "We thought you were too injured to continue."

I stride through the grassy, green forest, twisting between the spreading trees and sparkling moss. It would be all unicorns and rainbows in this place if it wasn't for the blood about to be shed.

I don't have the advantage of a spellcaster to make my voice heard, but as I reach the dais, I give it my best shot. "You mean you hoped I was."

My comment draws gasps from the crowd, but I'm beyond caring. I ignore Elwyn's sputtering and lift my arms in defiance at the other champions.

"Well now, which of you boys is going to be brave enough to attack me first? Because we all know that's why we're here."

Despite my bravado, I have a big problem: I don't have a weapon.

That's okay, Marbella, I tell myself. *You'll just have to steal one. And hope it has metal in it.*

23

MARBELLA

Nobody moves.

Rhydian licks his lips and disgust crawls all over me. Off to my left, Baelen watches him and at least five other men whose grins make me want to throw up.

I can see Baelen calculating each move, every step to get to them before they get to me. He's wearing fine armor and carrying multiple daggers, a sword, and a bow and arrows at his back. His hands twitch to the dagger at his hip every time he looks at Rhydian. Baelen may have spoken up against this trial, but now that we're here, maiming the other man won't be enough.

His gaze meets mine for a moment and the ferocity in his face scares me. He's barely Baelen right now. He's a Rath to his bones and the other men don't know what they've asked for. He's just waiting for them to make a move and give him an excuse.

"Come on!" I scream, my chest heaving, and fists clenched. There's lightning inside me. I can feel it under my skin. The same way there's a gargoyle's growl in my throat. I just need a way to let it out. I just need a weapon.

I roar at the other men. "You can either get a piece of me now or when one of you wins. Let's get on with it."

Sebastian's in a defensive position—he and Baelen seem to have figured out some way of signaling each other—but Jasper…

I do a double-take. Jasper's actually smiling. No, more like grinning like an elven cat.

"Holy lurking shadow panthers!" he shouts, drawing attention away from me. He leaves his position beside a spreading oak and strides toward me with a gusty laugh.

"Listen to the mouth on this woman." He bellows each word, laughing as he goes. "I, for one, would rather take her for life than have a small piece right now and let it be the last."

He's got within ten feet of me without anyone stopping him, close enough that I can see the dagger he's lifting out of the scabbard at his waist. *Holy lurking shadow panthers*, he hasn't forgotten what I did with the last dagger I held, and he knows I need a weapon.

His mouth might be laughing, but his eyes aren't. That's the Jasper I know. With a flick of his wrist, he pitches the weapon neatly into the ground at my feet.

"Which is why…" The grin drops off his face as he turns to the others, drawing his sword. "Anyone who wants a piece of her goes through me first."

As I leap forward to pluck the dagger out of the ground, I break the stand-off. Rhydian's five lackeys charge toward me, but Baelen's plan is as clear as the moss sparkling on the stones beside those beautiful trees. Jasper and I are the not-so-helpless bait. Baelen and Sebastian are the predators. The other men, well, they're the mush in between.

I pick up the dagger as the first man reaches me. It looks like Rhydian is cunning enough to let someone else take the first shot so he can figure out my weaknesses.

I'm pleased to discover that my new weapon is made entirely of steel. Electricity shrieks through my arm, lighting up the dagger, my hand, and my torso. The high-pitched crackling sizzles a warning and Jasper's smart enough to side-step and stay out of harm's way. He allows the attacking man through, but that's fine with me. I greet my attacker with a snarl and an armored foot to his face. The shimmer husks lining my boots may as well be iron cracking across his cheekbone.

He stumbles backward, and I give him one last chance. *Don't get up.*

The fool jumps back to his feet, dagger drawn, aiming for my shoulder. My lightning illuminates his face as he flies toward me.

He's aiming high, so I drop to my knees, driving my dagger into his left thigh. His scream is drowned out by the screech of electricity. I use my free fist to thump his other kneecap. I can't hurt his knee through his armor, but I push both his legs out from under him, using his forward momentum and the strength of the Storm to flip him bodily over me. He lands with a crash on to his back.

By then, Jasper fights two other men, and Baelen and Sebastian are battling another four. Rhydian continues to keep his distance from all of them. He's not the only one staying back. Another man hasn't moved from his position at the end of the arena. None of the other men are bothering with the loner, and I don't have time to identify him.

Before my attacker can recover, I slide across the floor, banging against the shield that protects the dais, and bounce off it. On the dais, the Elven Command jumps backward. Elwyn Elder moves so fast that he knocks over his chair. The hourglass wobbles and one of them grabs it before it smashes.

I drop to the man's side, holding the dagger in both hands, ready to plunge it into his heart. I recognize him now. "Garrett of the House of Glory. Do you yield? Or would you rather bleed to death?"

He clutches his thigh, trying to stop the flow of blood. His efforts aren't doing him much good. He's lost his dagger, and I draw his sword before he can reach for it too. Now there are two blazing weapons in my hands. I keep the barest safe distance from him so I don't electrocute him.

Despite the threat in front of him, all he can do is stare beyond me at the Elven Command where the powerful men watch from so close by, protected by their spellcast shield. Gideon Glory takes a step forward, his robes floating around him. The fury on his face is like a dagger itself.

That's when I realize that each member of the Elven Command has a grandson in the arena. All of them are fighting against me right now except for Sebastian Splendor.

I shout at Garrett, "What did your grandfather tell you? What did Gideon Glory order you to do?"

The man looks at me and it's like he's seeing me for the first time. "You weren't supposed to be here. They wanted to force you out."

"I got that already. What else?"

He sucks in a breath, groaning and in pain. "They ordered us to take out Commander Rath by any means necessary. They don't want him to win."

Behind me, a man crashes across the arena and Baelen thunders after him, loosing arrows at the same time.

I swing back to Garrett. The Elven Command would always have a backup plan. "And what if I came to the fight? What then?"

"May the ancients forgive me, my grandfather told me to take your power. The first man you touch will have your power. He told me… He ordered me…"

I throw my head back and scream. "He told you a lie. My power will kill you."

I ram the dagger into the earth beside his neck. Lightning leaps from my hands and zaps his skin. It's the lightest touch, but he flinches, scooting away from me to escape the deadly energy.

Despite the threat, he shakes his head. "No, it's true. He said you're different. You're not like the other princesses. He said that one of us has to claim you and…" His eyes flick to the fighting men. "It can't be Baelen Rath."

The phoenix told me I was *something else*. Now I know why that sounded like a really bad thing. When I nominated myself for the trials, the Elven Command was unprepared. But while I was away on the mountain, they had the chance to think and plan. They had time to change the rules—because I changed them first. I opened that door and now they're running through it. Baelen told me he was a target. Now we both are.

"If you truly believe that you can take my power, then do it." I hold out my bare hand to him. It's bathed in energy that crackles at the edges, leaping beyond my palm in strikes and flashes. "Take my hand."

He reaches for me, even though it means letting go of his wound.

I can't believe it. He actually believes what his grandfather told him. He's going to try…

At the last moment, lightning leaps out and bites his hand. He cries out and snaps his hand back, nursing it and trying to press his wound again. His face is pale. He's lost a lot of blood and won't last much longer at this rate.

"*That* is what happens if you touch me. Now tell me that you yield." I ram the dagger into the ground again, closer to him this time. "Tell me that you yield!"

"I yield!" His voice cracks as his eyes meet those of his furious grandfather. "The House of Glory yields."

Inside the shield, Gideon Glory is like ice. He turns his back on his grandson. I jump to my feet and strike my fist against the shield. Lightning travels through, bending and wobbling the shield so much that Gideon flinches in alarm. If I struck it hard enough, I'm sure I could break through, and he must sense it.

I shout at him, disgusted that he turned away from his injured family member. "Come and get your grandson before he dies."

Then I take both weapons and spin to the battle raging behind me. Of the four elves who were fighting Baelen and Sebastian, only two remain standing. They're both large men and they're putting up a solid fight. The other two have dragged themselves to the side of the arena, seeking safety away from the battle. They both appear badly wounded.

The two fighting Jasper haven't given up so easily.

I launch myself at one of them, shoving him aside. I'm careful not to touch him with my bare hand, connecting only with his armor, but I allow electricity to flow through me for a second before I release him. He shudders, shaking as he collapses to the ground. He's alive, but he's not in good shape. I'd love to zap the other man too, but I'm angry enough to kill him. Despite the chaos, the Elven Command ordered that nobody be killed. If I break that rule, they'll force me out of the trials. Which is exactly what they want.

I throw a glance back at Jasper and the man he's now fighting one-on-one. Jasper is light on his feet and the other man is tiring fast. At least it's now a fair fight.

I step over the fallen man on my way to Rhydian, advancing on him behind his protective boulder. From across the room, Baelen suddenly increases his attack strategy against the man he's fighting. Every anxious look he casts in my direction tells me he wants me to stay with Jasper, but what Garrett told me drives me on. The men were ordered to take Baelen out of the competition. I'm not going to let that happen.

I round on Rhydian. "You don't get to sit this out waiting for everyone else to yield."

"Just waiting for you to come to me," Rhydian says without budging. "I figured you would eventually."

I grip my dagger in one hand and sword in the other so tight that my knuckles turn white. I circle around the boulder to find that he's clasping a dagger in each hand.

I'm three feet away from him when he suddenly shouts, "Now!"

There's a flicker of movement from the side of the arena closest to me. The two men who crawled over there have nocked arrows into their bows. I'm not sure what they're aiming at, because they don't seem to be pointing their weapons at my chest. They let loose and the arrows fly harmlessly to either side of me, easily missing my torso, but too late I realize their real targets…

My hands!

No! Pain explodes through my fingers as the arrows nick them. The wounds are only grazes, but I can't stop the reflex…

My fingers open, and I drop both my weapons. The lightning spirals away from me, draining away without the steel to harness it. The Storm's power goes with it.

I drop and stretch for the steel I need, but Rhydian's on me already. He plows into me, using his shoulder and brute force to knock me to the ground, following me down to the ground. I land beside the boulder, the grass cushioning my fall so I don't crack my head. With my body behind the rocks, I can only just see the rest of the arena.

The other men's attack strategy suddenly changes. The men fighting Jasper and Sebastian launch themselves forward, tackling both of my friends, and shoving them as far away from Baelen as they can. The two men with bows and arrows leap to their feet, shooting at Baelen as they run at him. Now there are three men circling Baelen, and their methods turn savage. Swords and daggers drawn, they bait him with cuts and nicks, but their real target seems to be his lower spine—his injury.

I have to get to him, but Rhydian knocks me down, his body a dead weight against mine. I jam my hands against his armor, pushing as hard as I can. I need to get him off me, but I can't let him touch my bare skin. Not just because of what the Elven Command believes, but because I couldn't stand it if he did.

Only my hands and head are exposed. I have to keep them away from him, which means I can't hit him.

Lucky me. Those don't seem to be his target.

He slices the dagger down the armor between my breasts, attempting to cut it open but the Elyria web doesn't break. He tries again, ramming the blade against me.

I scream as my chest burns, grabbing his armored sleeve to stop him. His blade can't cut through my armor, but the pressure against my chest is unbearable. Every blow forces the spider web into my torso, tearing against my ribs and the soft skin between them.

I kick my legs, trying to throw off his balance, but his hip rests against my groin, one knee keeping him balanced and straddling my right leg. He's turned far enough to the side that I can't kick any part of his body that matters.

"Get off me!"

His big face snarls down at me. "Not until I get what's mine."

"You insult my House!"

"Elves in the House of Mercy were bred to be insulted."

I retort. "The House of Valor once had integrity. Where is your honor?"

His lips draw back into a vile grin as he rams the knife at my chest, over and over in rapid succession, harder and faster. My attempts to hold his arm back are useless—gravity and his sheer weight give him the advantage.

Agonizing pain thumps through me with every blow and every rip against my skin.

It's too much. I scream, pushing at him, hitting back, thumping his arms and side, trying to make him stop. But the awful truth is that I can't stop him without touching him—my bare hands on his.

He rams the knife at me again, his sweat dripping down onto my face, and suddenly… suddenly… I understand…

He's trying to force me to touch him. He wants me to hit him, skin on skin. He wants me to grab his hand—even to head-butt him. Anything that means I willingly touch him…

Sobs tear out of me at the awful realization. "No…"

I press my hands against his armor where it's safe, squeeze my eyes shut, turn my face away, and close my mouth against the screams forcing their way into my throat. I have to bear the pain. I have to hold out long enough for Baelen to get to me. I won't connect with Rhydian's skin.

I won't do it. "I won't do it."

"Yes, you will."

I open my eyes. My head is turned to Baelen. I can't see Jasper and Sebastian, which means they're still cornered, or they would have either run to Baelen or me.

Baelen is covered in blood. Two men lie on the ground at his feet, and I can't tell if they're alive or dead. He roars at the third, taking the brunt of the man's knife in his shoulder as he knocks into him, choosing to allow the blade to strike him in an effort to get close enough to grab his opponent's arm. The other man screams, and I can only guess what Baelen did—dislocated his arm, maybe ripped it from the socket. His opponents may have been trying to bait him, but they've well and truly released the Rath monster now.

Rhydian says, "He won't get to you in time. You will submit to me."

My torso is on fire. Rhydian's hateful face is inches from mine. If he can't make me touch him, he'll simply drop his face to mine, a single kiss to drain the fight out of me. But what's most agonizing is that he's right. It will take Baelen ten seconds to reach me across the distance, and Rhydian can take what he wants in far less time than that.

I'm sobbing but I don't care that I'm showing emotion, because I have to release this fear and anger somehow as Rhydian's face lowers to mine…

Another man appears above him, his outline watery through the tears and sweat in my eyes. A voice I don't recognize says, "No, she won't."

A club swings down, arching toward Rhydian's head. It knocks him right off me, rendering him unconscious at the same time. He drops like a dead weight off to the side, but his legs are still tangled in mine. I scramble away from him, kicking hard, as the man above me quickly drops the club, nocks an arrow into his bow, and shoots the final man still fighting Baelen. The arrow lodges in the man's leg. It's the opening Baelen needs to knock him out with the hilt of his sword.

I press up against the boulder, kicking the last of Rhydian's weight off me, as the new man drops to his knees, finally coming into focus.

Eli Elder makes his movements slow, leaning back on his heels and folding his hands in his lap, making it clear he doesn't intend to come any closer.

I'm almost too bruised to speak. My throat aches and my lungs… oh my lungs burn so badly. "Eli?"

"I wasn't going to fight."

"It was you… standing at the back."

He nods. "But I couldn't let that go on. I wouldn't be alive if it wasn't for you." His eyes are crystal-clear blue, his eyelids tapered at the edges like the rest of his House, his mouth set in a serious line. "I was tired and I was about to let go."

I'm not sure what he's talking about. Then I remember the mountain. He was the one who lost his grip and almost fell to his death.

"I heard your voice, and it saved my life," he says. "So I want you to know that I don't agree with what the Elven Command is doing —what my grandfather's doing. He's always been difficult, but he's never been like this before. Something's got a hold of him. He isn't himself. None of them are."

"Get away from her!" Baelen appears, chest heaving, sword bloody, pointing it at Eli.

Eli rises to his feet, his hands splayed out to show he isn't a threat. He holds his bow lightly between his thumb and forefinger, letting it swing to make it clear he doesn't intend to use it. "If you need my help, Princess, call on me. Until then…"

He drops his bow to the floor and raises his voice. "The House of Elder yields!" He nudges Rhydian with the tip of his boot. "So does the House of Valor. May it regain its dignity in times to come."

He retreats to the side as Baelen drops to me, his hands hovering over me but never making contact. "Are you hurt?"

I don't know how to answer. Pain thrums through every nerve in my chest, but I need to peel off my armor to know how much damage has been done.

What scares me more is the way Baelen's hands shake. He's either in shock or he's moving on pure adrenaline alone. Beneath the blood, his face is far too pale, his movements erratic. He's lost a lot of blood, and everything screams at me that he needs help but he won't seek it until I answer him.

"No, I'm fine," I whisper the lie and know he doesn't believe me, but what else can I say? I'm not dead. Rhydian didn't touch me. Those are the important things.

Up on the dais, the last grain of sand slides through the hourglass and a trumpet blares. Five men are still standing. The two that cornered Jasper and Sebastian both jump away from them, hands raised, their job done. The others are either unconscious or have already yielded.

Other than the final note of the trumpet, the arena is deathly silent. Up high, in the viewing levels, female elves stand on their feet, watching me, watching Baelen, watching the Elven Command. One of the women, dressed in fine robes, suddenly strides forward, her movements graceful and regal. The others make way for her, making it clear she's a woman of high position. As she approaches the shield, I recognize her as Sebastian's mother from the House of Splendor. Teilo Splendor, one of the Elven Commanders, is her father.

In one swift move she strikes her fist against the shield, holding it there, glaring at her father. Her mouth moves, but I can't hear what she says. Then she turns and strides from the arena. One by one, the other women follow her, thumping their fists against the shield before turning their backs on the Elven Command.

Sebastian and Jasper appear at my side. Sebastian's expression is filled with regret and sadness. "My mother's right. We don't treat our women like this."

My only concern is for Baelen. "Help Baelen, please. I don't know what they've done to him, but I'm worried."

Sebastian catches Baelen as he sways, working with Jasper to lift

Baelen to his feet. It takes both of them to shoulder his weight, neither of them quite as tall nor broad in the shoulders as Baelen is.

"Healers!" Sebastian roars into the quiet. "We need healers!"

Suddenly, healers flood the arena, racing to each of the champions, but Baelen struggles against them. "No, I have to stay with Marbella."

Jasper and Sebastian coax him all the way to his feet as the healers cut Baelen's armor from his body. Each piece drops to the ground in front of me and as his back is exposed, the cuts become apparent—deep and ugly, crisscrossing his spine, some so deep he's lucky they didn't sever the bone.

"They fought dirty," Jasper says to him. "Without honor. You can't help the Princess unless you recover. Come on."

"Go, Baelen," I whisper, hoping he will accept their help.

His eyes meet mine, a last tug on my heart, before he allows them to help him walk away.

I use the boulder as leverage to push myself to my feet. A female healer approaches me, but I shake my head at her. "There's nothing you can do."

She retreats with a deep bow to me.

The steel dagger rests in the grass. The only way I'm going to make it back to my quarters is with the Storm's help. The cold steel on my fingers is like balm, the electricity an energy boost. I'll crash soon, but for now, I stumble over to the dais, my body glowing.

Teilo Splendor holds his head low, his hands limp at his sides. His daughter's demonstration has clearly hit the mark with him. The others… not so much.

"This isn't the outcome you wanted," I say, surprised at how calm I sound. "I don't know why you're targeting Commander Rath but—"

"Because he refuses to follow orders!" Pedr Bounty thuds across the dais right up to the shield. He's one of the two Elven Commanders who still has a champion in the trials now that the Houses of Elder, Glory, and Valor are eliminated. "The gargoyle threat is imminent, but he refuses to act."

"What gargoyle threat?" I challenge, growing increasingly angry. "What are a few nests? You've hurt more elves in these trials—more champions on this day alone—than the gargoyles have hurt in hundreds of years!"

Shame washes over his strong features, but he's undeterred. "An invasion is only months away. We need to strike first."

"They're not invading. They're running away. Something's driving them out of Erador and we are the lesser of two evils."

He scowls at me. "How do you know that?"

I lean forward. "Because you sent me into a mountain with gargoyle nests on it and I happened to come across one."

He sucks in a sharp breath. The Commanders behind him react swiftly, shooting questions at me.

"Tell us where it is!"

"Tell us now!"

"Why didn't you kill it?"

And last, "How did you escape?"

I grind my teeth, refusing to answer any of them. "What does Commander Rath say we should do?"

Pedr Bounty glowers. "He says we should send scouts across the border and gather more information before we make a decision."

"Well, that sounds wise to me." Except that they won't do it. They're too proud and stubborn. I can tell by their expressions. "As for these trials... I'll see you at the next one."

I make it to the doors. One of the guards has the sense to yell, "Stand back!" as he pushes the door open for me and keeps his distance from the electricity crackling around me.

Jordan is right there with Elise, struggling against the guards outside. Two guards lie on the ground. Another is about to meet Jordan's fist as she screams, "Let me through! Let me—"

She races to me as soon as she sees me, calling the Storm Command who swarm me. I drop the dagger to the ground, so I don't hurt them. I've never been so happy to be surrounded by my nunnery as I am right now.

"They wouldn't let us in. Those brutes and their spellcasters..."

I eye Elise with alarm. She's bristling. Her hair is out of place, her dress is dirty, and her face is smudged. "If they'd kept me away from you for one second longer, I was going to send them to meet the ancients."

She presses her lips together, her anger vanishing into fear. "I saw what Commander Rath looked like when they brought him out and I… I was so afraid for you…"

I can't tell her that I'm okay, because I'm not. I'm so far from okay right now, but I do need her help. "I need to know when Commander Rath recovers, and I need you to give him a message. I want him to come and see me as soon as he can. Can you tell him that for me?"

"Of course. Anything."

"Okay, then. Please get me home."

24

MARBELLA

I peel my armor off in front of the mirror in my bathing room. My arms are dotted with black bruises. So is my collarbone, the skin between my breasts, and all across my ribs and stomach. The only mercy is that he left my breasts alone, preferring instead to slam his knife around them. On top of the bruises are grazes from the pressure of the knife point.

Jordan prepared an ice bath for me and now I slide into it gingerly. The icy water stings and numbs at the same time. She also left me with a pitcher of water and about a thousand cups already filled along the wide edge of the bath.

"Hydrate while you bathe," she'd ordered. "I want every one of those cups empty before you leave this room."

I sip the first one, running my finger across the graze on the back of my hand. Such a small thing to make me drop my weapons, but they knew exactly where to aim. They'd planned it all in advance: how to disarm me, how to stop Jasper and Sebastian from helping Baelen, how to keep Baelen from getting to me. All while attacking me. Jordan had warned me not to underestimate my opponents, but I'd never expected them to fight without honor.

I stay in the bath far longer than I should, untying my hair to float around me and obscure the bruises. My eyelids eventually droop, my battered body finally numb to the throbbing pain. I

163

don't want to get out. I don't want the pain to return. I wonder how soon I can ask Jordan to prepare another ice bath?

A commotion outside the bathing room door startles me into action. Sharp conversation thrums through the wooden door. The sound of urgent voices slips into the bathing room, but nobody knocks.

I emerge from the bath and gulp the final mouthful of the water Jordan ordered me to drink, reaching for my robe. As I wrap it around me, leaving the tie loose because of my aching ribs. I lean up against the door, trying to find out what awaits me on the other side of it.

Elise sounds flustered. That's twice today. Really not a good sign. "I know what I said, but I'm sure she didn't mean right now…"

I grab the door handle and swing it wide. "Baelen."

He straightens from a half-lean against a chair at the side of my bedroom, his focus zeroing in on me as soon as I appear. "You said to come as soon as I could. That's now. I could. So I'm here."

His forehead crinkles, and it's suddenly so adorable that I can't help but smile. I press my lips together, trying to stop. "But you must be hurt. You have to go back—"

"No."

I swallow. "Not even if I order you? For your own sake?"

"No."

"Then at least let Elise take a look at you. Elise?"

She puts on her business face and doesn't take any nonsense. He's wearing a loose white shirt and blue pants buttoned at the waist. "Lift," she orders, gesturing at his shirt.

I'm not prepared for the sight of his bare chest and stomach. He may as well be sculpted from male perfection; his wide, fully muscled shoulders taper through his broad chest to his waist, every part of him radiating strength. It's not the wounds that freeze me, but the memory of his chest against mine, of skin on skin, and… it's never enough. A little bit of me breaks apart, knowing that I'll never have that again. He's broader now, bigger, tougher than he was then, and he carries scars he didn't have before. The sight of him makes my heart ache.

I find his eyes across the room. He hasn't stopped focusing on me. Terrified that he'll read my thoughts, I shake myself, concentrating on the present. At least the new wounds across his chest are minor.

Elise clicks her tongue. "That's not too bad, I suppose."

"It wasn't all my blood," he mutters.

"Turn."

He plants his feet, shaking his head, stubbornly refusing, but she lifts her eyebrows. It's just her and Jordan inside my room so it's not like my entire Storm Command is watching.

"Please?" Elise asks.

Slowly, he swivels and lifts his shirt again. His back has been cleaned, but the wounds are gruesome. I grind my teeth. The other men had found all the gaps in his armor, stabbing and shredding over and over.

Jordan gasps. "Those cowards."

Elise sighs. "Okay, sit and lean forward, please. The healers have done an adequate job, but I can do better."

For the next ten minutes, she works on his back while he rests his head in his hands, quietly accepting her help. She can't spellcast his wounds because of the protective spells from the trials, but she's deft with a needle. Somewhere in the middle, Jordan hands him a pack of ice for his face, which is blue and yellow in places. By the time Elise has finished, I've found my way over to my bed, perching on the edge of it. My room is simply furnished with a large bed, a bedside table, and a small table and chairs on the far side, which is where Baelen sits now. Finally, his wounds are neatly stitched and patched to Elise's satisfaction.

"Better," she says.

Baelen raises his eyes up to her as if seeking permission to stand. I bury a smile. Elise has a way of commanding obedience but somehow manages to do it in a way that isn't demeaning or offensive.

I slide off the bed. "Jordan, Elise, I'd like you to leave us now, please."

"What?" Elise and Jordan both swing to me at once, the agitation in their rapid glances telling me they thought they heard me wrong.

"I need you both to leave this room."

"I don't think…" Elise starts, but Jordan is louder.

"That's not going to happen."

"Please, Jordan," I say. "I need you to do this for me."

"No," she says, eyes wide, clearly shocked. "I'm not allowed to leave you alone. I won't break that rule. I can't…"

Her shoulders shake and her face suddenly crumbles. "I always follow the rules. Even if I don't like it. Even if it breaks my heart…" She struggles to regain her composure, but the floodgates have opened and she can't hold it in. My order has triggered all her emotions. She presses her hand against her heart. "I follow the rules even if it kills me."

"You're right," I say. "You always do the right thing. You didn't speak to Sebastian when you could have all those mornings you saw him. You didn't object when he offered me his heartstone, even though it broke your heart. You've never once made me feel guilty about it or blamed me for it. You have more integrity than the Elven Command. And that's why I trust you right now."

Her eyes brim with tears, her head tips forward, and her shoulders slump, but she doesn't budge.

"I won't force you to break the rules, Jordan. So this is what I'm going to do instead…" I cross my room so that I'm standing just inside the entrance to my bathroom. "You aren't breaking any rules now, because this is my bathing room. It's the only place you're required to leave me alone."

"The bathing room? Seriously?" She stares at me. Then she covers her mouth with a laugh-sob, swiping at her tears with her other hand. "Oh, Princess…"

She glances at Baelen, who hovers nearby and is definitely as concerned about my intentions as Jordan. He shakes his head, this great beast of a man looking like he doesn't want to step in the wrong direction in case he breaks something. "I don't think this is a good idea."

Baelen's disquiet seems to have the opposite effect on Jordan. She appears to make a decision. "Okay, then."

Elise wraps her arms around Jordan's shoulders and together they leave my bedroom, nudging the door closed behind them.

I signal Baelen to step inside. "Commander Rath, if you will?"

I'm not sure if he'll follow me, but he crosses the distance with a worried crease in his forehead. I don't take any chances. As Baelen clears the door to the bathroom, I close it and press up against it.

He dwarfs the small space. The bath is full of water. There's nowhere to sit. He can't seem to decide where he should stand. If I were him, I wouldn't know either.

The same furrow wrinkles his forehead, but he keeps his voice gentle as he says, "Show me, Marbella."

My hair drapes across the front of my robe, obscuring the damage that lies beneath. I draw it across my neck out of the way and slide the top of the robe across one shoulder, revealing the bruises.

Baelen suddenly vibrates with tension, his Rath heritage surfacing. "I should have killed him. I *will* kill him."

"I didn't ask you in here to show you this or to encourage you to seek revenge," I say.

He pauses, comes back to me, and tilts his head, questioning.

I run my eyes across his high cheekbones and the single unruly patch of hair on the side of his head, the curve of his lips, and the cut of his jaw. He is hard and unyielding, never falling even when the other champions came at him with everything they had, but I remember when his lips weren't pressed in such angry lines. I remember when they were soft and gentle, planting kisses against my throat.

My breath hitches. I try to breathe normally as I take a step forward. He takes a step back, just like he should, except that he's slow and reluctant.

"I need you to do something for me now that we're alone," I say.

His eyes light up and, for a second, I imagine the light of his heartstone burning inside him. He doesn't take his eyes off me, running his gaze from my long hair draped across my shoulder, along the arch of my neck, down to the curve of my waist. The edge of my robe splits open at the bottom as I take another step forward, the material falling on either side of my thigh.

He takes another step backward, but there's nowhere to go now that he's hard up against the wall.

My heart thumps. I lift my arm. "I need you to take my hand."

25

———

MARBELLA

"Marbella." He closes the distance between us, but right when he's about to touch my outstretched hand, he stops, caution flooding his features. "Why?"

I can't ignore the question in his eyes. "The Elven Command has been spinning a lie for centuries that the Storm Princess's husband can share her power to help her in the Vault. It's not true. It never has been. Except that now they believe it is true for me. They believe that the first man I choose to touch will inherit the power of the Storm."

"That's why they came after you today, isn't it?"

"In the arena today, Garrett Glory told me he was ordered to take my power by force. I can't let that happen. I won't let them try again. I'm not even sure that I believe them, but if it's going to happen, then it has to be my choice."

He studies the floor. "You want me to touch you so that someone else doesn't."

I stop before I say "yes." I can't let him misunderstand me. I clear my throat. "When you bound yourself to me, and then told me it was so you could tell me secrets, I felt the same way you feel now."

He remains pinned in place. "Which is?"

"Like you cut my heart into pieces."

His eyes widen, but I hurry on. "So I'm going to tell you right away… even though it scares me… I'm not asking you to take my

168

hand so that I can get the better of the Elven Command or to beat them. I'm asking you because…"

I take a deep breath, exhale, then swallow against the dryness in my mouth, suddenly terrified, and trying to calm my nerves. I focus on a point on his broad shoulders, not sure if I can find my voice if I look him in the eyes.

"I'm asking you as me. Not as the princess. But as me, Marbella Mercy. I'm asking you to take my hand because I want you to. Because it's what I want."

I finally look up and the agony on his face shakes me to the core.

"Marbella, if I touch you right now…" He turns away from me, staring at the water. Particles of ice still float on the surface, quickly melting. Deep concentration hijacks his posture and it's like a wall shoots up between us.

Without looking at me he asks, "Do you remember…"

"Yes."

The corner of his mouth tugs up but only for a moment. "Then you know I can't take your hand."

He angles around me, maneuvering against the bath, bumping into the mirror, making sure he follows the widest path to avoid coming anywhere near me. I can't do anything to stop him. He's going to leave, and I don't want him to, but I have no choice.

I let my arm swing down by my side.

He stops beside me. "I don't want your hand, Marbella. I want all of you."

Shivers run to my toes. The distance between us is agonizing. He's hurt and I'm hurt, but I'd collide with him in two seconds if he gave me any indication that's what he wanted.

"The only way I can have a life with you is if I win," he says. "If I touch you now, I'll forfeit the trials and I'll never have another chance."

I don't think before I speak. "No, you don't understand. I can't let you win."

His sudden confusion crashes over me. I've given him every reason to believe that I want him to win. I can't tell him that the protocols will only end in death: either he will try to kill me, or I'll have to kill him first.

I whisper. "I can't let anyone win."

"Why?" He searches my face, seeking an answer to explain my declaration. "Something's wrong. Tell me what it is."

All the things I want to say rush into my head. *The protocols are cursed. If I win, everyone will live. If I don't, my husband will kill me, and the Storm will be unleashed—unless I kill him first. And if it's you... Baelen... I won't be able to do it.*

I can't tell him any of that because knowing about the curse will kill him. I scrunch my hands into the material at my sides, suddenly shocked to realize that my sash has slipped its knot and by tugging on it, I've made it worse.

I stop moving but it's too late. The sash gives way. The material drops gently to my sides. The only thing keeping it from sliding apart completely is that it's caught on the inner curve of my breasts. I try not to breathe or move. Even the slightest movement will be my undoing.

Baelen freezes, but he doesn't take his eyes from my face.

Damn. His self-control is absolute. It always was. The memory of his younger voice rips through me: *"May I have your permission?"*

My shoulders sink. I ignore my robe and all the skin I'm revealing. It's all ugly bruises anyway. "I can't explain. I wish I could."

"Then..." He sidesteps me, swinging the door open, but pauses in the doorway, filling it with his big body. He's suddenly frozen there, half-turned, the black thread from the new stitches showing through his white shirt like crisscrossing tracks across his back. One hand flexes against the door frame.

Please stay. I take the chance to give it one last try. I swallow my pride, knowing that I'm not above begging. But only this once. "Please, Baelen, take my hand. I'll never ask you for anything else. Just this. Please."

"No."

Stubborn man!

I inhale a scream of frustration. There aren't enough glares in the world to hurl at his disappearing back. Even if his back is so broken that it breaks my heart to see it.

My bedroom door clicks and then he's gone.

I've had enough. I've been grabbed at, beaten up, accosted,

pushed around, backed into a corner, and every man except the one I want is trying to get his hands on me. Literally.

Stupid trials! I catch sight of myself in the mirror. I look far too small without my storm suit or armor on. Far too vulnerable.

Stupid mirror, stupid bruises, stupid bath, stupid robe. I scream. "Stupid self-control!"

I rip off the robe, hurl it to the floor, and stomp on it. Not a great idea when my body's still sore and aching. The impact shudders through my calf and up my thigh. "Ouch."

I drop to the floor, dragging the robe around me as Jordan races into the room. She takes one look at me curled up on the floor and goes into attack mode.

"What did he do?" She looks fit to run after him and pummel him herself.

"Nothing. He didn't do anything." I rest my head against the edge of the bath, pushing my hair out of my eyes, pretending I don't have tears in them. "Nothing at all."

26

BAELEN

I grip the doorframe so hard, I sense it shift beneath my palm, threatening to crack.

I want to turn back to Marbella, take the hand she's offering, take what she wants to give, drown in her soft skin, forget myself, forget the trials and all the rules, inhale her soft breaths, taste her lips, steal this moment with her.

"Please, Baelen, take my hand. I'll never ask you for anything else. Just this. Please."

She's begging me. It shocks me to my core that she would beg me. I would do anything for her. Without question. But the plea in her voice, the desperation in her eyes, it's nothing to do with love and everything to do with survival. I recognize it. I know what it's like to have no options left. But inside my head is all one big mess of wanting to touch her—wanting her more than anything—and not wanting to lose her.

My self-control slips. I nearly turn back, but then her declaration repeats on me:

I can't let you win.

The fear in her eyes tells me there's more to it. There's a reason. It's bigger than not wanting me in her life, although she might mean that she doesn't. Whatever the reason, she's willing to give up on us because of it.

She's willing to place her hand in mine one last time and then

172

cast me out of her life forever.

Pain courses through me. It strikes through my chest so hard, I can't breathe. My hand flexes on the doorframe. I try to inhale, try to draw air into my lungs.

The pain of the wounds in my back is nothing compared to this.

My heart cracks, breaks.

I can't fight the hurt. "No."

She inhales behind me as if she's about to speak again, but I can't stay in her presence. My legs are numb as I cross her bedroom and pass her carefully made bed—it was never so neat when I knew her, as if she controls what little she can now.

I want to roar, want to shout, rage against the invisible barriers between us. My numb fingers grip her bedroom door, open it, and close it behind me with a quiet click.

Jordan and Elise wait a mere step outside, casting me alarmed glances, and I'm suddenly afraid that my pain is etched across my face, visible for the world to see.

Without speaking, I stride away from them, my boots hammering the floor, a harsh beat that pounds through my head. The edges of my vision cloud and my focus becomes pinpoint.

Battle. Fight. Rage.

I head for the training room, ignoring the glances cast my way as I make my way from Marbella's quarters to the military compound, ignoring the hush that falls over the training room as soon as I enter and stride toward the only free training post. The soldiers around me stop what they're doing to follow my path. Sunlight streams through the open window beside the post, glowing around me. The wounds on my back are no doubt visible through my shirt, making their eyes widen. *Damn wounds.*

I rip my shirt off, not caring that the damage is fully visible. I fought like a demon in that arena. My father trained me to close off the memories of battle, not to relive them, but the angry memories resurface. The other men had baited me. Stabbed at me. They thought I would fall, but all they did was release the wild inside me. I willingly impaled myself for leverage, taking daggers without pain. Ripped a man's arm from its socket. Broke another's leg. Blinded another with a dagger to his eye. Covered myself in their blood and yet…

I couldn't protect Marbella.

The one woman I vowed I would always protect.

The painful bruises dotting her body between the folds of her robe were a harsh reminder that I couldn't defend her.

Is it any surprise that she doesn't want me in her life?

With a roar, my fist collides with the wooden post, a single hit that cracks it clean down the middle. The training post—my only tangible target right now—splits before my eyes.

Useless piece of...

My next fist crashes against the falling wood, smashing the upper portion toward the lower stump. I drop to my knee for greater impact, forcing the two pieces together. The broken upper piece shatters against the stump, but the collision jars through me, finally an impact that I can feel.

I should have killed Rhydian Valor.

I rise up from my lowered stance, pulling back my shoulders, tilting my head into the sunlight streaming around me. Its warmth was once calming, like a promise of hope.

Marbella and I stand under the same sun.

That single thought carried me through the dark days of waiting, but not anymore. It's not enough anymore.

I turn away from the sun into a silence that feels catastrophic. I brace for my soldiers' reactions to my sudden and willful aggression.

I'm humbled that each one stands, head lowered, fist to chest, granting me a gesture of respect. The nearest man steps forward, raising his eyes to mine. "You honored your House today, Commander Rath. You fought for the Storm Princess with honor."

Would my father think so? He taught me to fight with integrity and intelligence, never with rage. *"You are the last,"* he told me. *"You can't afford to give in to emotion. To lose focus is to die."*

My fists remain closed at my sides. All I can do is nod.

I bend to the broken training post, spread my shirt across the ground, and load it up with the broken pieces, pulling the edges of the shirt around them to form a stack that I leverage into my arms. I carry the entire bundle all the way to the back of the dinner hall, where I add it to the pile of firewood. There's no point putting the shirt back on. It's covered in splinters of wood.

I plant my hands on my thighs, breathing out slowly.

I need to stop feeling.

I need a tavern and a bottle of strong drink.

My mind clears for long enough to signal my legs to move. I run through the military compound, sucking air into my lungs, my feet flying as I dart through alleyways toward the same shady tavern where I found Sebastian the other night. I avoid the public paths, remaining out of sight, taking the back ways, the shadowy corridors.

I only slow down when I reach the door, shoving it open and entering the gloom. Somehow, it's darker during the day. A handful of elves sit at various tables, but they turn back to their drinks as soon as I enter.

Approaching the tavernkeeper at the counter, I say, "The House of Rath will reimburse you."

He gives me a grin, wipes his hands on his apron, and splays his arms wide at the various bottles lining the shelf behind him. "Be my guest."

I point at the largest one I can see but grab his arm before he turns to retrieve it. "You will not allow Rhydian Valor to step foot inside this place while I am here. Otherwise, you will have a murder on your hands."

The tavernkeeper's grin grows broad. "Rest easy, Commander. The House of Rath's coin is worth more to me than that of Valor."

I accept the bottle he hands me, sucking it down without stopping to breathe. I deposit it onto the counter while the tavernkeeper stares at me with increasingly wide eyes.

"Another."

Four bottles of wine later, each one consumed slower than the last, I stumble from the tavern onto the cobbled street, my mind dull and hazy. It's dark now that night has fallen. A cool breeze dances across my cheeks and the stitches across my bare back.

That breeze… that malicious wind… it snatched Marbella's ribbon clean out of my fingers, lured us from safety, enticed her to the edge of the cliff, where she was willing to give up everything—willing to give up her life—for me.

The wind took everything from me.

I head back to the military compound, somehow managing to

find my way through the dark streets without a lamp, avoiding other elves at every turn, relying on three years of prowling through dark places to get me home safely.

Once there, I stare at my door, confused. I thought I was coming home, but this isn't it. This is not my bedroom.

I'm vaguely aware of the flustered female elves around me, all dressed in gray suits and carrying weapons—Marbella's Storm Command, speaking in hushed voices.

I wanted to go home, but somehow, I found my way back to Marbella.

One of them, a graceful blonde woman, spins away from me, calling for Jordan.

I drop my head against the wooden surface of Marbella's door, flex my hands against it, and consider how easy it would be to break it down the same way I cracked the training post. Too easy, and yet impossible.

I slide down it, hunching to the side, one shoulder pressed hard up against the door, my legs in a kneeling position.

Jordan's worried face comes into focus. "Commander Rath, are you okay? Are you hurt?"

I groan. "The wind stole it, Jordan."

She glances at the other women. "Stole what?"

"The blue ribbon…"

Pieces of the past rush through my memory, the last night I saw Marbella, her lavender cloak spread across the rocky earth cushioning our knees, not nearly as soft as her lips.

You have my permission.

Now I have no permission. None.

I can't even fight for her because she can't let me win.

"The lavender cloak," I whisper, my hands falling to my sides, palms open against the ground. "The wind stole it all."

Jordan studies me with a growing crease in her forehead as I stare past her at a spot on the opposite wall. There's nothing artificial here. No paintings or expensive furniture, but Marbella is surrounded by something much more priceless: friends who would protect her with their lives.

They surround me now and I'm alert enough to recognize the battle stances they're taking, the way they hold their weapons ready. I may be able to command them, but Marbella's sanctity comes first.

"Commander Rath?" Jordan asks.

I focus on her, gritting my teeth. "I'm going to kill Rhydian Valor."

"Hmm." She turns to the woman on her right—the one with blonde hair and bright blue eyes, who moves with a calm grace. "Reisha, can you please hail one of the messengers to fetch Macsen Mercy? We need him here right away."

The blonde woman immediately spins and disappears down the corridor at a deft run, leaving me with Jordan and nearly twenty other women. I suspect I've interrupted their change of rotation, since there are usually only ten women around Marbella at any given time.

Jordan kneels at my side, quietly placing a hand on my arm, her head bowed. "You will get through this," she murmurs. "We all will."

"When will it end, Jordan?" I whisper. "When will the memories leave me in peace?" My voice turns to a growl. "When will that damn blue ribbon stop spinning in the wind?"

She doesn't answer, the curtain of her dark brown hair obscuring her face.

When Macsen finally arrives, Jordan lets go of my arm. Macsen reaches for me, bending to pull my arm over his shoulder and help me stand. "Come on, brother. Let's get your wretched ass out of here."

By the time the cold night air hits my face, I'm more sober than I want to be.

"You need to be alert for the next trial," Macsen says, supporting me as I attempt to stay steady on my feet. "There's a rumor that it will be the compatibility test."

No, not that. I'll be forced to tell the truth about a lavender cloak and a blue ribbon.

I grab Macsen's arm. "Fetch me another bottle."

He gives me a stern shake of his head. "Baelen, you've had enough."

"No," I say, sheer determination coursing through me. "I haven't."

27

———

MARBELLA

Because I'd stayed in the Storm Vault for two days straight, it didn't need subduing this afternoon, so I remain hidden away in my bedroom after Baelen leaves—even eating in there before finally collapsing into a deep sleep that night.

But even in my dreams, I can't get away from him. His voice invades my sleep in the dark of night and I toss and turn, trying to ignore the ache in my chest. Finally, the early morning glow from the skylight wakes me before I want to be awake. Jordan bustles around me, folding blankets and pushing clothing into my closet much too noisily.

She pauses when she sees I'm awake. "How are you feeling?"

"It's not the bruises that hurt."

Okay, so I said that out loud. Not what I intended, but I'll have to live with it. I locate my spare pillow wrapped in the sheets beside me and pull it into a hug. She keeps shooting glances at me, and it makes me feel like I missed something… Now that I think of it, the foggy memories of Baelen's voice in the night seem a little too real in the light of day…

I pluck at my sheets, not wanting to sound too concerned. "I had a dream that Commander Rath was here in the middle of the night. Was that a dream or…?"

"He was here."

I sit bolt upright. "What?"

178

"He was completely intoxicated so we sent him away."

Baelen was drunk? That was a first.

"Don't worry, we sent someone to fetch your brother to take him away. We weren't sure if Commander Rath would make it home safely otherwise."

"I'm… stunned. What did he say?"

She perches on the end of my bed. She hasn't put her boots on, which means she wasn't really trying to wake me up. Every time she flexes her toes, they enter a shaft of light shining from the ceiling. Even her feet move with purpose.

"He ah… said a lot of things. Mostly about killing Rhydian Valor and everyone associated with him. But he also kept repeating something about a lavender cloak and a blue ribbon? He kept saying that the wind stole the ribbon—that it took everything. Does that mean anything to you?"

I slide back under the covers, pulling them up around my neck. My heartbeat increases as I remember his younger fingers looping through the blue ribbon I used to wear in my hair, sliding through my braid, loosening it, letting it fall over my shoulders…

"The ribbon was the only nice thing I owned," I say. "It was pale, like the color of blue ice. Which is ironic, considering what I became."

Jordan slides from the base of the bed to the floor in front of me, crossing her legs and picking at the hem of her pants leg. "When Sebastian handed you his heartstone, I dealt with it by focusing on you and my duty to protect you. I pushed everything else out of my mind. You need to do the same thing now. Your life depends on these protocols and they're getting more dangerous. You need to empty your mind and focus."

She rises, always graceful, and brushes herself off. "It's a new day."

"I'm lucky to have you." I loosen my hold on the pillow, letting it go, sliding my feet to the floor, and planting them firmly on it. The Elven Command has stopped following the traditional sequence of protocols, but at some point, they have to have a compatibility test. Sebastian Splendor will be eliminated then and my friend's heart can mend.

"It's a new day," I murmur. "Let's start it with a walk. It's time to make some changes."

BAELEN WOULDN'T APPROVE, BUT I WEAR A SIMPLE, LOOSE DRESS when I leave my quarters. I can't bear anything pressing against my skin, not even the strap that would help me carry a wooden staff. To compensate, my ladies are armed to the teeth: full body armor, swords, daggers, bows and arrows. They even wear matching headpieces and smear red dust across their eyes to make themselves look fierce. Jordan, in particular, is ferocious. She's the tallest of them, carrying red-feathered arrows and weapons with blood-red handles.

My destination is the armory. To avoid the majority of elves, we take the less busy path along the river. It doesn't take more than a glance from my warriors for passersby to get out of the way.

Halfway along the river, an object sails over my ladies' heads. With lightning reflexes, Jordan snatches it out of the air, crushing it. Oddly, she doesn't look worried. We don't stop and I trust my warriors to be on the alert, but Jordan falls back and opens her fist to show me what she caught.

Lavender petals from a gladiolus flower float to the grass.

I crane my neck to see the elf who threw it. "What does this mean?"

"The gladiolus flower symbolizes honor and strength," Jordan says. "I'm sure she meant for me to catch it, not crush it."

"Who?"

In response to my question, my ladies separate long enough for me to glimpse a young woman running to keep up beside us. She has bare feet, wears a patched dress, and is clearly from a minor House. She can't be more than eleven-years-old. As soon as she sees me, she cries, "Have courage, Princess. We're with you."

Then she veers off, racing swiftly away.

I open my palm for Jordan to drop the flower into it. It's an incredible gift from a stranger, let alone a young woman who could hardly afford it. I tuck it away in my pocket.

I jolt as another female voice cries from nearby. "Have courage, Princess!"

"We're with you, Princess!"

"Have strength!"

"You honor us!"

"Jordan," I whisper. "What's going on?"

"I wish I could show you, but it's best if we keep you protected." She grins. "But I think it's fair to say that you have support."

The cries of encouragement continue all along the river, only fading once we reach the more populated trading district. We make a straight line for the armory and my ladies clear a path without any issues.

Jordan swings the doors open. "This is the Storm Command," she announces. "Clear the building!"

The male and female workers file out around us. The head armorer pauses to speak with Jordan for a moment, before departing without causing a problem. A flash of silver coin tells me why that went so smoothly.

"They're used to us coming and going, but we don't often ask them to leave," Jordan explains, since I've never been here before. Something I intend to change today.

The protective circle opens to reveal walls of weapons of every kind. I head straight for the daggers, looking them over. When I point to one, Jordan gets it down and tests it for weight and balance. She shakes her head until the fourth one. It's smaller than the others, but that's a good thing because it can be concealed more easily.

"Now, what we need is..." She chooses from three different types of holsters that one of my Storm Command has produced and hands the chosen one to me. I shimmy my dress up and attach the soft belt around my thigh, pulling it tight and firm. A flat leather pouch is firmly attached at the side.

Another one of my Storm Command hands Jordan a pair of leather gloves. Not taking any chances, Jordan places both the gloves and the dagger on a nearby wooden table. I pull on the gloves and reach for the weapon.

If this works…

I brace for the storm's power as I pick up the dagger.

Nothing happens and I grin. The leather provides a protective barrier between me and the metal. I slide the dagger into the pouch at my thigh. It won't light up until I touch it with my bare hands.

Now that I can carry weapons, arrogant men like Rhydian Valor won't get the better of me again. I spin to face my smiling Storm Command. "How many of these can I carry at once?"

When we get back to my quarters, Elise paces in the hallway. As soon as she sees me, she pounces. "The compatibility test has been announced."

The happiness I felt at being able to protect myself dissolves. I brace for what she's about to tell me. I'm ready for anything.

"They're sticking with the traditional test."

I blink at her. "Really? No tricks, no traps?"

"It looks like it."

Jordan is cautious beside me. "That's a good thing, isn't it? It's the same test we did."

I can't help but worry. "It should be, but it seems too straight forward."

Elise urges me down the corridor. "The Elven Command has had a lot of backlash about the last trial. I think they're trying to regain control. Keeping with the traditional test is the smart thing to do."

I head to my bedroom, pull on the gloves, and unclasp the belt around my thigh. We ended up finding one with multiple pockets for my right leg, along with one for my opposite knee and one for my waist. I can't have too many daggers. I lay them out on the table one after the other while Elise gapes.

"Princess…?"

I grit my teeth. "I won't be defenseless again. And from now on, I will carry gloves so I can punch the lights out of any man who means to harm me."

She gasps beside me and to my surprise, tears suddenly slide down her cheeks. "I'm sorry I didn't think of that before."

I spin to her. "Elise, no, this isn't your fault. We didn't know what the Elven Command was planning. Or how far they'd go. Now we'll be prepared."

She gulps and nods. She pulls herself upright, smoothing down her dress. "The test is tomorrow. Before you go in, I will check the room myself. I won't allow any tricks."

"Thank you, Elise. I know you'll make sure it's safe."

I study my new weapons. I won't be going unprepared.

28

MARBELLA

I sit in a darkened room and face an empty chair. A transparent screen rests between me and the other side of the room. Elise swept both sides and tested the screen to make sure it can't be broken. The man who sits opposite me won't be able to get to me.

Still, I carry as many weapons as I can. From now on, the weapons belts will be the first thing I put on in the morning and the last thing I take off at night. I'm wearing a flowing silk dress with multiple folds to hide the bulk underneath. My gloves are tucked into a pocket at the side.

I suppose I look demure, waiting primly in the chair, my hair in a single braid resting across my shoulder.

The Elven Command watches from the side, also behind a transparent screen. Elise sits with them, but her seat is moved to the side. They can hear everything but can't control the outcome. Each champion will bring his heartstone to this test and after completing it, the Heartstone Chest will either accept his stone back or refuse it. There's no tricking it.

The only thing the Elven Command can control is the order in which the champions enter the room. The door opens at the side, and I hold my breath, waiting to see who's first.

Jasper Grace strides into the room. He's leaner than Baelen but has a way of carrying himself that somehow fits with his House. I

184

wouldn't call it graceful, but he carries himself with an efficiency of movement that makes it clear he can move fast if he wants to. He takes a knee beside the empty chair, head bowed. "Princess."

"Hello, Jasper."

He sits without hesitation, and I have to admire the fact that he didn't pause. His head shoots up as the magic takes hold, his brown eyes widening ever so slightly at the strange, compelling sensation he's now feeling.

The compatibility test is as much about truth as personality. The spells cast over the champion's chair force him to tell the truth and speak his mind even if he doesn't want to.

It's also incredibly unfair because my chair isn't spellcast at all. I can tell as many lies and ask as many questions as I want.

He speaks first, compelled to say what he's thinking. "Are you okay?" he asks. "Are you still hurt?"

"I'm fine now, thank you Jasper."

"I can't stop seeing the arena, replaying it in my head. I couldn't get to Commander Rath. I couldn't get to you. I can still hear you scream." He grips the handles on the chair, one fist clenched over his heartstone. His jaw flexes and I know he doesn't want to tell me any of this.

I interrupt him so he doesn't have to continue. "I have a question for you, Jasper."

He looks relieved and grateful, but his grip on the heartstone remains strong.

I lean forward and try not to smile. "Did you peek?"

His forehead crinkles, but his expression quickly clears. He remembers the night on the mountains when I had to remove the top of my suit to patch my back.

"No," he says.

"Good." *Let the Elven Command puzzle over that one.* "Do you have any family?"

"I have a sister. Younger."

I ask him other questions about his family, favorite things, and childhood. He slowly relaxes. He tells me about his grandmother who used to sing stories to him as a boy. He tells me about his sister who sews roses out of silk for the major Houses. He tells me about military training and meeting my brother there. He doesn't smile. He never does.

I avoid any questions that really matter. Until the last one. It could be dangerous, but I set my features into a pleasant expression and keep it glued to my face. No matter what he says, I can't react.

"I'm sorry to push you on this," I say. "But I need to know… which story you believed about the night I became the Storm Princess."

"I don't want to tell you that."

"Why not?" I ask.

"Because you don't want to think about it. Not really."

My composure slips. Somehow this man reads me too well. And all without giving anything about his own emotions away.

I tense. Breathe. Relax. "You're right. I hate remembering it. But it's just a story. It can't hurt me."

He nods. "Some people say that you deliberately climbed the mountain during the storm because you wanted to be the Princess. Other people say you were in the right place at the right time. Some people say that you climbed the mountain because you intended to jump off and kill yourself but the Storm got to you first."

I blink. That's one I hadn't heard before.

"But the story I believe…" He doesn't grip the sides of the chair anymore. He leans forward, watching me watching him. His brown eyes soften as his lips part.

"The only story that holds truth for me is the one where you took the lightning strike for someone else. You did it to protect someone."

The blood drains from my face. Despite all my efforts not to show any emotion, I can't find my voice. I whisper. "Thank you, Jasper. For telling me the truth."

He jumps out of the chair. He glares at it. But he quickly buries his discomfort and turns to me with military precision. "Princess."

Then he takes a knee, bowing to me again before striding out of the room. I fix my eyes on a point in the distance and force my face into an expression of nothingness, serenity, anything other than the storm of emotions I actually feel.

The door opens again.

Sebastian Splendor enters the room, bows beside the chair, but pauses, his brow furrowing at it. He slides into it but he's already gripping the armrests, his knuckles white around his heartstone.

He doesn't want to be here. I don't want him here either. I want him out of the trials and with Jordan where he belongs. That's okay because I'm going to make sure that happens.

I lean forward, raising my voice, shooting fire straight at him. "Who do you love, Sebastian Splendor?"

"Jordan. Always."

"Could you ever, in a million years, love me?"

He shakes his head. "I'm sorry, Princess. My heart is hers."

"Thank you, Sebastian. For telling me the truth."

He leaps out of the chair and spins to me, his face pale. He glimpses his grandfather through the transparent shield at the side and instantly Sebastian becomes wooden and emotionless. He drops to a knee. "Princess."

Three champions remain and Baelen is one of them. I hold my breath, but the next to appear is Pedr Bounty's grandson. He was the one who held Jasper back.

He pauses beside the chair, twisting his heartstone in his hands, glancing between where I sit and the Elven Command watching from the side. Like all the champions, he's big and brawny, the perfect choice for blocking another man.

I won't go easy on this man.

"They can't help you," I say. "This is the part where you have to face yourself."

He slides into the chair, staring at a point past my ear.

I remain silent until his gaze finally flicks to mine.

"What do you see when you look at me?" I ask.

He struggles, shifting in the chair, refusing to answer.

I don't smile. I don't feel anything. "You can't get out until I say the words that will release you. Does that make you feel helpless?"

"Yes."

"Do you think that's how I felt when Rhydian Valor's body pressed on top of mine? When he stabbed me over and over again?"

"Yes."

"Do you want to shout? Fight back? Escape?"

"N-no."

I lift my eyebrows. "Why not?"

"Because I deserve to feel this way."

"Hmm. I'm going to ask you again: what do you see when you look at me?"

"I see a…" His brow creases as he looks me over from my head to my toes, from my braid down the lines of my dress to my ankles. Sweat breaks out on his forehead. "I don't have the words."

I narrow my eyes and spit the order. "Try!"

He jolts like I punched him. "I see a storm of power and light. I see burning and chaos. I see a girl on a mountain. The wind's beating her, lightning's striking, and claws are ripping, but she's fighting back. I see death and life. The only safe place is beside her. Beside *you*."

He thumps the armrest. Shakes his head. Grips his heartstone so hard I'm concerned he might break it. He's breathing way too hard. "I see my death. And I don't know if you're the one killing me or saving me."

My lips part. I almost fly out of my chair. I itch for the steel so close to my thigh. "I should kill you for what you did."

"Yes." He wipes the sweat from his eyes but doesn't say anything else.

I stare at the floor for a long time. "I'm going to tell you what to do but it's up to you whether you do it."

He waits.

"Leave this place and never look back. Leave your House and all its trappings. Find a woman who can bear to love you, build her a house, and give her children who will miss you when you die. But whatever you do…" I lift my eyes to his. "Do not cross paths with me again."

He nods.

"Thank you, Gwynn. For telling me the truth."

He's the slowest to get up. He takes a knee, bows, and pauses on the floor. "You won't see me again, Princess."

Then he rises and strides from the room.

The second-to-last man enters the room. This time it's the one who cornered Sebastian. If Rhydian Valor is a gorilla, this man is an ox, thick and bullish. Unlike the man before him, he saunters into the room, his heartstone held casually in his hand. He drops into the chair.

Ice drips from my tongue. "You forgot to bow."

"Why should I bow to—"

The magic takes hold. His head snaps up so fast it sounds like a breaking log. "I should have bowed."

"Hmm."

He's from a major House but not one that's represented on the Elven Command, which means it's likely he's been raised with all the privilege and none of the responsibility.

I tap my fingers across my knee. "Explain to me why you didn't bow."

"The Princess's job is to serve. She's the one who should be bowing."

"Who taught you that rubbish?"

"My father."

"And who is your father?"

"Phillip of the House of Faith."

I file that name away. "Is he a good father?"

"No, he's a drunk. He beats the servants and treats my mother badly." His eyes widen. Shame turns his face red.

"Then why do you believe a word he says?"

"I…" Now he's fighting the magic. His knee bounces up and down, jiggling. He fidgets with the heartstone. "Because he's my father."

"Not good enough! You made enemies in that arena. Men I would never want as *my* enemies. But worst of all, you made an enemy of the Storm. What is your next move?"

"I thought I'd win. I beat Sebastian Splendor. That means I'm good enough."

I swallow a laugh. "Look around you and have another think about that."

His gaze darts around the empty room and meets the Elven Command. As much as I've lost all respect for them, they present a picture of regal power. Sebastian's grandfather, in particular, doesn't look impressed.

The man says, "I only did what they wanted."

"Yes, but do you think they're going to protect you? Is your father going to protect you? Is *anyone* going to protect you… from me?"

Let this sniveling idiot make it through the trials. I'll be happy to kill him. Without realizing it, my hand moved to my thigh, seeking the steel resting there and the power that comes with it. I wonder if an electrified dagger could break through the shield…

He shakes his head, compelled to answer. "No. They won't."

I lean forward. "Then what is your next move?"

"I… don't know." He presses his lips together, visibly fighting the impulse to speak. His fingernails dig into the heartstone so hard they're bleeding. "I don't like this. I can't stop saying what I'm thinking."

"It's called the truth."

"I don't like it." He tugs at the chair, breathing hard. He's panicking but I have no sympathy for him.

"Am I going to die?" he asks.

I want to scream at him, but I swallow it down. "Yes."

"I don't want to die here."

"Then don't. It's your choice."

His hands quake against the armrests, banging against them. "I don't want to go home. I hate it there."

"Then don't do that either."

He jolts like I shot electricity through him. "What?"

I consider the floor, unable to stand looking at him. "Find a new home. You must have made it through the endurance test somehow. Find another mountain to climb."

"Brute strength," he says. "It's all I'm good for… my father says."

Ah, nothing like a label to define a man's belief about who he is. "Then use it to kick him out."

His leg stops jiggling. "What?"

"Your father. Go home and give him the boot. I don't think the Elven Command will object. Let him live with the pigs where he belongs. Be a better master to your workers. Be a better son for your mother."

He stares at me through the shield. The cogs may be turning slowly in his mind, but they are finally turning. "If I do that, will you show me mercy?"

"I'll do better than that: I won't give you another thought."

He tilts his head, appraising me. "Okay then."

He shifts gears. Again, it's slow, but he gets there. "You're more complex than I thought you were."

I sigh. "Thank you, Harmon. For telling me the truth."

He steps out of the chair. This time he takes a knee and bows before leaving the room. I swallow the unpleasant taste in my mouth and think calming thoughts to wipe that interaction from my mind.

Baelen is last and I don't want to admit to myself that I'm tired. Dealing with the last two men was draining. I try to stay relaxed as I stare at the door, waiting for it to open.

It remains closed.

I wait. I fold my legs again. And again. And I wait some more.

Five minutes later, I'm worried. I check out the Elven Command. What if they've done something to stop Baelen getting here? What if this is the latest in their scheming? But they're fidgeting too. If that's any indication, they aren't responsible for the delay.

The door finally opens, and I almost leap out of my chair. I gasp as Baelen stumbles into the room. I try to see what's wrong. *Is he hurt?*

He lumbers over to the chair. His forehead puckers. He stares at it, tapping his heartstone against his thigh. Then he feels his way into the seat, fumbling and almost dropping the stone in the process.

"This is a nice chair." He pats the armrest, leaning to one side of it.

Wait...

My jaw drops. "Baelen Rath! Are you... still drunk?"

He rubs his forehead, squinting at me. "No. Maybe?"

"But that's two days now," I scold him. "How much longer do you intend to be inebriated?"

"As long as it takes."

"To what?"

"Get you out of my head." His grin disappears but he continues without pause, waggling his finger in the air. "Did you know that the color blue is supposed to be calming?"

"I've heard that."

He growls as if he's beyond disappointed. "Well, it's not. I've tried looking at it from all angles and it's not."

"What are you…?" *What is he talking about?*

He leans so far forward he almost tips out of the chair. He presses his finger against the shield between us. "Do you know what I need?"

I fold my arms across my chest. "I can't imagine."

He points at my shoulder. At least, I think he points at my shoulder. I can't be sure because his finger sways between the wall and the back of my chair.

"I need…" He purses his lips. He taps his finger against the shield again. "Nope… I forgot."

I'm not going to get any sense out of him. This interaction is pointless and the only thing I can control is ending it.

"Well, thank you, Baelen. For telling me the truth. Now get out of my sight."

"You're welcome." He slithers out of the chair, wobbles, and somehow clambers to his feet. "Uh?"

I point. "The door's that way."

I wait only long enough for it to close behind him before huffing in exasperation. The Elven Command looks as astonished as I am.

Teilo Splendor clears his throat and announces through the shield, "Princess, you must wait here until the champions have presented their heartstones to the chest. Which… might take some champions longer than others."

The other elves cough, but Teilo continues. "Your advisor may be present to verify the proceedings, but you may not know the outcome until we announce it tomorrow morning. Your advisor will return when it's time for you to leave this room."

The Elven Command files out and then I wait. And fume. And worry. But mostly, I fume. How could he treat the compatibility test with so much disrespect? Such a lack of care? To turn up barely able to string two words together. By the time Elise returns, I'm fit to explode.

I jump to my feet. "That man! Take me to his quarters."

She blocks me before I can take another step. "Princess, you can't go to the soldier's barracks."

I make a wide circle around her and stride from the room. "Don't tell me what I can't do right now, Elise."

I call my Storm Command to me. Jordan and Elise have an exchange of wide eyes when I announce where we're going.

"Are you sure that's a good idea, Princess?" Jordan asks.

"The best I've had today," I growl. "Let's go."

It takes half an hour to get there but my anger just gets worse. For him to turn up to my quarters in the middle of the night was one thing, but to take the compatibility test when he couldn't even stay upright…

My Storm Command wears full body armor every day now. They pose a commanding force marching through the archway into the military compound. It's their job to know every part of the city so they don't need to stop for directions. They escort me into the heart of the soldier's barracks to an imposing building made of sandstone.

The soldiers standing guard do a double take.

My demand makes them jump. "Where is Commander Rath?"

They both bow. One of them points. "To the right along the corridor, Princess. It's the door at the end."

I don't wait for my ladies to close the gap. Instead of surrounding me along the narrow corridor, they form two lines, one on each side of me, giving me full access to the door ahead. When we reach it, Jordan knocks and pushes it open without waiting for a response.

"The Storm Princess," she announces, wise enough to step immediately out of my way.

The room is twice the size of my bedroom. Maps cover the walls, and chairs are scattered throughout the room. An enormous desk the size of the one in the War Room rests under wide windows on the opposite side.

My brother leans against the table, his posture relaxed. I haven't seen him since the Heartstone Ceremony, but he's been busy acting as a proxy for Baelen, looking after Rath land while Baelen is busy with the trials. Macsen gives me a wide smile. "Welcome, sister."

Baelen sits on one of the chairs in front of the table, his head in his hands. I don't care that he winces with every thud of my boots across the wooden floor.

"Baelen Rath, what is wrong with you?"

"Don't shout, Marbella. My head hurts."

"Oh your head hurts? What about your reputation? Do you have any idea how hard it was for me to sit across from those… those… *monsters*? And to think that I actually made them afraid of you. And then you blow in like a stale breeze without a sensible word to give me."

"I had to protect you."

"How was that protecting me?"

He jumps to his feet and towers over me in two seconds flat. Getting up so suddenly was clearly a bad idea because he flinches and grips his head. He sways and groans, but manages to focus on me. "Think about how dangerous the chair of truth is for us."

"But… I wouldn't ask you any difficult questions."

"Marbella, please, give me a scrap of mercy. I can't say out loud what I'm thinking when I'm around you. I've been drinking for two days hoping that I could defeat that chair."

"One day," my brother interrupts. "You've been drinking for one day to defeat the chair."

Baelen glares at him.

Macsen isn't deterred. "The first day's drinking was for reasons he won't tell me about, but he got the idea for beating the chair after that."

I plant my hands on my hips. "Well, it worked."

Baelen presses his palm to his temple. "A bit too well." He sinks into the nearest chair. "Ah, my head."

I whirl to my brother. "Macsen, please pour a bucket of icy water over Commander Rath's head. It seems to need numbing."

I stalk out of the room, my fury remaining strong until I'm halfway home. Then it dissolves like ice in the sun. I don't want to admit that Baelen's right. Acting the fool is far better than saying something he doesn't want to say in front of the Command— especially something that could hurt me.

My anger has evaporated by the time I reach my quarters. It's replaced with worry about the results of the test. For all I know, the Heartstone Chest could have spat Baelen's heartstone back at him and he could be out of the trials.

That's what I want… isn't it? I don't want any of them to be compatible because then I'd be the last elf standing and the curse would be over.

For what might be the first time ever, I look forward to taming the Storm that afternoon because it will stop me from thinking about the outcome of the test.

29

———

MARBELLA

The next morning, the arena is as gorgeously laid out as it was on the day of the Heartstone Ceremony. The Elven Command has worked hard to erase every sign of the battle that occurred here four days ago. Their spellcasters have turned the space into a lush garden. I'm not sure who is responsible —or whether the Elven Command understands the meaning—but gladiolus flowers adorn every pillar, cascading across the walls, and drape from the second level.

Just like at the Heartstone Ceremony, the Elven Command takes up most of the dais and the remaining five champions wait at the base of it.

To my surprise, that morning the advisor from the House of Bounty approached Elise to pass on a message to me: Pedr Bounty's grandson apologized that he would be present in the arena, but the spells forced him to be here. He promised that he would not raise his eyes beyond the floor and would leave as soon as the spells released him.

Now, Elwyn Elder moves to the center of the dais to hush the crowd. "I ask the Storm Princess to step forward."

I press my hands to my sides. I've opted for simplicity today, wearing a gray suit like the ones I wear jogging, but my weapons belts are on display and accessible if I need them. I step from my entrance room onto the stage.

196

Sound assaults me as soon as I appear. I flinch. I whirl to the crowd, on my guard, as the uproar continues. And then I realize… they're cheering. Calling my name. *Our princess! Our princess!* Petals rain down on me from the second level. I turn in a circle, stunned and beyond words. How and when did this happen?

The cheering goes on for so long that I have to raise my arms for quiet. Finally, the crowd settles down and I stand to the side, waiting for Elwyn Elder to continue.

He doesn't look at me, but his countenance is icy. He won't like being upstaged. "The results of the compatibility test will now be announced."

At the base of the dais, the champions wait in their black robes. True to his word, Gwynn Bounty doesn't look up. Harmon Faith has fixed his focus on the wall behind me. In fact, all of them have found some point in the room to fixate on. Even Baelen stands perfectly still, not looking at me.

What's happened since yesterday? Why aren't any of them looking at me? A shiver suddenly runs to my toes.

Elwyn Elder smiles. "Three men were found to be compatible."

Three? The room suddenly spins. Sebastian can't be compatible so that means one of the monsters is. Or both of them. The thought makes me nauseous, but I tell myself that I should be glad. It will be so much easier to kill one of them if they win.

"The following compatible men will approach the dais. The others will leave immediately."

Elwyn pauses, dragging out his moment of power. "Jasper Grace."

Jasper strides up the steps and positions himself to my right, eyes down. I can't figure out his expression, but that's nothing new. I try not to read into it.

"Sebastian Splendor."

What? No!

I take a step back. Sebastian climbs the steps, his hands balled into fists, but not at me. He's the first of the champions to look up, throwing daggers at Elwyn Elder. He positions himself in front of me, blocking my view of the other champions on the arena floor.

I'm choking. I can't breathe. How is this man compatible when his heart belongs to someone else? I shake my head at Sebastian. *No.*

He drops his gaze without responding.

"And the final compatible man..." Elwyn's mouth pinches like this is the first distasteful thing he's done today. "The final man is Baelen Rath."

Baelen approaches the dais, still fixated on a point at the back of the room. He takes his place to my left. There's enough distance for me to take stock of all three men. Jasper and Sebastian both cast imposing figures, but standing beside them Baelen is a Rath through and through. He's the biggest. The strongest. The one with the most scars. But these three men have fought side-by-side. They're friends. They're loyal to each other. And...

I'm the only one who can yield.

In a final fight between two of these men, one will have to kill the other.

Now I understand why they're so subdued. There are only a few more chances for elimination. They must each be assessing the odds, the possible outcomes. From their point of view, the only way all of them come out alive is if *I* make it to the final fight and exercise my right to yield to my opponent.

Except that I already told Baelen I wouldn't do that.

I never should have told him that. I grip my stomach, trying to calm my breathing, to halt my overwhelming panic. I can't kill any of them. I don't want them to die. I want to scream. Why did it have to be these three men?

I understand why Jasper is compatible with me. He's from a minor House. He knows what it's like to be poor, and looked down on. He's worked hard to get where he is, using his determination, courage, and persistence to be his House champion.

But how is Sebastian still a contender? There's no way we're compatible. His heart belongs to Jordan and my own bleeds for them. She stands off to the side, focused on me, avoiding looking at him as if she can shield herself from what's going on around her.

Elwyn Elder instructs the three men to leave the dais. At some point, the eliminated men have already left, and I don't give them a second thought.

Jasper and Baelen are both wooden as they take the steps, but

Sebastian has located Jordan. One glance from him is all it takes. She presses the heel of her palm to her heart. Elise pulls her close but it's too late. Tears slide down the cheeks of my fearless protector. Jordan turns away before anyone else sees and five ladies from my Storm Command step up to form a visual barrier around her to protect her.

Sebastian is stricken pale. He stops at the top of the steps, his fists clenched, shoulders drawn back. For a second I think he's going to confront the Elven Command. His House forced him into this position, tearing him and Jordan apart. As he throws a look of anger at his grandfather, I finally see the hatred he's kept hidden for so long.

He continues down the steps to take his place beside Baelen. That's when it strikes me why Sebastian's still here. His heart is broken in the same way that mine was torn apart seven years ago. Neither of us can have what we want, and our pain unites us. Our broken hearts link us. They make us mirror each other.

We are compatible in exactly the wrong way.

There are three men left. This is my last chance to use my power to veto one of them.

Elwyn clears his throat. "The next trial—"

"Stop!"

Elwyn stares at me, his eyebrows raised.

"I wish to exercise my right of veto," I say.

The crowd gasps. Elwyn glances at the Elven Command. He clearly wasn't expecting me to do this, but I haven't played by their rules all along, so I'm not about to start now. "The princess has that right."

My heart is pounding, banging against my chest. I don't have a chance of calming down, but as long as I can get the words out, I'll be okay. "First I want to acknowledge that the vetoing of a House comes with an obligation. The vetoed House can make a request of me."

"That is correct," Elwyn says, "But it must be something that the princess is capable of fulfilling without harm to herself or her... reputation."

Oh, the hypocrisy. They'd tried to hurt both me and my reputation during the battle in this arena. I smother my distaste for

Elwyn as I step down from the dais, pausing at the base of the stairs.

Baelen meets my eyes for the first time. He's somber and clearly sober. I now regret my anger at him the day before. At the time when I'd stormed into the barracks, he already knew the outcome of the test. I picture him sitting with his head in his hands as I'd burst into the room. Now I know that it wasn't just because his head hurt.

Right now, I have to conceal my intentions. No House wants to be vetoed because of the dishonor that comes with it. There's nobody left in Baelen's House to try to stop me, so I head in his direction.

Confusion spreads across his face, followed by resignation. Maybe he thinks I'm still angry at him. Maybe he guesses that I'm trying to save his life. Maybe he understands that I'm not coming for him at all.

Beside him, Sebastian's expression becomes more and more blank and absent as he sees his chances of being with Jordan disappear with every step I take. Once I use my veto power, only two men will remain, which means there's only one more chance for elimination before the final fight to the death.

Jasper, on the other hand, looks surprised. I know from our time on the mountain that he's loyal to Baelen. He's also observant. He wouldn't expect me to willingly dishonor Baelen by knocking him out of the trials.

A quick glance behind me tells me that every member of the Elven Command is gloating. They want nothing more than for Baelen to be out of the trials.

I focus on Baelen. *I can do this.* Three feet away from him, I close my eyes and drop to a knee, my head down. At the same time, I raise my voice, knowing that I have to speak more clearly than ever before.

"I veto…"

I have one more moment to consider my choice. I could still veto Baelen, push him away, and keep him safe from everything in my life. But I know what I have to do.

"I veto the House of Splendor."

There's a moment of silence as the meaning of my declaration sinks in. Then the arena bursts into commotion. Sebastian's advisor appears behind him, shouting and shaking his fist. Every elf in the whole arena is speaking, some shouting—well, that's mostly the Elven Command.

I keep my focus on Sebastian.

Feeling returns to his face. His eyes widen and his legs buckle, but he remains upright. He sucks in a breath so deep, it's like he hasn't breathed for days. His shock hits me like a physical force. Tears burn the back of my eyes at the agony he's been bearing.

I shout above his advisor's rage. "Sebastian of the House of Splendor. Name your price."

His advisor screams, "Gold! Silver! Elevation to the highest House! A Splendor woman admitted into her Storm Command."

I wait for Sebastian to take a moment, to take it all in. Then, very deliberately, I point toward my Storm Command. They've pulled Jordan forward, tear-streaked and shocked. Sebastian has one chance to be with her.

I fill my voice with thunder so loud that the entire room quiets. Even the advisor shuts up.

"Sebastian of the House of Splendor. I am obligated to do one thing for you and one thing only. This is to compensate you for taking away your chance to share the power of the Storm. Only you can name your price." I glower at his advisor. "Consider your request wisely."

Sebastian pulls himself together, looking between me and Jordan. He has to choose his words carefully. He has to get it right. Just asking me to release Jordan from my Storm Command won't be enough to make sure they can be together.

"You will… marry me to Jordan of the House of Splendor," he says.

Relief floods me. I can't stop the smile breaking across my face. He got it right. "Yes, I will. And since married women can't be part of my guard, she will leave my service. Name your day and she will be your wife."

"Tomorrow."

I laugh. "Okay."

He's practically thrumming, he's so happy. He can't take his eyes off her. His silver-green eyes glow for the first time since the

Heartstone Ceremony and it strikes me how dull they've been through all of this, like part of him was missing. *She* was missing.

"Go to her," I whisper. "Never let anyone tear you apart."

High in the viewing levels, I catch sight of a flurry of silks. Sebastian's mother rises to her feet. She starts singing through her tears and I know it's not just because I made her son happy. She knows I just saved his life. "Spin gold, shelter silver."

The women in the arena follow her lead and to my surprise the men join in, their voices rising in song.

"Our Princess! Full of mercy! Full of strength!"

Sebastian veers toward me before he passes by. "Princess, I can never repay you enough, but I can give you the gift of knowledge. I heard the old ones talking. The final fight is about your worst fear. Know your fears and overcome them."

Then he's gone, striding to Jordan, lifting her up into his arms. My friend is laughing and crying as they disappear from the arena. My heart expands to see them so happy, but dread soon overcomes me.

My worst fear? It already happened. My worst fear was a lightning strike. The one I wasn't expecting. I try to shake it off, but anxiety remains like a fog around me.

The Elven Command has no chance of regaining control, so they declare proceedings closed without announcing the next trial. The crowd is still singing as Elise urges me back into the protection of the Storm Command and to my quarters. "The Elven Command will send notice of the next trial this evening. In the meantime, it looks like you have a wedding to prepare for."

And the Storm to subdue. The Storm has gone very easy on me for the last few days. I'm grateful because my body has taken a beating. I'm still bruised, and it will take a few more days for the yellow marks to disappear.

On the way to the Vault, my Storm Command gifts me with smiles and nods at every opportunity. For the first time, Jordan isn't among them, and I miss her. I'm happier than I've been in a really long time, but I'm also sad to be losing one of my best friends. Once Jordan is married, I won't be able to see her again. Elise walks quietly beside me. She's the only one who doesn't smile.

When we enter the safety of the Vault's waiting room, and

nobody else can see or hear us, she says, "I know how much that cost you."

I pause at the door to the Vault. The Storm is building beyond it, stronger today but not nearly the worst I've seen.

"I couldn't be selfish," I say.

"To veto Commander Rath and save his life wouldn't have been selfish."

I have no words. I run my hand across my eyes, angry at myself for the way my hands suddenly shake. "I offered him my hand."

Her forehead puckers. "Your hand? Like... your hand in marriage?"

"No." I turn my palm up. "I wanted him to take my hand."

"Ah."

"The Elven Command believes that the first man I touch will inherit the power of the storm—to be able to control it like I can." I remember Baelen skirting around me in my small bathing room, bumping into everything in his effort to avoid me. "He wouldn't touch me because he knew it would eliminate him. But now I wish I'd tried harder. I should have tried harder."

She has no words to console me. There's nothing to be said. I don't regret my choice to veto Sebastian, but it meant I gave up my one guaranteed power to save Baelen's life. I open the door to the Vault and step through it, hoping that it will rage against me, because right now I need something to fight, something that I know how to win.

30

MARBELLA

Jordan returns to my quarters that evening at dinnertime. She's glowing, but I barely have the chance to say two words to her before the message arrives from the Elven Command about the next trial.

Elise reads from the delivered parchment: "The next trial will be a game of wits, designed to eliminate one champion. The champions are to present themselves to the…" She pauses, throwing a questioning glance my way. "…to the War Room at the ninth hour tomorrow morning. Only the Elven Command and the champions' advisors may accompany them."

She rolls up the parchment, her brow furrowed. "That's all it says."

"So it's a test of intelligence in the War Room?" I shrug it off. There's no way I'm going to let it darken my last few hours with Jordan. I slap my hand over my knee. "Well, I'm not going to get any smarter overnight and I'm pretty sure I can handle a trial and a wedding in the same day so… I order no more talk about it tonight. Let's eat and enjoy our time with our Storm Commander before she gets married tomorrow evening."

My ladies break into smiles and cheering. Jordan glows all through the meal, but she's also full of purpose. Finishing her food opposite me, she says, "You need a new Storm Commander."

"Jordan, it's fine. Elise will put in a request once you're married.

Thanks to you, the Storm Command works like clockwork. It can wait a day."

She nods and tops off my glass of water. I give her a look, since she doesn't need to wait on me hand and foot.

"You did this amazing thing for me," she says. "I can't ever repay you."

"All this talk of repayment. Be happy. That's all I want." I click my tongue. I can't help it. "And maybe name one of your children after me."

She turns bright pink, stacking her dishes in a pile on the table. By the time she's done rearranging the cups and plates, she's become very quiet. "I'm going to miss you, Marbella Mercy."

I bite my lower lip. "Hey, you said my name."

"I did."

"I'm going to miss you too, Jordan."

She clears her throat. "All right then, I'm still in charge here so I'll stay tonight and—"

"Get ready here tomorrow? I'm sorry that I have to go out in the morning for the trial, but I'll be back in the afternoon. What are you going to wear?"

"Um…" She glances down at her gray suit.

"Oh no. Nope. Not that." I push my plate away and stand up on my chair. "Storm Command, attention! We have an emergency."

All of them swivel to me and I'm impressed with how quickly they drop their knives and forks. They're ready for anything. Which is good because…

I grin. "Jordan needs a dress."

For the next few hours, I forget everything except my friend's happiness. My ladies show me just how multi-talented they are when they pull together enough material to not only sew a dress, but also make it on the spot with the same craftsmanship they used to make my armor. It's a fine, green silk with a bodice that hugs Jordan's curves and flows gently from her hips. At midnight, when they're finished and Jordan tries it on, Elise adds the final touches by spellcasting one of the silver candlesticks into fine filigree to adorn the skirt and rest across Jordan's shoulders.

My ladies hug each other, and some of them start to cry. "Happy tears," they say. I know this is a side of them that nobody else will ever see—that they will never let anyone else see because they are warriors to their core. But they're also friends and aren't afraid to show their emotions around each other.

As Jordan twirls in her new dress, she gives me a grin and her true character shines through when she hitches up the skirt to reveal a weapons belt just like mine around her thigh and knee.

"I approve," I whisper, as my ladies surround her, and I wish I could hug them instead of keeping my distance.

Finally, Elise points at the ornate clock on the wall. "You need to get some rest."

"Is it too much to ask for tomorrow not to arrive at all? I'd like to stay in this moment for a while longer."

"I understand. But really, it's time for sleep now." She gives me her stern look, the one I know comes from concern for my wellbeing. The Elven Command's message about the next trial was obscure. I know the time and place but not much more. I'll need all my wits about me if I'm going to succeed. Which means I need rest. Reluctantly, I leave my friends, not sure how much sleep I'll get ahead of tomorrow, finally falling asleep to the patter of rainfall outside.

I'M THE FIRST TO ARRIVE AT THE WAR ROOM. I LEAVE THE STORM Command at the door and only Elise accompanies me inside, one step behind me. The Elven Command waits in a line at the front of the room behind the War Table. The whole space looks very different from the last time I was here, battling my Storm Command and learning how to fight again. There are three chairs spaced apart in the open part of the room, but otherwise, it's empty.

Osian Valor is the first of the Elven Command to greet me. I'm sure that's intended to throw me off balance given what happened with Rhydian. He gives me a thin smile. "Welcome, Princess. Please take a seat while we wait for the other two champions."

Jasper and Baelen arrive at the same time, their advisors in tow.

I assess the gap between us when they sit down, conscious that they are both doing the same. None of us trusts the Elven Command not to turn the tables on us.

Our advisors take their places behind us as Osian Valor clears his throat. "For this challenge, we have invoked the power of the Heartstone Chest. It is able to discern from the heartstones contained within it, your minds' true thoughts and your hearts' true desires. But this game is not about knowing your own thoughts, it is about knowing your enemy's."

He claps his hands and from nowhere, barriers shoot up between the three of us. There are now walls between us stretching from floor to ceiling. I can't see Baelen or Jasper, but I can see the Elven Command in front of me.

Elise whispers at my back, "Steady, Princess. Don't react."

Osian waits with one eyebrow raised as if he expected one or more of us to protest. When we don't, he claps his hands again. Less alarming this time, a small table appears in front of me.

"For this challenge you will be presented with two cups," he says. "Each cup will have a certain meaning." He paces the floor, taking his time. "You must choose which one to drink. The only way to remain in the game is to choose the same cup as one of your opponents. As soon as you choose a different cup from the other two champions, you will be eliminated, and the game is over."

I take deep breaths as my head spins about the rules. I have to choose the same cup as Baelen or Jasper. If I'm the odd one out, I'll be eliminated.

Osian grins. "Oh, and just to make things interesting, the substance you'll be drinking won't assist clear thinking." He waves his hands at the War Table. "Much like the fog of war and decisions made in battle."

He claps his hands again and two goblets appear side-by-side on the table in front of me.

"You may not lift up a cup unless you are prepared to drink from it. You will know when one of your opponents is eliminated because a bell will chime. Now, make your choice." Osian Valor steps back in line with the other Elven Commanders and I'm guessing that's all he has to say.

I assess the goblets in front of me. One is gold. The other is silver. Otherwise, they're identical in shape and form.

Gold or silver? Which would Baelen choose? What about Jasper? I only have to choose the same as one of them. But which one should I try to copy?

Although… what if they don't choose according to their own instincts? What if they choose the one they think *I* would choose? If that's the case, then I should choose the one I would pick, not the one they would pick.

Umm…

My brain is already boggling.

Okay, focus Marbella. Concentrate on what you know. I take a deep breath. I know that Baelen's bound himself to me and that that compulsion will urge him to pick the same cup as me. Jasper is loyal to Baelen so he would follow the same footsteps. Which means, I need to know which one I would choose.

Which is…?

One of the Elven Commanders shuffles a little, and I catch the movement from the corner of my eye. The others haven't moved, but they're all staring at me. Is it possible that I'm the last one to choose or are they trying to psyche me out by making me think I am?

Ignore them.

Would I spin gold or shelter silver? Would I welcome the morning sun or pay homage to the moon? Would I spill blood or dig a grave? I come from poverty so I would never dare drink from a gold cup, yet even silver is too valuable for the House of Mercy. The golden husks of the shimmer beetle plate my armor, but the silver threads from the Elyria spider line it…

I gasp. The image of the gargoyle's cave is suddenly bright in my memory: those silver threads that only glowed once the golden lamp was extinguished, their beauty hidden except by the light of the moon.

Shelter silver.

I pick up the silver goblet before I can second-guess myself. The clear liquid bites my tongue as it slides down my throat. It's sweet and cloying, sticking to the insides of my cheeks like syrup. It's not alcohol. At least, not like any alcohol I've ever tasted.

I place the cup back on the table and wait to hear if the bell chimes—if it does, it means that one of us chose differently. If it doesn't, it means we all chose the same.

There's a moment of pause. The Elven Command doesn't look pleased. Osian Valor claps his hands.

The cups disappear. A moment later, two new cups replace them.

Since we're going another round, that means we all chose the same, which means Baelen and Jasper are trying to choose like me. As long as I'm true to myself, then I can't go wrong. Unless… I'm wrong about that and they chose the silver cup for reasons personal to themselves and it's all a big fluke?

Stop it, Marbella. Focus!

Both of the new goblets are made of red glass. They're transparent enough to see that there's an object resting inside the bottom of each of them. The scrape of chairs nearby tells me that Baelen and Jasper have stood up to see inside their cups.

As soon as I do the same, I realize it's a mistake. The blood rushes from my head and I sway, dropping back into my seat. I sense Elise shift behind me, but the Elven Command lifts their hands in unison.

"Advisors step back. You may not assist your champions."

They're talking to all the advisors, which means it's not just me that's been affected by what we just drank from the silver goblet. Whatever was in that drink has left me light-headed and woozy.

I find my seat and the world stops swimming as soon as I sit down, but that's not going to help me because I still can't see what's inside the cups to know how to choose. *Curses.*

I rest my chin on the table and peer hard at each goblet. From the brief glimpse I had from the top, the two objects were both circular, but different, so I can't simply choose between left and right. I need to know what's inside the cups, and I can't tilt them toward me because that would mean partially lifting them.

I remember the speech I gave Jasper on the mountain when I thought he was belittling me. I'd told him not to make the mistake of thinking I was fragile. Which means I have to stand up and work through the pain. Baelen and Jasper would too.

Gripping the table, I brace myself against the oncoming

dizziness. I see inside only one of the cups before the world spins so hard that I have to sit down again. It was a coin.

I brace and go again. This time the nausea is worse, and I barely make it up far enough to glimpse the second cup's contents: a miniature rose.

I thud back into my chair, closing my eyes and waiting for the world to stop spinning. A choice between a rose or a coin is a choice between beauty or wealth. Two vices that could define an elf's motivations.

Unless… the rose isn't a symbol of beauty but of something more personal. Jasper told me that his sister made roses from silk. On top of that, Baelen was the only one who came from a major House and enjoyed the benefits of wealth—yet he'd turned his back on it to disappear for three years.

I drink from the cup with the rose in it, and once again, the sugary syrup lines my mouth. I swallow as little as I can this time and wait for the chime.

Once again, there's silence.

Osian Valor claps his hands.

Two new cups appear. My vision blurs as I try to focus on them, but the distinction is clear enough I don't need to examine them that carefully: one is large and the other is small. I swallow a laugh and reach for the small one. Maybe it's not a reference to my height —I'm sure there must be some deeper meaning, like the large cup representing gluttony or something like that—but the small one is the one for me.

I take the smallest sip and the Elven Command is definitely not happy. But neither is my head. Up might be down for all I know right now. After drinking from that cup, the table warps at the edges, and the figures of the Elven Command bend and sway in the distance like grass in a gentle breeze. Osian Valor's head looks like a fleshy blob on his shoulders and his robe appears to melt into the floor. Whatever they're giving us to drink, it's definitely messing with my head.

Two more cups later, Osian Valor claps his hands, and the sound thuds through my head like drums. I swear if that man claps his hands one more time… I'd like to believe I'd leap up and make him stop, but actually, probably, what I'll do is hurl. Every sound, even the quiet scuffle of feet, thrums through my head like a sledgehammer.

As two new cups appear, I can barely focus.

I slide from my chair, resting my chin on the table to try to see what's in front of me. If this is how Baelen felt at the compatibility test, it's no wonder he needed help finding the door. I squeeze my eyes shut, open them, and give everything to the effort to focus.

Each of these new cups has an image engraved on it, but both engravings are faint, fine, and hard to see.

As I focus on the one on the right, the image lifts off the surface of the cup, coming alive. It's a rope, twisting and twirling. No, not a rope, something more elegant, more precious. It's a ribbon, swirling loose in the air, floating away before I can catch it. It's a blue ribbon stolen by the wind.

I reach for that cup, dragging it from the table as I slide to the floor. I take a sip before I hit the ground, lying on my side, shutting my eyes and hugging the cup close, not caring that the liquid makes a puddle on the floor beside me.

The bell chimes.

My eyes shoot open. The chime means someone chose differently, but… who?

I refocus on the cup I'm holding.

Oh, no… It's not a ribbon. It's a… fishhook?

I drag myself upright, clinging to the table, focusing on the other cup before Osian Valor can clap his hands and make it disappear. The other goblet is etched with three wavy lines curling at the end like waves in the sea or… no, it's a representation of wind in the clouds. I drop my head into my hands. The other cup had a symbol of the storm. Baelen and Jasper would have chosen that one because it represents me.

I chose the wrong one.

I'm eliminated.

I'm out of the trials.

31

MARBELLA

I lean forward in my chair as the tables and partitions disappear, scrubbing at my face, unwilling to meet the eyes of what are no doubt five, gloating, happy Elven Commanders. They wanted me out of the trials and now they've succeeded. Even though the instruments of the game are gone, the wooziness remains, although when I screw up the courage to raise my head, I find that the room doesn't swim as much as it did before.

Osian Valor wears a deep crease between his eyebrows. Not exactly what I'd expected. He and the others look perplexed, exchanging glances among themselves and shuffling on the spot. Their reactions become clearer as my vision sharpens rapidly.

"One of you chose differently," Osian says. "But it was during a test where we did not expect it. For some tests the outcome is more expected than others. Those tests aren't meant to distinguish you from each other so much as to test your… endurance."

I glare at him. He means so that they can give us more cups and drug us more.

He looks to the other Commanders before resuming. "Before we reveal who is eliminated, we would like to know why you each chose the cup you did."

Because of whatever stupid hallucinogen you put in the drinks you rotten, old… I sigh. There aren't enough names right now.

Jasper leans back in his chair, his arms folded. His expression is as hidden as always, and his reply is just as concealed. "I thought it was obvious."

Yes, it was, unless you weren't looking at the right cup because you got caught up on a fishhook that you thought was a ribbon. I continue the tirade against myself in my mind because I know that as soon as I stop berating myself—as soon as I run out of names to call the Elven Command or myself—I'll have to face the fact that Baelen and Jasper will meet each other in the final battle. These two friends who have fought side-by-side will now be fighting each other. My heart squeezes. My internal rant against myself goes up in smoke and I force myself to breathe.

Baelen is quieter. He doesn't look up. "Because of a memory."

I consider his answer for a moment. It's also concealed, but more than Jasper's, it could apply to either of the cups.

"Because of whatever you put in the drink," I say.

Osian scratches his head. "Well, this places us in a very difficult position. One we'd hoped to avoid at all costs. But what's done is done."

He steps toward me. "Storm Princess Marbella of the House of Mercy, you will meet Baelen of the House of Rath in the final battle two days from now."

I definitely didn't hear that right. "I… what?"

"Princess, you and Commander Rath chose the same cup. Jasper of the House of Grace is eliminated."

"I… No…" I'm out of my seat in one second flat. "How?"

"Well, that is what we would also like to know. But I don't think we ever will."

"No, you're lying."

He steps back and Elwyn Elder takes his place. "Sit down, Princess. Put your weapon away."

Without realizing, I've reached for the steel at my side. My hand glows, not yet lit up, but threatening to. The Elven Command shuffles backward. There's no shield between us this time.

Without taking his eyes off me, Elwyn raises his voice, "Commander Rath, which cup did you choose?"

Baelen stares at me. It's the first time he's met my eyes today. His are just as piercing as always, just as perceptive, but now there's a question in them. "The one with the weird vertical squiggle on it that might have turned out to be… a fishhook."

"And Jasper, which one did you choose?"

Jasper is frozen. "The wind in the clouds."

I release my weapons. I don't wait for Elwyn to ask me. "I chose the fishhook." *Because of a memory.* Baelen must have seen a blue ribbon too. The one the wind stole. The memory was so strong that we'd both hallucinated it. My heart wrenches and I can't stop myself pressing the heel of my palm to my chest. Baelen turns away from me again, and I can't read his expression. I can't read his body language. I feel like my heart's cracking apart.

There's a wall between us now. It's the same wall that existed on the first day when he offered me his heartstone in the Storm Vault. I might not be able to see this new barrier, but it's there.

Elwyn says, "Princess, in light of the fact that Baelen Rath is the Commander of the Elven Army, which is a position of great importance to elven security, and the fact that he is the last of his House and his death would be, quite frankly, a tragedy… do you wish to exercise your right to yield at this point in time?"

I can't look at Baelen as I speak. I want to tell myself that this is not happening, but it is. "No."

"What?" It's Jasper. For the first time, his guard is down, his true emotions showing through, and those emotions right now are raw and horrified. "Marbella, what are you saying? You can't fight Commander Rath. You have to yield. You have to—"

Baelen's voice is soft but compelling. "Jasper, stop." He still doesn't look at me, fixated on a point on the wall the same way he was when they announced the compatibility results. "The princess has to do what she must."

"But that's… No… What's happening here?" Jasper looks from me to Baelen, swinging between us like he might find something logical or believable between the two of us.

I focus on the Elven Command. "Are we done here?"

Elwyn nods. "We will send details of the final battle after the wedding."

I skip a beat. I remind myself that he's talking about Jordan's wedding. For a second, I thought he meant mine. I spin and stride through the wide doors, leaving Baelen and Jasper behind.

And that's when everything blurs. Elise runs to keep up with me. She's speaking, but I can't hear her. All I hear is Baelen calling me, "the princess." Not Marbella anymore, but "Princess," like I'm a stranger. Like he never knew me at all.

He won't come near me now. No more appearances in the Storm Vault, no more random arrivals at my quarters. He'll stay away. And that's for the best.

"Find a way," I growl to Elise, stopping her mid-speech.

As she blinks back at me, shocked into silence by the savagery of my order, my voice cracks. "Please find a way, because I'd rather die than kill him."

"Yes, Princess."

But I know she doesn't think there's any hope.

JORDAN JUMPS TO HER FEET AS SOON AS WE ARRIVE. "I CAN'T GET married tonight. Not now."

I cast a glance around the living area. A plate of food sits untouched on the table, and she's worn a valley through the wool pile rug with all her pacing.

"I heard about the outcome," she says as the rest of the Storm Command disperses behind me. They are subdued, deflated, all of them feeling the damage I feel.

My shoulders sink. "That was fast." If Jordan has heard already, then the news will be flying around Erawind by now.

Her eyes fill with tears, and I almost break down as she says, "You need me by your side. I can't abandon you now."

I fight the tears burning behind my eyes. Now, more than ever, I must hold myself together. I'm broken inside, shattering into tiny pieces, but if I show Jordan how I really feel, she'll sacrifice her own happiness to protect me. "No, Jordan, you have to get married. Your happiness is the only reason I'm still standing right now. If you and Sebastian can be together then there's something good in my world —something good that I helped to create. If it wasn't for you…" My voice cracks. I can't go on, can't speak, but I push through. "You are the only happiness I have right now. Your happiness is the only thing keeping me alive."

A tear drips down her cheek. She takes a step toward me as if she'll break all the rules and wrap her arms around me to comfort me. "But—"

I suck in a breath, drawing on every icy needle of rain that the Storm ever threw at me so I can numb my emotions and shove them aside. The Storm's power dulls the sharpness of my sadness enough for me to pull myself together and stare her down. "You're getting married tonight." I soften my order with, "Please. I want you to. I *need* you to."

She worries at her bottom lip. "Okay, but I'm not leaving the city until after the… until after…"

"Thank you, Jordan," I whisper.

"Promise me, if you're in trouble in the final battle, you'll yield and not die." She leans forward and I know there's more. This is the part where she'd take my hand while she tells me something I don't want to hear.

Her gaze is gentle, almost apologetic, but also unyielding, as she says, "Commander Rath is the most ferocious fighter anyone's ever seen. The only reason those men got the upper hand in the arena was because he didn't expect them to fight without honor. As soon as he realized what they were doing, he changed… I didn't see it, but Sebastian told me that he practically tore their limbs off. I didn't have the privilege of seeing the Raths at the height of their power, but if they were anything like Commander Rath…" She shudders. "You're about to enter a battle to the death. You *must* yield if your life is threatened."

"I promise I won't die. I do. Really."

And this is the part where I'd lean forward and take *her* hands, if I could. "But… I need you to promise me something too."

I search for the right words, knowing I'm clutching at straws, knowing she won't like it, but it's the only option open to me right now. "I asked you once to protect Commander Rath if his life was in danger during the trials. I need you to make sure my Storm Command keeps that promise."

Her eyes shoot wide and the blood drains from her face. She drops into her chair, her pale face turned up to me. "Wait, after everything I just said to you about Commander Rath killing you, about his ferocity in battle and how worried I am for your safety... You want us to protect *him*... against *you*?"

I join her at the table, keeping my voice low. Elise has already hurried away in search of answers and the rest of the Storm Command is changing shift. I have a rare chance to speak with Jordan more openly than I've been able to before now.

"Jordan, I know that Baelen Rath will be the most dangerous opponent I've ever faced." For so many reasons, not just because he's the most fearsome fighter, but because he has the ability to cut my heart into emotional shreds. "But I know that he would never willingly choose to kill me. I *chose* to enter these trials. He had no choice. If, by some miracle, I get the upper hand and I'm about to strike a fatal blow, then yes. I need you to get in the way. I need you... to make it impossible for me to kill him."

She's giving me a different look now, one that says I'm telling her something she suspected for a long time. "You really don't want him to die."

I swallow. "I need to find a way to force the Elven Command to call off the fight. For both our sakes. But at the same time, I need to be declared the winner."

"I don't understand, Princess. If you don't want him to die, then why don't you want him to be your husband?"

"Because..." I haven't been able to tell Jordan about the curse. Even telling Elise was a risk. But now I grapple with a reason that Jordan might understand. Something. Anything that might make sense without revealing the truth.

Then I land on it: a reason that could be believed. "Because... the Elven Command lied about a man being able to share the power of the storm. If anyone except me steps foot in the Storm Vault, the Storm will kill them. Mai told me that her husband barely survived. I... can't risk killing Commander Rath. The same way I can't risk killing him in the final battle."

She digests that for a moment before saying, "But... why not just tell him to wait outside the Vault? You've been warned about it so you know he should stay out of it."

Okay, so it wasn't a very convincing reason after all. My mind turns blank every direction I turn for a better one.

She continues without giving me an inch. "And... having a husband isn't just about helping with the storm. I've heard that a husband can be quite worthwhile for... other reasons." Her face flames, but she presses on. "Reasons that I'm certain would be more than adequate with a man like Commander Rath."

I stare at her in shock. We've gone from talking about Baelen ripping me limb from limb to talking about... *other reasons*. My heart crumbles as she continues to look at me with concern. I know she doesn't just mean sex. She means comfort, support, knowing that someone has my back, that they care about me and care about how I feel and what I think.

My gaze drops to my lap because I can't keep my face blank right now. I can't hide what I feel. I have to push it all out of my head and forget about the idea of someone loving me, because the memory of *other reasons* already caused me to choose a cup I shouldn't have chosen.

A sad smile curves Jordan's lips and I realize that she's not going to press me further when she says, "You don't have to tell me your real reasons. I wish you would, but I know you must not be able to. Which is why I'm going to trust you. I'll do as you ask. I will make sure that the Storm Command protects Commander Rath."

I exhale some of my pent up fear and sadness. "Thank you, Jordan."

"Now," she says, pushing the plate of food toward me with a gentle smile. "Eat before you subdue the Storm today, because afterward, you have a wedding to preside over."

I do as she asks and then I head to the Storm Vault to complete my daily task that has somehow become the only place I feel safe— and the only thing I feel safe doing. But the Storm today is... different.

When I step into the Vault, the lightning sputters, half-formed thunder cuts off into silence, and the rain starts and stops, pouring one moment and disappearing the next.

I turn my hands upward, squinting as raindrops fall on my head, trying to call the lightning to me. It dances across my skin and for a moment, it feels like normal, but then it jolts upward, as if it's shuddering. Like I'm suddenly shuddering.

"Something's wrong." I study the storm above me. So far there's been lightning, rain, and thunder, but no wind. Not like the other day when there was plenty of it.

Fat drops of rain start to fall in front of my feet, but don't land on me. "What's wrong, Storm?" I've progressed from calling it "Beast", to now calling it what I think it should be called: simply "Storm."

An enormous water drop falls past my face, the width of my hand. It splashes at my feet, sloshing upward. A full five seconds later, another one follows it. Each splash sounds out a word.

It... isn't... my... fault.

"What isn't?"

It... isn't... me.

I shake my head and repeat. "What isn't? I don't understand you."

I... can't...

I wait for more. But that's it. That's all there is. The lightning sputters and dies. There are no more water drops. No more rain. The Storm calms and I have no idea what it was trying to tell me.

I leave the Storm Vault feeling baffled. I stop inside the first room where Elise waits for me, wishing Baelen would appear like he had before. I take the opportunity to tell Elise what I asked Jordan to do—to keep Baelen safe.

Elise hangs her head, her shoulders slumping. "I wish I had a better plan to offer you."

I slump into the chair at the side of the room. "Why am I doing this, Elise? Why am I trying to win? Why... can't I just yield like everyone wants me to? Like *I* want to."

Elise sighs. "I understand your frustration, but even if you put aside the disaster of a raging storm that will happen if you die, the curse will force Commander Rath to kill you. He's an honorable man and it will destroy him once he realizes what he's done. Then the storm will be unleashed and kill him anyway. You won't have saved him after all—"

"No, stop." My hand shoots into the air, silencing her. "What did you just say?"

"I said that if Commander Rath kills you, the Storm will be unleashed and kill him anyway."

"No." The room suddenly becomes crystal clear, all of its

corners and lines stark in my vision. I pick myself up and plant my hands on the translucent panels at the side. Elise's elegant form is reflected in them, but I stare past her into the silent, dark Vault beyond.

"On the day that the Storm first spoke to me, it told me that my husband would kill me. But it never said anything about being unleashed. In fact... wouldn't it be happy to be free? It wouldn't warn me about it so that I could stop it from happening."

"What are you saying?"

I whisper, "Baelen won't die, because the Storm won't be free."

Elise gapes at me. "Princess, I don't follow."

"If the Elven Command knows about the curse... or even created it..." I shudder. "Then that's why they were desperate to eliminate Baelen. That's why they've done everything they can to have one of their grandsons take my power. They don't want Baelen to win because they can't control him..."

"Princess Marbella Mercy, you need to start making sense right now!" Elise stomps her foot but worry chases the anger off her face. "Because you're scaring me right now and I don't mind admitting it."

I itch for my weapons belts, wanting the comfort of knowing I can unleash the Storm's power. *My* storm power. The power that, for some reason, I'm the first to use as a weapon.

"If I yield to Baelen, I'll marry him, touch him, and transfer to him the power to control the Storm," I say. "As soon as I do, the curse will be triggered, and he'll kill me. But the storm won't be unleashed because he will control it."

Elise's jaw drops. "He'll be the first Storm Prince."

32

____

MARBELLA

The idea of Baelen Rath as a Storm Prince… Why does that feel so right to me? Why am I not shrieking and ranting right now? Maybe it's the shock of my realization keeping me numb. Maybe it's knowing that if everything goes wrong for me, if I die, then the Storm's power will be in hands that I trust. Baelen's hands. The Elven Command won't be able to make Baelen use it in any dishonorable or evil way like they could try with someone else.

I lean against the panel, my breath frosting against the cold darkness inside the Vault. "I thought someone wanted to unleash the Storm, but it's not about that at all. It's about taking control of it."

Elise hovers beside me. "That would explain why the curse was created now. You're the first princess who can transfer her power to another elf. You're also the first to use the storm as a weapon, which means it's a deadly power to control."

"I could decimate a battlefield." I study my fingers pressed up against the panels. "Given what I can do with a single steel knife, cover me in steel armor and the results could be devastating."

"No other princess has done what you have. Even Mai was a passive vessel."

"Are you sure? I saw her slow time."

"I did my research," she says. "After I saw what you did when

221

Commander Rath was here, I had a very frank discussion with Mai's advisor. Mai was able to harness the remnant power of thunder and she could water her garden from her fingertips for a few hours after each visit to the Storm Vault, but she couldn't weaponize the Storm like you can."

"I guess I hoped I wasn't completely alone in this."

"I'm sorry, Princess. What you can do has never happened before."

I run my hand through my hair, wringing out the water from my braid. "What I find unbelievable is the idea that all I have to do is touch another man to pass my power on to him. What if I accidentally bump into someone walking through the square one day?"

What if the gargoyle I met on the mountain had leaned just a little closer? And why didn't anything happen when he picked me up inside his wings to deposit me inside the cave? Or... maybe something did happen and now there's a super-charged-storm-controlling-gargoyle raging around Scepter Peak?

I almost laugh, but it's shallow and quickly dies in my throat. "Elise, I have a lot of questions, but what I really need to know is whether the Elven Command actually knows about the curse or worse... if they created it to take control of the Storm. They've been talking about launching an attack on the gargoyles. The Storm would be the perfect way to do that."

She chews her lip. "I don't want to believe they'd create the curse. They've always been proud, arrogant..."

"Control freaks?"

Her eyebrows lift as if punctuating her response. "Yes, but they've never been deliberately reckless or cruel before. My guess is that they found out about it and thought they'd use it to their advantage." She shakes her head. "Maybe the question we should be asking is how was the curse created? Deep magic can only be manipulated through life itself."

I nod. "When I flew with the phoenix, it told me that the storm was created when a female gargoyle gave her life for revenge."

"Which means that this curse was created from death." Elise's gaze flashes across the Vault. "I need to look into recent deaths. That should lead us to whoever is doing this."

"Thank you, Elise. I know you won't let me down."

"Well… at least now I have a place to start." She squares her shoulders as she leads the way out of the waiting room.

When we reach my quarters, I find Jordan already dressed and half of the Storm Command fussing over her hair and the other half making a bouquet of white lilies for her. Her dress drapes across the chair she's sitting on, her elegant appearance only ruined by the puffy eyes she reveals when she looks up.

"This is my last time in this room," she says as I draw near, my storm boots squelching. "I won't be allowed in this place again."

"True. But one glance from Sebastian and this moment of sadness will be forgotten forever. Remember, *other reasons*."

She breaks into a gorgeous smile, and I leave her with the Storm Command while I retreat to my bedroom with a minimal guard. I stare into the abyss that is my closet. My wardrobe isn't exactly stocked with weddings in mind. Come to think of it, it's not even stocked with my own wedding in mind. I own multiple storm suits, several gray body suits for exercising, and a few casual dresses. I have the cloak I wore to the Heartstone Ceremony, and I have my armor. And… that's it.

One of my ladies appears in the doorway. She's as tall as Jordan, but the opposite in appearance: blonde, blue-eyed, and stealthy as a shadow panther. She's just as deadly as Jordan with a bow and arrow and, well, every other kind of weapon. But most importantly, she's calm, quietly intelligent, and always thinks before she acts. She doesn't know it yet, but I want her to take over from Jordan.

"Yes, Reisha?"

"If I may, Princess. This gift was left for you." She places a large, white box on my bed. "Elise checked it over for spells and I've assessed it for threats. It's safe for you to open."

I run my hand over the top. "Who is it from?"

"I believe Commander Rath's advisor brought it to the door, Princess." She bows and retreats to the side of the room where two other ladies wait, giving me as much privacy as they can, while still watching over me.

I chew my lip with uncertainty as I open the box. The lid is light and lifts off easily. Inside the box, a note rests on top of the contents, which are wrapped in material. I recognize Baelen's scrawl, written in the same graphite he used to draw with.

My mother wore this on the night she met my father.

I want you to have it.

B.

The silken cover slides between my fingertips as I push it aside. Baelen's mother fell ill with a deadly fever when Baelen was ten-years-old. She was pregnant at the time and neither she nor his baby sister survived. The impact on Baelen was… indescribable. He didn't become bitter, angry, or reclusive, but he was somehow set apart from everyone else afterward. The only person he reached out to, and connected with—for some reason I'll never understand—was me. Maybe it was because I never pushed him to talk when he didn't want to, never assumed he was happy when he wasn't, never asked anything from him. I was just… *there*. His father refused to remarry despite pressure from the other Houses and Baelen became the only heir to the Rath name.

I slide the wrapping open to reveal the dress beneath. It rustles into my arms, a deep purple with a plunging gauzy neckline, fitted through the bodice and waist, and falling to a cascade of silk folds from the hips. Delicate fabric flowers adorn the base of the bodice and drip across the waist and hips. It's elegant but also understated, and most importantly, it won't outshine Jordan's dress.

I place it carefully back into the box while I bathe and dry my hair. I opt not to tie my hair back into my usual braid, leaving it out, tucked behind my ears, and falling in waves to my waist.

I don't even consider not wearing the dress. I've told Baelen I won't yield. In fact, the whole city knows. But he chose to send me this anyway. I can't try to read anything into it other than what he said in his note: It was important to him, and he wants me to have it. I allow myself to feel grateful for his thoughtful gift.

When I pull on the dress, I discover that the folds concealed two high slits running up each leg. I ponder what to do with my weapons belts. They'll be visible and obvious, and it feels wrong to take daggers to a wedding. Even if I could conceal them, it wouldn't feel right. I study my gloves and belts, trying to decide what to do with them until Reisha speaks up from the side of the room.

"How are you at catching?" she asks.

"Not bad. I guess."

"Then, carry your gloves, but let me hold the weapons for you and I promise I'll get them to you if you need them."

When I nod my agreement, her expression becomes stern, "But I also promise you, you *won't* need them, because we aren't going to let anything happen to ruin this night."

She means it—not just for me but for Jordan whom they all love. My Storm Command is made up of twenty women who live to protect me. Their whole lives are contained within these walls. They don't have boyfriends or husbands. They just have each other. And they have me.

When I emerge, Jordan is ready and so is my Storm Command. They've opted for full battle dress and I'm quietly relieved. I have no doubt they could handle themselves in silk dresses, but I'm much more comfortable with them presenting a formidable force. They are my protectors, my security, and my defenders. I'm lucky to also call them my friends.

"Princess," Jordan says, "it's been an honor."

"The honor is all mine."

I proceed ahead of her since I need to arrive first. The wedding is taking place under the spreading oak in the middle of the courtyard. Jordan doesn't know yet, but Elise has spellcast the open space with glittering lanterns and twinkling stars—and a protective shield that only allows family and friends inside the area. We have the whole courtyard to ourselves.

Jordan waits just inside the courtyard, hidden from view by a line of my ladies. My feet walk the path of rose petals strewn along the way to the oak. A line of my warriors walks on either side of me, giving me a clear view of what lies ahead.

Sebastian waits under the oak. His cousin, Simon, stands beside him. It seems like a lifetime ago that I thought Simon was going to be the champion in the trials. Now he's smiling, a far cry from the tension of the Heartstone Ceremony. Guests sit on gilded seats on either side of the wide path. I recognize Sebastian's mother and, of course, his grandfather, Teilo Splendor. I hold my breath, waiting to see if Baelen is among them.

I don't see him.

I push away my disappointment. I wanted him to know that I

accepted his gift. And if I'm really honest, I'll admit that I wanted him to see me in it. The dress is beautiful and fits me perfectly. But tonight isn't about me or the trials. It's about Jordan.

I'm surprised when I locate Jasper among the guests, though. As everyone rises to their feet, he gives me a nod, forever serious, his earlier emotions hidden again. I acknowledge him with my own nod before moving to the front.

"Sebastian," I greet him as I pass by.

"Princess."

I stand before the trunk of the tree, briefly noting that a small table has been placed there like I asked. At the back of the crowd, Elise gestures to a choir of elves. They begin to sing as Jordan approaches. She's flanked on either side by warriors, and tears glisten in her eyes. From the moment she appears, Sebastian can't tear his eyes off her. She reaches his side, and he takes her hand in his. For a moment, their foreheads touch, before drawing apart and giving me their attention.

I lift my voice when the choir falls silent. "There are moments in our lives that pass too quickly but leave us forever changed. This is one of those moments. Sebastian and Jordan have waited their whole lives to be here together, and we are blessed to share this time with them."

I turn to Simon. "Simon Splendor, please place the rings on the table. Don't hand them directly to me."

He looks uncertain. This is the part that everyone's nervous about—me handling metal—but I'm not worried. I've learned quickly to control my power.

When he places the rings on the table, I take one in each hand, placing them in my palms and turning them upward. I keep a leash on the power raging through me, so the gold rings rest quietly against my skin.

"Sebastian and Jordan, may your love be as gentle as a summer rain shower."

I let go of the storm, just a little, and rain seeps from the surface of my skin, dripping upward against the force of gravity. The onlookers gasp, but I ignore them, concentrating on the rings.

"May your love be as powerful as thunder."

I let go a little more to allow pressure to thud through my

hands, pushing the rings upward, floating them in the air above my palms, and sustaining the suspension while I continue speaking.

"May your love burn as brightly as lightning in a clear sky."

My hands light up and so do the rings, glittering with the lightning burning around them.

"And may your love… be as eternal as the air we breathe."

I take a breath and blow gently over the rings. With the puff of air, the lightning fades, the raindrops disperse, and the rings lower to my palms.

I take each one between my thumb and forefinger. "Please hold out your hands, but stay very still."

Jordan and Sebastian do as I ask, and I carefully drop their rings into their palms, making sure I keep my distance as much as I can. I quickly step back, putting a large gap between us again. I'm vaguely aware that Reisha and my ladies are keeping a very close eye all around me. It makes me insanely happy to see that they haven't taken their eyes off Teilo Splendor in the first row.

After that, Jordan and Sebastian make their oaths and place the rings on each other's fingers. They clasp hands. Normally, this is the part where I would place my hands over theirs, acknowledging them as now united. I can't do that, but I hope that my gesture with the rings makes up for it.

Instead of wrapping their hands between mine, I clasp my hands in front of me and declare, "You are married."

He kisses her without a moment's hesitation, and she returns his kiss, fresh tears sliding down her cheeks as they melt into each other. I tear away from their happiness and step out of the way, taking myself off to the side, guarded once more as guests move forward to congratulate them.

Elise quickly joins me so I'm not alone inside the Storm Command's protective circle, and I appreciate her presence beside me.

"They'll tell stories about this," she says with a warm smile. "Nobody's marriage has been blessed by a Storm Princess before."

Sebastian and Jordan are truly happy. I'm glad Jordan will stay in the city until the final battle is over, but another big part of me wants her and Sebastian to run as far away as they can from it all. They don't need death tainting their first days as husband and wife. "What happens now? I hadn't thought past this moment," I admit.

"Food and dancing. You'll need to stay for that, but we've set up a table over there so you can keep your distance from everyone." Her lips thin in disapproval as she glares at Teilo Splendor.

When she said I should keep my distance from everyone, she mostly means him. He's the only member of the Elven Command who is present, and I'm grateful for that. I couldn't stand sharing this moment of happiness with all those men. I want to ask Elise if she's found out anything about recent deaths or the Elven Command's involvement in the curse, but I don't want to taint the moment. It will be easier to talk in a sound bubble in my quarters.

"I appreciate that you arranged the table for me." Maybe. Maybe I hate it too, because I want to dance and talk with the guests, instead of always watching from a distance while others live their lives.

I find my seat, remaining at my table while the Storm Command forms a semi-circle behind me and along my sides. I watch the dancing and revelry unfold in front of me. It's hard not to find it contagious, but at the same time, I can't breathe properly. With every passing second, I get closer to the battle in two day's time.

All the guests leave me alone, even Jasper keeps his distance which is probably just as well—there's no explanation I can give him that would make things better—but toward the end of the night, Sebastian's mother approaches my table. She bows. "Princess."

"You're Sahara Splendor," I say.

"I am." She has the same eyes as Sebastian—a glistening silver-green. She's curvy and graceful in a rose-gold gown that swathes her shoulders and drapes across her hips. Her voice lilts as she talks, reminding me that the Splendor House is known for its beautiful singing voices.

She looks directly at me with unexpected intensity, as she says, "It's a beautiful love story destined to end in tragedy, isn't it?"

I eye her with caution. Jordan and Sebastian are chatting happily with guests on the other side of the space that's been cleared for dancing. They haven't left each other's sides. "There will be no tragedy here. I won't allow it."

She rushes to speak. "No, I don't mean my son and his lovely wife. I mean you and Commander Rath."

"What did you say?" Anger shoots through me like a hot iron slamming across my spine. I can't control it. She's approached me out of the blue and now she tells me that Baelen and I are some sort of tragedy unfolding, like we're here for everyone's entertainment. I shoot to my feet. The air thumps. Thunder crashes across the courtyard. Time slows. The dancing and music slow and then stop, plunging us into heavy, angry silence.

Sahara glances around, but she doesn't seem surprised or worried. I'm the one who is shocked as I realize she's checking that nobody's moving.

"I'm sorry to cause you grief, but I needed a way to ignite your thunder." She spins back to me. "I've been speaking with Mai Reverie, and I understand you can only slow time for a few minutes."

"Mai told you?" I'm incredulous and disbelieving. Mai wouldn't tell anyone that secret unless she trusted them completely. And the only other people I thought Mai trusted were her husband, Darian, and her advisor, Rebecca.

Sahara ignores my question. "Which is why I'm going to speak plainly. Commander Rath is one of my son's true friends—a loyal friendship that I refuse to forsake. But the Commander bound himself to you, vowing to love and protect you, and now you hold his life in your hands. Will you really not yield? Or will you kill him?"

I glare at her. "You're missing the third option: will he kill me?"

Her eyes widen. "But that's not an option. He can't kill you."

"Yes, he can—"

"He bound himself to you. He can't harm you. Not even to protect himself. Not even to defend himself against you."

Everything spins around me. My stomach lurches and my vision blurs. I stumble back against my chair, coming up hard against its edges. "But…"

She studies me. It would be very hard for her to miss my shock right now; it's rising off me in waves. "You didn't realize." It's a statement, not a question. "You thought that the deep magic from the Heartstone Protocols would override his oath and allow him to fight you?"

"Yes!"

Her eyes glisten and her Splendor heritage shines in them. "You hold the power now, Princess."

"I won't kill him."

She stands straighter and her eyes light up with hope. "Then you'll yield? Despite what you said before?"

"No. I can't do that either." I grip the edge of the table to prevent myself from sliding beneath it. My knuckles burn white hot against the wood. "I know that makes no sense. But I have no choice. I have to win, but I can't kill him."

She leans forward, assessing me. It isn't a cold calculation, it's a look as old as time, a woman's wisdom when she understands there are no good choices but a choice must be made. "Then you need a solution—a solution that I can provide."

I jolt backward, not trusting her closeness. "Why are you doing this?"

"Because I owe you an enormous debt and I see a way to repay it." She leans back too, giving me space, and cautiously sweeps her hand out in a gesture at our surroundings. "Do you like the flowers?"

I hadn't noticed before, but I do now. Gladiolus flowers are scattered among the roses glistening on the ground, their gentle lavender petals mingling with the red rose petals. "Are you the reason for the flowers?"

"Not just me. I condemned the way you were treated during the battle in the arena. It was abhorrent. Beyond belief. I went to Mai Reverie immediately to seek her council about what I could do to protect you. I knew there was very little I could do to defend you physically, but if I could unite the people in your favor then you would have their support. I suggested the flowers and Mai grew them herself, hundreds of them."

I want to thank her—I know I have to thank Mai and I *will*—but I still don't know if I can trust Sahara.

"Then you saved my son's life," she says. "I knew that no matter what trial the Elven Command chose to administer, Sebastian would choose to die rather than fight his friends. Especially because he thought he'd lost Jordan." She pauses, sucking in her breath. "The only way I can repay you for saving his life is by saving a life that you… care about."

I zero in on her, choosing to ignore her comment about me caring about Baelen. I can't acknowledge that to anyone. I can't speak it aloud because then I'll break down. I grip the table harder, not caring that the power of thunder gives me the strength to press so hard that splinters break off beneath my palms. I'm probably drawing blood, but if I stop holding onto this table right now, I'll lose my hold on my emotions. "Can you call off the battle? Can you make your father put a stop to it?"

"No, I'm sorry, but… are you aware that I'm a healer?"

When I shake my head, a jerky side-to-side motion, she says, "I've saved the lives of many beloved sons. And husbands. And lov—"

I snap, cutting her off. "Where are you going with this?"

"I don't mind saying that I'm quite talented, especially in knowing which medicines to administer. Medicines aren't spells of course, so they can be given to champions despite the protective spells."

She pulls a vial from the delicate rose-gold clutch she holds in her hands. The vial is small, the size of a thimble, and sparkles gold too. "This one slows the heartbeat so much that it looks like someone's dead. All you have to do is nick them and they fall within moments. And this one… revives them."

The second vial is silver. She places both side-by-side on the table. She leans toward me, whispering, "Spin gold, shelter silver. He is worth more than both, yes?"

I stare at the vials as her footsteps retreat. One vial to make it look like he's dead. The other to wake him up when it's all over… Is this actually possible? Could this be the solution I desperately need?

When I look up again, she's gone. Not wasting another moment, I scoop up the vials and hide them inside one of my gloves. I'm just in time before the dancers come alive around me again. Everything resumes as if nothing happened, and Sahara Splendor doesn't look back. She glides over to her son and gives him a hug, drawing

Jordan into her embrace as well. The love between them is so strong that any suspicion I had about Sahara's motives melts away.

The celebration might be continuing around me as if nothing's changed, but something has changed. Sahara Splendor just gave me hope. My first real hope that I can keep Baelen alive.

33

BAELEN

The winged stallion soars across the night sky above the Revenant mountains, my homeland spread out beneath us. I glance at Macsen, a silhouette on the stallion he rides beside me. We have to reach Scepter Peak in time.

As we fly across the next valley, flickering lamps traveling up the mountain range tell me that the battalion of soldiers is close to the gargoyle's nest.

"There!" Macsen's shout is carried away in the wind.

I urge my stallion down toward the ground, preparing to leap from its back. There isn't time to slow down. Beside me, Macsen slips both legs over one side of his horse, ready to somersault to the ground as soon as we're near enough.

The soldiers pressing through the snow cover lift their lamps as soon as we soar overhead. The captain at their head calls a command to stop. He's the same man who helped me during the night patrols leading up to the Heartstone Ceremony. I leap from my horse, somersaulting and landing on my feet at a run. Macsen lands several steps behind me, running to a halt nearby.

We're both wearing armor and carrying as many weapons as we could grab in the minutes we had to prepare before taking off on the stallions.

"Commander Rath!" The captain hurries forward, holding his lamp high.

I rise to my full height. "Captain, your orders have changed."

He considers me for a moment. Even in the dim light, it's impossible to miss the relief that washes across his features. "The Elven Command sent us here to deal with the gargoyle threat. They ordered us to keep the mission secret. We were not to speak of it to anyone—including you."

The Elven Command sent a whole battalion of soldiers into Rath land to kill one gargoyle and his children.

The captain meets my eyes. He won't ask me how I found out. I won't tell him that it was Jasper, who has been quietly monitoring the movement of all troops from the city while Macsen arranged House of Mercy elves to monitor the border to Rath land and report back about any unusual movement.

Everyone who opposes the Elven Command is at the wedding tonight. They expected me to be there too. It killed me to miss it, but I won't allow a gargoyle family to be killed because I want to indulge in a moment of happiness.

The captain's breath frosts in the air as he asks, "What are *your* orders, Commander?"

"Go home, Captain. The gargoyle threat is not yours to fight this night."

"Thank you, Commander."

He signals for the troops to turn around, but none of them moves and for a moment, my heart sinks. Are they going to disobey me?

The captain considers the quiet battalion for a moment, and I can't identify his intentions before he turns back to me. "We heard about the outcome of the trial of wits," he says. "You will face the Storm Princess in battle. We also heard that the Princess won't yield. Yet… her survival is necessary for our survival. Without her, the Storm will rage."

I swallow. Clear my throat. "My duty to protect Erawind is more important than my life."

He gives me a quiet nod. "It has been an honor to serve with you, Commander."

The battalion of soldiers stands tall, each tapping his chest, saluting me. Then they turn and head quietly down the mountain again. It's a long trek back to the border of Rath land, where they left a herd of winged stallions to take them home again.

Once they're gone, I turn to Macsen. "The Elven Command will have a backup plan. We have to hurry."

He doesn't waste any time, taking off ahead of me up the peak. The location of the gargoyle's nest is only two hundred feet away, wedged between rock faces in a shallow cave. It's the same man that Marbella saved.

He's smart, moving his nest every few days to a new location. I lost track of him a few days ago, but unfortunately, the Elven Command didn't. It baffles me how they found out. The only remaining possibility is that they're somehow using flying creatures—birds—to surveil the mountains, but that would take sorcery of a kind that is outlawed in Erawind.

I hurry after Macsen, darting through the snow flurry, my eyes adjusting to the dark as I run. I catch up to him at the top of the next peak. He crouches at the entrance to a maze of rock faces. The entries and exits to the nest will be narrow. We'll have to proceed one at a time.

No matter how many soldiers the Elven Command sends, they would never survive a battle with a gargoyle like this one—he would pick them off one by one. Even an approach from above is difficult in this location; the jagged outcrops make landing a flying creature nearly impossible.

I know these peaks well.

I also know there are better places to hide. My goal tonight is to convince the gargoyle to relocate to one of them.

I grip Macsen's shoulder. "I'll go first."

He shakes his head. "It's my job to keep you alive, Baelen."

"Macsen." My shoulders slump. "Marbella has chosen her path. I don't know why, but she made it clear that she won't yield—"

"She wouldn't say that."

He didn't believe me when I told him. He didn't believe Jasper, either. The soldier's salute just now doesn't seem to have convinced him, either.

I close my eyes against his denial. Ever since Marbella offered me her hand, my heart has been dying a slow death. A small part of me still feels something, but I've tucked my feelings away, far from where I can reach them.

Now, I have to make the most of the days I have left.

"I'm living on borrowed time, Macsen. I can't control what happens in the final fight, but I can control what I do between now and then. If one of us dies tonight, it will be me."

A deep, unhappy crease appears across his forehead. "I don't think so."

He spins to the opening, but I was ready for his stubborn behavior and I'm not afraid to use dirty tactics to stop him. I step forward at the same time he does, ram my shoulder against his, and use his sideways momentum to push him off track, slipping my foot across his. He jolts, trips, then rights himself, but not fast enough.

I dodge his outstretched hand and slip through the narrow opening into the tight pass between the rocks. The constricted corridor extends for fifty paces before it lets out into the clearing with the shallow cave.

I'm sure Macsen wants to shout at me right now, but that would be foolhardy this close to the nest. He doesn't make a sound as he follows my steps.

The clearing is dark up ahead, the low hanging outcrop obscuring the stars. I slow my approach, taking deep breaths, preparing myself. It's been a long time since I fought a gargoyle—or more importantly, it's been a long time since a gargoyle saw me as a threat. It leaves a sick feeling in my stomach that this gargoyle thinks I'm here to kill his children.

I grip the stone wall for a moment, pushing away the memory of tiny running feet through the wilderness, a little girl's sobbing scream, and the moment when I made a choice about who I really am. That was when I decided that my race does not determine whom I protect.

I reach for the string of talons and claws that used to hang around my neck before I remember that I left it far behind me, the same place I left the last three years of my life. All I have now to prove to this gargoyle that I mean no harm is my actions.

Leaving my weapons fully harnessed, I extend my hand back at Macsen, planting my palm against his chest: *Stop*.

When he edges forward, I give him a firm shake of my head. I want him to stay out of sight.

Lifting my hands up in front of me, I splay my fingers to show that I don't hold a weapon, and then I move, inch by slow inch, into the clearing.

I clear the entrance.

The air shifts to my right, the slightest movement.

My instincts kick in.

I duck the enormous fist aimed for my emerging head—a blow that would have crushed my skull against the rocks. I dart forward at a crouch and retaliate with a fist swung back into the gargoyle's knee cap.

He roars, his wings spreading, and his wing daggers pointing down. I keep moving but he follows me, quick and agile. His fist meets my cheek but luckily my movement lessens the impact. I fight back with two quick blows perfectly landed on his cheek and temple.

His eyes widen for a second, clearly surprised that I survived the crushing blow to my face just now, let alone hit back with fists that, well, he might try to hide it, but I hurt him. He inhales, his eyes widening further—this time for reasons I can't fathom—but he shakes it off.

His response is to rain blows onto me. He can't spread his wings fully in the confined space, but he uses them to catch the air and gain height, slamming each fist down onto my head and shoulders. Bare to the waist, his muscles ripple across his chest with every movement.

I keep moving, block several blows with my own fists, and flow with the others. I'll only be in real trouble if he pins me against the rock.

Or if he decides to use his wing daggers.

I hit back, my own crushing blows to his side, chest, chin. A thin line of blood trickles from his split lip.

His clawed foot flies toward me, attempting to knock me against the rocks, but I dodge it. The rock face cracks where he hit it. Fissures speed through the mottled surface and chips fall from up high.

He growls as I dart away from him, his threatening snarls

becoming fierce and anxious when I stop between him and the cave, a threat between him and his children, the most dangerous place I could put myself.

"I'm here to warn you, not harm you," I say.

His chest heaves, growls filling the air around us. "All elves are murderers."

"Gargoyles have their share of evil, too." I slowly reach for the weapons harness around my waist, sliding the clasp loose to remove it and hold it high. I throw it to the entrance at the side of the clearing. Macsen remains concealed inside the corridor. I can barely distinguish his shape from the boulders around the space.

I say, "I know you're running from a great evil that has taken over your land."

He doesn't trust me—even without my weapons. He prowls toward me, circling the clearing, and I let him come.

"How do you know this?" he demands.

"The same way I know that a talon crow's neck can be snapped by using its tusks against it. The same way I know how to remove a shadow panther's claw. The same way I know that the threat the gargoyles now face originated from your village."

He follows my pointed finger to the mark on his hip, inhaling sharply. The fine silvery shape is the size of a small coin. It is the mark of his clan, but he has cut into it many times, as if he has tried to obliterate it. He hates his origins.

He's close enough to grab me, but I've deliberately positioned myself with the only opening at my back. If he wants to pin me, he'll have to swing me to the side or drive me all the way to the back of the cave past his children. He won't expose them to violence.

"You are stronger than most elves," he growls. "But you will meet your maker this night."

I nod. "If that is meant to be."

I dodge his next fist and hit back with my full strength, a punch to his stomach that carries what's left of my heart with it. I need him to survive. He has nested quietly on Rath land, never hurting or threatening any elf, only wishing to protect his children.

My fist connects, energy bursting from me, ribbons of crimson light snapping around my fingers. With a crack, blood-red flames ignite between us.

Shocked by the contact, I jolt backward, the firelight fading as fast as it appeared.

The gargoyle also leaps back, the breath whooshing out of his lungs, his eyes wide. He sucks in a deep breath, rubbing his chest while he regains his balance…

His voice is a startled whisper. "You smell like scorched earth."

"I am…" I don't know what he's talking about, but I have to stop this fight because I'm not sure what will happen next. The energy I just felt was dangerous, lethal. I can't let it out again. My voice rises to a near command. "I am Baelen of the House of Rath. This is my land. I give you permission to nest on it."

My declaration falls into a shocked silence.

He's stunned. "You give me… I have your permission to…" He shakes himself. "But I am a gargoyle!"

"Why does that make a difference?"

He blinks at me. He doesn't believe me. *How can I make him see that I am not his enemy?*

Golden light glints at the edge of my vision. I crouch slowly, arms held wide, and scoop the yellow object from the ground, holding it up to him. "Do you know what this is?"

He shakes his head.

"It's a Shimmer Beetle husk. The hardest substance in Erawind. Each year, these beetles shed their husks. They cast off the old and embrace the new. I believe that elves and gargoyles can do that too. Cast off the past and start fresh. One husk at a time."

He begins to pace side to side, the furrow in his brow growing deep. "If you aren't here to kill me, then why are you here?"

"A battalion of elven soldiers was sent here against their will to harm you. I turned them away, but more will come unless you accept my help."

"They will not kill me."

"Maybe so, but can you say the same for your children?" I exhale slowly, not daring to look at the babies snuggled in the nest behind and to my right. Any hint of threat to them will ignite the gargoyle's protective instincts and the conversation will be over. "I know a better place to hide. One where you won't be found."

It's a hiding spot that I had planned to use as a backup plan if I needed to disappear, but that seems pointless now.

"I'm asking you to trust me," I say.

"You are the second elf to surprise me," the gargoyle growls. "I will trust you for now, but only because that elf there had several chances to shoot me and didn't."

He points to where Macsen hovers in the dark.

Macsen promptly steps into the clearing, lowering his nocked bow and removing the arrow. He leans against the side of the opening with a grin aimed at me. "Mark the gargoyle's words, Baelen. This truce is because of me."

I relax, most of the tension leaving my body as I turn back to the gargoyle. "Please pack your things as quickly as you can. We'll carry whatever you need. We have a long trek ahead of us tonight. I promise by tomorrow, you will be safe."

As I relocate myself to the other side of the clearing, away from his children, I cast my eyes upward to the patch of sky visible between the overhang and the rock face.

The battalion was only the first wave. I'm prepared for what the Elven Command will try next. No matter what it is, it will be easier than facing Marbella in the arena.

34

GRAYSON

I pace my room like the caged animal that I am.

Elwyn Elder plants his feet next to the ornate desk that sits alongside the plush couches that line my room, his obstinate form framed by the golden wallpaper that covers the walls. The room is suffocating in its opulence, a typical space for one of the favored in the House of Glory, except that in my case, the silken curtains that fall straight and closed, giving the illusion of windows where there are none.

I don't belong here. Never have.

He snaps, "Don't forget where your allegiances lie, boy. The battalion has failed. Baelen Rath turned the soldiers back despite the threat to his land. You will go. *Now*. You will finish that gargoyle once and for all—"

"I will not."

His puffy cheeks grow red with rage, but he reins it in, taking deep breaths. "Remember what the gargoyles did to your mother. You have a chance for revenge. Go, Grayson, fight the gargoyle. Do it for her!"

Anger has always been my friend, but right now it's my enemy. I'm in danger of killing this old man if he mentions my mother one more time. "*No!*"

I storm toward him and he backpedals as fast as his legs can

241

carry him, hitting the wall behind him. "Why not, Grayson?" He spits. "Surely, you don't pity the gargoyles?"

I fist my hands, closing the gap between us. "You forget what I am."

I'm seconds away from hurting him when Gideon bursts into the room. "Grayson! Step back!"

He hurries toward me, palms out, the only Glory elf who isn't afraid to stand near me. His expression is full of concern. "What's wrong, son?"

I step away from Elwyn, turning my disappointment on Gideon. "Was this your plan?"

"What plan?"

"To kill the gargoyle on Rath land."

He sighs. "We need it eradicated, Grayson. I know it's a terrible business, but that gargoyle has threatened the local villagers, stealing their food. The House of Mercy has so little to live on as it is…"

Gideon has told me many times about how the Rath fortune has been squandered. Now, he says, "Baelen Rath is a warrior, a soldier first. He's a good commander, but he has no skill for the day to day task of caring for his people."

I take his speech with a grain of salt. I've crept out to see Rath land for myself. The House of Mercy is one of the happiest minor Houses I've come across. They're treated with respect and allowed to make decisions that other minor Houses are forbidden from making. They love Baelen Rath with such genuine feeling that it takes my breath away. For all accounts, he trusts them without question. The only thing that causes them grief is the possibility that they might lose him.

Still, I know Gideon worries about the order of things. The balance of power between the major and minor Houses hangs on a thread. If that balance were broken, our land would descend into war. The gargoyles are the tinder that could light the spark.

"Gideon," I say. "I know you think this is the right course of action, but I can't do this."

He casts me a worried glance before he exhales slowly. "I know it will be difficult for you, but you are our last hope. We've tried everything else. You've carried out other tasks for us. May I ask what troubles you about this one?"

"I draw the line at infanticide."

"Ah, the babies," he murmurs. "They will perish without their parent."

If I could close the gap and touch him, I would grip his shoulder and ask him why. *Why does he think I could do this?* It's true that I'm a killer. I *have* killed. Too easily. Not even fair fights. There's no such thing as a fair fight against me. But I will never harm a child.

He nods his head, raising his eyes to mine. "I'm sorry we asked you to do this. You are right to refuse."

I step back with a nod to Gideon and a glare at Elwyn. I might not always agree with Gideon, may not always see things the way he does, but he's all I've got. He's the only voice of reason among the Elven Commanders. Elwyn, Pedr, and Osian are always bullheaded. I've never met Teilo, but the others don't speak highly of him.

Elwyn snarls at Gideon before he storms out. "That gargoyle will be the death of us."

Gideon lets him go, his expression remaining serious. "The final fight in the Protocols is approaching. I need you to remain alert and ready. The Storm Princess is unpredictable. We don't know what her motives are, and I fear..." He rubs his forehead and lets out a sigh. "I fear for the future."

I stand as close to him as I dare. He's the only father I've ever known.

I was born hated, feared, and shunned. I could have been killed as a child. Gideon stood between me and death.

"I have your back," I say. "I won't let anything happen to you."

35

———————

MARBELLA

The morning after the wedding, there aren't any messages from the Elven Command about the final battle. I was expecting something already, but Elise makes reassuring noises at me. "They're bound to send word soon. In the meantime, we need to talk."

She drops us into a sound bubble at the breakfast table. She hasn't touched her food and neither have I. Anxiety builds inside me with every passing minute that we don't hear from the Elven Command.

I try to not look at the door for the thousandth time expecting a messenger to arrive. "What have you found out?"

Her forehead crinkles. "There have only been five deaths in the past month. It's actually the least in terms of averages. Of those, four were elderly and their passing was expected. The fifth was a woman who had been ill for some time; also expected."

"None of the deaths were untimely?"

"I'm afraid not."

"Well…" I grasp at straws. "What about disappearances? Deaths that might have been covered up?"

"I looked into those as well. There was one disappearance, but the woman was found safe and well."

"Then we're no closer to figuring out the origins of the curse." This is not the news that I need right now. I glance at the door

244

again. I need to know about the final battle, and I need to know who's behind the curse. By the look of things, I'm not going to get either of those pieces of information any time soon.

Elise prods at her plate. She's been slowly turning her eggs into mush as we talked. "The only thing I can think is... no... it's not likely..."

"What Elise? I'll take any information right now, even something unlikely."

She drops her fork. It clatters against the side of her plate, but she's too distracted to notice. "What if the death hasn't happened yet?"

"But... the final battle's supposed to be tomorrow. That would mean someone has to die today." I'm going to leap out of my skin now. If what she said is true, then any minute now the curse could be completed, and I have no way of knowing who is going to die so I can stop it from happening. "The victim could be anyone."

She chews her lip, momentarily silent, her gaze flashing around the room. My Storm Command is used to Elise and I having private conversations—and they'd expect us to have even more in the lead up to the fight—so they don't pay us any attention. "Actually... I can't be sure but... I think such a terrible curse would have to stem from a connection with the Storm."

"Then... someone in my Storm Command?" I stare at her, fear rising fast inside me. "Jordan? You?"

Her voice drops to a whisper. "I don't know, but we need to remain vigilant. I'll send word to Jordan to keep a look out for anything suspicious and to be on her guard. I think you need a Storm Commander sooner rather than later. Did you have anyone in mind?"

"Reisha Gild," I say without hesitation.

"Okay then, I'll make that happen. In the meantime, stay calm. This is all just maybes. We don't know any of this for certain." She's back to her usual calm self and I'm incredibly grateful for the way she balances me out. My emotions are going haywire. The threat of losing Baelen is already tearing me apart. I can't lose anyone else close to me. Even "maybe" is too much possibility for me.

I spend the rest of the morning secretly watching over my Storm Command instead of them watching over me, keeping track of where each of them is at all times and whether any of them seem ill or different in any way. By the time we finish lunch, there's still no word from the Elven Command and I'm way past edgy. The battle is supposed to be tomorrow. They didn't take this long with any of the other trials.

When it's time to subdue the Storm, I take off at a run to the Storm Vault, my ladies shooting concerned glances at me, but keeping pace around me. Even Elise rushes beside me, not speaking. She knows I can't make conversation right now.

Even without touching steel, I'm crackling at the edges. The lightning inside me is being fed by my anxiety, and it needs to find a way out or I'm going to explode.

When we get there, I race through the inner rooms, but I pause before entering the Vault itself. "Elise, I need you to go back out there. You need to watch over my Storm Command and make sure nothing happens to them."

"But, Princess… you need me here."

"I'm fine. I'm not in danger, but they are. I need to know they're safe and you're the only one who knows there's a threat. Go. Please."

It's clear she doesn't want to leave me. Her entire life is built around protecting me, especially while I'm in the Storm Vault— she's never left me while I've been subduing the Storm.

"Please," I say. "I know you don't want to leave me, but I need you to protect them."

She bows her head. "Yes, Princess. I'll make sure nothing happens."

"Okay, I'll be out as soon as I can." I wait for her to leave and then I step into the Vault without another moment's hesitation.

Lightning leaps straight to me, giant threads of it twisting around my torso and legs, hugging me close. There's a hurricane brewing in the center of the room, the biggest I've ever seen. I step into it willingly and, for the first time ever, the wind can't pick me up. The whirlwind blows from the right so I push back at it, both hands up at my side. It beats at me, whipping my hair across my face, but I don't lose my footing, leaning into the wind. In fact, the pressure against my body soothes my frayed nerves as I push through, one step after the other, grateful for the release of energy inside me. Finally, I make it to the quiet center, but I pause before stepping out of the hurricane, not ready to face the silence yet.

Thunder booms overhead so loud it makes my bones rattle. I turn my back to the pounding wind and tilt my palms up, allowing lightning to trickle upward, wispy like smoke. The wind quickly rips it away. I listen carefully to the Storm, hoping to hear it speak. It had tried so hard to say something to me yesterday.

Today, it remains silent.

I step into the quiet center, tilt my head back, and close my eyes, waiting for the rain. It doesn't come. Too soon, the hurricane begins to die down, the wind faltering like the rain did yesterday.

"What's wrong, Storm?"

I wait, listening, but it doesn't answer. Maybe there's nothing wrong. Maybe I'm just getting stronger and that means I'm subduing it faster. I'm about to turn away from the quiet center and head through the dying hurricane again, when light suddenly streaks from above me, striking through the hurricane's core. At the same time, the hurricane springs back into life.

A scream fills the air around me. It's the Storm's voice, shrieking like a wailing banshee: *He's here! He's here and I can speak!*

I crouch into a defensive position, ready for anything. "Who's here?"

A wind tunnel splits off from the hurricane, the hissing sound forming the Storm's voice. *It's not me! It's not my fault!*

That's what it said yesterday, but I have no idea what it's talking about. I shout back at it, "Stop speaking to me in riddles!"

The wind tunnel whips around me, spinning from one spot to another. Somehow it avoids colliding with me while it says: *I couldn't see it before. I can only escape the Storm Vault when there's a natural storm outside and even then, only a very small part of me can escape. I finally saw it two nights ago, but I couldn't tell you. I tried so hard, but I can only speak when he's here.*

A fine mist of rain washes across my face and drips to the floor where I think my jaw is located right about now. That's the most the Storm has ever spoken to me. Much of what it said doesn't make sense, but the fact that it's talking to me in sentences is, well, unexpected would be an understatement.

"There was a rain shower two nights ago," I say, latching onto the only thing the Storm said that makes sense.

A tiny part of me escaped and I saw her. She's dying! She's being killed for the curse.

Fear shoots through me like electricity, a thousand bolts of it. "Who's dying? Tell me!"

The reverent one. The one before you. But it's not my fault. I didn't do it! I wanted to warn you, but I couldn't speak...

Mai Reverie is dying!

I'm already running, pulling as much of the Storm's power to me as I race to the side of the Vault and yank open the door. I'll need as much of the Storm as I can hold to fight whatever's hurting Mai.

I'm so afraid for her that I make it halfway through the waiting room before I see Baelen. I never expected to see him in this place again.

I skid to a halt, my boots squeaking. I'm braced and uncertain. He's locked in a fighting stance, eyes closed, and there's no mistaking the ribbons of heartstone light curling around his shoulders and neck. He shudders, shaking open his eyes, finally focusing on me.

Suddenly something the Storm said becomes frighteningly clear: *I can only speak when he's here.*

The first time the Storm ever spoke to me to warn me about the curse was the very first time Baelen Rath stepped into the Vault's waiting room to offer me his heartstone. That was also the first time it spoke to Mai. The second time it spoke to me, he was waiting for me before the first trial. He wasn't here yesterday when it couldn't speak, but now he is.

He shakes his head again, releasing his body from its locked stance, clears his throat, and focuses on a point past my shoulder. "I'm only here as part of my duties as Commander of the Elven Army. I need to report—"

"There's no time." Whatever he was going to tell me, it's nothing compared to the urgency of saving my friend. I can't even allow myself a small moment of wishing he'd come to see me for any reason other than duty. "I have to go. I'm sorry, Baelen."

His focus zooms in on me for the split second it takes me to reach the next door.

"Wait, Marbella."

The shock of hearing him say my name freezes me long enough for him to stride to my side. Concern radiates from him in waves so strong that they hit me square in the heart. "What's wrong? Tell me."

For a moment I pretend that the last few days never happened, that I'm not going to fight him tomorrow. This is Baelen whom I trust with my life. "Mai Reverie's in danger. I can't explain. I have to go to her right away."

He doesn't ask any more questions, but instead shoves the door open for me, keeping it wide while I run through. Instead of remaining behind, he sticks to my heels. "I'm coming with you."

There's no time to argue. I shoot through the final door, shouting for my Storm Command to stand clear. The last thing I want is to hurt one of them while I'm full of Storm.

"Reisha, take me to Mai Reverie's quarters. She's in danger!"

Reisha wastes no time with questions, trusting my commands, ordering two women ahead to clear the way while the others form a running wall around me. Baelen stays behind our group, but a quick glance tells me he's close behind us.

"Where's Elise?" I ask Reisha as we dash through the corridors out into the courtyard.

She hesitates long enough that I know I won't like her answer. "The Elven Command called her to see them. It's about the final battle."

My heart can't possibly plummet any further than it has already. "Did they say anything else?"

She shakes her head. "I'm sorry, Princess. I don't know anything else."

I grind out my words in between sucking in breaths to continue running. "I need her." She's a healer as well as a spellcaster and if Mai's hurt then I'm going to need one. "Reisha, we need a healer. We need… Sahara Splendor!"

I don't have to say anything else. Reisha calls out a command to the elf on her left and the woman breaks off, sprinting away. I can only hope that Sahara hasn't left the city yet to return to her home.

That would be unlikely since Jordan and Sebastian are staying here for now.

We race across the square and through the outer wall of Mai's quarters, finding her advisor Rebecca lying on her side beside a sculpted stone ornament in the garden. Reisha checks her. "Unconscious," she says.

My Storm Command splits open to reveal that Mai's door is closed and her windows shuttered. One side of my Command opens even further to allow Baelen to step through to me. It surprises me that he doesn't have to say anything to them. They just let him through without question and I'm not sure how I feel about that. But I told them to protect him, so a very large part of me is grateful that they're treating him with trust.

I return my focus to Mai's closed door. An open door means no threat, but a closed one like this...

Reisha strides up to it, gasping when her hand connects with the wooden paneling. She snatches her hand back. "There's something very dangerous inside this place."

Baelen morphs into a Rath as Reisha speaks. He doesn't draw the dagger he carries at his hip, but he doesn't have to in order to appear fearsome. My lips almost lift at the memory of him standing outside the Storm Vault, standing way too close to me that first day, telling me that danger doesn't bother him. I've never seen fear in his eyes except once, and that wasn't fear for himself.

I must be channeling his fearlessness, because I say, "Then we're going in to find out what it is." I signal to the rest of the Storm Command. "I'm going to open this door. Once I'm inside, follow me. Carefully."

Reisha nods and copies the signal to those around her. The door is sealed with magic. It feels like the Storm's power but there's something off about it, something not quite right.

I press my palms flat against the door, feeling the same electrical zap that Reisha must have felt. It bites my hand, unpleasant and unnatural, resembling lightning, but I can tell the difference. It's not genuine lightning. The Storm was right—this isn't the Storm's doing.

I trickle real lightning through my fingers, allowing it to flow through the wood. Scorch marks spark on the door's surface as the force flowing from me targets the lock and hinges keeping the door closed and upright.

The hinges warp, buckling under the force I'm exerting. With a blast of wind from my hands, the fastenings at either side of the door give way with a *snap*. My ladies don't even flinch. They're already focused on what's inside the room, taking up fighting stances, weapons drawn and ready.

The door falls downward like a closing drawbridge, falling on its face toward the inside. But halfway down it stops, floating. An outward force pushes back at us from inside the room. I harness the wind again and push against the door, harder, and it falls down like a welcome mat at my feet.

My now clear view into the room shows me that it's been destroyed. The table has been thrown onto its side, books strewn across the floor, pages ripped out. Scrolls float in the air, suspended. The golden curtains are drawn and billow against the windows as if the room is full of wind. But like the force keeping the door closed, this isn't from the Storm.

"The Storm," Reisha whispers while Baelen hangs back, allowing me to make my assessment.

"No. This is not the Storm." Anyone else would think that the Storm was at work here, that a hurricane has ripped through Mai's quarters, but I can tell the difference. "This is spellcasting."

There's a groan from what looks like a pile of material in the center of the room. The material shifts, rising a little to reveal that it's Mai herself bent forward over her knees.

She rests in a puddle of silk. Her slender arms flop at her sides, her shoulders slumped. Her hair is draped across her face. Like her Reverie kin, her hair is as red as blood, but there's something very wrong with it. Something very wrong with her skin, too. Liquid drips from the top of her scalp all the way to the floor, pooling in the silken crevices of her dress. She's raining from the inside. Except that it's tainted with blood.

I race to her, sliding in the debris, skidding to a stop before I touch her or come into contact with the strange liquid pooling around her knees. I don't care about the rules right now, but I'm worried that I could hurt her. Just because she was a Storm

Princess once doesn't mean she can handle the Storm's power, especially not now when something's clearly hurting her.

"Mai, talk to me! Are you okay?"

I can't see her face behind all her hair. Her voice is forced. "You need to leave."

My forehead creases as I try to detect her intentions from her body language. My instincts are screaming that she's a threat to me, but I won't leave her, not when she needs my help. "Mai, tell me what happened."

"Make them leave!"

I glance back to my Storm Command as they file into the room, forming a shield at my back. They're staring at something to Mai's left and I risk a quick glance in that direction. Partially hidden behind Mai, a body floats inches above the floor. It's Mai's husband, Darian. His hair hangs across his face and I can't tell if he's alive or dead.

I don't want to tell my ladies to leave because I don't want to be alone with Mai. Not because I'm afraid, but because the Storm is an angry force inside me and it's rising to meet the dark spell that's been cast over Mai. Lightning crackles under the surface of my skin and I don't know whether that's a good thing or bad. A fight between these two forces can only lead to destruction.

I hesitate too long.

Mai screams. "Leave!"

A gust of unnatural wind shrieks through my ladies. It plucks them into the air, one by one, as they struggle and shout. They fight it, but each one of them is cast from the room, hands outstretched, some sliding through the door while others fly into the gardens beyond. At the same time, the wind tries to suck me upward too, plucking at my clothing and my legs, demanding that I leave.

I've fought worse than this. As I harness the lightning inside me, it reveals itself in snaking tendrils around my arms and legs. I won't release it, but I need its power to keep me anchored against the dark force around me. I shake my head. "You can't move me, Mai. I'm staying. I'm going to help you."

A glow reaches me from the corner of my eye and Baelen steps up beside me. His heartstone light burns fierce against his skin, a deep burn around his torso and arms. The false wind swirls around him in the same way it rips at me, but he doesn't budge. It can't move him either. As he draws near to me, the light around him blends with mine, red and blue swirling into a brilliant purple glow between us.

I feel… stronger. Calmer. Like half of me was missing and it's returned to me. I meet Baelen's eyes, not really sure what's happening, just knowing that together we can beat the evil in this room.

As if admitting defeat, the wind lifts the door behind us, slamming it closed again.

We're alone with Mai, and it's as if some of the spell lifts from her. She doesn't lift her head and blood-rain continues to trickle from her fingers, drip-dripping onto her dress. But she slumps forward, and when she speaks her voice sounds more like her own.

"The Storm attacked us. Here in my home. It killed Darian. My husband… is dead." She tries to twist in his direction, but unlike me, the wind is pushing her around, beating at her and forcing her forward. No wonder she was bent double when we got here.

My heart crumbles. Darian was Mai's whole world. "Mai, please let me help you."

"Darian tried to help me, but the Storm killed him as soon as he touched me."

I push against the wind, inch by inch, edging closer until I'm right in front of her. "The Storm didn't do this to you. This isn't the Storm. It's some kind of spell. Targeting you and Darius so it looks like the Storm."

Up close, I search for her eyes beneath her hair. They're wide, her pupils dilated. Tears track down her cheeks. She's in pain but she's trying to hide it.

"A spell?" she whispers. "A spell killed my husband and now it's killing me. Get out, Marbella. Please. While you still can."

"I'm not leaving you, Mai." I turn to Baelen. "The spell has targeted Mai and Darius. It won't hurt us."

I hope.

I continue. "If I could carry her myself, I would."

"I'll do it," he says. "We have to get her out of here so Sahara can help her."

Without hesitation, he ploughs through the opposing force,

pushing against the wind so that it takes on the appearance of water streaming around his calves and thighs. It plasters his clothes against his body, clinging to his muscular chest. He slides one arm around Mai's back, ready to scoop her up into his arms, but at the last moment, he flinches.

For a moment, I fear he's hurt, but then he says, "Marbella, she's…" His agonized eyes meet mine. "Her body, it's frozen. She hasn't moved because she *can't*."

He lifts her easily and she doesn't fight him. As he pulls her up against his chest, her head tips back and her hair drips across his arms, but her arms are stiff and wooden and her legs are bent at the knees without moving, set at an awkward angle.

"Her limbs are already dead. The spell's killing her from the toes up."

"Baelen…"

He meets my eyes across her head. "I'll get her out."

He pushes against the wind, leaning into it and I follow in the slipstream, conserving my energy for the task of getting the door open. When he reaches it, I slip around him, discovering that it's much harder to pull open than it was to push from the outside. I grip the handle and pull as hard as I can but even without any hinges, the suction inside the room is too strong.

"Stand clear, I'm going to use the Storm." I plant both palms against the paneling and let loose thunder and lightning at the same time.

The door explodes outward, shards flying, but before they can fly into my waiting Storm Command, time slows. Splinters halt in the air. At the same time, the spell behind me makes a harsh sucking sound, trying to pull us back into the room like water rushing down a drain.

"Baelen! Get down!" It's the only warning I can give him before letting loose a blast of lightning into the center of the room. The explosion pushes us outward into the garden and at the same time the spell finally cracks, splintering, its force dissolving. Every floating object inside the room thuds to the floor. Darian falls too, and the smallest hope I had that he was still alive fades as his lifeless eyes stare back at me.

Baelen is already hurrying down the path. Time speeds up as

Sahara Splendor rushes toward us with Elise at her side, both of them hauling medical pouches.

"Hurry!" I shout. "Mai's dying!"

Baelen sets her down on a grassy patch at the side of the front path and retreats to allow Sahara full access. The elegant woman wastes no time assessing Mai. "Paralysis. Fever… Necrosis!" She gasps. "Her body's shutting down. Is this the Storm?"

"No!" Rage spirals through me. "Someone wanted it to look that way. It's a spell. A cursed spell made to look like the Storm."

I pace back and forth as Sahara and Elise work over Mai. They examine Mai together, speaking quietly, conferring with each other. As they deliberate, Elise forms a bubble between her palms. Rainbow light swirls inside it. She tips her hands at an angle toward Sahara so she can inspect the spell. As soon as Sahara nods, Elise rolls her hands gently across the bubble's surface, pressing inward, until the bubble shrinks to the size of a marble and then smaller. Finally, it forms a droplet that rolls off her finger across Mai's lips. I hold my breath, hoping…

Sahara shakes her head, desperation flooding her posture. "That should have worked."

Elise's response is to conjure another spell, and then another, while Sahara injects medicines into Mai's limbs. But the more they shake their heads and run their hands over their eyes—the more spells and medicines they try—the more I know they're going to fail. My hands begin to shake and my heart thuds so hard in my chest it feels like it's going to crash out of me.

"They can't save her." Sobs rise in waves, riding through my body, crippling me. Sahara is the most talented healer and Elise is the most talented spellcaster, but even they can't stop the spell that is killing Mai limb by limb. I clutch my stomach, doubling over as the pain of losing my friend intensifies. "I'm going to lose her."

Baelen's quiet voice anchors me, helping me rise without touching me. "Marbella, I'm here. Tell me what you need."

What do I need? Nobody ever asked me what I need. I need Mai to live. I need the trials to be over. I need to know that the Storm won't be unleashed. I need to not fight Baelen tomorrow.

I need… Baelen.

The light I'd seen caressing his skin is gone now. He casts a shadow over me, blocking out the mid-afternoon sunlight, but it feels like shelter. A place to hide from the terrified glances my ladies give me, the anguish taking the form of tears streaming down Elise's cheeks, the way Sahara slumps her head into her hands and begins stroking Mai's hair, trying to make her comfortable.

Would it be so terrible if I told Baelen what I feel?

"I need… a gladiolus flower."

He nods, flooding me with sunlight as he stoops to pick one for me, choosing one with delicate white flowers. I turn my palm up to receive it and he drops it into my waiting hand.

Elise interrupts our conversation, visibly shaking in front of us. She's expended a lot of energy conjuring spells and Baelen steps up fast, allowing her to lean on him before she topples over.

Elise says, "Mai's asking for you."

My feet are lead as I cross the distance—five short steps that feel like a thousand. I drop to my knees beside Mai. Her breathing is short and sharp, her lungs constricted, her knees bent, and her hands folded across her chest.

She whispers, "I'm glad it wasn't the Storm. She's… angry and hurt. I don't know why she became the Storm, but she's not… truly evil."

"I will find out who did this to you, Mai. I will find them and I will—"

"No… Don't live for revenge."

"Justice," I say. "Not revenge." I place the gladiolus flower against her cheek. My voice cracks, my throat tightening, and I have to swallow back my tears. "For honor. And strength. For everything you've done for me."

She smiles as she inhales. "Thank you for bringing me… to my garden…" Her gaze flicks upward and I sense Baelen's presence beside me. "You must… find… each other."

The spell reaches her throat, stopping her breathing as it spreads across her face. She closes her eyes, peaceful, as her last breath exhales between her lips.

"Mai…" I drop my head to her chest, knowing that I can't hurt her now.

I wrap my arms around her and let my tears fall, dripping across her porcelain features as I place my cheek to hers.

The place is suddenly swarming with spellcasters—the Elven Command's lackeys—trying to see Mai, clicking their tongues at the destruction of her quarters, but Baelen stands watch over me while I mourn, refusing to let anyone near me, keeping them all at bay until I rise and stumble into the safe circle of my Storm Command.

I've lost Mai.

The curse is set.

36

———

MARBELLA

"We don't have to talk about it." Elise stares through the windows of the living area. The distant forest is a crisp green wash of spreading foliage, but it's a blur to both of us.

"I need to know how she died."

She sighs. "Multiple spells were layered over each other. Sahara and I couldn't counter all of them in time. I suspect they were planted while Mai was at the healing center after that day you learned about the curse."

"The day the rain spoke to her?"

"Yes, but the spells were cleverly masked. This kind of sorcery was outlawed after the old king died. The very first Elven Command—the one that was appointed after the king's death—was supposed to have destroyed all the books containing this kind of dark magic."

She leans forward, eyes cast down, hands folded in her lap. "Marbella… I can't help but think about the fact that it happened while you were subduing the Storm."

"It wasn't the Storm." I've been repeating that statement for hours since Mai's death, so many times that I'm exhausted by the repetition. First to the Elven Command's spellcasters, then to the healers. I'm just waiting to say it to the Elven Command themselves and for them to look at me with the same disbelief as everyone else:

258

as far as they're concerned, if it looks like the Storm, then it must be the Storm.

"What I mean is that whoever killed Mai chose to do it at the time of day when everyone knows you're busy in the Vault. At the same time, I was called to see the Elven Command, so I wasn't around either."

"What are you saying?"

"I'm saying that you're right: someone designed this to look like an act of the Storm. Because the Storm is the perfect scapegoat." She meets my eyes. "You're the only one who can tell the difference and you weren't supposed to be there."

"But I was there, because the real Storm warned me."

Elise crushes her hands together and for the first time, she's angry. "Why didn't it warn you sooner?"

"It couldn't. It told me that a small part of it can only escape the Vault when there's a natural storm outside. It didn't see Mai's death in time." I don't tell her the part about why it couldn't speak—I still can't process the idea that Baelen's presence in the Vault somehow gives the Storm a voice.

Elise shakes the angry tension out of her hands, smoothing down her dress. "Ah. So that's it. Elves have speculated for a very long time about how the Storm is able to choose another princess when it's locked inside the Vault."

I sigh. "It certainly explains why princesses are chosen during a naturally occurring storm. Like I was." I don't have the energy to think about that right now, so I change the subject. "When is her funeral?"

"The Elven Command has declared that tomorrow is a day of mourning. She'll be buried at sunrise as requested by her House. The House of Reverie will wear black until the end of this coming winter. And the House of Gild will wear black armbands in honor of Darian."

"And… the final battle? What did the Command say when they called for you?"

"They wanted to explain that the delay was because they were considering the consequences."

"That's it? That's all they said?"

"That's all." She rubs her eyes. "They were all there in the room with me. If they had something to do with Mai's death, well… I'm their alibi."

"Tell me, Elise, were any of the Elven Commanders spellcasters in their early years?"

Elise thinks for a moment. "Not Elwyn Elder, Pedr Bounty, or Osian Valor. They were all military." She purses her lips in thought. "Teilo Splendor is the only one I'm certain used to spellcast. But I heard a rumor once that Gideon Glory also dabbled in the magical arts."

"Then those are the two I need to watch out for."

She nods, but I pause, remembering something else. "Commander Rath came to the Vault today. He wanted to give me a report… Do you know what it was about?"

She shakes her head and rises from her seat as the sun sinks into the horizon beyond us. "You need food and rest, Princess. The funeral is at dawn. Come now, eat and sleep. The final battle is delayed for now. Tomorrow is for Mai."

The House of Reverie stands tall, their blood-red hair a striking contrast against their black clothing, but even more of a contrast are the swaths of flowers they carry, wreaths of all kinds ready to place on Mai's coffin. A second coffin waits beside hers and black armbands flutter against the biceps of every present member of the House of Gild, a line of elves carrying ribbons containing threads of gold and silver to lie across his casket.

We'd walked in the darkness along the river and through the forest to a vast clearing where the four kings and queens who reigned since we left the surface of the Earth are buried under stone monuments. The first two Storm Princesses are already buried here too, and one day… this is where I will rest.

Each King and Queen, and Storm Princess, rests under a different gravestone specific to them. Five children from the House of Reverie carry the sapling that will be planted on Mai's grave to grow into a sturdy ash tree.

We wait in silence around the coffins. There are no words at an elven funeral because nothing can be said to lessen the loss we feel, and no words can be enough to express the value of the life that has been lost. Instead, we wait for the sun to rise.

My ladies surround me. I decided to wear my armor in honor of the promise I made to Mai—to fight for myself. As the sun appears over the horizon, shedding soft light across the clearing, the coffin bearers lower the caskets into the ground and each elf approaches to pay homage to the ones we've lost. The Elven Command goes first, filing between the coffins one by one. I'm close enough to study them as they pass, but trying to see beneath the façade they paste over themselves is almost impossible. Only Teilo Splendor is visibly upset, his shoulders sunken lower than usual, his cloak dragging on the ground.

Elwyn Elder pauses long enough to glare at me, cloaked in his pride. Always too proud. Pedr Bounty casts an imposing figure beside him, shoulders squared. Gideon Glory and Osian Valor are completely unreadable, blank, although when I look up again, I find Gideon's stare on me too.

For a moment, it feels like he reached out and touched me, like a stroke inside my mind. I jolt, not certain what I just felt. Mind-reading is outlawed. He wouldn't try, would he? I'm not about to take any chances. I harness the Storm's power, using the wind to cool my body and blow out the crawling feeling inside my mind. The breeze ruffles his robes and he scowls before moving on.

I'm entitled to go next, but I'd sent a message to Mai and Darian's families yesterday that I wanted them to proceed before me. Elise told me that her mother had broken down and cried when she heard. I never understood why Princesses were so harshly separated from their families, never allowed to see them. But I was beginning to realize that it was to keep us isolated and without allies. As Mai told me, it was to make sure I never became too powerful.

Now, her family and Darian's lay their wreaths and ribbons quietly, heads bowed, tears flowing freely as they say their final goodbyes. I follow them, placing one hand on each coffin, close enough to touch at the same time. I close my eyes, remembering only good things—the flowers Mai cultivated for me, the love between her and her husband, and the way she'd encouraged me to believe in myself.

I leave the clearing with my ladies silently following behind me. Along the way, I pull my gloves back on, protecting myself, and Reisha hands me my weapons' belts. I pause to secure them around my thigh and when I resume walking, I discover that I'm not alone.

Baelen walks silently beside me, not speaking. Once again, my ladies allow him to form part of my protective circle. We stay that way for a long time as we follow the path through the forest and along the river. Eventually, my brother and Jasper join us, walking in silence behind my circle.

The city is quiet. Nobody will work today. All activities will be kept to a minimum out of respect for Mai. Despite everything that Baelen and I will face after this, it feels right to walk with him as the sun lifts into the sky. I lift my eyes with it, imagining the phoenix sailing across the sun's face, reminding me that our sun was once the glowing Elven Queen.

When we reach the city gates and Baelen breaks off to head back to the military compound, I don't think. On instinct, I reach for his hand and catch his fingers in mine.

My breath hitches as I realize what I've done, surprise at my own actions shooting through me.

He freezes, missing a stunned beat, until he sees that I'm wearing gloves. Even then, he doesn't relax. I can't feel anything through the thick leather, only the shape of his palm dwarfing mine, my fingers wrapped around his for a brief moment before I allow his hand to slip away, afraid now of what I've done.

His hand flexes, fingers curling around mine, and for a moment I think he's not going to let me go after all, but the haunted look in his eyes… shreds my heart into tiny pieces…

"Forgive me," I whisper, chomping my lower lip and stepping away, urging my ladies as quickly as possible through the gates, needing to put distance between myself and Baelen Rath.

He steps clear, allowing us to pass, his powerful silhouette stark against the sunlight, his cloak billowing as the breeze picks up. Macsen and Jasper join him, three mighty warriors watching me retreat.

THE ELVEN COMMAND FINALLY CALLS FOR US THE FOLLOWING morning. There are no chairs and partitions in the War Room this time, no game of wit waiting to trick me. Only the five Elven Commanders waiting in a neat line in front of the War Table. And Baelen. He stands alone on the far side of the room, without his advisor this time.

Elwyn Elder steps forward first. Teilo remains on the far right, while the other three occupy the middle. Gideon Glory doesn't take his eyes off me, his stare burning into me with the same intensity as the day before. But this time, I'm cloaked in the Storm. He might try, but he can't touch me or my mind.

Elwyn says, "We've called you both here this morning because we have two problems we need to address."

He produces a scroll, his palm obscuring the House emblem marking the side of it, and pulls out the parchment inside of it. "We've received these documents evidencing the last will and testament of Baelen of the House of Rath, duly signed and witnessed."

My gaze shoots to Baelen. His last will and testament? But… no…

Elwyn clears his throat, a pointed gesture of disapproval, but Baelen doesn't react—not even to my anxious stare. *What are you doing, Baelen?*

The merest hint of challenge enters Baelen's posture as he returns the Elven Commanders' critical stares without budging. Given that Elwyn said we were here to discuss problems, I'm guessing the Elven Command doesn't like what Baelen's done. I already know I don't.

"As the last of his line, Commander Rath has the right to decide the fate of Rath land. According to these documents…" Elwyn's fist grips the paper so hard it crushes beneath his fingers. "If Commander Rath is incapacitated, the House of Mercy will become guardian of all Rath land and possessions. They will not only be responsible for its upkeep but entitled to all its profits."

Well, no wonder the Elven Command is angry. They would have expected the substantial profits from Rath land to be divided equally between the Major Houses. In fact, judging from Baelen's stony glare, I'm guessing they demanded it from him. *Was that what he'd come to tell me the other day?*

Elwyn continues, "However, it is the ownership of the land that concerns us the most. We understand that, in the case of Commander Rath's death, ownership of Rath land and all Rath possessions will pass to… Marbella Mercy."

I didn't hear that right. I can't have. I blurt before I think, "But elves from my House can't own land."

"Actually, you can." Teilo Splendor edges forward, earning a sharp look from Elwyn for interrupting. "According to law, because you are a princess, you are entitled to hold property regardless of the House you came from."

This is news to me. News the other men clearly never wanted me to know. Mai had warned me that I wasn't being told everything. For the first time, a glimmer of a smile touches Baelen's lips, but it's a sad smile. His gaze slips to mine then slides away again.

Does he really believe he'll die in this battle? That I could ever hurt him?

The fact that he's written his will fills me with fear. I swallow a gasp as I remember that he gave me his mother's dress. And I suddenly wonder: what if it wasn't a gift? What if it was his way of saying goodbye?

Whatever was left of my heart cracks in two. Sound slips my lips before I can stop it. "No."

Teilo clears his throat before I have the chance to launch into a full-scale outburst. "Which brings us to the second and more pressing problem. We understand that you don't intend to yield, Princess, and at the same time, the Commander appears determined to fall on his sword. We believe we have a solution."

I grit my teeth so hard, the crack sounds across the room. "What is it?"

"An additional trial." His eyes gleam, the Splendor sheen making them appear like a cat's eyes in the dark. "It won't replace the final fight, but it could prevent it."

"How?"

"We propose that you each undertake an additional battle. But not against each other. If you each win your fight, well, then there will be a final fight after all. But if one of you loses this additional battle, the other will be declared the winner."

"Who are we fighting?" Baelen speaks for the first time since we entered the room and all I can hear is distrust. I'm certain it's reflected in my own face.

Elwyn Elder nudges up beside Teilo. He takes center stage and smiles for the first time. I really don't like that expression on his face.

He announces, "You will each fight a gargoyle."

37

MARBELLA

"You didn't!" Baelen advances on Elwyn so fast the Elven Commander backpedals into the table.

Teilo jumps out of the way, much faster than I expected for the older elf. Baelen stops inches from Elwyn, staring him down, and it strikes me just how massive Baelen is, making the older man appear small and fragile.

Elwyn hisses, "Calm yourself, Commander. We didn't trap any of them."

Baelen takes a step back but doesn't give Elwyn or the others any space. He speaks slowly and deliberately. He doesn't take his eyes off the other men, but it doesn't take me long to realize that he's speaking to me, not them.

"On the night of Jordan and Sebastian's wedding, the Elven Command saw fit to send a battalion of soldiers to Scepter Peak without my knowledge. Their mission was to capture and kill the gargoyles nesting there. Luckily, your brother found out about it, and we tracked down the battalion that night. I ordered the troops to return home before there was any bloodshed." Baelen half turns to me. "I came to report this to you before Mai Reverie was murdered."

Elwyn sucks in a breath sharp enough to echo in the deathly quiet room. He hasn't reacted to any of Baelen's accusations, until this. Baelen called it *murder*... not death. Elwyn's eyes narrow, his mouth pinches, and his cheeks flame. He definitely doesn't like what Baelen just said.

Baelen doesn't move from his imposing stance. "Now they say they want us to fight gargoyles."

Teilo Splendor is the only one of the older men who looks troubled. He takes glances at the others, looking genuinely thrown and confused as he lets go of the table where he'd caught his balance. I consider him for a moment as he straightens his robes. He was also at the wedding for his grandson when the battalion was sent into the mountains. Is it possible that he didn't know? It's the first sign I've ever seen of a split in the Elven Command.

"The gargoyles won't be real," Teilo says. "They will be simulations."

I focus on him while Baelen keeps Elwyn pinned. "Explain, please."

"We will use the Heartstone Chest in the same way that we used it for the game of wit—to create a scenario unique to each of you. The only danger is… we will not see what you see. You will fight the gargoyle in your mind. To us, you will both simply be sitting in the Chairs of Truth, but to you it will be very real. It will be like… a dream from which you can't escape until either you or the gargoyle is dead."

I consider him again. "So, once we start, we can't stop."

"Correct. For that reason, we will allow you to have as many Storm Commanders around you as you need to protect your body while your mind is elsewhere." He turns to the rest of the Elven Command and for the first time, there's a thread of anger in his voice. "Your body must remain sacred until you choose to share your power."

Well, he's certainly the first Elven Commander to think so.

"If you can't see what we see, how will you know if we've won or lost?"

Teilo says, "If you lose, the Heartstone Chest will open and reject your heartstone."

"I don't like it." Baelen takes a step back, this time toward me, placing himself protectively between me and the Elven Command. "Princess, you'll be too exposed."

He's right. It's bound to be a trick. If my mind is elsewhere, if I don't know what's going on around me, I'll be vulnerable to attack. Not only that, but I won't be able to see Baelen to know if he's okay. A shudder racks my spine at what could happen while I'm in the simulation.

"You might not like it," Elwyn spits, "but our decision is made. You will present yourselves to the arena tomorrow morning at the ninth hour. You are dismissed."

I spin to Elise. She's wide-eyed, waiting closer to the door. Her lips part but I shake my head. Whatever she wants to say will have to wait. Baelen is also tight-lipped as he leaves the War Room with me.

Halfway down the corridor, right before I reach the safety of my Storm Command, he murmurs, "Be careful. Don't trust them."

I spin to him, keeping my voice low, not much above a whisper. "Wait, Baelen, please."

He stops in the middle of the corridor, but his expression is hooded, tense. I need him to hear what I have to say, but I'm not sure if he will. Maybe he'll hear the words, but he won't really hear *me*. There's a thick invisible wall between us and it gets wider with every passing second. Maybe he thinks he's making this easier for me by pushing me away, but he isn't. As fast as he's building a barrier between us, the more clarity I have about the choice I need to make.

The Elven Command might try to delay the inevitable, but neither one of us will lose against the gargoyle tomorrow. And when that happens, we will fight each other. I have Sahara's potions —my last source of hope. But if they don't work, if I can't pull it off in a way that convinces the Elven Command that I've won, then either Baelen or I will die. And the truth is… I made my decision a long time ago about which one of us I would protect.

I meet his guarded eyes, knowing that if I don't speak now, I'll regret it. He believes that I would rather kill him than yield and I need him to know that's not true. I need him to know that will never be true.

My throat constricts and I can barely get sound out. "Seven years ago, I made a choice."

He doesn't react and I'm not sure if he heard me, but I keep going. "I wouldn't let you die then. I won't let you die now. When I have to choose between you or me, I'll always choose you."

A crease mars his forehead and confusion swirls in his eyes, but it only takes a beat for him to process what I said. I know that he really heard me when he sucks in a sharp breath. He flinches and it's like I punched him in the heart.

I can't tell him about the curse, I can't tell him why, but I just told him that it's my life or his.

"Marbella… please tell me what's going on. You have to let me help you."

"I can't." I shrug through the tears threatening to spill from my eyes. I'm tired of keeping them in. I've been keeping all my emotions bottled up for days now, trying to stay calm, trying to stay focused, trying to believe that we'll both live. But it's too much and the weight of it all is dragging me beneath the surface.

I'm suddenly swimming in tears and trying to blink them away. Baelen takes a step toward me, clearly without thinking, because his arms flex upward as if on instinct and he reaches out to gather me into his arms.

Before he can get anywhere near me, the blunted end of a spear lands on his chest, halting him.

"Remember where you are." The quiet warning comes from Reisha, now my fiercest protector. She shoots a warning glance at the far end of the corridor just as the Elven Command appears there, exiting the War Room.

At the same time, Elise circles me, wedging herself between me and Baelen, ushering me away. "Quickly, Princess. We need to leave. *Now*. Commander Rath, I suggest you do the same."

38

BAELEN

The War Room's walls are like a coffin around me. The Elven Commanders stand at the head of the room—my gravediggers. They've wanted me dead from the moment I came back. Now they're telling us they want us to fight gargoyles in a dream as a way to avoid my death. Everyone in this room knows that the last thing they want is to keep me alive.

"I don't like it." I step back toward Marbella, standing close enough to her that I can inhale the scent of her hair. Lavender. Just like her old cloak. I allow myself to be distracted for a moment, to indulge one last time in being near her. Then I close off the last tiny spark of life inside me and focus on my only remaining goal: keeping her alive.

In the last two days I've done everything I needed to do: relocated the gargoyle to safety, wrote my will, and said goodbye to Marbella's family. When I die, my lands will go to Marbella as they should. As they would if my promise to her all those years ago had come true.

Now, my only purpose is to be the warrior I was trained to be, the protector I vowed to be. "Princess, you'll be too exposed."

Elwyn's cheeks grow red. "You might not like it, but our decision is made. You are dismissed."

I remain behind Marbella as she turns to leave, making myself a barrier between her and the Elven Command. Elise waits for her at

270

the door. She starts to speak but Marbella gives her a quick shake of her head. I remain quiet, quickly catching up to Marbella to walk beside her.

I can't leave her without warning her, hoping she'll hear me when I murmur, "Be careful. Don't trust them."

I expect her to nod and continue on her way, but she spins to me, her voice barely louder than a whisper. "Wait, Baelen, please."

She could ask me to do anything and I would. I just… can't allow myself to feel anything when I do it.

I stop in the middle of the corridor with her, my heartbeat calm and in control while her hair floats around her shoulders and her eyes beg me… for something… I don't know what. She's only an arm's length away but there may as well be a chasm between us.

She knows I won't lose against the gargoyle. She won't, either. This dream fight only delays the inevitable.

She meets my eyes, her own full of fire, as if she's feeling for both of us now. She swallows hard, forcing sound out of her throat. "Seven years ago, I made a choice."

Lightning blasts in my memory, tearing through my hearing, but it's the desperate push of her hands, both palms against my chest, and her scream of fear that I remember most. It was the final look in her eyes that told me she wouldn't let me die. That she would dare death to claim her if it meant saving me.

"I wouldn't let you die then," she says. "I won't let you die now. When I have to choose between you or me, I'll choose you."

My forehead creases, her words reaching me from far away.

When I have to choose… I'll choose you.

She saved my life seven years go. Now she's telling me she will again.

I suck in a breath. My heart kicks, a punching beat that slams my chest. Feeling rushes into my numb hands and feet, my cold arms and legs, my frozen heart. But… if she's telling me she'll choose my life over hers…

I won't let that happen.

Damn this space between us. I need to hold her. I need her to talk to me. Something's wrong and I have no idea what it is or how to fix it.

"Marbella… please tell me what's going on. You have to let me help you."

"I can't." She takes a breath and it hitches. She swallows, blinking rapidly. Tears fill her eyes, spilling down her cheeks as she fights them. I'm stricken to see her cry. It breaks my heart all over again.

I'm moving before I know it, my arms rising to gather her into my chest.

I step right into the blunted end of a spear.

Reisha's urgent hiss brings me back to myself. She casts a warning glance in the direction of the Elven Command as they emerge from the War Room. "Remember where you are!"

Elise immediately steps between Marbella and me, forcing me farther away from her.

"Quickly, Princess. We need to leave. *Now*." She speaks rapidly, giving me a pointed stare. "Commander Rath, I suggest you do the same."

I have no choice but to take the nearest exit, but as I leave the corridor behind, I inhale a breath of fresh air.

Losing Marbella from my heart was like being half alive.

My mission hasn't changed. My goal is to protect her at all costs. But now I'll do it with a whole heart.

39

MARBELLA

I have no choice but to hurry down the corridor, glancing back to see Baelen take a side exit. I gasp for breath as we emerge from the building into fresh air. Elise immediately drops us into a sound bubble.

"That was dangerous," she says.

"I know, I'm sorry. But he would have stopped before he touched me—"

"No, I don't mean Commander Rath. I mean the Elven Command."

I eye her with alarm. "What is it, Elise?"

She speaks in a rush. "I felt it, Princess. I couldn't see it before, but I'm certain now. One of those men is using sorcery."

My heart skips a beat. "Which one?"

"I thought it would be Teilo Splendor, since he studied spellcasting, but it's not him. In fact, he's the only one who isn't tainted. I'm not sure if that's because he's chosen not to be part of it or because he really doesn't know about it, but surely he has to suspect—"

"Elise! Who is it?"

"Gideon Glory." She shudders, her whole body quaking, causing her to miss a step. Her breathing increases and her hands shake. "The darkness around him was more terrible than anything I've ever seen. Now that he's killed Mai and set the curse, the shadow around his body is… I can't even…"

"And the others? You said they're tainted? Is he controlling them?"

"There weren't any binding spells around them. They aren't wielding sorcery but they're willing participants."

I sway, trying not to lose my footing. "They murdered Mai. They want my power."

"Which means they still think they can get it somehow."

"How, Elise? If Baelen dies, then I win, and they can't touch me. If I yield and Baelen wins, then *he'll* get my power, not them."

"They must have a way they think they can get it." Her concerned eyes meet mine. "I'm worried, Princess. Something isn't right about this next trial. I'm worried they've concocted this plan so they have the chance to attack you."

I exhale, dread and fear mixing in my stomach. "I'm going to need every one of my ladies in that arena tomorrow morning. Please, can you get a message to Jordan and Sahara? I'll need them there too."

"Of course."

"I'll wear my armor. And gloves. Please find out if there's any Elyria web left, and I'll sew the gloves onto the armor. I'll sew myself into a freaking facemask if I have to. I'm not going to make it easy for them."

Elise is thoughtful beside me. She stops shaking as we consider my defense, seeming to find courage in knowing we have a plan. "I will spellcast a shield around you. If any of them try to get near you, I'll cloak their bodies, so they won't be able to make contact."

I don't ask her if spellcasting can defeat the dark sorcery Gideon Glory is wielding. I suspect that it can't, but saying so won't help. All we can do is try.

40

MARBELLA

The roar inside the arena the next morning hits me as soon as I enter it. The Elven Command is expecting me to take my place inside the side room and appear at their beck and call, but I don't plan on doing anything they want today.

My ladies stand proud and strong in four rows of five, marching behind me. Unlike the first battle I fought in this arena, the onlookers part to let us in, heeding Elise's cry. It doesn't hurt that she spellcasts her voice to project loudly over the top of them. Every one of my twenty ladies is present and armed with daggers, swords, bows and arrows, their body armor and headpieces gleaming, and the skin around their eyes painted red for war.

The entire lower level of the arena is empty except for the dais at the other end where the Elven Command already waits—always standing higher than us. In contrast, the upper levels are packed with elves. I'm not sure what everyone expects to see—Baelen and I will be sitting in chairs, unmoving the whole time.

Speaking of which, the chairs are two lonely pieces of furniture, both wooden and basic in shape and size. They face each other, positioned closer than I'd expected, maybe only ten feet apart. Otherwise, there's a wide, empty space all around them lit brightly from skylights in the ceiling above.

Elise leans toward me. She has to lift her voice above the din. "The dais isn't shielded, but the upper levels are."

275

That means there's no barrier between me and the Elven Command.

Reisha steps up on my other side so she and Elise flank me as we enter the arena. "Commander Rath is a few minutes behind us."

I hold my wooden headpiece in my gloved hands. My ladies made me a veil out of canvas threads to cover my face. It's not unbreakable like the Elyria web, but once I tie it to the neckline of my armor it will pose a challenge for anyone who wants to get past it. "Okay, let's go."

As I approach the chairs, Elwyn Elder steps forward, indicating the chair to my left. I consider taking the one to the right, just to annoy him, but the chair will be connected to the Heartstone Chest, so I have to sit in the correct one. The chest itself rests on the dais. It's closed. It will only open if one of us loses our fight.

I take my place beside my chair, but don't sit down yet, as my Storm Command fans out around me, leaving a gap so I have a clear view of Baelen's seat. The watching crowd finally quiets, an expectant hush falling over them.

Baelen appears at the entrance and I'm relieved to see he isn't alone. Far from it actually. Jasper leads a small band of soldiers, a handful of men that Baelen must trust with his life. The only one missing is Macsen—he sent me word this morning that he was returning to Rath land at Baelen's request. What he didn't say was loud and clear: he needs to make sure that Baelen's home, and all the elves who live there including our parents, remain safe.

Sebastian, Jordan, and Sahara arrive last. When they're close enough, Jordan breaks off to join my group, while Sebastian joins Baelen's, and Sahara takes up neutral territory between the two of us. Elise steps away then to examine the chairs and the chest. I know I should pay attention to what she's doing, but it's hard to focus on anything other than Baelen.

Like me, he's wearing full body armor, but to my surprise, it's not military issue like the armor he wore in the last battle. This armor has no chinks, no weaknesses. This armor belongs to the House of Rath.

Every inch of him is covered in finely sculpted metal plates overlapping and linking together to protect his torso, legs, arms, and neck, the metallic curves decorated in red and black markings, making him appear even larger and more formidable than he already is. At the same time, joints in the armor allow him to move with speed and grace as he takes position in front of his chair, facing me.

A shiver speeds down my spine as he focuses on me across the distance with surprising intensity, not guarded any more. I jolt as I realize that the barrier he'd been building between us is gone and now there's… *damn*… where did that look in his eyes come from? He inhales and it's like his body sucks me forward, calling to me across the distance while a slow smile spreads across his face. I can almost hear his voice inside my mind. *Come here, Marbella.*

I have to clamp down on my legs before they obey.

Just in time, Jasper cuts into my line of sight, dropping to a knee before he gets too close. He lands halfway between Baelen and me, too far away for me to hear anything he might want to say. I crane forward, concerned, but Elise heads straight for him, speaking to him for a moment before he heads back to Baelen's group.

She crosses the distance. "Sorry about that, Princess, but I needed a way to let Commander Rath know what I'm about to tell you: there's a thread of pure deep magic between the Heartstone Chest and each chair. The thread connected to his chair belongs to his heartstone and the one connected to your chair belongs to your heartstone. So far everything is untainted and correct."

She shuffles. "Also, Jasper wanted me to give you a message."

I bite my lip, glancing across the distance to Jasper and Baelen as they stand silently waiting. "Yes?"

"He said that he doesn't know what's going on, but he understands now that you don't have a choice."

"Thank you, Elise." I close my eyes for a brief moment, unwilling to reveal how much that means to me. Jasper and I had kept each other alive on Scepter Peak. He'd proven he was truly loyal to Baelen and he'd proven to me that he was completely trustworthy: a rare combination. But when he'd heard me say I wouldn't yield, he'd looked at me as if I was a monster. Now, he is willing to trust me again.

A single drummer beats a rhythm at the side of the dais. There are no spellcasters present with the Elven Command. Gideon Glory must believe that he doesn't need them. In the bright morning light, his skin shimmers a faint golden color, even more luminescent than usual.

He steps forward and raises his hands for attention, his robes sliding down his arms, revealing the faint golden tattoos that members of his House like to wear. On the inner skin of each arm is a single wing, each now framing his face.

"Our people! Welcome to the penultimate battle to determine the fate of the champions. Each champion will submit to a simulation in which they will fight a gargoyle." He pauses as the crowd ignites once more, giving them time to settle down. "We will know the outcome when the Heartstone Chest opens to reject the stone of the champion who loses his… or her… fight."

He stops playing to the crowd for a moment, giving me and Baelen his attention. "Once you sit, the simulation will begin." His gaze lingers on me for a moment, and I brace for any attempt to touch me with sorcery.

"Please," he says with a smile, gesturing to each chair in a fluid motion. "Be seated."

I turn away from him, giving him no more of my attention. Reisha leans into me with Jordan and Elise close behind her. "We vow to you, Princess," Reisha says, "We will protect you. And we haven't forgotten our promise. We will protect Commander Rath as well."

"Thank you, my beautiful friends."

I inhale. Exhale. I turn to face Baelen, wishing I could throw my thoughts across the distance. *Be safe.*

He gives me an acknowledging nod as he pulls his headpiece on. I do the same, tying the veil firmly to the neckline of my armor. The chair is a yawning gap in my vision, but it's the Elven Command's sorcery that worries me more.

I time my movements to Baelen's, following him into the chair in unison, jolting as the deep magic takes hold. It's like a magnet running through every bone in my body, compelling me to stay seated.

I thought I'd have to close my eyes, but my vision changes immediately. Baelen's silhouette blurs and blends into an encroaching darkness. I try to hold on to his image within my sight, but I can't fight the deep black like nighttime falling across everything. It surrounds me, consuming the arena, my ladies, the soldiers, the Elven Command, even the chair itself and, last of all, Baelen is completely gone and there's nothing but dark.

I float inside it, regulating my breathing, mentally preparing myself. The darkness lifts and I'm ready for anything.

Except this.

My armor's gone. The wind whips at my hair. I stand across from the edge of a cliff. Baelen sits at the edge with his back to me. From across his shoulder I see a pen and paper in his hands. But he's not the *now* Baelen, he's the *then* Baelen.

I glance at myself, at my hands and my dress—the old, patched one I used to wear. My faded lavender cloak drapes around my shoulders to ward against the cold. My hair is tied in a long braid and my blue ribbon—the only pretty thing I own—flutters against my side.

I'm eighteen.

This is the day I became the Storm Princess.

I don't want to be here! The shriek inside my mind fades as I keep walking. My older self's thoughts are consumed and destroyed as I merge completely with my younger self, until I forget why I'm here... I don't know what I was afraid of just now... because Baelen's here and nothing can hurt me.

I pass the shallow cave on my left that's deep enough to provide shelter. The cliff's edge opposite the cave is a sheer drop down thousands of feet. I'm breathing heavily. I've just climbed up the side of the mountain along the secret path that Baelen showed me years before—a place to escape in the Rath mountains that nobody else knows how to get to.

In the beginning, we had an unspoken code to only come up here when the other wasn't here. It was a place to be alone. He told me about it after he found me crying behind one of the outer buildings when we were eleven, my knees and hands bleeding after one of the visiting Valor boys knocked me over.

But now... It's his place and mine.

I step across the stones, navigating the rocky ground, and slide down next to him, my legs dangling over the edge. The drop is dizzying but it's funny how I don't feel fear when I'm near him.

I don't try to see what he's drawing. He's never offered to show me, and I respect that it's the one thing he keeps for himself. Most days he spends all day training and studying. Basically, learning how to kill gargoyles in every way possible.

He turns as if he's connected to me. "My father's sending me to military training tomorrow. This is the last time I can draw anything other than maps and military routes."

I take a moment to let my breathing even out. Then I nudge him, trying to coax out a smile. "Maybe they'll let you do military portraits. You know, the ones where all the elves take majestic positions and pretend they're in the middle of glorious battle."

He shrugs.

I raise my eyebrows. Not even a small smile?

But he's right. There's no use trying to make light of it. He's going away and at some point, I'm going to have to admit how that makes me feel. I exhale my emptiness into the breeze, closing my eyes, shutting out the view of the vast Rath lands far beneath us. "I don't want you to go, Baelen."

He closes the book, but I'm surprised when he hands it to me. "You may as well see it before my father burns it."

"Really? I can look at this?" I let it rest in my lap for a moment, running my hands over the cover. It's made of fine leather, black, a gift from his mother before she died. His father wouldn't really burn it. At least, I don't think so.

I turn it on its side, and it falls open to a picture of an elven girl. She's standing at the edge of this same cliff, her hair flowing and cloak billowing out, just like me a moment ago.

Baelen smiles for the first time, his eyes lighting up. "You thought I never saw you walk up the mountain."

I wish I could leap into the picture and stay in that moment. That heartbeat when I reach the top of the path, knowing that he's waiting for me. That moment right before he turns around—when he knows I'm here even before I speak.

I hand the book back to him. "It's beautiful, Baelen. But only because you drew it." I'm suddenly overtaken by an impulse I can't explain. "Don't give your father the chance to burn it. Set it free."

I jump to my feet, breaking into a wild grin. I take a last look at the picture as I gesture to the wide expanse. "Rip my picture out and let me fly with the wind."

In response, Baelen tucks the book under his arm. He rises to his full height, reminding me that he is a Rath. He towers over me and I'm suddenly very small but never afraid. His gaze runs over my face, from my forehead, to my cheeks, to my lips…

He's never looked at me this way before. Or… maybe he has but I was too afraid to see it. I hover, the smile draining from my face, uncertainty flooding me. "Baelen?"

He reaches for the ribbon at the end of my braid. The bow has come undone and for a moment I think he's going to tie it back up, except that he slides it loose instead, pulling the ribbon free. Without a word, he folds it in half and places it inside the book, a pale blue curl next to the picture of me, tucked away safely.

The book meets the ground slowly, deliberately. His chest rises and falls. His breathing is so even that he could be resting. He looks as purposeful as he does when he draws.

He closes the gap between us with a single powerful stride, stopping inches away from me. His chest is closer to mine than he's ever been before. His forefinger grazes my cheek, the lightest touch, tucking my hair behind my ear, following the curve of my neck down to my braid, loosening it from the bottom up until my hair cascades across my shoulders, flowing freely.

Shivers run up and down my spine as his hand remains tangled in my hair, his fingers light against the back of my neck, his thumb stroking the curve between my neck and shoulder. He tilts his head down to mine but doesn't move any closer.

"May I have your permission?"

I lift my lips to his, overwhelmed by the searching question in his eyes. As his hands run through my hair from my neck to my lower back, I sway into him, closing the gap.

"Yes."

When his lips touch mine, his hesitation is gone. He lifts me up to meet him, our bodies molding together. His kiss is soft and gentle at first. A light press of his lips against mine. He follows the shape of my lips from the corner to the curve at the top, gentle brushes sending tingles all the way down to my toes.

He tastes like a warm breeze, and I respond by fitting my lips to his, curve in curve, our mouths moving against each other until I gasp for breath. I tilt my head back and he follows the line of my cheeks and chin, planting kisses against my throat and up across my earlobe.

He lifts me, still kissing me, and carries me to the flat rocks at the side of the cave. When he sets me down on the lowest one, I find myself at eye height with him for the first time. His are serious, determined.

"I'll be gone for three years. I know it's a long time. But when I get back, I'll be able to make my own choices. I know it's a lot to ask but… will you wait for me?"

I pull back, but not too far, just far enough to run my hands across his cheeks and kiss the path my fingers follow.

I whisper, "I would wait a lifetime for you."

My lips graze against the fine stubble along his jaw, his cheekbones, finding his temple and the soft skin next to his ear…

He twitches and I stop, my fingertip resting lightly on his earlobe. "Baelen Rath, are you ticklish?"

He shivers against me. "Give me mercy, no. Not ticklish."

I gasp as he presses me close again, his lips crashing against mine. A burn grows inside me. It swirls across my lower back and through my stomach. His hands flatten against my spine, sliding beneath the back of my cloak. I rest my own hands across his shoulders only to find myself sliding my fingers behind his neck, drawing him closer still.

The sky rumbles above us, but I barely hear it. The first drop of rain lands on my cheek but Baelen kisses it away. Another one lands on my eyelashes, and he kisses that too. The wind tugs on my cloak, finally forcing me to look up.

Baelen keeps me close, his voice a rumble in my ear. "The storm's coming on fast. We won't make it down the mountain in time."

I answer, "It would be dangerous to try. We can stay here. It will blow over fast."

He takes my hand as I step down from the rock and leads me inside the cave, but he stops at the entrance. His book is still outside.

He looks back as his hand slides out of mine, holding on right to the end before letting go. He takes swift steps to retrieve the book, returning just before the clouds break and the rain falls.

I stop at one side of the cave as he backs up to the other. We've been caught in the rain once before. He stayed on his side of the cave, and I stayed on mine.

As clouds cover the afternoon sun and the sky darkens outside, so does the space around me. A match flares and Baelen lights the lamp he keeps at the back of the hollow, leaving the light on a rock to cast a soft glow around us.

He leans on his side of the cave, watching the rain fall outside, fat drops hitting the ground and running along the slight slope to the edge of the cliff beyond. I watch them too, knowing that we could stay like this for hours and when the rain stops, he will make sure I make it safely down the slippery rocks to the bottom of the mountain. He will see me home and then he'll be gone for three years. And I will wait for him without question.

I know he won't ask. I know it's my choice. I am the daughter of a servant in his father's house. He will never use his position or power to persuade me. He will never take advantage.

He won't speak. He'll wait in silence. He won't say the words.

So I say them to him. "I want to be yours."

He focuses on me, but remains where he is, and I realize that what I said could be interpreted in different ways. I leave my side of the cave as thunder rumbles outside. Closer to him, I reach for his hand, lifting it and placing it against my waist. His fingers flex around the small of my back and splay across my hip.

I reach up on my tiptoes to plant a kiss on his bottom lip and watch the question grow on his face. Then I untie the sash that keeps my cloak around my shoulders and let it drop to the ground.

"You have my permission."

41

MARBELLA

I hold my breath as Baelen leans toward me, his free hand cupping my cheek. He pauses before his lips meet mine, hesitating, his contemplation telling me he's thinking it through. I sway into him, closing the gap, and place a light kiss on his lips.

Then I wait, inches away from him, turning my face to the side as his slow breaths tickle my earlobe. He brushes my cheek with his but doesn't kiss me back. Not yet. I have to respect that. Just because I've decided what I want, doesn't mean he's decided it's the right thing for him—or for us.

Although… if he keeps nuzzling my ear like that, I'm not sure how I'll ever let him go. My hands find his sides and all the muscles of his stomach as I try to anchor myself somewhere, anywhere, while his lips taste the soft skin at the side of my neck. Shiver after shiver rocks my body because he's not only kissing my neck, but one of his hands rises from my hips and the other strokes down my side so that both end up resting against my rib cage, where his thumbs stroke the soft underside of my breasts through the thin material of my dress and underclothes.

I whimper as he glides his hands up my sides and over my shoulders, sliding through my hair and down my back, pulling me against him so my thighs are pressed against his. I tip my head

284

back, seeking his eyes, needing to know what he's thinking. Every part of me is alive, but he still hasn't kissed me back.

I tell myself I can accept his decision, whatever it is. There's no getting past his self-control or his perception. I've seen women from all the Major Houses throw themselves at him, sometimes in sickeningly obvious ways. He's the sole heir to the Rath fortune and that makes him a target. But I never saw him take a woman to his bedroom. From dinner parties and social events where I was required to serve guests, he'd turn away from women who would bed him in an instant, only to catch my eye across the room and gift me a smile, because he knew that *I* knew that he saw through all of them.

He's smiling at me now, a satisfied curve to his lips as he studies my own parted lips. I'm not sure what he's so pleased about. I can't help it if my breathing is coming short and fast or that my hands are pressed against the hard planes of his back. I definitely can't help that my lower half presses closer to his with every passing millisecond.

His voice is a low growl as he says, "I have wanted to kiss you for a very long time. But you are... so reserved, so cautious, so much my best friend... I couldn't tell if you felt the same way. But now..."

His smile transforms into intense need as his mouth swoops down to mine, finally fitting to the curve of my lips, grazing them and nudging them apart to taste my mouth with his tongue. Sensation rushes through me, deep inside, and I tug at the base of his shirt, urging him away from the rock face so I can slip my hands beneath it and explore the muscular shape of his back. In response, he pulls me upward, crushing me against him. I slide back to the ground as he sets me down to pull his shirt over his head. I've seen his naked chest before, but I was never allowed to look at him like I can now.

Instead of coming straight back to me, he stoops to lay my cloak across the hard ground near the cave's side, folding his shirt over the top of it. He kneels on the cloak, still clothed from the waist down, reaching out his hand for me. I hesitate. I know he doesn't expect me to, but I take hold of the bottom of my dress and pull it up and over my head. I'm still wearing underwear—underpants and a support top, but both are thin with age and don't cover much.

He inhales a quick breath and for a moment the need on his face almost takes over. He closes his eyes, the muscle at the side of his jaw clenching then finally relaxing, and when he opens his eyes, he's in control again.

He draws me down to the cloaked ground, both of us kneeling, his shirt cushioning my knees. He plants a kiss on my lips and follows the line of my chin and neck, down to the soft skin at the top of my breasts, caressing across the top of them, passing by to my stomach. As his lips descend, his hands follow them, kissing and touching every part of me from my back to my breasts to my inner thighs, brushing over my center, until I'm burning all over. The rain outside pounds down so loudly now that it smothers the sound of my moans as he takes his time touching me.

I kiss him back, discovering the hard muscles of his shoulders, neck, hips, and dragging at the top of his pants. I suddenly can't stand to be wearing this much clothing. The barrier between us is unbearable. I slide out of his arms, making him growl, "Come back." But I have to stand up to remove my underwear.

I slip out of my underpants and top, determined to return to him right away but I pause as his gaze takes all of me in, traveling from my toes to the tops of my legs, to my waist, breasts, lips, and finally landing on my eyes. I always imagined I'd feel incredibly awkward standing naked in front of a man for the first time, but I don't with Baelen. Not one bit.

A smile breaks across his face as he holds out his hand for me. His smile is reflected on my own face before I drop to meet him on the ground and he starts all over again, kissing and touching me until I don't know where I am anymore. At some point, he removes his own clothing, and it's my turn to growl at him to come back to me.

Finally, he pulls me with him as he sits with his back against the side of the cave, positioning me so that my legs straddle him. He kisses me once more, but draws back, his hands resting lightly on my hips, allowing me to choose what happens next.

I'm aware of my own body and his, but I'm not entirely sure how we're supposed to fit together. I'm suddenly frozen, my face flaming. I'm afraid that I'll do it all wrong and... *damn*... the way he's slowly dragging his hands up and down my sides and across my breasts isn't helping me at all.

He leans forward and kisses the hot burn on each of my cheeks, causing our lower halves to press against each other in ways that make me dizzy. He lifts me with ease, up and over him, and whispers, "Let's figure this out together."

A little bit of maneuvering later and whatever awkwardness I felt disappears as sensation floods me. I grip his shoulders as I lower myself completely over him, the intensity overwhelming me. I try to breathe, but only succeed in gasping. I'd thought my senses were already in overdrive, but I couldn't have been more wrong.

He plants his hands on my hips, holding me, unmoving, letting me catch up with my own body, letting me choose when to move, allowing me to control our actions. Without thinking about it, I rise, watching pleasure wash across his face, but he still doesn't move, letting me stay in control.

I slide back as my body adjusts to his, movement gets easier, and the ache inside me takes over. I forget about the storm outside, the dark, and the flickering lamp light. I don't hear the thunder or see the streaks of lightning across the far horizon. My whole world is here and now, moving with Baelen, building our own storm together inside this cave. A storm that consumes all of me, growing into an uncontrollable force.

I tilt my head back and grip his shoulders as I plunge against him and the world expands and contracts around me, a thousand stars burning and exploding. Crying out, I shatter against him, my cries lost in the boom of thunder outside the cave.

I descend into his arms, shivering, aftershocks rippling through me. I curl over him as he strokes my back, but as I kiss him, I realize... he hasn't lost control.

He wraps his arms around me, his voice low, insistent, barely contained. "Tell me you'll let me be yours, Marbella Mercy. Because I don't want this just once. I want this again. Not just today."

My lips part. "I'm yours, Baelen."

He places one arm behind my back, the other across my backside and lifts us up to a standing position, still connected, then he lowers me very gently onto my back on top of my cloak, using all of his strength to keep us together. I stretch out beneath him as he begins to move. Giving him everything I have, I wrap my legs around him, drowning in the intensity I see in his eyes.

Sensation builds inside me again, increasing with every stroke, but I push it away. I want to focus on him the same way he focused on me. I want him to know what it feels like to crash and shatter, to fall into my arms like I fell into his.

I touch every part of him that I can reach, reveling in the way his muscles tense and relax as he moves, loving the way he responds to my touch. Without realizing, my breathing speeds up, matching time with his as my body moves of its own accord. I can no longer hold back the intensity building within me, and it only takes one more plunge for ecstasy to ripple through me, coursing through every nerve ending.

My wide eyes meet his as everything pauses. Then he crashes into me and there's no way I can control my response. My hands push against the ground as I arch back, my body wanting to be as close to his as it can be. Where thousands of stars had shattered before, now the depth of my whole foundation shifts.

We fall into each other and tiny pieces of me float away into a place where nothing can ever tear us apart.

42

—————

MARBELLA

I come back to the sound of my name being whispered over and over as Baelen gathers me into his arms, both of us trembling hard. He pulls me in to his side, leaning back against the cave wall while I curl my legs over his. We stay that way for a long time as the roar of thunder and rain continues outside.

I find myself falling asleep against his chest. Until there's a strange rumbling in it, making my head and shoulders wobble. I look up at him in alarm only to find that he's chuckling. It's such a rare sight that I sit up and take it in for a moment, not caring that I'm still completely naked.

He grins and lifts an eyebrow at me. "Twice?"

I match his smile and slide against him, curling my upper leg around his and my arm across his broad chest. "Twice," I say with a satisfied growl. "I'll expect that again, thank you."

In three years' time.

My smile fades and I bury my head against his neck before he sees my happiness slip away. Being separated from him now feels like I'm about to lose an arm or a leg. I want to fight it with everything I have, stop time, stop tomorrow from coming.

As the rain eases outside, he lifts me up, kissing my forehead and cheeks. Without a word, he picks up our clothing, shaking my dress off before handing it to me. I pull everything back on reluctantly, including my cloak, wanting to stretch out the minutes.

When we're finally dressed again, I wait at the cave's entrance, watching the final drips of rain, while Baelen retrieves his drawing book.

The sky is still dark. Evening has arrived. There's an occasional streak of lightning in the distance, but the worst of the storm is over. When Baelen reaches me, he opens his book and pulls out my ribbon, running it through his fingers. He slides my hair forward, pulling the ribbon around it and tying it at the side of my neck.

I stop him, entwining my fingers with his. "I want you to have it."

"But if you go home without it…"

"My mother will have to believe that I lost it."

He hesitates. "When I get back, I'll bring you a thousand ribbons. All blue."

I kiss the side of his suddenly serious mouth. "I don't need a thousand ribbons." I slide the material free from my hair and wrap his hand around it. I ache to touch his skin again, search the contours of his face and neck and other parts of him that I'm suddenly not afraid to think about.

He kisses me back, the ribbon peeking from his fist. Dark clouds swirl outside as I press into him. My hair splays out and my purple coat floats upward. I suddenly feel… weightless.

At the same time, he whispers to me. "Marbella Mercy, I give you my heart."

The wind tugs at me, insistent, my coat billowing. "Baelen Rath, I—"

As I speak, the ribbon slips from his fingers, picked up by the wind, stolen right out of his fingertips. He snatches at it, but it whips upward. He steps out onto the ledge, chasing the twirling blue material. But I don't care about that scrap of cloth. All I care about is what I need to tell him: *I love you.*

I chase after him, closing the distance between us, tugging him to a stop and hurtling into him. He throws his arms around me, and we let the ribbon swirl upward, high above us, disappearing into the darkness.

"I don't need it," I say. "I only need you."

He leans down to kiss me but as I tilt my head back to accept his kiss…

A flash of light streaks high in the sky.

It's so bright that it tears the sound out of my throat. It's so sudden I don't have time to feel fear. It's so savage it drives the air from my lungs. It crackles and shrieks, drowning every other sound, filling me with a silent scream.

There's only reflex. Only instinct. Only knowing that Baelen's body protects me—that the lightning will strike him, kill him, and I can't let that happen. I push him away from me, away from the strike, with all the strength I have. He registers shock and surprise that I shoved him, but at the same time he follows my line of sight upward, sees the lightning, sees me standing beneath it…

As electricity lights up the space around us it illuminates his eyes and all the fear in them, fear I've never seen him show before. Fear for me, the same as I feel for him. He swivels and tries to get back to me, tries to cover me with his body again even though I don't want him to. But his feet collide with the rocky outcrop.

He slips on the wet rocks…

Falls…

Smashes his head against the overhanging stone…

"Bae—!" The lightning hits me, catching me in its burning rays. Pain rips through me, tearing me apart, sharp as a thousand daggers, hot as burning pokers, tearing me limb from limb. A scream shrieks through me, slashing through my throat.

But it's not a single lightning strike. Not a strike that hits and disappears. The lightning doesn't stop. It streams around me on and on. Pain shreds me into tiny pieces and it has no end. I can't move. I can't escape. All I can do is scream. Why hasn't it stopped? Why haven't I died?

The light is so bright it could be daylight on the cliff. Baelen lies on his side so close yet so far away from me, blood dripping from the deep slash down the side of his face and jaw. He doesn't move, and I can't tell if he's breathing. I can't tell if he's alive.

He has to be alive! I need get to him. I have to help him. I need to know if he's okay. I reach forward, pulling and struggling, trying to escape the storm's grip, pushing through the pain, stretching out my arms and hands as far as I can. I scream with effort trying to break the lightning's grasp.

But as soon as I lift my arms, I sense it—the lightning pulsing through me, *traveling* through me. My eyes widen with horror and realization, but it's too late. The lightning shrieks through me, through my hands, through my fingers, into the air, across the distance and… into Baelen.

The impact picks him up, a curl of electricity seizing him and lifting him high into the air. His unconscious body glows red and orange, suspended, connected to me through the shining thread. He shudders, jolts, burns. I'm hurting him even more than I already did by pushing him. I'm killing him.

It's my fault.

It's all my fault.

I scream with the effort to pull my hands back, trying to curl my fingers into fists and drag my elbows to my sides, forcing my hands down. Finally, finally, I break the connection. The lightning releases him and he plummets to the ground, half on the rocks, half on the ledge, smoke rising from his body in white curls. *What have I done?*

"Let me go!" I scream into the sky—at the lightning shining back and forth between me and the boiling clouds. It's a brilliant, white thread connecting me to the expanse above and it widens before my eyes, expanding beyond me, beyond the cliff's edge, ten feet wide and growing.

At the same time, the clouds explode into thunder and fireworks made of multi-colored lightning. The thunder crashes. The wind howls. A sheet of rain washes Baelen's blood from the stone.

No, this can't be… Sobs tear out of me, racking my body. I fight it with everything I have, kicking and struggling, not wanting it to be true.

This is not an ordinary storm. This is… *the* Storm.

I am the new Storm Princess.

43

MARBELLA

I leave my younger body.

I fall onto the wet stone on my hands and knees, clambering around to see my younger self suspended above the cliff's edge. I try to remember why I'm here, what's going on, but my thoughts are jumbled with the pain I just felt—the pain that's still reflected on my younger face.

The lightning had pinned me above the cliff for two hours, completely helpless. For two hours I watched Baelen bleed out in front of me, not knowing if he was alive or dead. The Storm didn't let me go until the spellcasters finally arrived and cast a spell around me similar to the one in the Vault. I'd pounded my fists against the spell cage, screaming at them to help Baelen first—*Help him, not me!* When they didn't listen to me, I threw myself against the cage so hard that I blacked out. I woke up in the Storm Vault. Baelen was gone, the nightmares began, and my future with him was over from that moment.

Now, I try to block out the sound of my younger voice screaming Baelen's name over and over again. I cross my hands over my chest and try to breathe.

This isn't real.

My thoughts finally come together to remind me: I'm in a simulation. True, it's a simulation based on a very real memory, but it isn't really happening again. It's all a vision inside my mind.

Teilo Splendor had told us that the Heartstone Chest would create a simulation that was unique to each of us. For some reason, the chest brought me back to this time, to this night. Everything up to this point was a memory. A memory that I'd tried very hard to forget, but it was an event in my life that had burned at the back of my mind for seven years. The Heartstone Chest must have brought me back for a reason, but… why?

I wipe my eyes, trying to clear my vision. My younger voice mutes and the lightning fades. The image of my other self is still there, but it's gauzy and transparent. Without the lightning, the cliff's edge becomes dark and shadowy.

On the other hand, Baelen's younger self remains perfectly clear, unmoving, stretched out over the rocks, right where he'd fallen and damaged his spine.

I clamber to my feet and race to his side. I couldn't help him seven years ago, but maybe I can now. Maybe the Heartstone Chest is giving me a chance. Nothing I do in the simulation will change the real past. It won't change what really happened, but maybe I can change how helpless I'd felt watching him die right before my eyes.

I reach for my cloak to bandage his wound, only to find that I'm wearing my armor again. Before I can look around for something else to help him, a shadow drops over me.

It's fleeting but undeniable. I spin, crouching, and study the darkness overhead, waiting for the shadow to appear again. It flies over me once more, and this time I follow its path as it circles overhead, gradually descending. The shape grows clearer and larger as the gargoyle soars toward me.

I glance back at Baelen. I may not be able to bind his wounds, but now I know why I'm here, why the heartstone brought me back to this place.

I'm here to protect him from the gargoyle.

Sebastian had told me I'd have to face my fears, and this is it. This is my worst fear, because no matter how hard I tried to protect Baelen on this cliff seven years ago, all I did was hurt him. This is my second chance—a chance to save him like I couldn't before.

I roar a challenge into the night sky as the beast thumps down onto the ledge, its wings outstretched. Instead of folding its wings to its sides, it keeps them aloft, ready to use the daggers at the pinpoints of its wings against me. This gargoyle is the kind the elves fear—glowing red eyes, horns stretching from two points on its stony skull, its teeth dripping as it growls. Its chest is broad and muscled, even larger than the gargoyle I faced on Scepter Peak. It doesn't make any difference that I know real gargoyles don't look like this. The real ones might be far more beautiful, but this one is just as dangerous.

I reach for my weapons, discovering that I have none. *Damn.* I've only got my fists and I'm pretty sure that's not going to help. I glance around as the gargoyle circles me. Without taking my eyes off it, I pick up the nearest rocks, two palm-sized ones. Not exactly knuckle dusters, but they'll pack more of a wallop than my bare fists.

Wait… *bare* fists. My gloves are gone. My hands shoot to my veil. It's gone too, but I'm still wearing my headpiece. It's not metal and it's blunt. It was only intended to keep my veil away from my eyes, but if I have to, I can use it as a weapon.

The gargoyle surveys the shimmery vision of my younger self, looking between it and Baelen, growling at him before turning its focus to me. It crouches, wing daggers pointed at me, and roars so loudly that its breath gusts across me like a stormy breeze. Lightning flickers in the distance, a backdrop of crackling electricity illuminating the beast's silhouette.

I don't wait for it to attack. I take a running jump, knowing I'll only get one shot at its head. The gargoyle braces as I leap but it doesn't use its wings to defend itself. My rock-filled right fist connects against the side of its face with a *thwack*. I'd intended to land the blow and use my own momentum to somersault over it, but the beast anticipated that. It twists, accepting the blow to its face, but swats me at the same time in one forceful move as it follows me down to the cliff's surface. For a moment, its bloodied face hovers over mine, as if it expects me to yield.

I may be winded and have a pounding headache on the way, but yielding is not going to happen.

One-two, I knock my fists into its face first and then follow with a two-footed kick, knocking the gargoyle backward and sliding myself out from under it at the same time. I jump to my feet and fly back at it, exchanging quick blows. It blocks and defends everything I throw at it but manages to get in a few hits of its own before circling me again.

The creature shakes its head, taking another assessing look at me, and I realize I'm in trouble. It was playing with me before. It charges at me, its wing daggers ripping through the air, scant inches from my arms as I jump backward. I have no idea if my armor made of Elyria web will protect me. The gargoyle on Scepter Peak had shown me that gargoyles and Elyria spiders live in harmony. For all I know, their wing daggers could be just as strong as the web. I don't plan on finding out.

The gargoyle drives me backward, knocking me up against the side of the cave. One of its daggers grazes my face. I can't let it pin me against the rock like the other one did. I scream out in pain, grab my wooden headpiece, and shove it right at the beast's eyes. Wood can't break that stony skin, but it causes the gargoyle to jolt backward, giving me a slim gap to slide through beneath its wing. As I do so…

A dagger! The beast is carrying a dagger!

I throw my hand back at the last moment and snatch the weapon, tearing it from the gargoyle's hip. I slide across the ledge toward Baelen as lightning springs to life around me. Glowing blue light snaps around my body, hissing and crackling.

The beast turns, realizes its weapon is gone, and charges at me. At the same time, thirty black spots appear above me.

More gargoyles! For a second, confusion overwhelms me. The Elven Command said I'd only have to fight one, not so many all at once. All the new gargoyles speed toward me, blurry forms, only seconds away. I can't let them reach me. I can't let them reach Baelen.

I draw on all of the Storm's wrath, vaguely aware that the first gargoyle has skidded to a halt, eyeing me with… surprise? It's hard to tell, but I don't have time to think.

Electricity crackles around me as I plant my feet and scream, "I won't let you hurt him!"

The gargoyle jolts, its voice a sharp growl. "You're protecting him from me?"

That's when the other gargoyles reach me, a cloud of them,

shrieking, mere feet away now. They reach for me and for the dagger.

With a shout, I drop to the cliff's surface, turn the dagger upside down, and ram its hilt against the stone with all my might.

The electrical *thud* reverberates around me, pulsing outward. Lightning streaks in a wide circle from my weapon, bashing into the oncoming attackers. Their teeth and claws light up, bony, glistening, wings snapping as the force hits them, hurling them backward.

All of them tumble away from me. Some of them drop from the sky, clinging to the ledge before sliding out of view. Others plummet down the cliff immediately, but most of them spill backward, the force of my lightning propelling them far, far away from me.

Their screams fade as I spin back to the male gargoyle. It alone is still standing, one arm flung across its eyes, braced against the storm raging around me.

Blood drips down the side of my face. I roar at it. "I will protect Baelen Rath to the death, because I love him!"

The gargoyle's eyes widen as my shout reaches it. I take a step back for momentum and then run toward it, electric dagger raised. The creature glances backward—it's dangerously close to the cliff's edge—before bracing for the strike. At least, I think it's going to brace, until the last moment, when it ducks, angles its right shoulder into my ribcage, and tackles me backward along the ledge where it forces me to the ground.

Oomph! The air leaves my lungs as I hit the ground. A ton of gargoyle male drops down on me, but at the last moment, its hand slides up behind my head, cushioning me from cracking open my skull, and its other hand punches the ground to stop its massive body from crushing me. The impact hurts, and it takes me a moment to catch my breath. Long enough for the beast to shift its paw to my dagger arm, pin it, and force my hand open, compelling me to release the weapon.

I struggle, kicking my legs and trying to get my arm free as it rises upward, straddling my hips. "Stop fighting me, Marbella."

"Never! I won't let you hurt him! You... what?"

It leans across me. I lie stunned as it whispers into my ear. "Stop fighting me."

I shiver, because there's something so familiar about the way it just leaned into me. "Wait… Who…? B-Baelen?"

He nods. "It's me."

I search his features as he helps me rise to my knees, trying to find anything that resembles the man I know. My lips form a startled *what the?*

"What's happening?" I ask. "This is supposed to be my simulation. You're not supposed to be here…"

He growls, "I didn't know it was you until you held the dagger. You're the only one who lights up at the touch of steel. That's when I recognized you."

"But what do you see when you look at me?"

A rattle of breath inside his chest sounds suspiciously like a chuckle. "Please don't be offended, but you look hideous."

I'm too stunned to be offended. "So, I look like a gargoyle to you, just like you look like a gargoyle to me?"

He sighs. "I should have known this was all wrong. Gargoyles don't look like this. Especially not female ones."

"Then, what's really going on right now? Have our simulations somehow combined in our minds?" Heat suddenly burns through me. I stare at him. "What happened in yours before you flew down here?"

He smiles, slow and strong, seeming to enjoy the blush that blazes across my cheeks. "A memory. One I haven't forgotten."

"Oh."

He clears his throat, suddenly serious. "Which ended when I hit my head." He gestures to his younger self. "After that, I floated way up high, and I thought the simulation was over, but then I plummeted back here. It felt like I was actually falling."

He shakes his head as he peers around us. "I can't see anything beyond this cliff. I can't see the arena. I don't know for sure, but it doesn't feel like I'm sitting in the chair anymore."

I think back to the moment when I fell out of my younger self. I'd fallen too, as if something had released me—or pulled me out. Had we both fallen out of the Chairs of Truth at that moment?

"Then… what does this mean? Are we stuck in the same vision, but our bodies are moving in real life now? Baelen, if that's true, we could have killed each other!"

I look around us, searching the sky, the cliff, the rocks, trying to find a clue about what's happening. It's too silent. Too quiet. There's no breeze, no moving clouds anymore. The simulation has… paused.

"What about the other gargoyles that attacked just now? If you look like a gargoyle to me, and this is somehow really happening, then who were they?" Fear shoots through me, sharp and terrifying. "Who did I hurt?"

His expression is shadowed. "There were too many of them to be the Elven Command."

I gasp. "My Storm Command. Our friends. They were trying to get the dagger away from me. They must have been trying to stop me from hurting you."

A shriek rises in my chest, but I push it down. I meet Baelen's eyes as panic threatens to overtake me. It's the first true panic I've felt in seven years when I thought he'd died. I don't know what's really going on around us, and not knowing whether my ladies are safe is killing me. "It has to be the Elven Command. They've done something to us, to the chairs. And now my Storm Command is hurt…"

Baelen doesn't pause a moment longer. Even in his current gargoyle form, the concern in his eyes shines through. He's already assessing an exit, a way down the mountain, reaching for my arm.

"We're in danger. We need to move." He scoops me upward, but just as he rises to his feet, he roars, his eyes shooting wide.

He pushes me away from him as if he's trying to protect me. I recognize the way his arms move forward in a quick, desperate motion. It's the same way I pushed him out of the path of the lightning strike.

I stumble backward, grazing my hands. "Baelen!"

He arches back against something I can't see, something that's clearly hurting him. With a sickening crack, one of his wings snaps right before my eyes. His line of sight descends to his chest, but I can't see a wound.

"Baelen!" I snatch up the dagger, ducking to avoid Baelen's wings as he spins. His outstretched fist connects with an invisible object. There's a *thud*. He hit something—whatever was hurting him.

"I can't see… I can't see it!" I wave my weapon around, trying to see where I need to attack, but there's only silence again.

Baelen drops to his knees. "Marbella, come here. Quickly."

I run to him, driving the dagger into the ground at the last moment, but within arm's length so I can reach it if I need it. I try to catch Baelen as he slides to his knees, one of his legs at an awkward angle.

"Baelen? Where are you hurt?"

He doesn't answer. His good wing curls over the top of me and pressure builds across my shoulder blades and lower back as he compels me toward his chest. He gathers all of me up inside his wing, even my feet, fitting the wing snug across my whole body, cocooning me. I have no choice but to turn my head into his neck, inhaling the scent of his skin. He smells like… icy rain and a warm, sun shower both at the same time.

I am small. And afraid. "Baelen?"

"Stay here, where it's safe, until the simulation ends. They won't come for you yet."

I don't think I want to hide here. Something has hurt him, and I can't see his wound, but it's bad. I know it's bad. Otherwise, he would get up and fight. Nothing could stop him. Nothing could keep him down. Pressure builds inside my chest, a world of fear and dread all balled up inside me, and I'm ready to scream.

He sighs. "Marbella Mercy… I love you too."

My heart stops. Whatever I want to say, whatever I feel, it all chokes inside me. His wing slides away from my back, releasing me enough to allow me to lift my head, using both hands to push away from his chest.

The cliff changes around me then, rearranging itself, rocky outcrops smoothing into sunlit walls. The space around me morphs back into the arena. My vision clears, changing as reality seeps in and the walls, the dais, and the upper levels become crystal clear. The upper levels are empty. The onlookers have gone. The arena is clear and quiet.

There's a groan to my right. Reisha lies on her stomach, trying to crawl toward me. Blood drips from cuts all over her body as she lifts her head, her outstretched hand dropping to the ground.

She's breathing hard, gasping out words. "We tried to stop you from fighting each other… but you were too strong… too strong…"

All around her, my Storm Command have fallen to the floor. Like dominos, my ladies lie scattered, their armor ripped apart, their bodies bleeding. Some of them are trying to get up, others don't move. Jordan and Elise lie among them, too far away to see if they're alive. Baelen's soldiers are scattered around us too, many groaning, others lying still, all of them shuddering like an electrical force has ripped through them.

My electrical force…

My Storm Command were the gargoyles in the simulation—the gargoyles I blasted from the sky. They were trying to help us, and I repelled them. I took out my own protection. And now the simulation has ended, but the Elven Command said it would only end when a gargoyle died.

I can't breathe. I can't look down. My heart isn't beating.

Baelen is still beneath me. He'd told me to stay inside his wings until the simulation ended.

I can't look down… I can't…

He morphs before my eyes, his sharp face and dripping teeth disappearing. He transforms back into himself and suddenly, his wounds blossom before my eyes. There are four slashes across his chest like the corners of a square, piercing right through his armor.

Four Elven Commanders stand behind him, each holding a sword that's bloodied and glows with an unnatural golden light. Among them, Gideon Glory's face is alight with the blaze of sorcery. His spells shimmer along the blades that he and the others hold. Wisps of sorcery waft around the Chairs of Truth lying broken on their sides nearby. Even now, golden ropes of sorcery slide across the ground toward me. Pedr Bounty rubs his side, and I can only guess that he was the one that Baelen thumped.

The Elven Commanders were the attackers we couldn't see. They stabbed Baelen in the back. They'd orchestrated it from the start. The Chairs of Truth had immersed us in a simulation—a real one—until Gideon Glory used his sorcery to break the chairs and pull our bodies out of them but kept our minds in a false vision.

They'd tried to trick me into killing Baelen and when I didn't...

Baelen's chest is still. His eyes are closed. A drop of blood slips from his mouth. Gravity forces his arms to slide down my sides, slipping away from my back where he'd held me until his last moment and told me that he loved me.

They killed him.

My heart rips apart inside my chest. It's beating so hard. Lightning and thunder, rain and wind build inside me. I can't lose him. I won't lose him.

As Gideon's sorcery takes hold of my arms and legs, I scream and scream and scream.

44

———

MARBELLA

Elwyn Elder rounds me and grabs me from behind, latching on to my armor and dragging me off Baelen. My skintight suit presses against my neck like a noose. He drags me across the floor, past the broken chairs to a clear space beyond them and drops me onto my back.

I can't move. The sorcery is like fire burning me and immobilizing my spine. Gideon Glory comes into view, leaning over me. So do Pedr Bounty and Osian Valor. The four Elven Commanders peer down at me while Gideon mutters beneath his breath, chanting over me. The other three raise a hand each and a golden thread extends between their palms, connecting into a circle when Gideon raises his too.

In unison, their hands lower toward me, one each toward my bare hands and my bare cheeks, lowering at exactly the same time.

They want my power. They *all* want my power. They wanted Baelen to die. They wanted the chance to kill him. They… I… my heart is… so torn I can't do anything but scream my grief. "You did this!"

They don't respond. Gideon's chanting grows more urgent and all four of their lined, old faces begin to glow as the sorcery keeps them joined, moving their hands as one, closer and closer to the surface of my body.

I scream, shouting at them, but there's nothing I can do to stop

303

them. How long had they planned this? How long had they schemed? There's a dagger at Gideon Glory's hip but I can't move my hand to reach it. They're going to take my power and then… they'll kill me.

Closer and closer.

I whimper as their hands touch my bare skin, connecting at the exact same moment.

"Finally," Gideon Glory exhales a sigh of sickening elation. Triumphant smiles break across all their faces, but I…

I feel nothing.

There's no surge of energy, no crackle of lightning, no pulse of thunder. Nothing of the Storm passes from me. It's like being empty, but not because they took my power—because it's not there to give.

I become very quiet, sensing… a heartbeat. It's slow. Very slow, almost like the sound of someone taking careful, cautious steps toward me except that there's nobody approaching me. I don't know where the heartbeat is coming from or who it belongs to. All I know is that it isn't mine and it doesn't belong to the four Elven Commanders whose evil grins are fading fast.

Their fingers claw into my skin, pressing deeper, frustration replacing their triumph.

"What's going on?" Elwyn Elder demands, a glare forming fast.

Gideon shakes his head, filled with confusion. "I don't understand… we should have her power by now."

"You said this would work!"

They argue back and forth, yanking on my arms, clawing at my cheeks, and I begin to laugh despite the pain, great big sob-laughs. Mostly because I've lost it, I've lost everything, but also because… "It didn't work."

Gideon Glory hisses at me, snarling a chant, his eyes glowing like golden orbs, but his sorcery washes over me like water off a swan's wings. At the back of everything, that slow, quiet heartbeat thrums and turns into a shield around me. The Elven Command has taken everything from me—they took Baelen, and now I'll never again see his smile or hear him laugh or hold his hand or join my body with his. There's nothing more they can do to hurt me.

Gideon's hold on my spine weakens. He chants harder, but his power is fading fast. I kick my legs, freeing one of them from the spell, and strike out at Osian Valor on my right hand side. He shouts as my armored foot cracks against his ribs, knocking him off balance. He tries to keep hold of my hand but falls to the floor. My hand is scratched and bruised from his raking fingernails, but it's free now. As quickly as I can, I grab hold of the dagger dangling so recklessly from Gideon's belt right beside me as he leans over me. Oh, the arrogance that he never thought I'd be able to reach for it.

He shrieks as my hand lights up on contact, struggling to get away from me, but I hook my fingers around his belt and press the sizzling dagger into his side. I whisper, "You killed Mai. You killed Baelen. You are nothing but evil."

He leaps to his feet, but I follow him up and so does the dagger, finding its target. His eyes fade. The only light cast over his body radiates from the Storm I wield.

As he falls, dead, I spin to the remaining three, finally in a position to see that Teilo Splendor lies across the far dais in a rumple of robes. I don't know what happened while I was in the simulation, but Teilo's head wound tells me that he tried to stop the others.

I'm suddenly cold as the adrenaline of escaping Gideon's sorcery wanes. I can't bear to look where Baelen lies. I drop to my knees, only knowing that I have to end this. If I'm the first princess to wield the Storm as a weapon, then I'm determined to make myself the last.

"You want the Storm," I say as the three remaining Elven Commanders scoot away from me. "Then you can have it."

I lift the bright dagger to my own heart, "Be free, Storm."

45

BAELEN

My heartbeat thuds in my ears. Slow. Fading.

It's like walking away from my life step by step. My consciousness separates from my body and the world turns white. No more lines, colors, or shapes. No more twirling ribbon or crackling light.

No more battles.

Everything around me disappears except Marbella's voice and the bright dagger she presses to her heart, somehow the brightest thing I see. Too bright.

"You want the storm," she cries. "You can have it!"

She's the reason I'm here. She is my reason.

A single, final thought rips through me.

Stop.

46

MARBELLA

Before I can drive the blade home, a *thud* freezes everything around me.

The dagger pauses at my chest, its tip refusing to budge. I'm not responsible for the pause in time. There's not a lot I can process right now, but I know it wasn't me who froze everything.

The three remaining Elven Commanders are caught between expressions of fear and rage, their glittering robes frozen in swirls as they scrambled to get away from me. My friends are frozen too, some half-rising, some on their knees.

I finally see Jasper and Sebastian, both stationary, but in the act of running toward Baelen, with Sahara right behind them. They don't look harmed like the others and their voices echo in my memory, like a dream that happened around me while I was unaware. *Get back! The Storm is too strong!* And lastly, Sahara shouting: *Take cover! We can't help him if we're dead.*

A drop of water hits my cheek, drawing my attention upward. A cool breeze swirls around me, creating soothing sensations across my scratched skin. I'm not sure where it's coming from until a soft, female voice speaks behind me.

"I'm here, Marbella."

I freeze like the people around me but not because the thunder has affected me. I know her voice. Sure, the last time I heard it she was wailing and shrieking, but there's no denying the lilt she speaks with, the gentle rush of sound like a waterfall lives beneath each spoken sound. I stand and turn slowly.

She's like an older version of the gargoyle baby I saw in the nest. Her skin is porcelain in texture and a soft caramel color. Her eyes are deep brown and framed with long dark lashes. Her hair rests across one shoulder and washes down her side to her slender hips, and she has the longest legs I've ever seen. They're only partially covered by the fine silver gown she wears. Her ears are round, not like mine, and she glows around the edges.

Her wings shimmer in a cascade like her voice, except that one is broken, the fine gossamer webbing torn and draping closer to her body to her left side.

"You're the Storm," I say, even though it's obvious.

"*We* are the Storm," she corrects me, her mouth drawing into a serious line. "You, me, and… him."

I follow the line of her arm and pointed finger, sucking in a sharp breath and spinning back to her before I see Baelen.

"Come with me," she says, gliding past me in his direction, not quite touching the ground.

"No."

She pauses. "Why are you afraid of him?"

I choke. "I'm not afraid of him. I can't look at him because if I don't look… I can pretend he's not… gone." I gasp against the pain clawing up through my stomach into my chest. I didn't think there was enough of my heart left to break any further, but pieces are tearing out of me one by one.

She pauses beside me, her dress swishing around her legs. "But… he's not dead."

Now I'm truly frozen. My heart leaps as everything else stops. "What?"

"Close your eyes, Marbella. Listen. Tell me what you hear."

I don't have to close my eyes to know what she's talking about. "I hear a heartbeat."

"And what do you feel in every part of this room?"

"Thunder."

"Well," she says with a gentle quirk of her eyebrow. "It's not my heartbeat and I didn't cause the thunder. Neither did you so…"

"Baelen!" I'm moving before I know it, racing past the Storm, and zigzagging around frozen people. I skid and drop to my knees at his side. I hover my hands above his face and neck, still afraid to touch him, but close enough to sense… he's warm.

My heart can't take any more pain. "I don't understand. You said he's the Storm too. How?"

"The Elven Command was right about you being able to share your power. But they were completely wrong about the timing. They couldn't take your power just now because you already gave it away."

She gives me a smile, but it's a sad one. "On the night you became the Storm Princess, you gave your power to Baelen Rath."

47

MARBELLA

"Let me show you." The Storm brushes her hands across the space above Baelen's chest, delicate gestures, painting colors in the air, images forming until I recognize my younger self wrapped in Baelen's arms on the stormy cliff. My ribbon is a curl of blue floating above us. It's moments before the lightning hit us.

"That first lightning strike wasn't me," the Storm says. "It was a natural storm and a natural strike. Deadly, for sure, but not me. I'd escaped into the clouds, and I saw it as it happened."

The lightning streaks down at us inside the image, illuminating my upturned face. I look away before I see myself push Baelen, but the Storm says, "This is important, Marbella. You need to see what you did."

I force myself to watch as the images play out, watching myself drive Baelen out of the way, shoving him as hard as I can to keep him safe. He slips, but there's something else… something I never realized…

My eyes widen as I watch my feet slide backward across the wet stone, my hands still outstretched, my lavender cloak billowing and weightless, tugging me, sliding me right out… past the edge… and the fear in Baelen's eyes…

"You were so determined to save him; you didn't know how close you were to the edge of the cliff. You slid right off. That first lightning strike would have killed Baelen if it wasn't for you." She meets my shocked eyes. "But *you* would have died if it wasn't for me."

Inside the image I can see now the brighter streak of lightning—the Storm's power—speeding toward me, overlaying the first natural strike to reach me first. The Storm's lightning catches me in its rays and even though it rips me apart, it slowly drags me back to the surface of the cliff.

"But… I…"

"Keep watching, Marbella," the Storm urges me. "Because what you did next changed everything."

I squeeze my eyes shut. "I know what happens next. I hurt Baelen. Badly."

Her eyebrows lift. She turns her hands mid-air, and the image turns with her. Baelen's image is now closer to me. "Is that what you think? Look again."

Inside the image, the cascade of lightning from my hands hits him. Unable to turn away now, I flinch and swallow a cry, squeezing my fingernails into my palms. But then… the wound on his face heals.

"Cauterized," I whisper. "But I saw him bleed for hours."

"That was the rain mixing with the blood he lost before this moment. You couldn't see from where you were."

At the same time, Baelen lights up. Crimson strands like the color of his heartstone curl around him. They pulse through his body right into his bones, even into his spine. I'd thought it was flame, that I'd burned him, but it's not.

It's red lightning.

"When I struck you, I gave you my power," the Storm explains. "When you struck him, you gave part of that power to him."

She reaches out and wraps her hand around my arm. It's like connecting with a shadow, unreal, transparent, but it anchors me to the spot.

"You bonded with him in a way that no Storm Princess has ever done before," she says. "He shares the Storm with you like no man ever has before. You are connected body and soul. I don't know how you managed to stay away from each other these past seven years."

"Then… Those times he came to the Storm Vault and I could suddenly fight back against you…" I'd seen what I thought was his heartstone light shining across his body, but was it actually… crimson lightning?

"He was harnessing his power without knowing it, combining his strength with yours."

"And when we were at Mai's, he stood beside me. The spell couldn't move him."

"Just like it couldn't move you."

"And… now?"

"Their blades injured him to the point of death, but his storm power keeps him alive," she says. "*Your* storm power keeps him alive." The image fades above his chest. "You know the truth now."

For the first time in seven years, I'm not afraid to touch Baelen's bare skin with mine. My hands shake and a sob rises in my throat, but I press my palm to his cheek.

A shudder runs through me at the contact. I've waited so long to be close to him again. His face is warm. A faint wash of bristles grazes my hand as I run my fingers across his jaw, aching for him to respond. "Wake up, Baelen."

He remains completely still. Tears slide down my cheeks. "If he's alive, why won't he wake up?"

Her eyes glisten with tears. "Marbella, I'm sorry. When I said the storm is keeping him alive, I didn't mean it healed him. Not this time. There's too much damage. He's alive, and he's suspended in this moment so the damage doesn't progress, but… he won't heal by ordinary medicine or spellcasting."

She pauses. "It is probably a small consolation, but I want you to know that he isn't cursed. The curse was destroyed when that sorcerer died." Her delicate lip curls as she points at Gideon Glory in distaste.

The curse is over. It's gone. Defeated. But I still face losing Baelen. Everything in my body aches. "Please tell me what to do. I won't stop until he comes back to me. Tell me how to help him."

She sucks in a breath. "You can't help him. Only my people can."

Her people? I take in her wings, her delicate skin, her rounded ears, and the fact that she is more beautiful than the men of her species—the gargoyles.

Her hand grips my arm. "If you want Baelen Rath to live, you must take him to the heart of Erador. You must take him to the gargoyles."

I stare at her in disbelief. She wants me to take the man I love into the heart of our sworn enemies. "How can they help him when nobody else can?"

"The female gargoyles have a place, deep inside Mount Erador. There is a spring, which is the only water source that flows directly from Earth's surface. They can harness deep magic there. Only deep magic can save him now."

There are so many problems with what she just said. The gargoyles will kill me on sight for starters. Baelen too. I can't just waltz into Erador and expect them to help me. I can't leave Erawind either—I have to stay with the Vault to subdue the storm —although looking at the Storm right now, I'm not sure that's a problem anymore.

Cautiously, I ask, "How are you here?"

She says, simply, "You freed me."

"Then why aren't you…" I wave my hands around. "Storming?"

"The Storm Vault never contained me. You did. I stayed there because that was where the first Storm Princess wanted me to stay. And the one after that. And you. Now, I'm here because you want me to be here. I'm calm because you want me to be calm." She leans forward with a hint of a smile. "Don't worry, if you die, I promise I will 'storm.'"

I glance around at the Elven Command. Then I consider all the hurt and wounded warriors, as well as my closest friends: Elise, Jordan, Reisha, and Jasper too. Even Sebastian and Sahara. If I'm going to leave, I can't leave them to the mercy of the Elven Command. That's *if* I'm going to leave, and I'm not even sure about that. "What if I don't want you to be calm?"

A large smile breaks across her face, deliciously wicked in the way it lights up her eyes. "Then I will rage at your command."

I close my eyes for a moment, exhaling my doubt and dread. Then I contemplate my frozen friends, deciding how I need this to play out. First, I need to know if what the Storm told me is true— that the only way to help Baelen is to take him to Erador. As a healer, Sahara can tell me whether that's true or not.

I cross the distance to her first. She's caught in a moment of despair, her line of sight trained on Baelen, running toward him. I brace in front of her, planting my feet and leaning forward to counter her momentum. Then I take hold of her wrist.

She comes alive, her legs moving, running straight into me, but I keep my hold and swing her around to slow her down.

She screams. "Princess!" Her eyes dart across the room where I was last placed. "But you…"

"Thunder," I say.

She knows about me being able to use thunder to slow time, so she catches up fast—especially given that everyone else is still frozen—but then her line of sight swivels back to me and she screams again as she catches sight of my hand on her arm. "Princess! Let go!"

"It's okay," I say. "Baelen has my power."

She's shaking. She doesn't argue with me. "We have to help him."

I'm relieved to know I was right about her: that she wouldn't get distracted by the details. "Please, I need your help."

I hurry with her to where Baelen lies. She immediately starts assessing his wounds, deftly peeling off parts of his armor, clicking her tongue unhappily.

"I need to know if there's anything you can do for him," I say. "I need to know if I have any alternatives."

"Alternatives to what?" she asks, but she's already distracted. "These wounds were caused by blades strengthened with sorcery. There's no other way to pierce Rath armor. His wounds are deep, but it's strange… He's not bleeding. It's almost like he's…"

"Paused?" I ask, using the Storm's description. "You're right. He used the thunder on himself. What I need to know is whether you can heal him?"

She shakes her head, stricken pale. "A mortal wound caused by sorcery can only be countered by deep magic."

Across the room, the Storm gives me a smug I-told-you-so shrug of her shoulders. I haven't figured out yet whether Sahara can see her. I'm guessing not when the older woman looks right through the Storm.

I return my attention to Sahara. "How do I find deep magic? Or create it? Or whatever it is that I do to get it?"

"Deep magic comes from life itself. You could give your life to save his, but somehow, I don't think he'd appreciate it." She gives me a sad smile. "There's only one other way, but it's very dangerous."

I sigh. "I have to go to Erador."

She blinks at me. "How did you know?" She waves her own question away. "It's only a whisper but being the daughter of an Elven Commander has some advantages, such as overhearing things I'm not meant to hear. They say there's a spring in the heart of Mount Erador—"

"Where the women can harness deep magic." I sink beside her. "I was hoping there was another way."

"Marbella… you're not thinking of going there?"

"Of course, I will. I love him."

Her eyes fill with tears. She tries to blink them away, but they drip down her cheeks. "What can I do to help?"

"I need to unfreeze all these people. Then I need you to get everyone out of here before the Elven Command wakes up. Gideon Glory is dead. He was the main sorcerer, but the others are just as dangerous. You have to get everyone far away from here. Including your father."

She chews her lip. "We can go to Rath land. It's the furthest from the city. Sebastian told me there are places to hide in the Rath mountains—Baelen showed him where."

"The House of Mercy controls Rath land now. They will protect you," I say. "My brother is already back at Rath land, and he will make sure you're safe. Thank you, Sahara."

"Marbella." She hesitates, but gently lays her hand over mine. It's a gesture I never thought I'd experience again—a consoling touch. "Be safe."

"I'll come back. I promise. The Elven Command is corrupt. It can't be allowed to continue. But I need to help Baelen first."

She nods while I rise to my feet.

"Storm!" I call, hoping I don't confuse Sahara too much by speaking to something that's not there. "A hurricane is called for.

Something that will whisk these men to a place where they can't get out for a while. And keep them frozen for as long as possible."

The Storm ponders my request for a moment. "The bottom of the river? A dungeon?" Her eyes light up. "No… I know… The Storm Vault."

How perfect. "You'll have to seal its doors."

"Of course." She grins. "With pleasure."

A mini tornado builds as I watch, catching the Elven Commanders in its pull and tug, spinning them round and round. It spins toward the doors, pushing them open with ease, and the Elven Commanders disappear from sight.

The Storm gives me a distracted smile.

"I wasn't sure if you'd stay here with me," I say.

"Of course. I stay where you are. But let me concentrate so I get this right."

I trust her to do what she says, and I can't waste any time by hovering over her. If I'd created the thunder, then I could release everyone at once, but since it was Baelen, I have to touch everyone to bring them out of it. That's twenty Storm Commanders and fifteen of Baelen's soldiers. After going so long without touching anyone at all, I brace myself for my senses to go haywire from sensory overload.

I brush my hand lightly across Jasper's arm and then Sebastian's. They're the least wounded and will be able to help the others. Also, I trust that Sahara will explain to them what's happening. I'm not sure how many difficult conversations I can handle right now. I don't try to stop them running forward like they were about to. Sahara's right there to catch up with them, drawing them to a stop before they race toward Baelen.

I cross the floor to Jordan, Elise, and Reisha next, but I'm not prepared for how emotional I am. They're all wounded because of me. I drop to my knees next to Jordan who lies between Elise and Reisha. I stroke Jordan's hair to wake her up, reaching across to touch Elise's arm at the same time. They both gasp, turning onto their backs, staring at the ceiling, trying to get their bearings.

"Princess?" Jordan tries to get up first, while Elise uses her elbow as leverage, wobbling and squinting at me.

"Sahara!" I call. "We need help over here."

"It's okay," Jordan says, holding up her hand. "I'm okay. Elise?"

Elise rubs the back of her head. "Just dazed. I'll be fine." She suddenly jolts upward with a new urgency. "Where is Commander Rath? What happened?"

"He's…" I swallow. There's no easy way to tell them what happened or that I'm leaving. It all tumbles out at once. "He's hurt, but I'm going to do everything I can to help him. But I have to leave you and I need you to be safe."

I help them to their feet, grateful that the pause in time must have given their bodies moments longer to heal.

"Princess, we're coming with you," Elise says. "Wherever you're going."

I shake my head. "I don't have a lot of time, but I need you to follow Sahara's instructions. The Elven Command is gone for now, but they won't be contained for long. I need to know you'll be safe. Promise me you won't come after me."

"Where are you going?" Jordan demands, always loyal. "You have to change your mind. Let us come with you."

"No, my dear friends." Before they can stop me, I hug them both at once, tears leaking down my cheeks even though they freeze, aghast.

Elise almost shrieks in my ear. "Princess! What are you doing touching us?"

"It's okay. Baelen has my power." It seems to be my new mantra, repeated everywhere I go.

"Oh. Okay then…" Jordan and Elise suddenly hug me back. A big, warm hug to make up for all the hugs I haven't been able to have. I haven't woken the rest of the Storm Command yet, but I wish I could hug them all.

"Look after each other," I whisper, pulling away before I don't have the strength to leave my friends.

Wiping the tears from my cheeks, I drop to Reisha next, making sure that Sahara is ready to tend to her. Then I walk around the rest of the group, quickly assessing who is least and most wounded, leaving the most badly wounded until last, waiting as long as I can to make sure Elise and Sahara are ready to help them.

Finally, I wake Teilo Splendor. He holds his head in his hand, squinting at me. "Princess, you're alive."

"Your daughter will tell you what needs to be done," I say, turning away from him.

"Forgive me," he calls. "I should have seen their betrayal, their sorcery."

I don't know what to say so I keep walking, returning to Baelen where the Storm is waiting again. My friends are all busy now, helping each other. I take a moment to close my eyes. I need to get to Erador as fast as possible, which means I need transport. I need a bird with fiery wings that isn't afraid to carry the Storm on its back.

Phoenix! I cry inside my mind. *You said I could call on you if I needed your help. Please help me.*

There's a brief moment of silence. Then…

I'm outside when you're ready.

I sink to Baelen's side as relief washes through me. But I have another problem. I whisper to the Storm, "I need to move Baelen, but I'm not sure how."

"Oh, that's easy. Wind will help us." She lifts her hands and Baelen's body rises off the ground. "Which way do you want to go?"

On any other day, I might have smiled at how easy she makes it look to float him upward with a mere lift of her hands. Now, I'm just grateful that it can be done. "Outside. A friend is waiting for us."

I rise to my feet, but before I can take two steps, Jasper blocks my path. His armor is dented. Like the others, he bears welts across his face and lower arms. I wince as I picture my lightning cutting across his body like whips.

"I'm coming with you," he says.

I shake my head, maneuvering around him, which is difficult now that more elves are awake. I already told Jordan and Elise that they couldn't come with me. I'm not changing my mind for Jasper. "No."

He swiftly steps into my path again. His eyes flick left to where the Storm hovers. For a second, I think he can see her, but then I realize he's looking past her to Jordan and Sebastian. They've taken a moment to embrace each other, their heads together, the relief on their faces visible even from here.

Jasper says, "If I'm going to leave my family, it has to be for something more than hiding out and surviving in the mountains."

"Jasper, I'm going into gargoyle country. I might never make it back."

"The same way you walked out of a gargoyle's nest?" His gaze is piercing. "You survived that. I think you have the chance to survive this."

My jaw drops. He has to be talking about the nest I found on Scepter Peak. He'd come upon me as I exited the nest, but I never suspected he knew it was there. "You knew it was a gargoyle nest?"

He shrugs. "It's not the first one I've encountered. You can use my help, Marbella. So can Baelen. He made me promise, right from that first trial, that I wouldn't let any harm come to you. I'm not going to break my promise to him. Let me come with you."

He stares at me with earnest eyes. He kept me alive on Scepter Peak—we kept each other alive. I wasn't expecting help, didn't think I'd need it, but where I'm headed, I'm going to need all the help I can get. Besides, he's really not going to budge and he's blocking the door. "I guess I can take one more. Follow me, please."

Baelen floats along beside me as I reach the doors. I'm not sure what Jasper makes of that, but I'm hoping he thinks I'm using the Storm's power to move Baelen on my own. It's close to the truth.

I pause there for a moment. Behind me, all the people I love— my family—are taking care of each other, preparing to leave, preparing to go into hiding. My heart tugs with the knowledge that I'm about to leave them, but I'm determined that I'll see them again. I will come back and end the Elven Command's reign over them.

I step out into the light with the Storm and Jasper on my heels.

The phoenix waits for me, its wings tucked in at its sides, taking up all the space across the wide, cobbled path.

Princess, it greets me.

"Thank you for helping me, Phoenix."

I gesture to Jasper to get on the phoenix's broad back and then turn to the Storm, keeping my voice low. "Please tell me you can tether Baelen to the phoenix."

"Of course," she says. "I'll do it this once, but I can teach you how to do it yourself. That way it will look less strange to your friend."

"Thank you. And his name is Jasper."

The Storm floats Baelen up onto the phoenix's back beside Jasper and a thin line of lightning appears around Baelen like a silver rope. The phoenix spreads its wings to allow the lightning to stretch all around its body, keeping Baelen in place. It's a good thing the bird is so enormous given that it's about to carry three of us.

"He won't fall," the Storm promises. "The phoenix has melded with the lightning so it's practically part of its own body." She lifts off the ground. "I will ride the wind. I'm ready when you are."

I climb on behind Baelen, placing his head in my lap and my hand over his heart, listening for the calm, slow thump of his heartbeat.

I vow to you, Baelen Rath, I will bring you back to me.

I don't know what Erador holds for me, but I will find the springs and heal Baelen. No matter what it takes.

The phoenix contemplates me with fiery eyes, spreading its wings and preparing to take flight. *Where do you wish to go, Princess?*

"To Erador," I say. "To the gargoyles."

EPILOGUE

GRAYSON GLORY

Gideon's body is heavy in my arms. Somehow I force myself to function, scooping him up from where he lies, still bloody, on the empty arena floor.

His eyes are closed. His hair drapes across my arms. I can touch him for the first time in my life, but only because he's already dead. The wound in his side is a gash that has torn my world apart. Anger burns deep inside me but it's like a lash uncoiling, a whip that will unfurl before it snaps.

Clutching Gideon to my chest, I draw on my power, close my eyes, and then… I'm gone from the arena, transporting myself back to Glory land in milliseconds.

In the next instant, I open my eyes to the immaculate gardens that surround the cage I call my home. I stumble along the stone path through a copse of trees until I reach the end of the garden. There the path stops, but I keep carrying Gideon along the rough track hewn through the forest that sits behind my home.

Moonlight flickers through the creaking branches above me, the darkness enveloping me.

I don't care if I trip. A fall would be a welcome relief to the pain that churns inside me. Gideon's body is far too light in my arms. He should be heavy, should be a burden.

I told him I had his back.

My foot catches on a tree root and I crash to the ground,

landing hard on my knees, pain cracking through my legs. It billows up through my chest, an overpowering surge.

I hated Gideon. Argued with him. Relied on him. He lied to me constantly but not always. He was the only certainty in my life. He was the one who spoke for me before I could speak for myself. I sometimes wished him dead, but I never wanted it to happen.

I tip my head back and roar into the dark night, letting go of the hold I keep on my power. It washes out from me in a ripple of burning heat. The debris beneath me catches alight and the trees burst into flames. Fire roars out from me in a circle, incinerating everything in its path until it burns itself out just as quickly.

I'm left kneeling in a clearing filled with ash, the trees burned to mere stumps for fifty paces all around me.

Placing Gideon's body on the ground, I begin to dig with my bare hands in the dirt, opening a grave for him.

With every handful of dirt, I remind myself: Marbella Mercy did this.

She did this.

Wherever she runs to, wherever she hides… I will find her.

Find out what happens next in
Storm Princess: Book 2.

Then complete the series with
Storm Princess: Book 3
the final book with no cliffhanger.

STORM PRINCESS: BOOK TWO

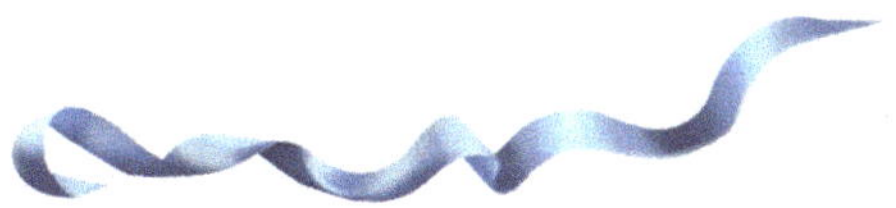

**"Marbella Mercy, I give you my heart.
I will love you, protect you, and honor you until the end of time.
Until death."**

Continue Marbella and Baelen's story in Storm Princess: Book 2.

Content information: Storm Princess: Book 2 is high fantasy romance, the second in the complete Storm Princess series.

Recommended reading age is 17+ for sex scenes, mature themes, violence, and language. Ends on a cliffhanger.

STORM PRINCESS: BOOK THREE

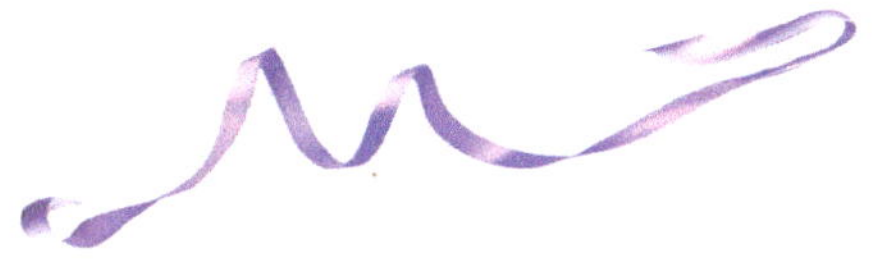

**"You are everything to me.
I would wait a thousand years to hear your voice, kiss your lips,
walk beside you."**

Complete Baelen and Marbella's story in Storm Princess: Book 3.

*Content information: Storm Princess: Book 3 is high fantasy romance, the
third and final book in the complete Storm Princess series.*

*Recommended reading age is 17+ for sex scenes, mature themes, violence,
and language. Ends on a cliffhanger.*

ALSO BY EVERLY FROST

STORM PRINCESS - COMPLETE

(Fantasy Romance)

1. Storm Princess: Book One

2. Storm Princess: Book Two

3. Storm Princess: Book Three

KINGDOM OF BETRAYAL

(Fantasy Romance)

1. A Sky Like Blood

2. A Sin Like Fire

3. A Soul Like Glass

DARK MAGIC SHIFTERS

(Dark Urban Fantasy Romance)

1. Wolf of Ashes

2. Bond of Flames

3. Crown of Fate

SUPERNATURAL LEGACY - COMPLETE

(Angels and Dragon Shifters)

1. Hunt the Night

2. Chase the Shadows

3. Slay the Dawn

4. Claim the Light

BRIGHT WICKED - COMPLETE

(Fantasy Romance)

1. Bright Wicked

2. Radiant Fierce

3. Infernal Dark

SOUL BITTEN SHIFTER - COMPLETE

(Dark Urban Fantasy Romance)

1. This Dark Wolf

2. This Broken Wolf

3. This Caged Wolf

4. This Cruel Blood

DEMON PACK - COMPLETE

(Dark Paranormal Romance)

1. Demon Pack

2. Demon Pack: Elimination

3. Demon Pack: Eternal

ASSASSIN'S MAGIC - COMPLETE

(Urban Fantasy Romance)

1. Assassin's Magic

2. Assassin's Mask

3. Assassin's Menace

4. Assassin's Maze

5. Assassin's Match

ASSASSIN'S ACADEMY - COMPLETE

(Dark Academy Romance)

1. Rebels

2. Revenge

3. Rogue

MORTALITY - COMPLETE

(Science-Fantasy Romance)

Mortality Complete Set: Books 1 to 4

1. Beyond the Ever Reach
2. Beneath the Guarding Stars
3. By the Icy Wild
4. Before the Raging Lion

<u>Stand-alone fiction - dark romance</u>

Corrupt Me: Immortal Vices and Virtues

ALSO BY JAYMIN EVE

STORM PRINCESS - COMPLETE

(Fantasy Romance)

1. Storm Princess: Book One

2. Storm Princess: Book Two

3. Storm Princess: Book Three

Shadow Beast Shifters

Book One: Rejected

Book Two: Reclaimed

Book Three: Reborn

Book Four: Deserted

Book Five: Compelled

Fallen Fae Gods

(Romantasy Duet)

1. Gilded Wings

2. Crimson Skies

Demon Pack

(Dark Paranormal Romance)

1. Demon Pack

2. Demon Pack: Elimination

3. Demon Pack: Eternal

Supernatural Academy

Year One

Year Two

Year Three

Supernatural Prison Trilogy (Urban Fantasy)

Book One: Dragon Marked

Book Two: Dragon Mystics

Book Three: Dragon Mated

Supernatural Prison Stories

Broken Compass

Magical Compass

Louis

Royals of Arbon Academy Series (Dark College Romance)

Book One: Princess Ballot

Book Two: Playboy Princes

Book Three: Poison Throne

Dark Legacy Series (Dark High School Romance)

Book One: Broken Wings

Book Two: Broken Trust

Book Three: Broken Legacy

Secret Keepers Series (Paranormal Romance)

Book One: House of Darken

Book Two: House of Imperial

Book Three: House of Leights

Book Four: House of Royale

Titans Saga

Book One: Releasing the Gods

Book Two: Wrath of the Gods

Book Three: Revenge of the Gods

Curse of the Gods Series (RH Fantasy Romance)

Book One: Trickery

Book Two: Persuasion

Book Three: Seduction

Book Four: Strength

Book 4.5: Neutral (Novella)

Book Five: Pain

NYC Mecca Series (YA Urban Fantasy)

Book One: Queen Heir

Book Two: Queen Alpha

Book Three: Queen Fae

Book Four: Queen Mecca

A Walker Saga (YA Fantasy Series)

Book One: First World

Book Two: Spurn

Book Three: Crais

Book Four: Regali

Book Five: Nephilius

Book Six: Dronish

Book Seven: Earth

Hive Trilogy (YA/NA Urban Fantasy)

Book One: Ash

Book Two: Anarchy

Book Three: Annihilate

Sinclair Stories (Contemporary Sports Romance)

Songbird

ABOUT THE AUTHORS

Jaymin Eve is the Wall Street Journal and USA Today Bestselling author of paranormal romance, urban fantasy, and sci-fi novels filled with epic love stories, great adventure, and plenty of laughs. She lives in Australia with her husband, two beautiful daughters, and a couple of crazy pets. To date, she has sold close to two million ebooks, and still can't believe that she gets to create fantasy worlds as a job.

Everly Frost is the USA Today Bestselling author of fantasy romance, urban fantasy and paranormal romance novels. She spent her childhood dreaming of other worlds and scribbling stories on the leftover blank pages at the back of school notebooks. She lives in Brisbane, Australia with her husband and two children.